A Ring of Truth
The Valiant
Chronicles: Book II

Val Tobin

This is a work of fiction and any resemblance to persons living or dead, or places, events or locales is purely coincidental. The names, characters, places, and incidents are products of the author's imagination or are used fictitiously

DEDICATION

To Bob, Jenn, Mark, Chanelle, Savannah, and Jack

ACKNOWLEDGMENTS

Editing by Alan Annand (Sextile) sextile.com and Kelly Hartigan
(XterraWeb) editing.xterraweb.com. Thank you, Alan and Kelly.
Thanks to Patti Roberts of Paradox
(paradoxbooktrailerproductions.blogspot.com.au/) for the amazing cover.
Dr. Alis Kennedy, Miigwech for help with the Aboriginal details and
reading my manuscript multiple times.
Judy Flinn, thank you for consulting on story, reading it through more than
once, and for all your help and support.
Thanks, also, Michelle Legere, Kathy Rinaldo, Val Cseh, Andrea Holmes,
Chris Brown, John Erwin, Susan Barbour, and Chris Jenkins for support,
advice, or beta reading.

CHAPTER 1

Carolyn Fairchild lay on a cot in a cell, a thin blanket draped over her waist. She shivered and sat up to pull the blanket over her feet. Even with socks on, she felt chilly. She reached under her pillow but found no more crackers. She'd eaten them all during the night.

Whenever crackers appeared with her meals lately, she squirrelled them away. They helped combat the all-day nausea. Carolyn was positive now it was morning sickness.

At first, she'd thought it was a stomach flu. But when she'd thrown up after eating, or even just smelling, any kind of meat, she'd realized she was pregnant. She'd told her captors she was vegetarian. When they'd continued to give her meat, she'd hurled it at them.

She'd kept at it, even after the female guard, Tasha, had blackened Carolyn's eye when a meat patty had smacked Tasha in the face. Then, last night's dinner had appeared minus the meat. But the substituted food wasn't the complete nourishment a pregnant woman needed. Carolyn worried the baby wasn't getting enough, leaving her with even less.

By her calculations, she'd been imprisoned for a month, making it early June. The morning sickness had started a few days ago, although without a window, marking the passage of time was a challenge.

Carolyn swung her legs onto the floor and leaned back against the cold brick of the wall. After a few deep breaths, she stood slowly. No sudden moves. She shuffled to the sink near her bed. Was it morning yet? If it were close to breakfast time, the guard would bring food soon. She'd better pee now or be caught with her pants down.

The Agency didn't allow her much privacy. If the guards wanted to watch her use the toilet, they could stand at the cell bars and get an eyeful. Most of the time, they ignored her. Occasionally someone was mean enough to try to catch her in the act.

So far, she'd seen only guards who monitored her, took her to the showers, or brought meals, and they rarely spoke to prisoners. The other day she'd grasped Deuce, a bearded, burly guard, by the arm. His reaction had been swift and brutal.

He'd flung Carolyn's hand away, opened her cell door, and slugged her in the face, all without a word. That had blackened her other eye. If any of them had a conscience, they hid it well.

Carolyn swallowed, and her stomach gurgled. She needed water to calm her queasiness. In her former affluent life, she wouldn't have dreamed of sipping water from the tap. It still revolted her, but it was the lesser evil between that and whole-body nausea. She cupped her hands and slurped the water.

The attempt to control the nausea made her break into a sweat. Carolyn ran hot water to rinse her face. A wave of dizziness hit her as she leaned over the sink. Her stomach lurched. Tears welled up at the thought of being trapped throughout her pregnancy. She didn't dare think beyond that.

Carolyn gripped the sink and inhaled deeply. She suppressed the tears and pivoted to glance through the bars to check for guards. All was quiet.

She slipped her pants and underwear down and sat on the toilet, stretching her T-shirt to cover herself as much as possible. Even without guards present, she hid her body. The cameras always watched.

After washing her hands, Carolyn baby-stepped to the bars and stood by the main door. A smaller trapdoor at floor level allowed the guards to deliver meals without entering the cell. Once, eating from a tray that had sat on the floor would've disgusted her. Now it was just another thing she did to survive.

Arnie Griffen, her friend and fellow alien abductee, was in the cell next door. The guards had warned them not to talk, and so far, he and Carolyn had risked only surreptitious whispers at night. They'd learned that if they both stretched their hands through the bars, they could touch fingers.

Until her morning sickness put an end to it, they'd reached out to one another each night. Now she couldn't lie on the floor, arm stretched out, without making herself ill. It'd been two nights since they'd touched.

Carolyn pressed her face to the bars and looked in both directions. Nothing moved. She could see part of each cell kitty-corner from hers. One was empty. In the other, a woman spent most of her time huddled, weeping on her cot.

When Carolyn had tried to talk to her, Weeper had threatened to tell the guards. Fear had washed out of the woman and into Carolyn, and she'd had to clear and shield herself. Since then, she spoke only to Arnie.

She hoped he was awake now. "Arnie?" A loud whisper. No response. Voice raised to normal speaking level, she tried again, and thought she heard him shift on his cot.

"Carr?" His cot creaked.

Thank God. "I need you, Arnie." Carolyn lay on the floor and reached her arm through the bars. A swell of nausea hit her—she'd pay for this stunt in a few minutes.

His fingers touched hers. "I've got you."

Relief flooded through her. "Can you hear me okay?"

"It's difficult, but yes."

She took a deep breath. "I'm pregnant." Telling him was risky, but she didn't want to be alone with it anymore.

Silence. But the grip on her fingers tightened.

"I'm scared. What'll happen if they find out? I won't be able to hide it for long."

"How far along?"

"A month. Since early May."

"Right before John died," Arnie said.

Here it was—the moment of truth. Carolyn was positive she'd gotten pregnant after her husband John had died. Which meant her unborn baby's father was Michael Valiant who'd kidnapped her to turn her over to the Agency.

Instead of surrendering her, he'd helped her escape. Along the way, they'd turned to each other for physical solace. Carolyn had believed she was infertile after her daughter Samantha was born and hadn't considered birth control. Michael knew her secrets and hadn't worried about birth control either. Now she was pregnant.

But she couldn't let Arnie know who her baby's father was. Michael, along with his partner Gerry "Torque" Muniz, had kidnapped Arnie and handed him over to the Agency. Carolyn kept silent.

"We have to escape," he said.

"I can't leave."

"What do you mean? Chances are slim we can manage it, but we should at least try."

"If I leave, they'll give Sam to the aliens."

"One of your hunches again?" Arnie was sceptical of her premonitions.

"No. They told me." Carolyn sighed. Better he believed the news came from Agency personnel than from the spirit world.

"Bastards. I'm here for you, no matter what."

"Thank you."

The steel doors clanked and rattled.

Her fingers slipped away from Arnie's. Bile rising, Carolyn rushed to the toilet. Her effort to stifle it only brought it up. She retched into the bowl as the guard appeared, pushing a food trolley. Breakfast was served.

CHAPTER 2

The dungeon door rattles. Two guards drag a woman into the cell and chain her to the wall across from Carolyn and Arnie. The woman is missing a hand, the stump wrapped in filthy, blood-soaked rags.

All prisoners are naked, all chained to the wall. The guards grab Carolyn and unchain her, catching her when she falls forward with a whimper. They half-drag, half-carry her to another section of the dungeon. The sight of the iron maiden, the rack, and other instruments of torture fills her with terror. She struggles, but their grip is firm.

As the guards lay her on the rack, Carolyn sobs and pleads, denying she's a witch, insisting they've made a terrible mistake. They remain impassive and when she's bound, leave.

A man Carolyn recognizes as Michael's former partner Torque enters the room. Another man, shorter, balding, with round, staring eyes—he reminds her of an owl—steps up and strokes her body. She trembles and pleads with him to release her, but the man's touch becomes more invasive. Carolyn closes her eyes and screams, a high, wailing shriek of despair.

The door bursts open. Michael. He tells the men someone has broken into the dungeon and is releasing the prisoners. The man molesting Carolyn hurries from the room. Michael pulls out a knife and attacks Torque.

Taken by surprise, Torque is no match for Michael, who kills Torque. Michael removes the restraints and lifts her into his arms. He races from the room towards the outside world and freedom. Carolyn tries to put her arms around his neck, but doesn't have strength to lift her arms. Her head flops against Michael's shoulder.

She hears shouts and footfalls. Guards. "Leave me." Voice hoarse from screaming, it comes out a croak. She wants Michael to escape. She loves him more than life.

Carolyn finds herself back in chains, wrists and ankles manacled. Trapped in the owl-eyed man's bedchamber, she's his possession. Did Michael escape? Did they kill him? Loss overwhelms her, and she bursts into wracking sobs. The man whose name she still doesn't know drags her into bed.

Tears streaming down her face, Carolyn wrenched awake. She leapt up and launched herself at the toilet, letting her breakfast fly when she reached the bowl. Stomach muscles ached from the unrelenting spasms. Drained, she slid onto the floor.

She lay there until she mustered the strength to drag herself to the sink. The void that was a placeholder for Michael had increased after that dream, and she'd give anything to hold him again. Carolyn rinsed her face and returned to bed. She flipped her tear-drenched pillow over to the dry side and waited for the guards to bring lunch.

***

Lunch was over: vegetable soup, which meant crackers. Score. Although still hungry, Carolyn tucked the packet under her pillow. While she used the toilet, she listened for footsteps and moved quickly. Most of her privates stayed private, even from camera eyes, by stretching her T-shirt to cover her crotch. But the awareness of being on display remained constant.

Still, it wasn't as degrading as a trip to the showers. That didn't happen often enough to feel clean, but too often to get over the humiliation of undressing in front of an audience. Usually a woman accompanied her, but not always. While most of her male escorts at least pretended to look away, others leered. So far, none had tried to touch her.

When guards came to take her for questioning, she lay curled up on the bed, blanket clutched to her chest, trying to sleep. For a moment, she thought they'd come to take her for a shower. *Why would that require two men?*

The taller man pulled the blanket off her. "Stand." His tone was neutral, as if he didn't care whether she obeyed him. But he'd slug her if she refused, so she stood.

When the other guard cuffed her hands, Carolyn considered protesting. Did they seriously think she'd fight? But she stayed quiet and shuffled between them down the corridor.

***

Carolyn gazed at the floor so Jim Cornell wouldn't see her reaction to whatever he said. Brown hair hung like a curtain over her face, though it wasn't much of a curtain. Michael had made her cut and dye her hair when they were trying to elude the Agency, and her blonde roots showed. Perhaps Cornell would let her fix it as it grew out. The thought bubbled hysteria up to the surface, and Carolyn choked back a sob of laughter.

She sat in a chair facing Cornell, who side-saddled the front of his desk, looming over her. Intimidation tactic, she thought, and it worked. Cuffs still bound her hands. The guards had left the key, so Cornell could remove them if he wanted, but she refused to ask him.

"Look at me, Carolyn."

What would he do if she disobeyed? Afraid of getting hit, she raised her head, and they locked gazes. A whimper escaped her when she recognized the owl-eyed man from her dream.

"Tsk. Both eyes blackened." He sounded contrite. "You were mistreated." Cornell said it as if it shocked him, as if it might be news to her. He reached out and touched her cheek with his index finger.

Carolyn recoiled and sucked in her breath with a terrified hiss.

"Don't be afraid." Gentle. "I won't hurt you. It's necessary for you to stay here, but we can try to get along."

Carolyn lowered her face again, the sting of tears in her eyes. She wouldn't cry in front of this monster. *Not. Going. To. Trust. Him.* She had to hang on to that.

"I don't know what Valiant told you, but maybe you should hear my side of it before you decide I'm the enemy. Have an early dinner with me, and we can talk. I'll remove those cuffs. The restraints weren't necessary, but it's protocol." Cornell leaned towards her.

She flinched when he cupped a warm hand around her cheek. Her body inclined away from the touch. Tenderly, Cornell smoothed the hair from her face. "I said I wouldn't hurt you. Hold up your wrists."

Carolyn raised her arms. He removed the cuffs and set them on the desk. She studied him. He was shorter than Michael—five foot seven to Michael's six feet, which made Cornell an inch shorter than Carolyn. His belly rounded over his belt. Bald on top, he had a monk's fringe of grey-flecked black hair. Round, thick-rimmed glasses cemented his resemblance to an owl.

She broke her silence. "You're Michael's boss? The one who ordered him to kill my husband and to kidnap Arnie and me?"

Cornell frowned, disappointed. "Is that what he told you?"

"Are you going to deny it? You know I'm psychic. If you lie, I'll know." She lied herself in this—she couldn't always see the falsehood. But in this case, she knew she'd guessed correctly.

"My dear lady … " He rose and walked across the room to a table set for dinner for two. Beside it, a sideboard displayed a buffet feast, most of it vegetarian. A large vegetable platter loaded with carrots, broccoli, celery, cauliflower, and other fresh, crunchy vegetables formed the centrepiece. In the middle of the platter sat a bowl containing a creamy white dressing. There was an antipasto platter with olives, pickles, melon balls, bruschetta, sun-dried tomatoes, and crisp crackers.

A cheese platter held a variety of cubed and sliced cheeses, most of which she couldn't identify. There was meat: various cold cuts, a mound of tuna salad, and one of salmon salad. An assortment of breads and buns overflowed a wicker basket. A bottle of wine chilled in a bucket on the table, along with a bottle of spring water.

They hadn't forgotten dessert. Petit fours, mini cheesecakes, éclairs, brownies, cookies, chocolate truffles, and other tasty treats sat next to the savoury platters. A coffee urn and teapot stood beside pitchers of milk and cream, and a bowl of raw sugar. It made her hungry and nauseated at the same time.

Her fear increased. She could hate them if they tortured her or were cruel, but how long could she fight them if they were nice to her? She swallowed and realized she salivated. When her stomach growled, Carolyn burst into tears.

CHAPTER 3

Arnie paced the width of the cell. Carolyn still wasn't back, and it made him crazy. Steel rattled, and Arnie glanced up in time to see a dinner tray slide through the small door. He checked out the guard who'd brought it. Tasha. She flashed him a grin.

When Arnie had first arrived here, he'd tried to stay aloof, no matter how hot Tasha was. But she'd been the only guard to pay any attention to him, and before long, he fantasized about seducing her and convincing her to help him and Carolyn escape. The fantasy grew more spectacular the longer Arnie remained trapped in this human zoo.

Tasha was gorgeous: long brown hair worn braided and twisted around her crown, and doe eyes the colour of mahogany. A petite five-foot-three powerhouse, fit and muscular, but not in an unfeminine bodybuilder way, she looked as if she'd be great in bed. The woman oozed sexy even in fatigues, and most of the time, she wore a tank top, no bra. Oh, Lord.

Arnie forced his thoughts back to Carolyn, and when he saw Tasha wasn't leaving, called to her, his voice worried and distracted.

She raised her brows. "Easy, sweetie. We're not supposed to talk, remember? Want them to think I've been a bad girl?"

Arnie swallowed and sweat broke out on his neck. She'd aroused him with that one simple question. He tried to reorient. "I'm worried about Carolyn. Is she okay?"

Tasha frowned and clenched her jaw.

He gulped. "Where is she?"

"Oh, Arnie." When Tasha said his name, it was like a caress.

He shivered. "Can you tell me?"

"Why?"

"Please? Are they bringing her back soon?"

"When they're finished with her."

Arnie's mouth went dry, and his stomach knotted.

She held out her hand. "Come here, sweetie."

He went to the door and gripped the bars. Tasha stroked his face, fingers gentle, caressing.

Arnie's eyes closed, and he sighed, relishing the contact. An ache spread through his loins, and his breathing became shallow and rapid. It'd been a long time since he'd had sex. Celibacy wasn't the norm for him.

When he opened his eyes, Tasha smiled, and it was spectacular. "Relax. Carolyn's getting acquainted with my boss. You'll get to meet him soon enough."

The blood drained from Arnie's face.

Her hand wandered to his crotch and rubbed the growing bulge. "Want to go to the showers?" The words carried a seductive undertone.

Arnie nodded, speechless. Tasha grabbed his hand and slid it under her top, and he explored her breasts, relishing the soft skin. When his fingers found a nipple, he pinched it and rolled it between his thumb and index finger.

She gasped, grabbed his hand, and pressed it between her legs. "Want that?"

He nodded, fearing he might come in his pants.

Tasha snickered, unlocked the cell door, and held out the handcuffs. Arnie stuck his hands out and she cuffed him.

The shower room had two shower stalls, both without doors, but Arnie had never seen anyone else in there. Tasha ordered him to the other side of the room and locked the door.

She crossed the floor like a predator creeping towards her prey and stood before him. Tasha dropped the cuffs on a nearby table. "Take off your clothes."

Arnie removed each article of clothing and set it on the table, the cold air making his skin prickle. Her eyes grew wide when he hooked his thumbs into the waistband of his briefs and slid them off. The briefs joined the pile of clothes on the table.

They stood together in silence while her gaze wandered over his naked body. Arnie flushed. Tasha chuckled and ordered him into the shower. When the water was flowing, she pulled off her tank top. She removed her holster and set it on the table.

The sight of the gun triggered thoughts of escape, and he couldn't stop staring at it. Then their gazes locked, and Arnie tensed. She'd caught him ogling the weapon.

Tasha laughed and wagged a finger in his direction. "Uh-uh. Don't even think about it. I don't want to shoot you, lover boy. Do what I say, and we'll have fun."

He looked away. Tasha terrified him, a new experience for Arnie, who'd never feared any woman. However, that didn't dampen his ardour. Another glance at her naked body aroused lust and desire. He decided to behave. She strode across the room and stepped into the shower stall.

"What if someone comes to the door?" he asked. Would discovery be worse for him or her?

"No one's coming. Just you. And me." A snicker. She did that often, as though everything was contemptuous. It was part of what made him fear her. She was gorgeous, sexy, and scarier than anyone he'd met.

He forgot everything, including Carolyn, when Tasha eased to her knees and took him in her mouth. He groaned. It'd been so long since he'd experienced this kind of pleasure. He panted and moaned, Tasha's busy mouth making his testicles pulse and shooting sensation through him. She pulled away when he grew thick and ready to burst.

"Not yet. Me first." Tasha stood and kissed him, rolling her tongue around his mouth. Arnie touched her breasts, and a pulse zapped from his mouth and hands to his loins.

"Yes, that's good," she whispered. "Now on your knees."

Arnie slid to the floor. Tasha leaned against the wall and gripped his head with her hands while he put his mouth where she directed. Hers to command, he got lost in the hedonistic moment, drowning under the water pouring from the shower and the demanding woman to whose thighs he clung.

Tasha screamed a climax and pulled him up, and he gasped for air, surprised to be alive. Stifled, claustrophobic, he pulled back, but she jumped into his arms, wrapping her legs around him and impaling herself on him. A moment later, Arnie let go with a loud moan that sounded more like pain than pleasure. His legs shook, knees on the verge of buckling.

She leapt to the ground and retreated. "Better?"

No, worse. Oh, God, I want to go home. Arnie nodded and tried to collect himself, but confusion set in. What was this? Where was his confident, carefree self? Why did he hate what just happened? Why did he feel violated, obliterated? The real Arnie had disappeared, and the doppelganger that replaced him was a snivelling coward, used and abused by a woman the size of a pixie.

In the past, he'd been the one to choreograph sex, to take control, even with the women who'd initiated it. He'd enjoyed women, giving them pleasure while using them for his own needs. Now he felt dirty and used. This place had turned him into a non-entity, a shell. What repulsed him most was how grateful he felt that Tasha had condescended to fuck him. Arnie burst into tears.

CHAPTER 4

Carolyn sobbed quietly, hands resting limp on her thighs. Too drained to muster the energy to wipe the tears, she let them fall. She wondered what Michael would do. *Not cry.* Thinking of Michael helped.

Cornell hurried to Carolyn's side and knelt beside her chair, but didn't try to touch her. He handed her a tissue from the box on the desk, and moved back, giving her space. She accepted the tissue but held it crumpled in her fist while the tears continued to fall.

"Stop, Carolyn." Cornell's voice was stern, but gentle.

Carolyn took a deep breath and calmed. She dabbed her eyes with the tissue and wiped her nose.

Cornell gripped her shoulder. "I want to help you. Things can be different, better."

"Why am I imprisoned here? What did I do to deserve this?"

"It's not what you did. It's what others want to do to you. You're here for protection. Let's have dinner together. You're hungry. You've been rejecting food, and haven't been getting enough calories to sustain yourself, never mind the baby you're carrying."

She froze. *Oh God, he knows.*

"Don't worry. Together we'll handle this. Allow the Agency to help."

"Trust the people who murdered John, kidnapped me and Arnie, and institutionalized Ralph Drummond? That's the solution? The Agency pushed Ralph until he committed suicide."

The shocked look on Cornell's face told Carolyn he hadn't expected her to know Ralph was dead.

"That's right. I know the Agency drove Ralph to suicide."

"Drummond had mental problems. That's why he checked into the hospital. The Agency didn't put him there." Cornell sounded hurt, offended.

"Let's consider for a moment that your every utterance is suspect. Ralph didn't voluntarily commit himself to a mental hospital. The Agency forced him. Agents stalked everyone in Ralph's UFO group, me included. The Agency bugged my home and phones. Why should I trust them?"

"Are those Michael Valiant's words? Valiant misled you so you'd follow him."

"No. I wanted Michael to forget about kidnapping me, which he did as soon as I proved to him that Torque murdered Jessica."

Michael's wife Jessica had died the same day John did, and Torque had killed them both. Carolyn stared Cornell down and waited for him to respond to this latest charge.

"Let's not hurl accusations. Sit and eat, and we'll have a civil discussion. Take care of yourself, for the sake of John's unborn child."

Carolyn fought the urge to look away, afraid to arouse his suspicions, struggling to hide that the baby was Michael's. She walked to the table, pulled out the chair nearest the door, and sat.

Cornell sat across from her, setting the napkin from his plate on his lap. Carolyn did the same with her napkin, keeping her movements slow and deliberate. Her stomach growled again, and she picked up the bottle of spring water. She filled her glass, trying to mask the sound.

He glanced at her and smiled. "It'll be okay. I promise."

Carolyn set the bottle back in the bucket. "Your promise is worthless."

"Eat. We'll talk when your blood sugar and hormones aren't muddling your thinking."

She ate. At first, she nibbled delicately on an apple, testing her stomach, and followed that with a few crackers and carrot sticks. When the food stayed down, she dared a piece of bread. After eating the processed white bread served in her cell, the fresh, whole-grain bread felt nourishing and alive. She gave a blissful sigh.

Cornell raised his head. "Good? Eat all you want. There's plenty."

Reluctant to admit how wonderful it was, she nodded, unable to deny it was delicious. She sipped the water, grateful it didn't come from a bathroom sink.

Cornell poured wine into his goblet and held up the bottle. Red wine, Cabernet Franc, from an estate in Niagara-on-the-Lake. "I assume you won't be having alcohol for a while?"

She shook her head. Cornell replaced the bottle in the bucket, picked up his glass, and sipped. When he set the wine glass back on the table, he said, "Want an update on your daughter?"

Carolyn leapt from her chair and lunged at him. "What have you done with Sam?"

Startled, he jumped up, faster than she would've expected a man of his girth to move. He pinned her against the wall, his face near hers. Carolyn smelled meat on his breath and her stomach roiled. She turned her face away and closed her eyes, a sob escaping her throat.

"Listen," he said. "Sam is fine. She's safer than anyone else on the planet right now except us. Understand?"

Carolyn nodded once, and Cornell eased the pressure on her arms. "Can I let you go? Or would I be risking another attack with that butter knife?"

She looked at her hand and almost laughed out loud. Her fist held a butter knife. She hadn't been aware she'd grabbed it. "Prove Sam is safe and she'll stay safe."

Cornell took the knife from Carolyn and set it on the table. He towed her to his desk and set her in the chair at the computer. A few mouse clicks brought up a view of the kitchen inside a home Carolyn didn't recognize.

"That's my house." Cornell changed the view. The living room. No one in sight. Backyard. There they were: Samantha and two boys. Sam wore a two-piece bathing suit and looked stunning. The two boys swam in the pool, and Sam reclined on a lounge chair in the shade, reading a book. She seemed content.

"Why is Sam at your house?" Carolyn put acid in her voice and Cornell tensed. Good.

"For protection." His voice was even. No trace of tension.

"I'm supposed to believe that?" She scowled. "Why did you steal my engagement ring?"

Carolyn had left her wedding band with Michael, but had kept her engagement ring. When the aliens brought her to the Agency, the guards had confiscated the engagement ring. Attempts to get it back had failed.

"We didn't steal the ring. Sam has it."

"Sam? Why?" She gasped, struck with a realization. "Sam was with you." She leapt up from the chair, and Cornell grabbed her again. This time, she remembered a self-defence technique Michael had taught her, and spun away from him. She grabbed the chair, used it as a shield.

"Let go of the chair." Cornell waved his hand, directing her. "No one will harm Sam. Let's discuss this rationally."

"Are you insane? You've kidnapped Sam. I'm your prisoner. You murdered John. And you ask me to be *rational*?"

"I didn't kidnap Sam. I hired her as a nanny. To keep her safe."

"Safe from what? You and the Agency are the biggest threats to our safety."

"There's more. Please release the chair. What are you planning to do? You can't leave here." Cornell pressed a button on the phone. When the receptionist answered, he said, "Helen, send in a guard, please."

The guard opened the door and peered into the room. "Yes, sir?"

"Just letting the lady here know you're right outside. That's all for now."

The guard closed the door.

"Let go of the chair."

"Or what? You'll beat me?"

"I told you I won't hurt you."

"You'll get a lackey to beat me?"

"No one'll hit you. Drop the chair and listen."

Carolyn hesitated. Michael had convinced her he'd protect her, but this was different. Silently she asked her angels and guides for help and pushed the chair away.

"The climate is changing. The environment's deteriorating. Bees are disappearing, and without the bees, no one will survive. Quakes, floods, and tsunamis will cause more devastation."

Carolyn swallowed and nodded.

Cornell continued. "We built underground facilities where communities of people can live when the environment won't support life anymore."

"I don't understand. If you can create an underground habitation, why can't you fix what's happening above ground?"

"That's why we've partnered with the aliens. They'll take over the ruins and heal the earth. It's beyond our capacity to fix things."

The conversation was getting surreal. Then she remembered. "You planned to turn Sam over to the aliens in my place. You say she'll be safe, but you're lying."

"That was then. You're here now. What makes you believe I considered that?"

Carolyn smiled, coldly. "Ralph told me. I talk to the dead, and they know the truth."

Cornell didn't reply.

"No comment?" she said, unable to resist a smirk.

"I'm protecting Sam. Even with the aliens, she would've been safe. She's living at my house, so they'd have returned her there. She'd have no recollection of the abductions, as you didn't."

"But they would've been abducting her, experimenting on her, making her infertile the way they did me."

"Clearly you're not infertile."

"I couldn't have another baby for nineteen years. The doctors said I couldn't conceive."

"Then how do you explain your current condition?"

"I can't. No doubt the aliens and the Agency are involved."

"I can protect Sam and bring her along when the time comes to go underground. But I'll only guarantee her safety if you cooperate."

"Cooperate how? What do you expect me to do? I doubt it will be something I'll want to do. What if I don't? Are you going to tell me you'll kill her? Hurt her? Turn her over to the aliens?"

His face darkened. "Get something straight. You're here, and you're staying. I have Sam, and if forced, I'll give her to the aliens. Cooperate, or I'll leave her on the surface. Do you want her to die of starvation, disease, or flood? Those things will happen up here."

"What happens to me and Arnie and the other prisoners when you go underground?"

"Depends on how useful you are. Become indispensable, and you can survive, join the rest of us underground. Be a nuisance, and you're as dead as everyone else."

"What do you want?"

"Right now? Tell me where to find Michael Valiant."

CHAPTER 5

Arnie believed he'd experienced more degradation than was tolerable when Michael Valiant had forced him into the trunk of Torque's car and brought him to this monkey house. But that didn't compare to the humiliation of sobbing in Tasha's arms now. Too embarrassed to meet Tasha's gaze, Arnie kept his head lowered. But if she thought him weak, she gave no sign.

She stroked Arnie's bare back and pressed his head to her shoulder. "Relax. Talk to me. Perhaps I can help you get clear of this, huh?"

He stopped crying. "What do you mean?" Was Tasha implying she'd help him escape? It didn't make sense. A short time ago, she'd threatened to kill him.

"Help me and I'll help you. Play nice, and your stay here can be comfortable. But you need to give me something."

Arnie tried to pull away, but she pressed him tight to her body. Tasha's naked flesh rubbed against his, and he felt himself stiffen.

"Yes," she said. "That's better."

Lust surged through Arnie, followed at once by rage. He gritted his teeth, remembering Carolyn. The Agency had her somewhere, and he had no idea where. It worked. The hard-on ebbed away along with his lust.

"Baby," Tasha purred, both hands stroking, caressing. "Don't do that. Come on now."

He struggled.

"No, darling. You go when I release you. Be nice. Let's talk."

Speaking out against Tasha felt like the most difficult thing Arnie ever had to do. But if he didn't take back his power, he'd fold and do whatever the Agency wanted. "Then let me go." A simple statement, but to Arnie, it meant everything, and when Tasha released him, it seemed a victory.

The room echoed with Tasha's laughter, and he deflated. Arnie waited for her to speak, but she remained silent, watchful. He shivered and gooseflesh prickled his arms and legs.

She picked up her clothes and got dressed.

Hands shaking with nerves and chills, Arnie reached for his T-shirt. Instantly, Tasha pulled her gun from its holster and pointed it at him. "No, sweetie. Not without my permission."

Arnie pulled his hand back. "I'm cold."

"Let's talk first."

"About what?"

"Who tipped Ralph Drummond off about the Agency?"

"An interrogation? That's why we had sex? Are you kidding?"

"Better than torture, sweetie. What's that saying? The way to a man's heart is through his stomach? But that's not the way to your heart, is it?" Tasha's hand snaked between his legs and gave his scrotum a squeeze.

Arnie gasped.

She chuckled, eyes sparkling. "Each correct response earns you one piece of clothing. The opposite of strip poker."

"Did you question Drummond?" A sinking sensation pelted him in the gut.

"No, honey. Drummond's dead."

Arnie's stomach clenched, and his knees wobbled. Dizzy, he pressed his hands onto the table and leaned forward, head drooping. Eyes closed, he let the tears flush out until the vertigo and nausea passed. "How?"

"I'm asking the questions. But I'll give you that one. Ralphie boy hanged himself."

"That can't be true. Ralph wouldn't hurt his family like that."

"What he did and why don't concern me. But now we can't question Drummond, tag, you're it."

Tears welled up again. This time, he stifled them. "Fuck you."

***

Carolyn cheered silently. *They can't find Michael.* She hoped her face didn't show her joy. "Why would I know where Michael is? I left him to surrender to the aliens."

"Valiant went to the alien base in Algonquin Park. What were his plans after that?"

"I don't know. That was the point of going to the base."

Anger flickered for an instant on Cornell's face, but when he spoke, his tone was neutral. "What did Valiant tell you about the base?"

Carolyn considered what to say. The truth would suffice because nothing she said could direct him to Michael. She truly had no idea where he was. "Michael said the aliens in Algonquin might help me avoid abduction by the hostiles."

That Michael had found the base and escaped the Agency delighted Carolyn. Relieved he was safe, she tried to sense any spirits around Cornell. She'd been at the Agency for a month, and no spirits had made contact. Was she blocked? Had the aliens done something during the last abduction? She didn't feel any different. Perhaps it was stress and the pregnancy.

Cornell stared at her.

She returned the stare and shrugged. "Sorry. Can't help you."

"Not an option. Cause and effect, Carolyn. I can reunite you with Sam, or I can have you executed. The choice is yours."

"I think the choice is yours."

"How hard do you want to make this? Consider, but not too long. We'll talk again. Give any of my people trouble, and I'll make sure you're uncomfortable. Work with us, and you'll earn rewards. How would you like decent clothes to wear? A private shower?"

Appalled, curses about to spill out, she stifled them, and instead asked her angels and guides for help. "Keep your bribes."

His face became a mask, and he buzzed the receptionist. "Send in the guards."

When the guards entered, Cornell sat behind the desk, staring at the computer. Without looking up, he said, "Get this woman out of here. The cuffs won't be necessary. She won't give you any trouble. If she does, don't hit her." He looked at Carolyn one last time. "But report it to me."

***

Carolyn braced herself as she and the guards neared her cell. She'd walked sedately between them all the way from Cornell's office, pretending to be docile and cowed. Her stomach fluttered in anticipation.

One guard pulled ahead and opened the door, while the other stood next to Carolyn, looking bored. This was it. Act now or miss the opportunity. Carolyn lunged for Arnie's cage and grabbed the bars, holding them in a firm grip.

She screamed his name, willing him to run to her. She wanted to hug him, ached to at least touch him. Carolyn stared at the empty room and realized Arnie wasn't there. A guard pried her fingers off the bars. Head bowed, she returned to her cell.

***

Tasha stood over Arnie. She'd forced him to sit in the only chair in the room. Made of metal, the chair intensified the chill spreading through his body.

"Drummond's source," Tasha said. "Talk."

18

"Fuck you."

Tasha laughed. "You just did, sweetie. Now talk, and I'll give you something to wear."

"There's not much to tell. I don't know his source."

"Oh, Arnie. You're so full of shit. It's a woman, and you fucked her. Your dick will be the death of you."

The blood drained from Arnie's face. "She never told me her name, and I didn't ask."

"Describe her."

"What will you do to her?"

"Nothing."

"What will the Agency do to her?"

"Not your concern."

"I disagree. The Agency thugs will hurt her, and it'll be my fault."

"Consider what'll happen to you if you don't talk." She leaned forward.

Arnie swallowed, his mouth dry. How could this be happening? He couldn't betray the contact. He hoped Dragonfly was trying to find others to blow the whistle to, or whatever the Agency did to him would be even more tragic.

He steeled himself. "Fuck you."

Tasha was quick. She handcuffed Arnie's hands to the chair and produced a knife from a hidden sheath at her waist.

"What's your biggest asset, Arnie?" His name still sounded like a caress when she said it. Tasha held the knife to his right eye. "Your beautiful blue eyes?"

Arnie closed his eyes.

She laughed. "Perhaps not." Tasha moved the knife down his cheek.

The knife scraped along his skin, and he felt blood trickle down his face. He suppressed a sob.

"Maybe your handsome face?"

He gritted his teeth, waiting for the sting to become excruciating pain.

"Guess where I'm headed."

Arnie groaned, anticipating the knife's descent. "Please, no." Finally reduced to begging.

"It would be a shame to turn you into a eunuch, wouldn't it, stud? Talk."

Ashamed, he gave her something. "She went by the name Dragonfly."

Tasha slapped him across the face. "Tell me something I don't know."

Arnie let out a gasp that was part sob. "What do you want? If you know already, why don't you find her?"

She punched him in the face, and he groaned as his head snapped back. She had a better right hook than most men. His stomach churned, and bile rose in his throat. "I'll be sick."

"I don't care."

He gagged on the vomit and swallowed it, eyes watering from the effort to hold it in.

Tasha slid the knife down his belly.

Arnie's breath became shallow. "Please." His voice pitched higher.

"Dragonfly."

"She's five-six. Muscular. Brown hair. Wore it short. Green eyes." The words spilled out, and once he'd started, he couldn't stop. He tried to clamp his lips together, but they kept going. "Said she worked at a base outside Toronto. Didn't say where."

"Good. You can put on something." She picked up Arnie's socks and slid them onto his feet.

Her touch revolted him now, and he flinched when her hand brushed his skin.

"Now, now." She'd noticed the flinch. "Just a bit more, sweetie. Remember, I can give you pleasure, too. Cooperate."

Arnie closed his eyes, ashamed at the betrayal. He should be man enough to bear anything Tasha did to him without giving Dragonfly away, but he couldn't. The terror of the pain was too intense.

Tasha flicked the knifepoint across his thigh, and Arnie felt the trickle of blood again.

"If I cut you, the aliens can heal you, and I can do it again. As many times as I want. It's marvellous. They can create living tissue, and it'll have your DNA. They'll reconnect nerves, so you'll experience it intensely every time. Want me to ask them to give you a bigger dick?"

"Stop. Please. I'll talk."

"Distinguishing marks?"

"A tattoo ... Small dragonfly on her right shoulder ... Details too vague ... Green and black ... Other colours. What more do you want?"

"Where did she live?"

"She didn't tell me anything personal. She never told me her name, for Chrissake. Please. Stop."

"Where was she getting her info?"

"She never told us that."

"Did she say why?"

"No."

It was silent for so long that Arnie opened his eyes. Tasha perched on the table watching, face serene. She smiled and held up the knife, his blood speckling the blade. She locked eyes with him and licked the blade, then her lips. "You taste delicious, sweetie."

Crazy fucking bitch. He fainted.

CHAPTER 6

Michael Valiant heard the roar of the South Nahanni River and ran towards it. Pursuit was close behind, and he was afraid they'd soon be near enough to score a hit if they fired. His lungs screamed for relief. He had to do something to speed his getaway.

Three agents tailed Michael, and *she* was one. Althaea Dayton—the biggest mistake and closest near miss of his life. Althaea and Michael had almost had an affair once. But that wouldn't stop her from pulling the trigger if she managed to get close enough to put a bullet in his brain. She'd have more reason than anyone else. The relationship hadn't ended well.

So Michael ran, telling himself that talking to Althaea would be fatal, because if he stopped running, it would be over for him. It was early June. Michael had been on the run for the last month—ever since he'd left Algonquin Park.

Undetected, he'd made his way north, a tribute to his skills and the ineptitude of the Agency's bureaucrats. After six hours in the air, not including a stopover in Calgary, Michael arrived in Yellowknife from Ottawa. Then he'd gone to Fort Simpson and chartered a floatplane to Nahanni National Park's Virginia Falls.

The end of May was a chilly and buggy time of year to be out in the wild above the sixtieth parallel. For once, he was grateful for climate warming.

Michael had made a possibly fatal mistake two nights ago.

He'd spotted an agent standing outside a log cabin. Althaea. He'd have recognized her anywhere. She oozed raw sexuality, a sensuous beauty he'd found almost irresistible during the brief time they were partners.

Althaea looked like a princess warrior—her long blonde hair tied back in a single braid, wearing army fatigues, and an assault rifle slung over her shoulder. A tank top showed off her muscled arms. She still gave off that feral energy Michael had wanted to tame years ago. That he'd turned her away from his bed—rejected her—might get him killed now. She wasn't the forgiving type.

Michael had already taken a few steps towards her before he realized she'd kill him without question. So he'd melted back into the trees. The mistake was that he didn't leave. Althaea wasn't alone, and one of the men with her spotted Michael.

Easy to blame her, but his own carelessness had exposed him. She still had the power to unnerve him, and he hated himself for it. How many people would pay for that mistake?

Briefly, Michael had lost the agents, but they'd found him again when he'd stopped for a rest. Two days of running had brought him to exhaustion and close to delirium. He'd lost his pack and hadn't eaten much. A canteen of water kept him from dehydrating, but it was almost empty. The sound of the river was like music for many reasons.

He burst through the trees a short sprint from the river. Water smashed over stones jutting up like worn teeth. *Only an idiot would enter the river here.*

Michael jumped, the water sweeping him under, and he hit a rock that tore his shirt and sliced open his left shoulder. Water surged over his head, but he resurfaced and grabbed a boulder.

Without thinking, he hauled himself up, but dropped back into the river when something smacked into his left shoulder. A bullet. He looked back. Three people approached the water. Two held back the third, keeping her from jumping in after him. The crazy bitch wanted to risk it.

Michael kicked off his shoes and swam with the current, but the injured arm threatened to sink him. The current would sweep him out of reach if Althaea didn't jump into the water. He might drown escaping, but at least he'd get away. When his head went under again, he kicked and focused on staying alive.

The shore sped past. The water's chill seeped into his bones, and he shivered, nauseated. He'd have to get to shore—soon or never. With an effort, he aimed himself at the opposite side and kicked.

Michael moved towards the far shore at glacial speed, though the current swept him farther from his pursuers. Eyes blurring, a wave of dizziness sank him. He kicked harder and got his head above water. Michael swallowed the bile rising in his throat. If he vomited here, he'd go under and die.

At least he was below Virginia Falls and wouldn't have to contend with a ninety-metre plunge. His efforts became increasingly feeble, and for a moment, he viewed his struggle from a vantage point above his body. Was he dying?

The shore approached. Inhospitable as the jagged rocks looked, they'd be a place to lay his head. *Just for a moment, God. Just let me rest for a moment.*

Although it brought heartache, he let his thoughts go to Carolyn. He missed her. Every day. She was so beautiful, so unusual. A sceptic, Michael hadn't known what to make of her psychic abilities. He'd scoffed at her claim that she was a medium, until she connected with Jessica, then Torque.

That she'd abandoned him in Algonquin puzzled and hurt Michael, though he assumed her reasons were altruistic. The wedding band she'd left behind hung around his neck on a chain, where it would stay until he found her again.

Michael's feet hit ground. His lungs ached, and he'd swallowed river water, but at least it was fresh. He'd stopped shaking only because he'd gone numb.

When the water was shallow enough, he stood, but his legs wouldn't support him. He crawled from the water, and lay with his head on the stones, eyes closed. *For a moment.*

Michael's body was freezing, his arms and legs prickling, his left shoulder burning. He clutched Carolyn's gold wedding band in his hand, squeezing so tight it dug into his palm. Okay. He could still feel, but drifted towards unconsciousness. *No. Not now.* If he lost consciousness, he'd die.

Blackness came.

Michael stood. He felt good. His shoulder didn't hurt. He swung his arms and did a few jumping jacks, marvelling at his energy. When he looked down, he saw the body lying in the mud and the stones and the wet.

The body belonged to a tall man. Close-cropped, dark hair spiked up, dishevelled from the water. Detached, Michael saw the body was his. He stared at the pallid skin, the closed eyes. The right hand still clutched the ring. Whoever found him would have a hard time prying his fingers open. *Yes. They won't get it until they pry it out of my cold, dead hand.*

He found that funny. *Ghosts have a sense of humour. Who knew?* Michael thought of Carolyn again. He'd failed her, his mission to sever her connection to the hostile aliens not completed. Now he wouldn't be able to find her, rescue her from the Agency, and have a life with her.

Who'd shot him? Althaea? Probably. She was a good shot. He hadn't died instantly, and that was enough for him to get away. Would humans find his body before the animals? The thought didn't upset him—he was simply curious.

If only he could see Carolyn one last time. At that thought, Nahanni faded away, and Michael found himself in an Agency cell. Carolyn lay on a cot. He thought of approaching her and suddenly was beside her bed.

She'd been trying to sleep, but sensed the presence. Her eyes peered into the dim light of the cell. Carolyn herself glowed with a light that attracted Michael. She'd be able to see him, and he wanted that more than anything else.

When her gaze landed on him, fear and dismay crossed her face. "No, Michael, no. Please. Don't be dead."

Her agony cut into him.

Tell her it'll be all right. He didn't know where that came from, but it was a good idea. "Carolyn, it'll be all right." When he spoke, it came out as a buzzing sound. Had she heard him?

Face contorted in agony, she shook her head and said, "How can it be all right? You're dead."

He supposed he was dead, but he denied it. "No."

She frowned, confused. "How did you die?"

"No." He said it again because it seemed right.

Her eyes widened, as if something had occurred to her. "Michael, I'm pregnant. It's your baby. Please. Help us. Help me save our baby."

Pregnant. How? She couldn't have any more kids.

Michael noticed someone next to Carolyn. The young girl appeared before him, more solid than was Carolyn, who seemed to be behind a curtain of haze. This girl, about eighteen, was clear and distinct. She had black hair, but Carolyn's eyes.

"Dad." The girl's voice was musical, comforting.

"I don't understand," Michael said.

"I'm your daughter. We'll be together soon."

At that, Carolyn screamed. "No, no. You can't both die."

The girl turned to Carolyn and smiled. "It's okay. I'll see you soon too. I'm Christina. You'll call me Tina. We'll all be together soon." Tina vanished.

Something tugged at Michael. A roar filled his head, like a jet taking off next to his ear. He turned back to Carolyn, to reassure her, to look at her one more time, but he found himself in a long, dark tunnel. His surroundings a blur, he moved rapidly.

When his pace slowed, he yearned for company. He hadn't met anyone in the tunnel, and he'd lost Carolyn and his daughter. The emptiness made his heart hurt.

Light surrounded him, and Michael sensed someone near him. Jessica.

She smiled, looking radiant in a flowing gown, and extended a hand. Michael clasped the hand and marvelled at its solidity. She spoke though her lips didn't move. "Michael. You can't stay here, but you're allowed to come with me for a time."

"I love you, Jess." He had to say it now. He'd missed his opportunity once before when she'd come to him in a dream.

"I know." She smiled, and his heart overflowed.

Michael stepped into a sunlit meadow.

"Go on ahead. To the light." She pointed, and his gaze followed her arm.

A brilliant light. If he'd seen it with his physical eyes, he'd have gone blind. He walked towards it, but ran when he absorbed the love and joy spilling from it. Home. He wanted to go into the light now, yearned for it.

But he paused and looked back. Jess waved, encouraging. As if from behind a waterfall, Michael saw Carolyn sobbing on her cot in the cell. He hesitated, not wanting to abandon her. But he had to leave right now. Carolyn would have to handle it. Michael turned back towards the brilliance, and a smile broke out on his face. That's where he belonged. Happy, he ran into the light.

CHAPTER 7

When Michael ran into the light, Carolyn screamed in despair. Arnie shouted her name, but she was too dazed to respond. Deuce and another male guard entered the cell and yanked her upright.

She struggled, not caring if they hit her or reported it to Cornell. They didn't strike her, but dragged her through the corridors to Cornell's office.

He stood in the doorway and pointed to a couch along the left wall. The guards dropped Carolyn onto the sofa, drained and limp, chin on chest. Sunlight from the window made her blink and squint.

She dragged her head up. The Agency boss sat in an armchair before her, wearing an eager expression. Her heart sank. He knew everything she'd said to Michael.

"Any news to share?" Cornell talked as if they were chatting over coffee.

"Go to hell."

"You must be upset. That's the closest you've come to swearing, angel girl."

She pulled her legs up and hugged them, resting her forehead on her knees.

"No, Carolyn. I want to see your face."

"Go to hell."

He sat on the couch and shifted closer to her.

"Don't touch me." Her voice held a warning note.

"The baby isn't John's." A statement. "You told Valiant it was his."

Carolyn remained silent. Cornell invaded her space, but made no physical contact. She closed her eyes, keeping her face buried.

"No wonder you didn't want to make that common knowledge. You slept with the man who killed your husband. Before John was even in the ground. Did Valiant rape you, or did you throw yourself at him?"

"Go to hell."

"This is boring. I'm trying to be patient, but if you won't talk, I'll give you to Tasha. She's my best interrogator."

Carolyn swallowed her fear, certain Cornell was truthful in the boast about Tasha's skills. "You said you wouldn't hurt me."

"If you don't cooperate, I'll renege. I don't have time to fuck around. You want to see Sam suffer? Or stay oblivious to all this, go back to school, finish her degree, and never know her life hinges on your playing nice?"

Carolyn raised her head, chin on knee, and glared at him. "How do you sleep at night? Be so cruel and live with yourself?"

"All for the greater good, angel. You don't understand because you don't have all the information. We're trying to save humanity. I can't let anyone interfere."

Her stomach knotted. *Lying.* She sighed. "You don't even believe that."

He pressed his lips together and frowned.

"Did that piss you off? You can't lie to me." What did he want? *Power.* "You're driven by power. It's a need stronger than greed in you. Greed is there, but it's all about power for you."

Cornell didn't reply, but stood and walked to the desk. He buzzed Helen. "Send the guards in, please."

The door opened, and the two guards entered.

"Chain her to the ceiling, standing." Cornell waved a hand, the sweep encompassing Carolyn and a spot in front of the desk.

Carolyn jumped to her feet. The guards grabbed her before she could take a step.

"No. Let go." She wrenched an arm free. Deuce recaptured it.

"Shut up." Cornell's voice was even, conversational. He motioned for the guards to continue.

They dragged Carolyn to the centre of the room. She shook, more from fear than from cold. Afraid the guards would hit her, she stopped struggling and sent a silent request for help to her angels and guides.

Deuce snapped cuffs on her wrists, and the other guard ran a chain through a ceiling hook. They looped the chain through the cuffs and hauled on it, yanking her up onto her tiptoes. Deuce clipped the chain in place. A nod from Cornell dismissed the guards.

Carolyn tried to move, but the chain held her in place. Cornell went behind her, put his arms around her waist, and squeezed tight. Cheek to cheek he held her as she thrashed and kicked.

"Stay still," Cornell whispered in her ear. "This'll go smoother if you behave."

Carolyn froze, but sobs quivered her body. "Please take off the chain."

"Too late. I asked you nicely. Now we'll do this my way."

Angels and guides, please help.

He pressed his body against hers and stroked her abdomen. Terrified, she feared he would rape her and moaned through clenched teeth. Tears streamed down her face. She focused on her breathing, calming herself enough to connect to any spirits or guides in the room.

Her left side grew cold, and her left arm tingled. Someone was here. *Torque.* Michael's former partner. *Torque, please help me. Tell me something I can give to Cornell that'll help me.*

Cornell whispered in her ear. "What did Valiant tell you about us?"

"Michael said you veil the lies with truth."

"What did he tell you about what's happening?"

"That the aliens were abducting me for my psychic abilities, but he didn't trust the Agency. Michael said it could all be lies. Please let me go."

Cornell's hands moved under Carolyn's shirt and stroked her belly. One hand slid under her waistband and threatened to slide lower.

She whimpered.

He released her and came around to stand in front of her. "You know rape is a weapon in wartime interrogations? No one admits it, but it works." He stroked her cheek.

She didn't reply, but the fear must have shown in her eyes, because he said, "It wouldn't be my first weapon of choice. But you need to work with me. I'd hate for Sam to experience anything like that."

"Please. I'll answer whatever questions you want. Please don't hurt her."

"I knew you'd be reasonable. I don't enjoy this, angel. I'd rather reward you than punish you, but you aren't giving me much choice." Cornell wiped her tears away with gentle fingers. "Where's Valiant?"

"Dead. Michael's spirit came to my cell." When she said it out loud, the loss overwhelmed her again, and she sobbed, closing her eyes so she wouldn't have to look at Cornell.

"Open your eyes, angel."

She did, but refused to meet his gaze.

Cornell put his hands on her shoulders. "How did Valiant die?"

"He didn't say."

"That's the first thing they tell you. Don't lie."

"I'm not. Michael said he wasn't dead, but I saw his spirit."

"What does that mean?"

"Michael appeared before me. I asked him how he died. He said 'no.' Maybe he was in denial or hadn't realized it yet."

Not dead.

She listened for more, not daring to hope Torque was trying to tell her Michael was alive. If it were true, she wouldn't tell Cornell. *Torque, please, give me something I can tell Cornell.* She waited, listened, and looked down and to the right.

Cornell's grip on her shoulders tightened, and he shook her. "What? Is Valiant here?"

"No. Torque."

"What's he saying?"

"Nothing. I feel him here."

Nahanni.

Carolyn didn't understand. *What is Nahanni, Torque?* As soon as Carolyn asked, she realized that's where Michael was. But she couldn't tell Cornell. He'd send agents there. Again, she silently asked Torque to give her something she could tell Cornell that would help her without hurting Michael.

Ionosphere.

Carolyn didn't understand that either, but didn't think it would hurt Michael. "Torque's saying something about the ionosphere."

"What about it?"

Carolyn waited.

Too much heat.

"Too much heat?" Carolyn repeated it as a question, not comprehending.

It meant something to Cornell because he went to his computer. He clicked his mouse and typed furiously. She watched him work. Her wrists and shoulders burned with the weight of her body hanging on the cuffs.

"Jim." Carolyn used his first name, trying to make it more personal.

He looked up in shock. Terror washed over her. Was he reacting to his name or to something on the computer screen?

"What is it?" There was fear in his voice, and her terror escalated.

"Please. Take the cuffs off," she whispered.

Cornell went to her and unlocked the cuffs. "How did you know?" His voice held panic.

Carolyn sank into a chair and swallowed, trying to clear the fear lodged in her solar plexus. Weary, she said, "What?"

"The ionosphere's heating up."

"What does that mean?"

"Trouble. Things might happen faster than we thought."

Carolyn's gasp seemed to snap Cornell back to himself. "You're going back. I've got work to do."

"Are we in danger?"

"Not your concern." He picked up the phone and called for the guards. He turned to her. "Say nothing to anyone. If you do, I'll be angry. Clear?"

Carolyn nodded.

"Say it." Cornell's voice was low, menacing.

"I understand."

The guards arrived and Cornell waved his hand at her. "Back to her cell."

They each grabbed an arm and dragged her away.

CHAPTER 8

Robert "Soaring Eagle" Holden guided the motorboat through the roiling waters of the South Nahanni River. The rapids weren't so bad here, and he could manoeuvre the boat with relative ease. His son Daniel sat in the front of the boat.

"We'll go ashore around that bend," Robert said. "We camped here last year, and I found some good herbs." Robert wild-crafted his own herbs and edible wild foods. He foraged most of it from Nahanni, leaving plenty for others, and never picked anything on the park's restricted list. But that still left him plenty of plants to add to his stores, so he visited the park throughout the spring, summer, and fall.

Robert and Danny lived in Tryst, a small town near Nahanni National Park, populated by people descended from Nahanni's original inhabitants. Robert was the closest the town had to a medical doctor, using mostly herbs to treat any afflictions that came his way. Forays into the park helped replenish his supply of natural medicines.

For the last four years, he'd been able to forage earlier each year, something he attributed to climate change. Spring started earlier; fall started later. In the north, it meant a longer growing season, a larger variety of vegetation. The warming trend benefited life above the sixtieth parallel, though Robert knew in his heart it was wrong. Any disruption to the delicate natural balance was likely to end in disaster.

But this trip involved more than gathering plants. An urgency to get into the park this week had overwhelmed him, even though, as far as the plants went, next week would've been better. Robert had been having premonitions, then dreams.

Last night, they'd camped in the Third Canyon, downstream of The Gate, a 460-metre-high limestone wall across from Pulpit Rock, which loomed like a sentinel. Anxious as they settled down for the night, Robert worried he was wasting time.

He slept fitfully and dreamed of a man who exposed the beings who'd abducted Robert. In the ensuing confrontation, Robert fought at his side. Aliens surrounded them, one tall, skinny alien grasping Robert by the throat and suffocating him.

He'd awakened to Danny shaking him, and though he'd told Danny it was just a dream, Robert had remained agitated. It was important for them to continue their journey along the river.

Danny pointed towards the rocky bank ahead. "Dad, there on the shore. It looks like a person."

Robert squinted against the sun and discerned a dark lump close to the water's edge. He would've mistaken it for driftwood if Danny hadn't said something. Robert's old eyes weren't what they used to be.

He considered himself in good shape, but his eyesight had always been poor. Since turning fifty-six, he could feel age catching up to the rest of his body. He was grateful Danny still had good eyes and the agility of a twenty-five-year-old.

Robert aimed the prow at the mass on the shore, easing the boat as close to the riverbank as was safe for the motor. They dragged the boat onto the rocks, anchored it, and then waded to the man lying there.

Through the torn shirt, Robert saw a bloody shoulder and recognized a gunshot wound and lacerations. He knelt. Two fingers on the man's neck established a faint pulse.

"Take the gear up the bank where it's dry," Robert said. "We'll need a fire. He's in shock and suffering from hypothermia. Lucky we came along. He wouldn't have lasted much longer without help."

The man clutched something in his fist. When Robert pried the fingers apart, he found a wedding band on a chain around the man's neck. Robert removed the chain. When the ring touched his palm, a shock went through him, and a slideshow of images flickered before him. He stuffed the ring in his pocket, snuffing out the glimpses into the man's life and that of the woman who'd owned the ring.

Robert glanced up to see Danny returning.

"Fire's ready, Dad. I've laid a sleeping bag out. We can put him there while we pitch the tent."

"Help me lift him. Good thing he's not conscious; otherwise, he'd be in pain."

They rolled the man onto his back, mindful of his wounded shoulder. Shock speared through Robert as he recognized the man from his dream.

Danny grabbed the man's arms, Robert his legs, and they hauled the stranger to the sleeping bag, setting him down gently. Robert peeled off the man's wet clothes and covered him with a blanket. To warm him with body heat, Robert climbed under the blanket with the man.

While the stranger's body warmed up, Robert examined the wound. No exit wound, so the bullet was still inside the shoulder. The slug had hit no internal organs, fractured no bones, and the cold water had minimized blood loss. Robert opened a medical kit and prepared to remove the bullet.

He'd had no formal medical training but what necessity had taught him about medicine and first aid. More knowledgeable about herbs and plants than about surgery, in an emergency, he could stitch up a wound. Although the wounded man was fortunate they'd found him, there was no guarantee he'd survive. But the odds had just improved.

"I have to treat his wound, and he'll need food and water when he wakes up," Robert said. *If he wakes up.*

Father and son stared at the man and then exchanged glances.

Danny said, "You think whoever shot him might still be around?"

Robert shrugged. "I don't know. I hope not. When he comes to, we'll ask him."

Danny nodded. For a moment, Robert considered leaving the man here. Strong premonitions spoke of danger, but the urgency to continue on the river had disappeared. Now he'd found the man, Robert had nowhere else he needed to be. They turned to their gear and prepared to set up camp.

CHAPTER 9

Crouched at the corner of his cage, Arnie reached his hand through the bars and called to Carolyn.

"Arnie." Carolyn's hushed voice sounded close.

"Are you okay? Are you hurt?" He kept his voice low. No telling what the guards would do if they caught them talking. This chat was necessary though. Arnie wanted to ensure she was okay, but had more on his mind than her physical condition.

"Cornell questioned me, but he didn't hurt me."

"Give me your hand, Carr."

When Carolyn's fingers touched his, Arnie grasped them and held tight. If he wanted to ask her anything, he'd better hurry. Prisoners were always on borrowed time when they talked to each other, and this conversation was riskier than most. "Who's Michael?"

A sharp intake of breath.

"You talked to someone named Michael this morning. Who is he?"

"Michael and I were together for a few days before the aliens caught me."

"You slept together? You're carrying his baby?"

"It's complicated, Arnie. The Agency killed Michael's wife and wanted to capture both of us. It just happened."

"I'm not one to judge. It's a shock, that's all. How do you know him?"

Her fingers tensed.

"Carr, what's wrong? Who is he?"

"Michael tried to kidnap me. I convinced him to help me instead."

"Did he have a partner?"

Another long pause.

"Carr?"

"Gerry Muniz. Michael called him 'Torque.' I'm sorry, Arnie. Michael and Torque are the guys who kidnapped you."

Arnie released Carolyn's fingers, snapped his hand away. "You slept with the guy who kidnapped me?" Spoken too loud. This could bring the guards in here, and if he saw Tasha, he'd shit his pants. He dropped to a loud whisper. "How could you do that to me? To John?" Arnie had an epiphany. "Michael killed John. You slept with the guy who killed John." This hurt. He'd never believed Carolyn could be that cold.

"Arnie, please. Don't do this. You don't understand."

"Did Michael kill John?" he said. She fucking owed him an answer.

"No. They'd ordered Michael to do it, but he hesitated, so Torque killed John."

"You fucking traitorous bitch. I can't talk to you anymore. John loved you and that's how you repay him? You fuck his killer?" He gripped the bars, tried to shake them, but they had no give.

"No. Arnie, please. We need each other right now."

"Do we? Or does the Agency need you to spy on me? What did they offer you? Sam? Sam's safety for what?" Arnie went to his cot and sat on it, leaning against the wall. He wanted to hit something. He returned to the bars.

Unbelievable. Carolyn had let herself be seduced by that psycho who'd kidnapped him. All these years, Arnie had stayed away from her because she'd made it clear she'd never betray John. John dies, and before he's even buried, she's banging not just any guy, but John's would-be assassin? It was that easy for Carolyn to turn her back on John? Fuck.

She was probably on their side now, doing that fucker's dirty work. Those bastards had stolen Carolyn from him. Arnie wished Michael were here right now. He'd tear that fucker apart. "Fucking assholes. Miserable rat bastards." Arnie planted himself in front of the camera, fists flailing. "I won't talk to her. Hear me? Take this fucking spy away."

"Arnie!"

"Shut up, Carolyn. I'm not talking to you." Arnie paced, uncertain what to do, trying not to think, unable to stop thinking.

Carolyn cried out again. "Please! You'll get hurt. The guards will come."

"I don't care. Tasha, you psycho bitch. Where the fuck are you?"

"Oh, God." Terror infused Carolyn's voice.

He stopped pacing. Footsteps approached. Arnie peered through the bars and staggered backwards when Tasha and Deuce appeared. His heart palpitated, anger evaporating and replaced by dread at what he'd brought on them.

"What do you want, Arnie? A little more Tasha time?" Tasha said. "Did you enjoy our chat the other day? I can arrange another. Or should I show your friend here a good time?"

"No. I'm sorry. I lost my temper." Arnie poured contrition into the words.

"We heard. It's all on tape, so no need to repeat it. Thanks for bringing it to our attention. I'll make sure you have extra food with your next meal as a reward. Now behave." She winked at him. "You kids don't make me come back here, or I'll knock your heads together."

Deuce laughed and smacked Tasha on the ass.

She turned on him. "You want to lose that hand?"

Fear flashed across the face of the brawny guard.

Tasha's fucking crazy. Even the guys who work with her know it. Arnie backed away from the bars and went to his cot.

After the guards left, Arnie tried to calm himself. The thought of Carolyn sleeping with someone other than John made him crazy. *Someone other than you, you mean? So that's how a jealous rage feels.*

Arnie had never felt that way about a woman. He'd desired Carolyn for years, but kept it under wraps, because she'd made it clear she considered him just a friend. Yet he'd always had it in the back of his mind that someday things might be different. When John had died, Arnie had thought perhaps he'd get his chance. Maye he'd be able to settle down with her, monogamous at last.

That she wouldn't reciprocate hadn't occurred to him. He'd assumed they'd never hooked up because she wouldn't cheat on John. It was a shock to realize the attraction wasn't mutual.

"Arnie." She sounded sad, frightened.

His heart skipped a beat. His outburst might cause her hardship. He didn't know what Tasha could do to Carolyn and didn't want to find out.

Face against the bars, he said, "I'm here."

"Arnie, I'm sorry this hurt you."

"Me too, Carr. But I had no right to talk to you that way. We've only got each other here." It dawned on Arnie that when Carolyn had communicated with Michael this morning, it was with his spirit. If true, then the guy was dead. This outburst had been over nothing. Arnie still had a chance. If he could get her out of here, they might go to Mexico and disappear.

Arnie crouched on the floor and stretched out his arm. "I'm holding out my hand." A moment later, Carolyn's fingers brushed against Arnie's, and he grasped them. "I've got you," he said.

CHAPTER 10

Michael regained consciousness. Eyes closed, he listened, trying to determine if he was in Agency hands or with someone else. A fire crackled nearby, warmth on the back of his head. His shoulder hurt, but he could tell someone had dressed the wound.

A sleeping bag piled with blankets insulated Michael from the brisk air. When he opened his eyes, he saw a tent and gear. A few metres away, a young man hovered over a camp stove, his back turned. Not Agency. Michael tried to rise. Nausea and pain overwhelmed him. His eyes misted, and he groaned. Someone shuffled nearby and pressed Michael back onto the sleeping bag.

"Don't move. You almost died."

The man who spoke came into Michael's field of vision, an older man with obvious native origins. The man had long black hair streaked with white and grey, his face lined and wrinkled. A smoker, Michael suspected. Nicotine stained the man's teeth and fingers.

Michael said, "Who are you? How'd I get here?"

The man smiled. "One thing at a time. Drink some water."

A canteen appeared in the man's fist, and he helped Michael shift onto his side and gulp the water.

"Slow down," the man said.

Michael eased up. "Thank you." He drank more water and sagged back onto the sleeping bag. "Did you dress my wound?"

"First I removed a bullet."

Michael nodded. "I'm grateful."

"I'm Robert Holden." He pointed to the other man. "My son, Danny, over there cooking stew. And you are?"

"Michael Valiant." Agency personnel called him "Mick," but if he never heard that name again, he'd be happy, so he kept it to himself.

"Hunting's restricted in the park. How'd you get shot? This wasn't a rifle, and I doubt it was an accident."

Michael hesitated and went with half-truths. "I'm with a government agency. Someone tried to stop me from doing what I'm supposed to do."

"RCMP?" Robert asked, referring to the Royal Canadian Mounted Police.

"No."

"Whom are you working for and why are you here?"

"The less you know, the better."

Robert frowned. "I'll need more than that. You're in no condition to go anywhere at the moment. Rest for at least the night. How good are they at tracking you?"

"Highly competent and determined." Michael thought of Althaea. "I'm glad you found me first. Do you have any weapons?"

"Two rifles."

"Is that it?"

"Yes."

"Where's my weapon?"

"With our gear, cleaned and ready to use. It should work fine."

"Thanks. I owe you."

Robert stood. "Dinner's almost ready. You should eat something. I applied herbs on your wound. That'll help you heal, but you need to build up your strength. You lost blood, and I assume you haven't eaten in a while."

Michael nodded.

"These people must want you bad."

"You could say that."

Robert's gaze held Michael's. "I looked through your wallet, Mr. Valiant. You have multiple identity cards. While you don't appear to pose a threat, I'm concerned about what you're not telling me. I didn't see an ID badge tying you to a government agency."

Michael kept his gaze locked on Robert's. "I'm covert ops. I don't want to attract trouble, and I don't want to cause any. Let me stay tonight, and I'll leave in the morning."

"Stay longer. That's a serious wound."

Michael nodded, relieved he'd get a night to recover. "Would you get my gun? If my pursuers show up, you'll be glad you did."

Robert went to the tent and returned with Michael's clothes, Glock, and holster. "Everything's dry. Danny's closer to your build. His shirt should fit, and here's a pair of shoes. Your watch and ring are in your jeans' pocket."

Michael sighed. "Thanks. Sorry to be trouble."

"No worries." Robert turned to Danny. "How's the stew coming?"

"Ready anytime you are."

Michael sat this time without wanting to pass out. Robert helped him put on a denim shirt. Danny was shorter than Michael, with a stocky build, so the sleeves stopped shy of Michael's wrists. The shirt fit otherwise and didn't put pressure on his wound when he moved his arms.

He finished dressing and washed. Danny ladled stew into bowls, and the three men sat by the fire to eat. Michael's hand went to the ring dangling from the chain around his neck. Carolyn. The sight of her in that Agency cell had enraged him. He had to get her out.

Danny indicated the ring. "Does that belong to your wife?"

"No. A woman I promised to help. I'm keeping it for her."

"You're wearing a wedding band. You're married?"

Michael lowered his eyes for a moment. "My wife Jessica died a month ago." It hurt to say it. "Jess was pregnant when she died."

"Sorry," Danny said.

"Thanks. What about you, Mr. Holden? Where's Mrs. Holden?"

"Margaret and I divorced years ago. She raised Danny, and I helped as much as possible. She's remarried with another family now."

"You never remarried?"

"Too many community responsibilities. I run a healing centre that keeps me busy."

"A remote place for a healing centre, isn't it?"

"Doctors up here are scarce. I learned what I could about healing, though I'm not a medical doctor. I follow the old traditions, use alternative therapies."

"What traditions?"

"Aside from healing with herbs and plants, I run sweat lodges, do soul retrieval, journeying, that type of thing. You were on a journey while you were unconscious, Mr. Valiant. I'd be interested to hear your experience."

Michael watched the flames, remembering. Danny threw another log into the fire pan. Smoke curled up in grey fingers. Michael turned back to them. "You're right. Something happened. How'd you know?"

"I can tell when a man's soul has wandered. You fragmented under trauma. You left your body and travelled to the spirit world."

"I remember parts of it," Michael said. "They sent me back for a reason I don't remember."

"Then it's not for you to see. Sometimes we get glimpses of what might happen, but a lot must unfold with no prior knowing."

Michael ate more stew. "Not to change the subject, but great stew. What's the meat?"

"Bison," Danny replied.

Michael nodded in appreciation.

"If you don't want to talk about it, Michael, that's okay," Robert said. "But if you don't mind sharing, we won't find it strange."

Michael noticed the change from "Mr. Valiant" to "Michael." A positive sign. He set down his now empty bowl and told them about dragging himself out of the river and collapsing, then finding himself standing over his body.

They listened, rapt, while he described how thinking about Carolyn had drawn him to her. Michael didn't mention her imprisonment in an Agency cell, but talked about seeing Tina and Jessica, the dark tunnel, and the light.

"The light was incredible. I experienced intense joy and love. Like I'd returned home after a long trip." Michael fell silent, and they watched him collect his thoughts.

"In the light, I saw everything I've ever done in my life and how it affected other people. The light showed me what it was like to be another person, because I experienced what they experienced, what they thought and felt. When I hurt them, or sometimes, brought them joy or happiness. The light knew everything I'd done. I was embarrassed, but it didn't judge. It left that to me."

Michael lowered his eyes, recalling how it'd happened so quickly. Given a second chance, he wanted to do better. Next time, he wanted a more positive review. He looked up again. "I realize we're all connected. That sounds like new-age bullshit, but it's what I learned. What I do affects me and everyone else. It wasn't easy to endure. I've done horrible things. I can't forgive myself, even if others do."

He looked to Robert. "Do you teach that in your shamanic work?"

"I help them figure it out for themselves, like you did. You describe a typical Near Death Experience, or NDE. Many people who've returned from the dead give similar reports."

"I wanted to stay, but they said I had something to finish. They showed me what it was, so I'd agree to come back, but they said I'd forget it when I returned here."

"That's not unusual," Robert said. "My guides sent me here to find you."

"What makes you think that?"

"We weren't planning to come to the park until next week. Intuition told me to come early. Obviously, it was to help you."

"You sound like Carolyn."

"Do you believe in aliens, Michael?"

Michael felt as if he'd stuck his finger in a light socket. He tried to make his voice sound normal. "Why do you ask?"

"This area has frequent UFO activity. I've had experiences myself. The extraterrestrial activity is the only thing here that might attract a covert ops agent. What's going on?"

Michael was honest. "Their base is here in the park. I've been getting guidance on which direction to take. Deadmen Valley."

"We can take you. It's down river."

"Too risky."

Robert had finished eating, and his bowl sat on the ground before him. He stared at it as if it were a rare gem. Then he looked up at Michael. "I had a dream someone was in my house. Something woke me, and a red light like from a laser shone on the bedroom wall. At first, I thought it was coming from outside. Then I realized that was impossible, because blinds covered the window. Afraid, I got up to investigate and found nothing. But I felt the alien presence. I don't remember getting back into bed. Next thing I know, I'm floating out through the ceiling. These aliens abducted me and performed experiments. If you're looking to make them stop, I want to help."

"Robert, you're an experiencer." Michael was incredulous.

"I'm an abductee. Call it what it is. 'Experiencer' makes it sound like tourism. The aliens kidnap us. We don't volunteer, and they don't ask permission. I've been waiting for you, Michael. I'm supposed to help you with this."

Michael hesitated. He didn't want to take Robert to the alien base. He might be a good tracker in the wilderness. But could he be invisible? Could he fight? Could he shoot someone? "Better we go our own ways. I'm not making a social call. I might have to shoot someone. Something."

"Understood. But I'm familiar with this area. If I don't go, intuition tells me you'll fail."

Michael glanced at Danny, then back to Robert. "He can't come."

"Agreed," Robert said.

"You're not going without me," Danny said.

"No, Danny," Robert said. "In my visions, you weren't there."

"Just because you didn't see me doesn't mean I'll be hurt if I go. I can help."

Michael said, "Sorry, Danny. Your father can come, but I can't be responsible for you."

Danny's face darkened. "I'm responsible for myself."

"Nothing personal. Come as far as Deadmen Valley. Robert should return in a day or two."

"What if he doesn't?"

"You get the hell out of here."

Robert placed a hand on Danny's shoulder. "I'll be back. Your mother would kill me if I took you."

"I'm an adult, Dad. I can make my own decisions."

"Not in this. You'll stay and watch the gear."

Danny, sulking, collected their bowls and went to the bucket to wash the dishes.

CHAPTER 11

Michael gazed at the river. Staying here made him uneasy. But he was too weak to help Danny and Robert pack up and move. They'd use the river tomorrow to get down to Deadmen Valley. He picked up his gun and pulled back the slide.

"Where's your rifle, Robert? Keep it close. You too, Danny."

Robert went to get the rifle, and Danny finished the dishes and did the same. They sat around the fire again, and Robert lit a cigarette. "Hope you don't mind if I smoke. It's my one vice."

Michael shrugged. "As long as I'm upwind, it doesn't matter. I'm surprised you smoke, considering the alternative therapies you do."

"When I was a kid, no one realized how addictive cigarettes were." Robert leaned back against a log. "You want to set watches?"

Michael nodded. "I'll take the first. I've slept enough."

Robert exhaled a cloud of smoke. "I'll take the second."

Michael stared at the river, wondering where Althaea was. He'd escaped her and her partners almost a full twenty-four hours ago. She wouldn't give up, knowing her, and she just needed to follow the river to find him. Something didn't feel right. Michael stood, gun in hand. "I want to look down the river."

"Want company?" Danny said.

"No thanks. Stay alert." Michael made his way to the water's edge and sat among the rocks. From there, he'd spot a boat if one showed up, and he'd definitely want to see Althaea before she spotted him.

Last time he saw her, she was transferring back to Nevada, and he was on his way to Canada, all triggered by the fiasco in France. They'd followed a spy to Paris, had neutralized the target, and Althaea had suggested they go back to her room to celebrate. Michael went, knowing she wanted to sleep with him. They'd been heading in that direction for a while.

When Cornell had first assigned Michael to be her partner, he'd tried to keep it a working relationship. That she was beautiful and sexy made it difficult, not impossible. But she was also smart and wild, and when he was with her, he wanted to take her, possess her.

She was aloof at first, making him want her even more. When he found that her reputation for being unattainable was true, a weight lifted. She was all business, and he hoped to keep it that way. But the more they worked together, the more respect they gained for each other, and the more comfortable they were with one another, the harder it was to remain detached.

That night in her hotel room, everything came crashing together. They shared drinks from the mini bar, on the sofa beside the bed. Neither wanted to say good night. Exhausted from the gruelling assignment, they both had a restless energy, after-effects of the hunt and kill.

Althaea touched Michael's arm when she said his name and laughed at his dry wit. He eased closer to her, drinking in her scent, while he tipped little bottles of rum into his mouth. She smiled, and his resolve melted under desire for her.

Without thinking, he leaned in and kissed her, tasting her. She responded instantly. He pulled her muscular body into the circle of his arms. His lips wandered from her mouth to the hollow of her throat, to the space between her breasts. When he reached down to rip her blouse open, he flashed on a memory of Jessica, head thrown back just so. He froze and released Althaea, almost dropping her on the floor.

"Mick? What is it?"

"You know what."

"I don't care if you're married."

"I do. Jess doesn't deserve this."

At first, she'd argued instead of pleaded, as if an affair could be made logical. "You want me. Don't deny it."

"I do want you, Ally. All I want is to rip off your clothes, throw you on the bed, and do things I've never done with anyone else. But I love Jess. It'd be just sex, and I don't operate that way."

"It's not just sex and you know it. I get you. You're unhappy. Jess doesn't understand you. She doesn't even know what you do for a living. I don't care if you stay married. I want to be with you. We're great together. The sex would be incredible. Jess won't know. It'd be just one more secret you keep from her. We can do this without hurting anyone."

She sounded so reasonable, his stomach turned. When he'd realized he'd thawed the ice queen, he'd puffed up with pride and virtually patted himself on the back. But after the triumph, came the shame.

If he did this, he'd lose Jess. Even if she never found out, he'd lose her, and the thought of life without her killed it for him. He stood, shook his head, told Althaea it couldn't happen, and left.

That's when the thawed ice queen turned into the abominable snow bitch. She threatened to tell Jess, threatened to kill Michael, to kill herself. Finally, she calmed down and got herself transferred to Nevada.

He'd always thought of Althaea as logical and pragmatic, and seeing her lose it had scared the shit out of him. He'd kept his gun handy twenty-four seven until she'd left for Nevada, and he and Jess had moved to Ontario.

Now here he was, gun in hand again, waiting for her to come after him, and this time, she had the Agency's blessing to kill him.

He searched the water in both directions, scanning the tree line on each side of the river, wishing he had binoculars. He relaxed a little after verifying nothing was coming towards him. But the camp was fifteen metres from the shore and visible. Anyone who came down the river would spot the boat and then the campsite.

Michael returned to camp, explaining his concerns to Robert and Danny. They helped him set up a lookout from which to keep an eye on the water. Robert had binoculars, and Michael scanned the far shore. He sat on a blanket sipping cedar tea and waited for Althaea to come back into his life.

CHAPTER 12

In the darkness, Carolyn Fairchild's daughter, Samantha, tiptoed into the Cornell's kitchen. She crept to the fridge and opened the freezer door, determined to find the ice cream. It was late—almost midnight—but sleep eluded her, and she needed comfort food. Unable to get the ice cream out of her head, she'd snuck out of the guesthouse and into the main house to get it.

Ever since her mom had turned up dead in Algonquin Park last month, Sam barely ate or slept. During the day, stomach in knots, she couldn't choke down anything. But at night, when sleep became the problem, she found that eating something rich and fatty helped her quell her stress and get a few hours rest.

Sam weighed herself every morning and found she'd lost five pounds in the last month. *I've invented the pie-cake-ice cream diet. No food during the day, but pastries and ice cream at night.*

The freezer light illuminated the tub of ice cream behind bags of frozen veggies. *Come to mama.*

As Sam reached for the ice cream, the kitchen lights came on. She jumped back, almost tripping over her own feet. She slammed the freezer door closed and turned.

Jim Cornell's wife, Virginia, stood glaring in the doorway, hands on hips. "What are you doing, Samantha?"

To Ginny—*excuse me*—Mrs. Cornell, she was always Samantha. Cornell called her Sam, as did the boys, and even the hired help. But with the Missus, it was always "Samantha," as if she were in permanent trouble. Sam's mother had only called her by her full name when angry. God, how she missed her mom.

"Just getting ice cream. There's none in the guesthouse. I can't sleep and thought it might help."

"No food after seven o'clock."

"Sorry, Mrs. Cornell."

"Samantha, you know we have this rule. What if the boys saw you? You're in a nightgown. At least have the decency to wear a robe."

"Sorry. I didn't expect to see anyone."

"Go back to bed. Buy ice cream tomorrow. Then you'll have it in the guesthouse."

"Okay." Sam turned to go leave.

"Samantha."

"Yes?" She turned back.

"When you enter this house, I expect you to be properly attired. Don't come in the house half-dressed."

"Okay." Sam returned to the guesthouse and locked the door. She flopped onto the sofa, turned on the TV, and channel surfed, not registering what was there.

Her stomach growled. She hadn't eaten today, but after that encounter with Ginny, she couldn't stomach any food. She went to the kitchen and opened the fridge. White wine. Alcohol helped her sleep, too, though she worried about making a habit of it. She poured a glass, took a sip, and warmth spread through her body. She set the glass on the coffee table and flicked through more channels.

Don't think. Damn. Oh, Mommy, Daddy. Why did you leave me? Sam picked up the wine again and sipped. Flick. Next channel. She was wide-awake. She wished Jim were home. He never minded when she slipped into the kitchen for a late-night snack. Sometimes he'd even join her. Ginny never bothered her when Jim was home.

Sam sipped the wine. Flick. Sip. Flick. Before she knew it, the glass was empty. Her legs tingled. Her head felt swoopy. She giggled. Was swoopy a word? She put her head on a sofa pillow and stared at the TV until her eyes closed.

When Sam awoke, she stretched and basked in the glow of the good night's sleep she'd had. She checked the time. Eight o'clock. Wow. She hadn't had more than a few hours' sleep in over a month. The boys would be already dressed and waiting for breakfast. She'd better get moving.

By the time she dressed and made her way to the house, it was almost eight-thirty. She unlocked the kitchen door and hurried inside. The boys, George and Wade, were finishing breakfast. Sam shot a look of gratitude at Marnie, the housekeeper. It was Sam's responsibility to get them their breakfast.

"Thanks, Marnie," Sam said. "I owe you."

"No problem, honey," Marnie said.

"Where is she?" Sam asked. No need to elaborate. Marnie knew whom Sam meant.

"Upstairs. I told her you'd set the table and put the food out. Don't worry. I know you've had trouble sleeping. Set an alarm clock so it doesn't happen again."

Sam glanced at the boys. They were staring at her. She smiled at them. Six-year-old George smiled back, his grin exposing a missing front tooth. Wade, twelve, tilted his head and said, "I won't tell my mom, Sam."

"Thanks, Wade." Sometimes she found Wade a little unsettling, like he was filing things away to use later.

Sam rushed them through breakfast. She got them to school on time, driving them in her mother's car, which the Cornells let her keep in their garage. When she arrived at the house, she returned to the kitchen, looking for Marnie.

She heard voices and paused, staying out of sight. If Ginny were there, she'd talk to Marnie later. Sam had no desire to face Ginny this morning and get nattered at about something stupid.

"I haven't had a moment's peace since she moved here," Ginny said. "What do you think of her, Marnie?"

"Seems nice. I'm sorry for her. It must be difficult to lose both parents so close together."

"I suppose. But she's rude and disruptive. She doesn't follow house rules. The boys see that, they'll act up themselves. They're so impressionable."

"It'll be fine. Maybe she needs time to adjust?"

"You're too kind, Marnie. Like it or not, Jim wants her here, for whatever reason." A mug thudded on the counter. Ginny was irritated.

Sam had heard enough. She slipped out of the house, heading to the guesthouse through the back gate. Once inside, she locked the door and got herself a glass of water from the purifier on the counter. That was all she could stomach. Her hands shook as she raised the glass to her lips.

She sat on the couch in the living room and turned on the TV. A sob caught in her throat. School wouldn't begin again until September. How would she manage that long? She was lonely.

Sure, she had Fox, her mother's cat, and she could invite a friend or two over, though Ginny didn't approve of them. But this aura of disdain where she lived hurt and confused Sam. She wished Jim were home. He made her feel safe and welcome. She picked up the phone and called Jim.

CHAPTER 13

Jim Cornell hung up the phone. He'd spent the last fifteen minutes trying to assure Samantha that his wife didn't have a problem with her. He buzzed Helen on speaker. "Get Tasha in here."

"Yes, sir."

Thank God, he'd moved Helen up here from Toronto. He didn't want to break in another receptionist. It was hard enough being away from his family. Cornell wished he could go home more often, for Sam's sake as much as anything else.

This last phone call worried him—the girl almost sounded depressed. She'd talked about returning to school in the fall, and he'd pretended to go along with the idea. Soon he'd talk her into changing her plans, get her to transfer to the university in Peterborough. He preferred to keep her close.

After investigating the information Carolyn had shared about the heating ionosphere, Cornell had grown concerned. It could cause more catastrophic storms. Hurricanes, tornadoes, and typhoons had already gotten stronger and more violent over the last few years, each storm worse than the last. Amp it up ten-fold by heating the ionosphere and it would be Armageddon.

A knock on the door, and Tasha poked her head in. She flashed him a smile, swaggered into the room, and dropped into a chair, legs stretched out, hands clasped behind her head.

"Congratulations," Cornell said. "I don't know how you got what you did from Arnie, but we've figured out who Dragonfly is."

Tasha gave him another huge grin. "I enjoy my work, sir. Who is she? Do I get to interrogate her?"

"Julie Helliwell. I'm having her transferred here. She suspects nothing. We'll let her think we trust her, see what she does with it. Let her hang herself."

"Anytime you want her taken down, just say the word."

"Of course."

"When do you expect her to start?"

"Tomorrow morning. I'll assign her to Arnie's block. We'll see what happens when she realizes she's guarding the person she's leaked information to."

Tasha smiled. "Okay. Thanks for the heads up. I can't wait to see the look on Arnie's face."

Cornell cringed. He had an aversion to Tasha's sadistic nature even though he made use of it. He didn't do what he did for pleasure, but for himself and his family. "We're done here," he said, voice clipped.

"Yes, sir." Tasha chilled him with a stare. Jesus, she was creepy. She stood and left the room without another word.

Cornell called his wife. The housekeeper answered, and he waited while Ginny came to the phone.

"Hello?" Ginny said.

"It's me. Checking in."

"Will you be home this weekend?"

"Doubtful." Richmond Hill was too far to commute from when he had to spend so much time in Peterborough. "I might get back for two days during the week. Everyone okay? How's Sam?"

"Fine." Ginny's tone sounded anything but fine.

"What's wrong?"

"I don't understand why we need this stranger in our guesthouse. I can't even invite friends over for a girls' weekend."

"Sure you can. There's room in the house. So they share the guest room. I have to keep her safe, which is easier to do if she's living with us. If it doesn't work out, she'll need to move here, but I don't have time to monitor her activities."

"Why can't Samantha go to someone else's home?"

"Because I can't divulge to anyone where she is. Trust me on this. Okay?"

A sigh floated up through the phone. For someone who had everything, Virginia complained a lot. Cornell waited for her reply.

"Yes. Okay." Ginny said it grudgingly.

"Sam's not even in the house, but sleeping under a different roof. And she's watching over the boys. What's the problem?"

"Do you watch her? Over the monitors? Do you?"

"Oh for the love of—I'm too busy to spy on the girl. You're supposed to be monitoring her. Do you know her whereabouts at all times? Because it's important. When you're keeping an eye on her, I don't have to check in as often on the monitors."

"Yes. She goes nowhere without my permission. After what happened to her parents, she's okay with it."

"Make her welcome. She feels like an intruder."

"Did she call you?"

"I check in with her regularly," he said.

"Samantha entered the house during the night. I thought someone had broken in, and it terrified me. She wanted ice cream. After seven."

"Sam's a scared young woman, Ginny. If she wants ice cream in the middle of the night, get her a bowl and spoon. Understand?"

"I'm supposed to cater to her?" Ginny's voice turned shrill.

Cornell leaned back in his chair. "Be nice. Promise me you'll do that."

Another sigh. "All right."

He changed the subject. "Are the boys okay?"

"You mean do they like having a gorgeous blonde in a bikini around? Yes, the boys are okay."

"I wasn't asking that. How are they doing? School okay?"

"No different than usual. They spend more time at home and bring their friends over to gawk. The girl has her friends over, too. I can't say no. They stick to the guesthouse or by the pool. I try to minimize the times she has friends here, but she'd go out more if I didn't let them come over."

"You're doing the right thing. It's better if she sticks close to home. I need to go, but I'll call you tonight after dinner." Cornell hung up the phone. He'd check in with Sam later, on the guesthouse phone, and make sure Ginny had eased up. She'd always been insecure and jealous.

Cornell knew it'd be difficult for his wife to have an attractive young girl living in the house. Not that Ginny was unattractive—she had a classy, mature style. Maybe a little on the heavy side, but she carried her weight well and still got him hard. But her insecurity made her a wild card.

The phone rang, and he snatched it up. "Yes?"

"Althaea Dayton on two-thirty-two." *Althaea? Wasn't she out in Nevada? What did she want from him?*

"Thanks, Helen."

He pressed the extension. "Cornell here."

"Hi, Jim. Long time."

"Althaea. How are you doing?"

"I've seen him." *Valiant. She had to be talking about Valiant.*

He exhaled slowly. "Where?"

"Nahanni. They transferred me here last year. Can't say I was pleased, but things happen for a reason. We use a cabin in the park when we're off duty. I was there with Stephenson and Moser. Valiant showed up. I'd seen he was wanted, of course."

Nahanni? What's in Nahanni? Cornell turned to his computer and pulled up a map of the Northwest Territories, zooming in on the park. An alien base.

"What happened?" He expected bad news. If Althaea had Valiant in custody, he would've heard about it already.

"We almost caught him. I shot him when he jumped into the river, but he escaped. The current was strong, and the guys wouldn't let me go after him."

"You shot Valiant?"

"Mick and I didn't part on good terms, and the details on this manhunt said we could use lethal force if necessary. I deemed it necessary."

"Did you try to find him?"

"We followed the river a ways, but didn't have a boat. We get choppered to the cabin, and there's a canoe, not a motor boat. No one would be crazy enough to shoot those rapids. But I have a plan."

"Spill."

Althaea told Cornell what she intended, and his smile grew wider while she talked. "I like it. Good work, Dayton. Keep me posted."

"Yes, sir."

He hung up. Valiant wasn't dead. Was Fairchild deliberately misleading him? One way to find out. He buzzed Helen.

"Yes, sir?"

"Have the guards bring Carolyn Fairchild to my office." Anger boiled up. If Fairchild had lied, she'd regret it, and she was damn well going to pitch in and help them locate Valiant now.

CHAPTER 14

Do you watch her? Over the monitors? Do you? The words rang in Sam's ears. She'd returned to the house again to find Marnie, but as she'd passed the library, she'd overheard Ginny on the phone. Sam hadn't intended to eavesdrop until she'd heard her name. She pressed against the wall and listened.

From the gist of it, she realized Ginny was talking to Cornell. When Ginny ask him if he watched Sam over the monitors, Sam's guts froze. He could watch her? The Cornells had cameras in the guesthouse? Sam hugged herself, body trembling. Was there a camera in her bedroom?

She ran down the hall, opened the front door, and slipped outside. On her way back to the guesthouse, the thought of cameras changed her mind. She sat on a lawn chair by the pool instead, head in her hands.

The patio door rolled open, catching her attention. Ginny. Sam's mouth went dry.

Ginny took a chair across from Sam. "I'm sorry about last night, Samantha." Her voice was warmer than it had been, but Sam didn't buy it. Cornell had probably told Ginny to make nice.

Sam wondered why he wanted her around so much. Maybe it wasn't just compassion. "I'm sorry too."

"I'm stressed lately."

What could be so stressful in Ginny's life? They were rich, and Ginny didn't have to work. She didn't even look after her own kids.

Sam nodded as if she understood.

"If you need a midnight snack, help yourself. Just wear appropriate attire, please."

"Okay. I'm sorry I never considered the boys walking in on me. I guess I'm distracted."

"With what?"

Sam stared at her. Did she really want to know? "I miss my parents. It's hard."

Sorrow flickered across Ginny's face. She patted Sam's hand. "I forget what it must be like for you, Samantha. I don't mean to be harsh."

Sam fought the urge to pull away and looked Ginny in the eyes. "Why am I here?"

"What do you mean?"

"Why does Mr. Cornell want me living here?"

"To help us with the kids. We need a nanny."

"Marnie was taking care of them just fine before I came here. Why me?"

"What are you implying? You think there's an ulterior motive for having you stay here?"

"Am I in danger?"

Ginny glanced away.

Sam's heart skipped a beat. That was it: Cornell thought she might be in danger.

"Jim's in a difficult position, with a great deal of responsibility. He can't talk about what he does, but when he says something is for the best, I trust him. You should, too."

"What's he afraid of?"

"I don't know. Perhaps nothing, but better to be safe, right?"

Sam nodded. But she still worried about cameras in her bedroom. What if Cornell was a perv, getting off watching her undress? Sam considered what to say. "I thought I saw a camera in the guesthouse, Mrs. Cornell. Am I being monitored?"

Ginny sucked in her breath. She hesitated, but only for a second. "Those are security cameras, Samantha. They're for your protection."

"I don't understand. Are they recording me? Is there one in my room? In my bathroom?"

"Of course not. They monitor the entryways, the windows. Are you accusing us of something? We don't deserve that." Ginny frowned, and her face grew dark.

Sam looked away, guilty. "I'm not accusing you. I felt weird about it. Wouldn't you?"

"No. I'd be happy the place is secure. Do you activate the alarm when you go to bed?"

Sam nodded, though it was a lie. She'd activate it if she ever went to bed. Since she hadn't been sleeping, just passing out on the sofa, she hadn't turned on the alarm.

"Are we okay?" Ginny asked.

"Yes. I'm sorry to be any trouble. I don't want to intrude on your family."

Ginny smiled, but there was no warmth in it. "You're not intruding. The boys enjoy your company, and it helps Marnie. So we're okay?"

Sam forced a smile. "Yes." But she wondered if anything would ever be okay again.

CHAPTER 15

Carolyn looked up when doors clanked in the corridor and two pairs of footsteps approached. The guards had already cleaned up today's last meal, so this visit had nothing to do with food for prisoners.

Heart freezing as always when the guards appeared at odd times, Carolyn huddled under a blanket. Terrified the guards were coming for her, but not wanting them to come for Arnie either, she choked back frightened sobs. Whenever the guards went to someone else, relief was also a stab of guilt. But it didn't stop her from praying they'd pass by both her and Arnie.

The guards stopped at her cell. Deuce and a woman Carolyn hadn't seen before. The shorthaired woman was muscular, but not as scary as Tasha. Deuce unlocked the door. Carolyn watched without moving as the two entered her cell.

"Get up." Deuce wrenched the blanket off Carolyn. "Let's go."

She stood before he could touch her, but he gave her a push towards the door anyway. "Grab her, Julie."

The woman grasped Carolyn's arm and steadied her when she stumbled. Carolyn tried to shake her arm loose, but Julie's grip was steel. The guards liked to show they could touch her whenever they wanted. They were never gentle, and she had the bruises to prove it.

They took her to Cornell's office. Increasingly uneasy, Carolyn crossed the threshold. Cornell was angry with her, but she didn't know why.

He looked up from his computer and motioned for the guards to plant her on the chair before his desk. A good sign—at least she wouldn't be chained to the ceiling this time.

The guards performed their duties silently. Carolyn assumed they wanted to heighten her sense of fear. It worked. Once she was in her seat, they left. She looked at the floor. Whatever Cornell said, she'd keep her reaction to herself. As usual, he didn't let her.

"Look at me, Carolyn."

She raised her head. He came around to perch on the front of his desk, looming over her. She swallowed, trying to suppress nervousness. Always cold in here, she shivered. He glared at her. Carolyn vowed to keep her face blank no matter what he said.

"He's alive."

She held her breath. Michael was alive. She tried not to flinch, but her eyes reacted.

Cornell didn't miss it. "You knew, didn't you?"

"I wasn't sure."

"You suspected, but kept it to yourself to protect him." Not asking, telling.

"I wasn't sure because Michael hadn't shown me how he died."

"But Torque told you Valiant lived, didn't he?"

Without thinking, she looked away, and it told Cornell he was right.

"This isn't a game, Carolyn. You must tell me what you know when you know it. Otherwise, there'll be repercussions for Sam and Arnie. This little oversight will cost your friend."

"No. Please." Carolyn regretted she hadn't realized the depth of their cruelty. "Leave Arnie alone. I'll do what you ask."

"You need to understand I'm not making empty threats." Cornell buzzed Helen. "Have Arnie taken to the interrogation room." He clicked off.

"No. Don't. I'll tell you whatever I can. Please don't hurt Arnie."

Cornell ignored her and buzzed Helen again. "Send in Julie and Deuce."

"Yes, sir."

The guards returned. Cornell waved his hand in Carolyn's direction. "Take her to interrogation."

"No!" she screamed. "You sick bastards. There's no reason."

The guards ignored her screams and hauled her from the room. Carolyn looked at Helen, who sat at her desk, staring as though Carolyn were a curiosity. She struggled to break away, but the guards were too strong for her. She screamed at Helen. "You work here? How can you go along with this?"

Helen's expression remained impassive.

The guards dragged Carolyn down the hall to a room she'd never seen. They'd chained Arnie shirtless to the ceiling. His eyes grew wide when he saw her. "What's going on, Carr? The guards said you'd explain what we're doing here."

Deuce shook her. "Tell him."

She sobbed, terrified. "Cornell said he thinks I'm not cooperating. He said …"

Deuce twisted her arm and pushed her up against the wall, yanking her from Julie's grasp. He shoved his face into hers. "Every time you refuse to obey, you increase his punishment."

Carolyn turned to Arnie, sobbing. "I told Cornell I'd tell them anything he wanted, but he wouldn't listen."

"Tell him what you kept to yourself."

Although she knew he'd take it as a stab in the back, she talked to protect Arnie. "Torque told me Michael was still alive."

Arnie grimaced at her words.

Deuce grabbed a whip Carolyn hadn't noticed hooked to the wall.

"No!" she screamed.

Julie pinned Carolyn and kept her turned towards Arnie. Deuce glared at her. "Here are the rules: every time you look away, he gets another; every time you speak, he gets extra."

Carolyn sobbed quietly. She thought she'd choke on her tears.

Deuce positioned himself behind Arnie and struck hard. Arnie screamed in agony. Deuce didn't pause. He hit Arnie again, the whip cutting into his back. Blood sprayed up and Carolyn gagged. When the whip cracked again and more blood flew from Arnie's back, she crumpled over and vomited on the floor. Julie pulled her up by the hair, forcing her to watch.

Arnie's screams were getting hoarse. Carolyn lost count of how many times Deuce struck Arnie until he lost consciousness. His spirit detached from his body. At first, it was a vague mist, and she thought she was hallucinating. The mist coalesced into a form, and Arnie's spirit stood next to his body.

"I can't feel it from here," he told her.

Afraid he was dead, Carolyn wanted to tell them to stop. But she feared that if she spoke, Deuce would continue beating Arnie, and she wasn't sure if he was dead or just out of body. She tried to communicate with him. *I love you, Arnie. Please don't die. Oh, God, I'm so sorry.*

Deuce dropped the whip, rubbed his hands together, and moved over to Carolyn. "We're done here."

"You killed him," Carolyn said.

Deuce checked for a pulse. "Nah. Just unconscious. Now move."

"You can't leave him like that."

"Someone will come for him. You're going back to Cornell."

"No."

Irritation crossed his face.

Terror engulfed Carolyn. Was that uncooperative? He might pick up the whip again. "Sorry. I didn't mean that. I'm coming."

They grabbed her arms and frog-marched her out again. She had one final glimpse of Arnie, hanging unconscious by his wrists, blood dripping onto the floor. Would he ever forgive her? She tried to stifle fresh sobs and gagged. She barely registered being dragged through reception to Cornell's office. The guards dumped her in the chair again.

Cornell leaned against his desk and smiled as if happy to welcome back a long-absent friend. "Give you a clearer picture of what'll happen if you hide anything else from me? This time, Arnie; next time, maybe Sam."

Carolyn clapped a hand to her mouth and jumped up. Cornell sprang clear of his desk. She dashed to the garbage can behind his desk and threw up in it. She knelt over it, gagging. When she raised her head from the trashcan, Cornell offered a box of tissues.

She wiped her mouth and blew her nose. He helped her up, led her to his ensuite bathroom, and stood in the doorway while she rinsed her face. When she finished, he led her back to the chair. Her stomach rumbled, ravenous—the baby wanting to be fed. If she didn't eat soon, she'd be sick again.

"I didn't want this," Cornell said.

She suppressed a sarcastic reply, afraid to speak. Who knew what they'd consider uncooperative behaviour? She kept her head lowered. If he wanted her to talk, he'd ask a direct question.

Cornell sat behind his desk, having satisfied his need to loom over her. "We have an idea where Valiant went. I need you to verify his location. We've set up a lab where you can do remote viewing. I don't care how long it takes or what's involved. Locate and track him. Help us set a trap for Valiant. You'll start today. If you don't, Arnie returns to the interrogation room, and you'll observe again."

"If you keep it up, you'll kill him. The aliens need him."

"The aliens can heal physical injuries. We can do this indefinitely, and Arnie won't die."

When the implications of that sank in, bile rose again in Carolyn's throat. Shaking, she bowed her head and prepared to betray the father of her unborn child.

CHAPTER 16

Julie Helliwell studied the guardroom monitors, flicking from one cell to another. She was only interested in Arnie's cell, but made it look as if she were viewing each prisoner. Her heart broke every time he appeared on screen, lying face down on his cot, back covered in bandages.

At least they'd given him first aid after beating him unconscious. It had killed her to hold Carolyn still and watch Deuce whip Arnie. If Julie had her way, she'd have beaten the shit out of Deuce. But it was her first day at the Peterborough compound, and she had to be careful, or they'd discover she was the Agency leak.

When Ralph Drummond had first introduced her to his friend and fellow abductee Arnie Griffen, Julie found herself attracted to him. It thrilled her when he showed it was mutual. Julie looked forward to meeting with Ralph and Arnie, and spilled more information to Ralph than she otherwise would have, wanting to impress Arnie.

Worried that Cornell might have had her transferred here because he suspected her, she'd kept her distance from Arnie. So far, no one treated her any differently, so she relaxed. Perhaps she was just paranoid.

She'd covered her tracks, never using her real name with Ralph and Arnie. But if their paths crossed, Arnie could betray her by accident. That had been foremost in Julie's mind when she'd brought Carolyn into the room to witness Arnie's whipping. His terror had been so great then, he hadn't given Julie a second glance. But she wouldn't be able to avoid him forever.

She saw an opportunity when Cornell summoned the guards to take Carolyn to the lab. Julie pulled a pad of sticky notes from the desk drawer and jotted "don't let on you know me" on it. She went to the infirmary and asked the nurse for a bottle of pain meds.

"Are these for you?" the nurse asked.

"No. Griffen's in pain. He's making too much noise and disturbing the others on the cellblock. I figured I'd give him something to shut him up."

The nurse handed over the pills.

Julie hurried to Arnie's cell, where he lay on the cot, eyes closed. She unlocked the door and hurried to his side, shielding his face from the camera with her body. "I brought you pain medication."

He nodded feebly and showed no sign he knew her. Had he forgotten her? Had she meant nothing to him? She pushed those thoughts aside. He'd recognize her sooner or later, and when he did, she didn't want it to be with witnesses or on camera.

She held the bottle out, the note stuck to it. "I'll get water. The nurse wrote the dosage on that paper."

Julie went to the sink and filled a paper cup halfway. She turned back to him. He stared at her, dull eyed, unseeing. She wanted to cry. "Sit." She said it roughly though it hurt to do it.

He made a half-hearted attempt to sit and groaned. She grasped his arm and helped him up, again blocking his face from the camera. Arnie looked at the bottle, plucked the paper off and read. He looked puzzled and then did a double take as he recognized Dragonfly. He closed his eyes a moment. When he opened them, his face was blank, his gaze glued to hers.

"Open the bottle and take two pills." Her voice warned discretion.

He exhaled in a hiss. His eyes continued to stare into hers. She watched while he put two pills in his mouth. Julie handed him the cup of water and he drank it. She took the pill bottle and the note back.

"Okay?" she asked.

He nodded. "I am now," he said.

***

In the lab, Carolyn sat in an armchair beside a table. The lights were dim. She had a notebook in her lap and a pencil in her hand. A digital recorder lay on the table. She leaned back, trying to get comfortable.

Cornell observed her from across the table. "Tell me everything you get even if you think it's irrelevant. Make notes and sketches. Discover where he is and with whom. Determine his intentions."

"What if I get nothing?" They wanted results, but what would they do if she failed? If they thought she was misleading them, they'd hurt Arnie or Sam.

"I trust your abilities. You know what'll happen if you lie. Failure isn't an option. Arnie's depending on you."

She closed her eyes and concentrated on Michael. She asked her angels and guides to help her connect. One thing she could do without alerting Cornell was warn Michael she was tracking him for the Agency.

Carolyn allowed her body to relax, letting it loosen from her toes through her body. She inhaled, engaging her abdomen, and took three deep breaths, easing herself into a meditative state. When her mind wandered, she brought it back to Michael. Open, she waited for information.

The impressions flowed, and she said aloud whatever she saw. "Mountains ... Trees, mostly evergreens ... A river ... Wide, with white caps and rapids ... Rocky shoreline." She fell silent, letting more information flow to her.

She continued. "Daylight ... Two men with him ... Natives ... Father and son." She described Robert and Danny, lingering on their features so she'd have more time to connect to Michael.

Help me talk to Michael, angels, please. Help him realize he has to beware. They're coming for him.

What image could she send him to make clear he was hunted? No guarantee it would work, but she had to try. She formed an image of Michael with guns pointed at him and raised a sense of urgency, of close pursuit. She beamed it at him with all she had.

Afraid her silence would tip off Cornell she was trying to send Michael a warning, Carolyn returned to receiving images. "Boat ... Aluminium ... Anchored at the riverbank."

A boat with landscape markers formed on the paper, a rough sketch, but passable. Carolyn stuck to major items, leaving out details, keeping Cornell ignorant of the full extent of her abilities. "Can't see a name on it. Might start with 'M.'"

She lied about not seeing the name of the boat. It said "Misty River" on the side. The 'M' would make them think she was trying, but couldn't quite get it. "They're camped ... One on watch, two sleeping."

She fell silent again. Michael was awake. If he were asleep, it would've been easier to communicate with him. She'd try later in her cell. "Camp stove ... A tent, near trees." She felt pain in her shoulder. "Injured ... Michael ... Wound's healing." She sent him Reiki. "It's going blank. I'm losing it." She opened her eyes.

Cornell stared at her, slack-jawed. He closed his mouth and leaned forward, beckoning for the notebook. She gave it to him.

"The pencil too. I'm not leaving you with a potential weapon."

She set it on the table. He stuck it in his shirt pocket. She hoped he'd let her return to her cell now so she could find out how Arnie was and send him Reiki too.

"You've earned a reward," Cornell said, sounding so pleased it made her stomach turn. "I'll see you get pyjamas to wear at night. And tomorrow morning, a private shower while the guard stays in the hall. I trust you won't cause any trouble."

"Thank you. That's kind." She hated herself for sounding like a sycophant.

Cornell motioned for her to stand. "We're done for today."

He ushered her out of the room, and the guards took her back to her cell.

***

Julie turned to leave Arnie and found Tasha and Deuce blocking the cell door.

"What are you doing?" Deuce asked.

"Just giving him pain meds."

"On whose authority?"

"I checked with the nurse. It was four hours since he'd had any. She said it was okay." Julie kept her voice steady, ready to fight. She'd take Arnie with her, but he was in no condition to help her fight their way out.

Tasha stared at her with amusement, and Julie's stomach sank. She'd seen that look before. Tasha expected a fight. Julie wondered again if they knew her connection to Arnie. Had Cornell transferred her here to expose her? If so, she'd played right into it.

"Hand over the bottle." Deuce held out his hand.

Julie slipped the note from it, hid it in her fist. She gave him the bottle.

Deuce grasped her wrist. "The note, too."

Julie dropped the note and kicked Deuce in the knee. She heard a snap, and he howled in pain. Tasha pulled her gun, but Julie grabbed Tasha's wrist and twisted. The weapon fired, a bullet drilling into the wall opposite the cell. The gun fell to the floor.

Deuce rose on his bum leg. He drew his pistol and aimed it at Arnie, still catatonic on his cot, oblivious to everything. "Stop, Julie, or I'll fucking blow his head off."

Julie ceased fighting. Tasha punched her in the face, and Julie dropped to the floor. Deuce kicked her in the stomach, causing her to curl up like a foetus.

Tasha retrieved her gun and held it over the wounded woman. "Good night, bitch." Tasha slammed the gun into Julie's head.

Everything went black.

CHAPTER 17

Michael glanced at his watch. Close to ten o'clock. Twilight in the land of the almost-midnight sun. The sun would set at 10:40 PM and rise again at 3:28 AM. His wounded shoulder stabbed him when he yawned and stretched, making him wince. He'd caught himself dozing off a few times.

At one point, he'd imagined Carolyn was with him. It made him uneasy. Ever since she'd come up, a sense of danger pressed on him. Michael wondered if she'd put images in his head. He'd seen guns pointed at him.

He'd trust the message and head out earlier than planned. Sleep now, wake Danny instead of Robert, and leave with Robert after Danny's watch. Michael scanned the area one more time. Nothing moved. He scoured the river. All clear. He half-expected to see Althaea roaring along the river in a motorboat, guns blazing. She was out there and waiting for her to pop up any minute made him crazy. Only action would release his tension.

He went to the tent and jostled Danny, who rolled over and opened his eyes. Michael motioned for him to get up and then waited outside. Moments later, Danny joined him.

"I thought my dad was taking the next watch."

"Change of plan. We've got to get moving. Wake us at dawn."

Michael entered the tent and crawled into the sleeping bag Danny had vacated. Robert snored lightly. Michael lay on his right side to spare his throbbing left shoulder, closed his eyes, and tried to relax.

He wondered if Carolyn was okay. The desire to go to her made focusing on his current goal difficult. Forced to be here while the Agency held her tormented him.

Michael pushed the distracting thoughts away and concentrated on what had to be done. The alien base pulled him, the being he'd met in Algonquin Park a constant presence. He'd lost the connection for a while after Althaea had shot him. The more pain he felt, the weaker the connection to the

62

aliens.

He gripped Carolyn's ring and his tension eased. Fatigue wrestled him to the mat, and he fell asleep.

***

Michael stands at the edge of the crowd, heart thudding against his chest as if trying to punch its way out. The gallows is too far away. He's too late. Carolyn and seven others are lined up behind the row of nooses. Five women and three men to be hanged, their bodies burned.

Excitement fuels the crowd as people shout, "Hang the witches!" Michael would happily take a cudgel to their brains if it'd help save Carolyn. He sees Jim Cornell standing next to the hangman.

Michael draws a knife and works his way through the crowd. If nothing else, he'll send Cornell to hell. Scaffold looming, his gaze fixes on Carolyn. She lifts her head and sees him, eyes growing wide. She shakes her head, warning him away. He draws nearer to his target.

Cornell whispers in Carolyn's ear. She turns and spits in his face. He grabs her arm and drags her to the nearest noose. His voice rings out above the crowd. "This one first."

The hangman puts a hood over Carolyn's head and slides the noose around her neck. Panicked, Michael rushes forward, but the faster he moves, the more distant she seems. Hands grab him, and he slashes blindly at them, screaming at Cornell to stop.

He arrives on the scaffold as the trapdoor opens and Carolyn drops into space. "No!" rips from his throat ...

Michael awoke, the word on his lips, but not vocalized. What a fucked-up dream. Sweat drenched his body. The dream prodded him with a sense of urgency, and he wanted to leave. But dawn hadn't yet arrived. Might as well rest while he could. Michael lay back on the sleeping bag, clutched Carolyn's ring, and closed his eyes, hoping this time sleep would be dreamless.

CHAPTER 18

When the guards brought Carolyn back from the lab, Tasha and Deuce were dragging Julie out of Arnie's cell. Deuce limped, and Julie was unconscious, her face bloody. Carolyn slumped on her cot, waiting until the guards left the cellblock before trying to get Arnie's attention.

The doors slammed behind the departing guards, and Carolyn pressed herself against the bars by Arnie's cell. She didn't know if he was conscious. What if they'd hurt him in the scuffle that got Julie banged up? She doubted Arnie had caused that damage.

Her first attempts to get his attention failed. Carolyn's voice stayed low and even, but after calling him for at least ten minutes, there'd been no response. "Arnie, even if you don't want to speak to me, please, tell me you're okay."

No sound, not even the cot's creak. If he was awake, he wasn't moving. Or he wasn't on the cot. Carolyn returned to her bed. They'd had their evening meal, so it was night, but she didn't know how late. Was he asleep? Surely, he couldn't have slept through Julie's beating.

Carolyn paced back and forth. Every pass she made, she paused and listened, hoping to hear he was awake and aware. While she walked, she sent Reiki to Arnie and Michael. When she scanned Michael's shoulder, the pain from his wound shocked her, and she sent him extra energy.

A cot creaked. *Arnie.*

She stopped pacing and listened. The cot creaked again, and she dashed to the bars of the cell. "Arnie?" She held her breath waiting, listening.

"Carr?"

Oh, thank God. "How badly are you hurt? I'm so sorry. I swear I'll do whatever they want so they won't hurt you again."

"Hold my hand?" His voice was weak, tired. Arnie was always so energized, so strong and confident. Now he sounded beaten, and not just physically.

She sank to the floor and stretched out her hand. "Arnie, I'm here." Her fingers wiggled.

He groaned, and his fingers caught hers.

Carolyn gave a squeeze, savouring the touch. "I've got you."

"Ralph's dead, Carr."

"I know."

"You do? Why didn't you tell me?"

"I communicated with him in a dream and was afraid you wouldn't believe me. I'm sorry Arnie."

"It's not your fault. You try to be strong, but these assholes break you. The Agency found Dragonfly because of me."

"Who's Dragonfly?"

"Julie. The new guard. Ralph's contact. Tasha made me tell everything I knew about her. They brought her here and beat the shit out of her. It's my fault. I couldn't take the pain and told them everything. Now they'll torture her, kill her."

Tears rolled down Carolyn's face. "You have to get away. They'll kill us when they're done with us."

"I'm not leaving without you. Not that I'd know how to escape even if you'd come with me."

"Cornell has Sam. I can't leave."

"Then we're not leaving."

"But if you got away, you could find Sam and take her somewhere safe." Hope surged.

"Are you forgetting the aliens can track us? They'd find me."

"There has to be a way. I'll meditate on it."

"All right." He squeezed her hand.

Affection fluttered in her heart, and she longed to hug him. She snatched her hand away when the doors to the cellblock opened and footsteps approached. Guards.

She climbed into bed, and Arnie's cot creaked as he did the same. She gripped her blanket like a child and waited to see whom the guards were coming for. Carolyn prayed they'd pass her and Arnie by, but suspected one of them was at risk.

She was right. Deuce and Tasha unlocked Arnie's cell door. Deuce still limped, and it looked like he had a tensor bandage at his knee.

"Get up." Tasha's harsh voice echoed through the cellblock.

The guards led Arnie past Carolyn's cell. When she saw his shirtless torso, back swathed in bandages, she burst into tears. Their footsteps faded. The cellblock doors slammed closed. Carolyn hugged her blanket and began the long vigil of waiting for Arnie's return. When she realized she was sucking her thumb, her sobs grew louder.

***

Arnie walked between Tasha and Deuce, not registering where they were going. When he realized they headed to the interrogation room, the terror failed to cut through the numbness.

Tasha opened the door, and Arnie preceded the guards into the room. This time, Julie hung by chained hands, her torso bare.

A table against the wall held a water jug and paper cups, along with an open black duffle bag. Arnie couldn't see what was in the bag, but was sure it wasn't party favours. A chair sat at the table. On the wall, the whip hung, waiting. Arnie shook and his extremities grew cold—so much for numb and impassive.

Tasha pushed Arnie in front of Julie. His gaze met hers though it was tough. One of her eyes had swollen shut. She looked unafraid and gave Arnie a half smile. "Don't give them anything."

Tasha laughed. "By the time we're done, you'll be begging to tell us everything. Griffen's here to help you along. His back's a write-off, but he can sacrifice other body parts to your cause." Tasha turned Arnie around to face her and gave him a chilling smile. "Thanks for helping us find the bitch. We haven't forgotten who provided the information to figure out Dragonfly's identity."

Before anyone could stop him, Arnie whirled away from Tasha and threw his arms around Julie. "I'm sorry," he whispered as he kissed her cheek.

Tasha wrenched him away. "Do that again and I'll string you up next to her. Screw orders. I'll fucking flay the skin off you if you make another move without my say-so."

Arnie hung his head but knew he'd won something. Not much, and it wouldn't last, but he'd defied them in a small way. He still felt Dragonfly's cheek against his lips.

Tasha motioned for Deuce to get the whip. The festivities were about to begin. Arnie braced himself. Before the end, he'd want to kill them. Could he get Tasha's gun and shoot them both? Anger and frustration bubbled up in him as he realized he'd never make it. At home, he used to work out, and even here, he did sit-ups, push-ups, and whatever he could manage in the confines of his cell. But he'd be no match for trained fighters.

Helpless, he looked into Julie's eyes. She gazed back, unflinching, conditioned to endure torture. She'd braced for the impending ordeal, but these psychos would compensate, and he'd be forced to watch. He wished he were back in his cell and felt a surge of guilt. It was his fault she was here; the least he could do was bear witness.

Deuce cracked the whip, cutting into Julie's back. She clenched her teeth and didn't cry out. He swung harder. Still she kept silent.

Arnie cracked. "Tell them what they want. They'll get it eventually."

Julie met his gaze and shook her head. "They haven't asked me anything yet."

Tasha laughed. "Yeah, we're just warming up."

"Deuce," Julie said.

Deuce grunted. "What?"

"My back's itchy. Scratch it for me?"

Arnie screamed. "No! What are you doing?"

Julie laughed, but the whiplash cut it short. A small cry escaped her as blood erupted from her back. Tasha stroked Arnie's chest. "This is turning me on."

Arnie wanted to vomit. "Don't touch me, you psycho."

Tasha blew into his ear. "Relax, cowboy. There's a chance you'll get out of here without a scratch." She gave his chest one last stroke, but removed her hands. Another point for Arnie.

Deuce paused, whip hanging limp in his hand, flushed face dripping with sweat. "Ask the bitch something, Tasha. If she passes out, we won't get anything."

Tasha snaked her arms around Arnie's waist and squeezed. "Where'd you two meet to fuck?"

Arnie opened his mouth to answer, but Tasha stifled him with her hand. "No. She'll tell me."

"Fuck you," Julie said. "I won't tell you shit."

"You can take a lot, Julie, but Griffen can't. He's already been through so much. Are you ready to sacrifice him?"

"You can't kill him. The aliens need him."

"There're things we can do the aliens will repair. Pull out finger nails, for instance."

Sweat broke on Arnie's neck. He trembled and his knees threatened to buckle.

Tasha said, "See what you've done? He's quaking with fear, and I haven't even started. Shall I hog-tie him and pull a few nails? I thought you preferred real men. This weenie caved as soon as I started interrogating him, and I barely scratched him."

"I'm sorry, Julie," Arnie said, voice breaking. "Tell them. What difference does it make? It was a random place." Unless it wasn't. Arnie tried to remember. Did he pick the place or Julie? Julie did. *Shit.*

What was she hiding? Or rather, *whom* was she hiding? If she were trying to protect someone she valued more than Arnie, they'd torture him. Tasha was out to break Julie even if she mutilated Arnie in the process.

Julie glared at Tasha. "I'll kill you for this."

"You're in no position to make threats. Die under interrogation or survive to be hanged, you're not leaving here alive."

Arnie tried to break out of Tasha's arms. "No!"

"Hold still. Don't make me tell you again. That's how the Agency penalizes traitors."

Arnie's mouth went dry. That was true for all prisoners, himself and Carolyn included. Carolyn had said it before, but he'd refused to believe it. He finally gave up thinking their captors might let them go back to their lives. One day, the aliens would no longer need them, and they'd be executed.

"Enough bullshit. Julie, where'd you two meet? Jog her memory, Deuce."

Deuce brought the whip down on Julie's back again. She gave a low moan, her head flopping forward. In the ensuing silence, she struggled to meet Tasha's gaze, but the effort seemed too great.

"Where did you meet?" Tasha screamed. "Tell me or Griffen loses a nail."

Julie tried to speak, but gagged, and her chin swayed on her chest.

"Lift her head, asshole. You're not supposed to kill her."

"I'm not. You're the one making me hit her," Deuce grumbled.

"A hotel on Yonge Street," Julie croaked. "The Traveller's Den in Thornhill."

Arnie tried not to betray the lie. Tasha grabbed his hair and yanked his head back, putting her mouth to his ear. "Is that true?"

Pain brought tears to his eyes. His reply was shaky and weak. "I-I-I … Y-yes."

"Fuck it. The bitch is lying. Hit her again, Deuce."

Deuce struck again with the whip.

Tasha shoved Arnie towards Deuce. "This fucker's backing her lies. Tie him to the chair. You two will not do this. This'll cost him."

Arnie screamed and struggled as Deuce dragged him to the chair. After they'd bound him, Tasha secured his arm to the table. Deuce reached into the duffle bag. When Arnie saw the pliers, he hollered and thrashed, but Tasha held him fast.

His terror escalated as the pliers got a purchase on the nail of his pinkie finger. Unbearable pain shot like an electric current into his brain. Arnie screamed long and loud, flinging tears and sweat from his face. He blacked out.

CHAPTER 19

They left the boat hidden among bushes on the riverbank. Danny camped amongst the trees, keeping watch over the area. If anyone appeared, he'd text Robert. Michael and Robert left Danny with the promise that Robert wouldn't enter the base though Michael suspected it was a promise they wouldn't be able to keep.

The two men walked for ten hours. Robert carried a backpack loaded with gear, and Michael focused on not collapsing. He carried a small duffle bag over his right shoulder—all he could manage though it frustrated him. They foraged most of the food they ate, and so didn't have to haul too much with them.

Michael was getting careless, his mind wandering, and the pain in his shoulder distracting him. He was grateful for Robert, who'd more than once spotted edible wild food Michael had overlooked.

Sometimes Michael sensed he'd veered off course and corrected. He recognized the path they followed even though he didn't know how he knew it. Most of the time, the alien intelligence from Algonquin guided him, while other times, he thought it was someone else.

Once, he caught a glimpse of Jessica as a light, translucent presence. His heart perceived her, and he hurried ahead so fast Robert almost lost sight of him, calling out for him to slow his pace. Afraid he was hallucinating, Michael stopped to let Robert catch up. The mist that was Jessica slipped away and left his heart aching.

They continued hiking. Up ahead, the trees thinned and patches of sky peeked through the foliage. Michael blundered into a clearing and sensed danger. Behind him, Robert's footsteps stopped.

Michael turned. Robert stood alert, a finger to his lips. Michael nodded. He felt like a deer surrounded by hunters. Silently, they stepped back into the forest.

"What is it?" Michael whispered.

"In the forest," Robert said so low Michael strained to hear it.

A butterfly fluttered across the clearing and that was all. He scanned the woods but saw nothing. He listened. Just forest sounds. A breeze stirred the leaves, and he caught a whiff of pine and cedar. A woodpecker tapped on a tree. Something stirred in the underbrush, charging towards the glade.

Michael drew his gun, prepared to shoot. A chipmunk darted out of the trees, across the grass, and into the underbrush. Michael laughed. "That little guy sounded like an elephant." He stepped out of the trees, gun still ready, but relaxed.

"Wait. No," Robert called out.

Michael continued cautiously. When he reached the centre of the clearing, the brush rustled again, and a caribou stepped from the trees. Tall and brown, antlers majestic, it moved towards Michael.

The caribou approached. Antlers tilting at Michael, it swung its head and knocked him onto his back. The animal stood over the man and their gazes locked. It planted a hoofed foot on either side of him and snorted, but didn't appear to want to hurt him.

He glanced at the gun in his hand and holstered it, hoping he wasn't making a mistake. His gaze fell onto the antlers. The beast raised a hoof, let it hover over Michael's chest, and planted it again near his injured shoulder. Abruptly, as if frightened by something, the caribou turned and ran back into the forest.

Michael lay on the ground, staring up at a cloudless patch of sky. How blue and magnificent it looked. Clouds scudded overhead, sailing swiftly on their way.

Robert stepped out of the bushes. "You hurt?" He leaned forward, cutting off Michael's view.

"Just stunned. That was strange."

"That was your power animal."

"What do you mean?"

"An animal sent to give you guidance. Caribou tells you to keep moving, take action."

"Did he have to knock me down to tell me?" Michael stood with Robert's help, and his left shoulder screamed in protest. "Examine my shoulder? It feels damp, but it's on fire. Is the bandage leaking?"

Robert opened Michael's shirt and inspected the bandage. "Not leaking. It'll be fine until we camp. Okay?"

"Yeah." Michael took a swig of water and weighed the direction to take. No surprise when he realized they'd follow the caribou's path. The two men stepped into the forest and continued their journey.

***

By the time they made camp, they'd left the river and foothills behind. They built no fire and ate what they'd foraged, supplemented with trail mix and jerky.

"I'll take the first watch," Michael said.

"Works for me." Robert climbed into his sleeping bag.

Michael sat wrapped in a blanket, his back against a log. The remaining daylight filtered through the trees. He reached inside his shirt and caught Carolyn's ring in his fist.

"You do that often," Robert said.

Michael met Robert's gaze and nodded. "It gives me faith we'll be together again."

"Her spirit's strong. When I held the ring, I got images of her."

"What did you see?"

Robert raised himself on one elbow. "Visions, but they scrolled through too quickly."

"Was it bad?" Michael's voice betrayed concern.

Robert shrugged. "I didn't want to intrude, so I didn't pay attention."

"If I let you hold it, can you tell me if she's okay?"

"Maybe. I can't control the images I receive." Robert held out his hand. "Want me to try?"

"Please." Michael removed ring from the chain and handed it over.

Robert held it in his left hand and closed his eyes. "You have a deep connection to this woman." He opened his eyes.

Michael shook his head, denying it. "I haven't known her long."

"She carries your child."

Michael sighed. "I'm aware of how it sounds. I met Carolyn right after my wife died. Her husband died around the same time."

"But you were watching her before then, and you were there when her husband died."

Michael noticed Robert was telling, not asking and had a sudden urge to take back the ring. *Might as well go all the way. I need to verify Carolyn's okay.* "My agency ordered me to kill John. When I hesitated, my partner did it."

Robert closed his eyes. "You've been together in other lifetimes, acting out the same drama in each lifetime. You fail every time."

Michael's mouth went dry. "What do you mean?"

Robert opened his eyes again. "I saw you—both—in other incarnations. There's a pattern. Others are involved, including the man who holds her captive now. Your partner too. You're with these men, then you meet her, you fall in love, and try to escape with her."

Michael shivered and pulled his blanket tighter. Sensing what Robert would say next, he held his breath. He recalled the dream in which Cornell hanged Carolyn.

Robert continued, "You kill your partner, but the other man gets her back. You try to rescue her, but fail. They kill her, or kill you. Either way, you lose each other, so you come back and do it all over."

"How can I stop this?"

"You'll figure it out. Each life, you bring what you learned from the previous one. Each life has a lesson and you evolve over lifetimes. When you don't resolve something in one life, you continue the lesson in the next."

"I could've died on the river the other day, and it would've ended it in this life."

"You hadn't fulfilled your purpose—which is something different than the lesson you're supposed to learn."

"Who decides that?"

"Some say we decide before we're born."

"What do you believe?"

"Creator decides."

Michael fell silent. What could he say to that? Was his dream a glimpse into a past lifetime? It'd explain why Carolyn felt so familiar to him, why they'd drawn together. "Can you tell me what's happening to her right now?"

Robert closed his eyes again. Fear clouded his face, and his eyes opened. He handed the ring back. "I'm sorry."

Michael scarcely dared breathe. "Where is she?"

Robert looked up at the darkening sky and pointed.

CHAPTER 20

Carolyn lay naked and shivering on the operating table. Why was she here less than a month since the last abduction? The aliens didn't even bother erasing her memory anymore as if keeping Carolyn oblivious no longer mattered. During certain procedures, however, they still anaesthetised her.

Once the aliens brought her here, she spent long periods alone, except for the blond humanoids who came and went. Even they ignored her when she tried to communicate with them. They didn't understand, or they didn't care?

Footsteps approached and Cornell appeared at her side. Carolyn had seen him here during an earlier abduction and assumed he often visited. She wished she could force him to trade places with her. She exhaled, trying to release her swelling anger, but failed.

"Why am I here?" Maybe she'd at least get answers.

"The aliens verified Valiant's the father. You'll carry the baby to term for them."

Carolyn tried to struggle, but paralysis was total.

"The aliens have been taking your babies for twenty years. Do you really think you were never pregnant since Sam?"

Horror overwhelmed her. "That can't be. I would've known."

"Consider it your contribution to science." Cornell sounded smug. "This'll be an interesting child, considering your psychic powers, and that Valiant is part alien." Cornell grinned.

The bastard's enjoying this. He was trying to break her. Tears welled up, and Carolyn held her breath for a moment. "Michael?" she whispered. Invoking him brought a moment of relief, as if he were there.

"Right. When Valiant's mother conceived him, the aliens mixed their DNA with his."

"No one is taking my baby."

Cornell chuckled. "Not your call. It'll be safe, don't worry. They'll raise the kid as one of them."

Carolyn thought of the blond humans she saw on the ship. "It'll never be one of them." She noted Cornell referred to the baby as "it." He didn't know it was a girl. Carolyn calmed herself and focused on getting information while he was in a sharing mood.

"Why would they want John's babies? He was neither psychic nor part alien. Was he?" Now Carolyn doubted everything.

Cornell shook his head. "In your case, the father's identity was mostly irrelevant. The aliens allowed you one pregnancy, to make sure everything functioned. After that, they harvested ova and any growing foetuses. You've had a few alien kids. Most of them were used in experiments. You've had babies with Arnie, and once he even fertilized you in the conventional way."

Carolyn gasped. "That's not true."

"Neither of you remember, but were both willing enough."

"That's sick. How many people are they abducting for experimentation?"

"Lots. It's unavoidable—the cost of doing business with them."

A wave of fear engulfed her. Cornell admitted this because there was no need to hide it, just as the aliens no longer cared if she remembered the abductions. "Why tell me this now?"

Cornell leaned down to whisper in her ear. "It's almost over. Your blissful ignorance doesn't matter anymore."

Michael. Part alien. Was that possible? Carolyn supposed so. The aliens were capable of anything. Loss and grief swamped her as she looked back on twenty years. She and John had been so full of hope trying for another child. At first, it'd been a game. She'd tracked the days she was fertile, and they got creative finding time alone while Sam was little.

How many attempts had succeeded? How many babies had the aliens plundered from her womb? The urge to struggle became overwhelming. Carolyn shot Cornell a look of hatred. His hand rested on her shoulder, and she fumed, frustrated she couldn't shake it off.

"We didn't have a say in whom the aliens selected," Cornell said. "They have their own method of selection. Feel good, angel, knowing you helped save some of us. Our species will survive."

"But it'll be a colony of psychos. I want no part of that."

"Sam will be. I'll keep her safe for you. Soon she'll be an orphan. Sorry." Cornell sounded genuinely regretful.

Carolyn tried to gather saliva in her mouth to spit at him, but her mouth was dry. She grunted with the effort and frustration of struggling against the paralysis. "Get away from me!" Carolyn screamed, hoping an alien would intervene if she got too agitated. None came.

Cornell put a hand on her thigh, a gentle touch that sent chills through her body. She remembered her dream, lying on the rack, and what he'd done to her. Heart racing, she pleaded. "Please don't touch me."

He stared at her. "Such a beautiful body." He said it absently, talking to himself more than her. Fingers brushed her skin like feathers. His hand drifted to her belly, ran a finger lightly over a stretch mark, one of the few souvenirs of her first pregnancy. "It doesn't have to happen this way. I can save you." He touched her cheek, cupped her face in his hand.

She wanted to turn away, but couldn't escape his eyes. It became difficult to breathe, and Carolyn fought for air.

Cornell stroked her cheek, brushed a wisp of hair from her forehead. "I tried to be good to you, but you wouldn't let me. We could've had a better relationship. Still can. We'll talk when you get back." For a moment, he looked as if he would kiss her. He leaned forward, but then straightened up and walked away.

Carolyn shuddered. After he'd left, she screamed and cried, and there was no stopping her tears now.

CHAPTER 21

Arnie awoke on his stomach, his back still a mess. Eyes closed, he listened. Silence. He tried to orient and realized he was on a cot. They'd returned him to his cell? His throbbing right hand reminded him what had happened.

He shivered with both fear and cold under the thin Agency blanket. A quick inventory found him naked from the waist up. Gauze wrapped his little finger. Tasha had ripped the nail off, but someone had bandaged it. *The Agency taketh away and the Agency giveth. Fucktards.*

What had they done to Dragonfly? *Julie. Her name is Julie.*

They might have already killed her. Did she tell them what they wanted? He hoped not. He hoped she'd confounded and obfuscated. Arnie wasn't sure what "obfuscate" meant, but he'd heard Carolyn use it once, and it sounded appropriate.

Arnie's mind rambled. Whoever had treated his hand must have drugged him too. It'd be so easy to go back to sleep. Locked up in a cell he had few options and nothing useful to do. He couldn't even help himself, let alone Carolyn or Julie.

Worry for his mother consumed him then. She probably still suffered over his "death." According to Carolyn, Valiant and his partner had faked Arnie's death when they'd abducted him. Everyone Arnie knew thought he was dead.

Fury overwhelmed him whenever he pictured his frail mother struggling to cope with a death that hadn't happened. He wished he could make someone pay for it. But he was so tired. Sleep would be a welcome escape.

Arnie rose and went to the cell bars. "Carolyn." No response. "Carolyn?" *Please answer.* "Carolyn." Now Arnie used a normal speaking voice. Stomach knotted, he feared he'd attract attention if a guard was nearby.

"Arnie, I'm here."

Relieved, Arnie sank to the floor and reached out his good hand. Thankfully, Carolyn was on his right, and he always reached out to her with his left hand.

"Here's my hand," Carolyn said, and their fingers met.

Arnie heard sobbing. What had they done to her while they were torturing him? How much shit did the fucking Agency expect them to take? This place was sucking the life out of them. That it led to their execution was just the blood on the bowel movement.

"What happened?" he said.

"They took me again."

No need to specify. Alien bastards.

"Cornell said the aliens verified Michael is the baby's father."

Arnie wanted to pull his hand away, but squeezed her hand tighter. She needed him. He needed her.

"Cornell told me something you should know."

"What?" Fear churned in Arnie's gut. Cornell never shared good news.

"He said I've been pregnant many times since Sam and ovulating regularly."

"What's that mean?"

"The aliens have been harvesting my eggs and conceived foetuses. They kept my babies."

"Son of a bitch."

"There's more."

Arnie fought the urge to hit something. What could be worse than that?

"A few of the babies were yours."

Arnie went numb. There was a sound in his head like ocean surf.

"Artificial insemination?" *I have children with Carolyn?*

"Not always artificial." Carolyn fell silent.

Arnie shook his head at what that implied. Naked sex. That was just crazy. Relief washed over him. "I'd remember that. Cornell lied to mess with your head."

"The aliens would've erased that memory along with the others. But maybe we recognize it at an unconscious level. Perhaps that's why we're so close."

"I don't believe it." But he did. With all his heart. "Oh God," he whispered.

To his horror, she said, "There's more."

"What else?" Arnie gritted his teeth.

"The aliens will take this baby when it's born." She sobbed out loud, in great gasps.

Arnie's arm was numb, but his grip tightened on her hand. "Why would they let you carry this baby just to take it?"

77

"For their own purposes. It doesn't matter how I feel."

"We have to escape."

"If I do, they'll hurt Sam."

"We'll find Sam and rescue her too. Isn't she at Cornell's house? We'll find it and take her away."

"How are we going to rescue her?"

The despair in her voice chilled him. Usually Carolyn gave warnings or vetoed ideas based on premonitions. Now she'd discarded this idea without checking. He realized she'd been using her intuition less often. "What do your guides say?" He had to help her recover from whatever hell Cornell had put her through.

"I don't know."

"Ask."

"You don't believe. Why are you saying that?"

"You believe, and you've always asked for help from your guides. What happened?"

"I'm tired. Everything's heavy. I can't meditate. What if the aliens or the Agency disconnected me from my guides?"

"If so, they wouldn't make you do remote viewing."

"Okay. But do me a favour."

"Anything."

"You ask too. We need all the help we can get."

"Okay. I will," Arnie promised. It couldn't hurt.

CHAPTER 22

Danny set the frying pan with the fresh three-pound lake trout on the camp stove. He'd taken a risk coming out of hiding to catch and cook the fish, but it'd be worth it. He sipped a mug of cedar tea while he watched it fry.

How much longer should he wait? It'd been almost twenty hours since his dad had gone off with the stranger who'd ruined their trip. He built a small fire in the fire pan. Michael had told him not to, but the air was cold, and Danny reasoned that whoever had been chasing Michael was long gone. It'd been over two days since they'd found Michael, and they'd seen no one else. Valiant was paranoid.

Danny checked the fish. Trout done, he turned off the stove. He carried the frying pan to the fire using a towel and set down the pan. The fish's flesh flaked away when he picked at it with a fork, and it was delicious.

Something in the sky caught his attention. A helicopter passed soundlessly overhead. Not one of the tour copters that frequented the park, but a military chopper. Should he put out the fire? No. Military was government, and they weren't interested in him. He thought of whoever hunted Michael as "the bad guys," whatever that meant.

The bad guys weren't the government—especially not the military. They were the good guys, protecting Canada. Still, Danny felt uneasy, and when the chopper disappeared over the mountains, he was relieved.

He finished the trout and his tea and then cleaned up. As afternoon became evening, the sun still high in the sky, the chopper came around a few more times. After the third pass, Danny extinguished the fire, probably too late. Even though Danny had used dry wood and had stripped the bark to minimize smoke, they would've seen it if they had binoculars or heat sensors.

Danny went to the tent and took out his rifle. Should he text his father about the choppers? Had he and Michael seen them from where they were?

Danny checked his cell and found no messages. He'd wait and see. If anyone found him, he'd say he was in the park by himself, wild crafting— what he and his dad had started out doing anyway. He had the picked herbs to prove it.

Tension eased, Danny returned the rifle to the tent and picked up a digital reader. He settled down to read while he waited for his dad to show up or darkness to fall.

***

Althaea Dayton stepped from the helicopter and motioned for Stephenson and Moser to move toward the camp. They'd have to hurry before it dawned on the young man camped nearby that they were coming for him. The helicopter ran silent, the blades making use of stealth technology, but he'd likely seen it circling overhead.

Althaea indicated to Stephenson and Moser to come at the campsite from the other side. She approached the tent and waited for the others to get in position. After five minutes, she stepped into the clearing. All was quiet.

It was past midnight. The man might be asleep, but she couldn't take any chances. If armed and ready, he might panic and fire. Stephenson and Moser converged from opposite directions, signalling all clear. Althaea peered into the tent.

The man was armed, but not ready. A rifle lay beyond his reach as he sat on his sleeping bag reading by the soft glow of a digital reader. Althaea sliced open the tent with her knife and grabbed the man before he could move. She dragged him from the tent. He grunted and struggled, his efforts feeble and futile.

When he saw the three agents, his eyes widened, but he showed no fear. He stopped struggling and relaxed. "Are you military?" he asked.

So that's why he wasn't afraid. The guy assumed he was in secure hands. She continued the charade. "Yes. We're looking for someone."

The young man's eyes grew wider and now she saw fear. Without saying anything, he'd told her he'd seen Michael, and he knew who they were. She couldn't let him live. But first, he'd tell them everything he knew about Valiant and what he was up to in Nahanni.

"Hold him," she said, and her partners complied.

Althaea took a deep breath. This wasn't something she enjoyed, but it had to be done. She crouched before the young man and held her knife to his throat. "Let's talk about Michael Valiant," she said.

CHAPTER 23

Michael checked his gun. The suppressor was on, the weapon cocked and ready. He watched the guards patrolling behind them. Michael and Robert had managed to slip past the Agency patrols and now huddled between dense brush and the side of a cliff.

The journey had taken them southwest of the South Nahanni River, into the heart of Deadmen Valley. Trees and scrub had given way to grass, the loss of cover forcing them to wait until twilight to cross the open. The rocks and sparse vegetation gave them scant protection, and Michael was anxious to get inside the mountain.

The path to the base entrance was here; they just couldn't see it. They'd seen a helicopter come and go from this direction, and Michael's intuitive guide had led to this spot. His left hand drifted up to grab Carolyn's ring. It dawned on him that he didn't compulsively run a hand through his hair anymore—he grabbed at the ring.

Wonder what Torque would think? Michael closed his eyes, trying to sense where the entrance was. Where was the inner voice that had taken him thousands of miles out of his Goddamn way? *Where are you when I need you, boys? Hello? Can you hear me now?*

Robert stared at Michael, no doubt wondering what they'd do next. Michael wondered the same thing. Suddenly a desire to walk the perimeter of the cliff washed over him, and he was back in the game. He waited for the guards to pass.

The sentries went by every fifteen minutes. Five minutes after the guards walked past, they'd move. But they'd have to be careful not to expose themselves to the cameras. Michael checked his watch. Time.

He motioned for Robert to follow, and they crept forward, moving from cover to cover. Michael kept tabs on the urge to follow the perimeter of the rock wall. After a hundred metres, Michael lost the compulsion to keep walking. He stopped short and Robert almost collided with him.

"Sorry," Michael muttered under his breath. He scanned the area. The entrance had to be near, or he'd want to continue walking. Above them, a trail cut through the rocks. They'd have to climb the almost vertical slope. Michael's shoulder throbbed at the prospect, but he ignored it.

He nudged Robert and pointed upwards. Michael picked his way through the rocks and stones, found footholds where he could, and grasped whatever looked strong enough to hold his weight. They'd have to hurry. If they got past the twenty-five-metre mark, the rocks below would conceal them. Until then, they were like bugs on a windshield. Michael quickened the pace.

The next time he stopped, Michael looked at the ground far below. Perhaps they'd make it after all.

***

Carolyn pulled out of a trance. "That's everything."

Once again, Cornell had her in the lab, notebook and pencil in hand, connected to Michael. He and another man climbed the side of a mountain. She told Cornell, hoping he wouldn't be able to narrow it down to any specific location.

Mountain ranges were huge, and he could be anywhere. But Carolyn sensed Cornell knew more than he let on, and she'd just told him where Michael was.

Whenever she connected to Michael, Carolyn tried to warn him of the Agency pursuit. So far, she didn't think she'd succeeded. There'd been no inner knowing she'd reached him. She begged the angels to protect him, and sent telepathic messages to his guides and angels, asking them to warn Michael.

Carolyn still felt bogged down as if a fog surrounded her and blocked her from reaching out. She'd experienced it the night before when she'd agreed to call on her angels and guides to help her and Arnie escape.

"Try again." Cornell sounded angry, impatient.

The irritation in his voice was a good sign, indicating the clues she'd provided weren't enough. Carolyn tried not to betray her spasm of happiness, but closed her eyes and connected to Michael.

She saw a caribou.

Something in her expression must have changed because Cornell shifted in his chair. "What?" A demand.

"It's probably nothing," Carolyn replied, opening her eyes. It probably was nothing. What would that give him?

"I don't care. Tell me."

"I saw a caribou."

"A real caribou?"

"I guess." *No, a figurative one.* She didn't say it aloud, fear censoring everything she said here. Maybe it wasn't real. Then she realized it was Michael's spirit animal guide and remained silent. Let the Agency grunts search for a herd of caribou.

"Try again." Cornell didn't sound irritated this time.

She relaxed, eyes closed, and reconnected to Michael. Two men with guns appeared below him, but were unaware of his presence. This would pinpoint Michael's location, so Carolyn kept her face a blank mask. She needed something less significant, less specific. "There's a faint trail. I'm losing it. The images are fading. It's gone."

"Draw it."

"I suck at drawing."

"I don't care."

Carolyn opened her eyes and sketched a narrow trail along the edge of a mountain. The fugitives were getting to higher elevations. Scrub brush. Boulders. Rocks. Powdery snow coating everything. Carolyn sketched the rough shape of what she saw through Michael's eyes and tossed the finished drawing on the table. "That's everything."

Cornell picked up the sketch, glanced at it, and pocketed it. "We're done here."

The guards entered, and Carolyn prepared to return to her cell.

***

Cornell rushed back to his office, shouting to Helen to get Althaea on the phone. The phone rang as he reached his desk. "Ally?"

"What's up, Jim? Sounds as if there's news."

"Valiant is climbing the mountain. I'm emailing you a sketch of the trail. No doubt, he's found one of the access routes to the base. Figure out which path he's using and get him. The son of a bitch has been free too long."

"I'll call you when we have him."

Cornell hung up the phone and gave Helen the sketches, instructing her to scan them in and email them to Althaea. He returned to his office, optimistic that by day's end, they'd have Valiant in custody.

He fought an urge to book a flight to the Northwest Territories. Valiant would be transferred here—drugged, so the bastard couldn't escape. Cornell wasn't going to trust anyone to get Valiant here without chains and sedatives. No way would he risk having to do another manhunt.

It'd be a pleasure to tell Valiant they'd give his baby to the aliens. Cornell thought back to when he'd held Valiant captive in Algonquin. He'd told Michael the Agency would brainwash Carolyn, making her believe

Valiant was her enemy and Cornell was her lover.

Cornell had been bluffing—what an expensive endeavour that would be. But it might be worth attempting. He'd have to commandeer resources, but no one would question it when he proved how useful Fairchild could be as one of them. Perhaps she'd even pull the trigger on Valiant.

CHAPTER 24

Michael and Robert had been climbing for hours. The air was chilly, and a thin coating of snow blanketed everything. If the cold became extreme, it'd penetrate the layers Michael wore. He'd lost his parka escaping Althaea, and while Danny had provided turtlenecks and sweaters, Michael had refused to take the young man's only parka.

Helicopters came and went for the last few hours. Once, Michael had thought he heard Carolyn calling, but attributed it to fatigue. It'd felt nice to be reminded of her voice even though she'd sounded alarmed. Michael had taken it as a sign to be more cautious and had slowed their pace. He constantly checked for an ambush or pursuit.

Robert expressed concern that Danny might be in danger, and Michael tried to reassure him, but had his doubts. Worry nagged Michael whenever he remembered Danny.

They approached another bend in the trail, and Michael raised his gun. So far, they hadn't encountered even a bird, but he didn't trust the silence. He motioned for Robert to halt and peered around the curve.

The trail grew wider here. Wind picked up, blowing through the surrounding scrub brush. The air smelled fresh and clean, and the view was spectacular. Across the tree-covered mountain, in the valley far below, the river sparkled in sunshine.

Michael inhaled, refreshed, and stepped out from behind the shelter of the cliff face. Robert followed. Five metres from the bend, six men and one woman appeared, surrounding Michael and Robert.

"We've been expecting you," Althaea said. "Cornell has been forcing your little 'ho' to track you, Mick." She smiled.

Michael's stomach twisted. Maybe he *had* sensed Carolyn earlier. He didn't react. Althaea stared, licked her lips—a habit. Michael remembered kissing those lips.

"Let Robert go." Michael figured he'd start with the obvious. "This doesn't concern him."

"He's involved more than you know. Daniel is on his way to becoming part of the Nahanni legends. You're going back to Cornell."

Robert took a step towards Althaea, and the agents raised their weapons.

"What do you mean? What happened to Danny?" Robert's voice shook.

"We found him where you left him, though he didn't want to admit he'd seen you, Mick." Althaea looked at Michael as if she wanted everyone to know this was his fault. "We persuaded him to talk, but couldn't let him go, so he's now one of the headless men."

Robert screamed in rage and ran at Althaea.

Michael grabbed him, held him back. "They'll shoot you."

"I don't care."

"You'll join him soon enough," Althaea said. "Bring them."

They handcuffed Michael and Robert, and Althaea led them up the trail. Before long, she dropped back to walk with Michael. "You'll die and it won't be quick. Was she worth it?"

When he didn't reply, Althaea's pretty face clouded over. Michael turned away, scouring the surrounding area, trying to sense Carolyn. If she'd connected with him, perhaps he could hear her voice again. It'd be preferable to listening to Althaea prattle on about the terrible things they'd do to them.

The trail continued though the grade wasn't steep. The group approached an opening in the mountain, like the mouth of a cave, which a moment before hadn't been visible. They stepped into a dim tunnel, lights spaced three metres apart. Robert walked as though in a daze, grief etched on his face. Michael wished he could help Robert and regretted bringing him.

Althaea took Michael's arm as though they were on an afternoon stroll. He tried to shake her off, but she held firm. "Stop it, or I'll slug you." She said it low, so the others couldn't overhear.

"Try it," Michael replied, not so low.

She grinned at him. "Come on, Mick. I meant something to you once. We were soul mates."

Michael tried to detect mockery, but heard none. "You don't know what that means, Ally." The nickname slipped out.

Once, he used to love the familiarity of calling her that. They'd had many intimate dinners together, times when Jess had been far away and out of mind. His heart stabbed with longing for Jessie.

Althaea drew closer to Michael. She stuck her gun back in its holster and brought her other hand up to squeeze his arm. "I've missed you."

"You have a funny way of reconnecting."

"How did you expect me to react when you rejected me?"

"I expected you to understand that I love my wife."

"You no longer have a wife. It didn't take you long to get over her death."

Michael fought the urge to push Althaea away. If she thought he was cooperating, he'd find the opening he needed. "I still love Jessica, and the Agency murdered her."

"There's no proof of that."

"I have all the proof I need."

The tunnel forked and two agents split away, leaving four guards. Althaea's group followed the tunnel leading to the left.

After walking for fifteen minutes, they halted at a double row of empty cells. Althaea stopped at the first one and removed Robert's handcuffs. She opened the door and motioned for him to step inside.

Like an automaton, Robert stepped into the cage, and she slammed the door shut behind him. He moved to the single cot in the room and sat, dropping his head in his hands.

Althaea dismissed Robert's guards and tugged on Michael's arm. "Next one's yours."

After Althaea removed the cuffs, Michael entered the cell, Althaea once again clinging to his arm.

"Wait outside," she said to the two remaining guards. Althaea released Michael's arm and motioned him to sit.

"I'll stand, thanks."

"I can force you."

Michael sat.

"The abductions are ending," she said.

"Why tell me?"

"I want to see your face when I tell you that the bitch you impregnated is scheduled to be terminated as soon as the baby is born. The others will be executed—the ones the aliens don't keep permanently. They might keep your girlfriend, and you'll never see her again."

Michael kept his face blank. "Old news. If you've nothing else to offer, leave."

"No reaction? I guess she meant little to you. That makes me feel better. You just wanted to fuck her. Did you rape her?"

"I love her."

She grimaced. "You can't. After your wife, there's me."

"Althaea, what do you expect to happen here? There's nothing between us. We had something. *Had.* It's long gone. You didn't respect me or my marriage. Whatever I felt for you died when you reacted like a crazy, jealous stalker."

Althaea flinched. Michael stood. She took a step backwards. *Good.*

"Sit, Mick."

Michael made a move as though to comply, but lunged for her gun. Althaea had braced herself and beat him to it. She snatched the gun from its holster and hit Michael on the side of the head with it. Dazed, he grasped her wrist and twisted her hand, but the gun remained firm in her grasp. When the two guards pulled him off her, Michael knew he'd failed.

Althaea snarled. "Hold him for me."

They braced Michael between them. She stared into his eyes. "I'll enjoy what Cornell does to you, but frankly, I can't wait that long."

Fluid as a dancer when she moved, Althaea swung her fist and smashed it into his face. Michael's nose spurted blood, and she backed up. But she wasn't done. She hit him in the stomach, and he'd have doubled over if the guards hadn't been holding him. Althaea used him as her punching bag, avoiding blows that would knock him unconscious.

His breathing became ragged and laboured. By tomorrow, he'd have two black eyes. When she'd had enough, Althaea wound up for the last strike. She raised the gun and hit Michael in the head. At last, everything went dark.

CHAPTER 25

"We have him."

The words, coming at him over his speakerphone and said by Althaea Dayton, energized Cornell. It gave him the infusion of hope he'd needed ever since Valiant escaped from the Algonquin base. Cornell wished Althaea were here so he could hug her. "Good work, Ally. Are plans underway to get Valiant here ASAP?"

"Yes, sir. I'll deliver him myself. What do you want us to do with Robert Holden?"

"Keep him locked up. The aliens need him for a while. When they're through with him, terminate him."

"Yes, sir."

"We'll celebrate when you get here." He hung up.

Things were looking positive. If only he could get Carolyn Fairchild on their side. Despite her desire to help Valiant escape, she'd been invaluable in helping the Agency locate and capture him. If Cornell could get her on board with what they were doing, she'd be more useful. He called Helen again.

"I want to take Fairchild underground with us. Once the baby's born, we'll put her through the training programme. But I want nothing to interfere with the baby's development. Schedule it for two months after the baby's due date."

"Yes, sir."

He disconnected. Yes, that'd work out well. They'd have to manipulate her mind, and Carolyn would view him as a benefactor—perhaps more— and Valiant as an enemy. Cornell recalled her beautiful, naked body and felt himself grow hard.

***

When Michael regained consciousness, every part of his body throbbed, his head most of all. He sat, but it made him woozy. To control the dizziness and nausea, he closed his eyes. He probably had a concussion and would have to force himself to stay awake.

An idea formed. He waited a few minutes, listening for guards, and then called out to Robert. A cot creaked.

"Michael? How badly are you hurt?"

"I'll manage. You okay?"

"We never should have left Danny alone."

"I'm sorry. We should have sent him back to town."

"I've connected with him in spirit."

"Did it help you?"

"Yes." Robert lowered his voice. "Danny explained what you need done."

"That makes things easier."

Michael kept Robert chatting for another fifteen minutes, mostly about family. Halfway through a statement he was making, Michael dropped to the floor and shook as though convulsing, eyes rolling back in his head. Robert screamed for the guards.

At the sound of footsteps, Michael feigned unconsciousness. Robert shouted to the guards that Michael was in trouble. The cell door rattled and clanged. Eyes shut, body limp, and breath deep and slow. He sensed the guards nearby. A guard checked Michael's pulse at the throat. He itched to leap up, but forced himself to lie still.

"Pulse is fine," the guard said. "Should we take him to the infirmary?"

"No. Just put him on the cot. It'll be safer to bring the doc here. Grab him. I'll cover you in case he's faking."

The guard's hands slid under Michael's armpits and dragged him along the floor. The scenario he wanted to play out scrolled through his mind, and he estimated the other guard's location by his breathing.

Now.

He leapt up, turned, and grabbed the guard holding him. Michael shoved the guard towards the wall. The guard holding the gun tried to get a clear shot and failed when his partner slammed him into the wall. A fight for the gun had the three men grabbing and struggling. The gun fired, and one guard dropped to the floor.

The remaining guard jumped on Michael, and they struggled for control of the weapon. A wave of dizziness hit Michael, but he held on, though his eyes blurred. Time was running out. Any moment, Althaea or more guards would appear. Michael dug down deep and mustered a burst of energy. He punched his opponent in the gut, shoved a knee between them, and wrested the gun from the guard's hands.

He hit the guard on the side of the face, making him pitch backwards. Michael fired, hitting the guard in the chest and then fired again, this time hitting the face. It was over.

"Michael?"

"Wait, Robert." Michael snatched the keys and another gun from a guard. He hurried to Robert's cell, handed him a weapon. As Michael struggled to free Robert, the cellblock door crashed open.

"Company," Michael said. "Get ready."

Two guards appeared. Michael shot one guard and pushed Robert back into the cell as the other guard fired her weapon. Michael dropped to the ground, returning fire, and the woman fell. But she wasn't out. Her gun aimed at Michael, her gaze locked on his, finger poised to squeeze the trigger. Robert's weapon discharged first. The guard slumped to the ground and didn't move.

"Thanks. You saved my life." Michael jumped up. The guard's lifeless eyes stared up at him.

"This way." Without waiting to see if Robert followed, Michael ran down the corridor.

The route took them past the guardroom. Michael motioned for Robert to get down and crouched by the open door.

"You wait here. Boyd, come with me." Althaea.

Michael heard the sound of guns drawing from holsters. He snatched the weapon from Althaea as she stepped out the door. Her body a human shield, he shot Boyd in the head. Robert stepped into the breach and fired at the remaining guard. He missed and had to jump back as the man raised his gun and fired.

The fight lasted five minutes. Michael coldcocked Althaea and focused on putting the last guard down. When it was done, he picked Althaea up and slung her over his shoulder. "She'll help me get into where I need to go," he said, in answer to Robert's puzzled look.

They continued down the corridor, but still hadn't found the room Michael was looking for when Althaea stirred. He set her down, handcuffing her with her own cuffs before she was fully awake.

Her eyes opened, focused, and then widened in shock. She struggled to back away, but he grabbed her arm and hauled her to her feet. "You're coming along for the ride, Althaea."

"You won't escape."

"I'm not trying to." He gave her a shove, and she stumbled forward. "Walk. Follow the corridor. No turns."

"Whatever you've got planned won't work. They'll find the bodies and come after you."

He ignored her. Instead, he said, "You know, I always wondered why aliens would need us—the Agency, I mean, not the people they abduct—

that one's obvious. You know what I figured out?"

"What?" She sounded genuinely curious.

"They physically can't fight and need soldiers. They're incapable of doing their own dirty work."

She remained silent, lips pressed together, eyes narrowed. He'd nailed it.

They continued to walk, Michael leading the way. Somewhere, the benevolent alien he'd met in Algonquin guided him. Althaea stopped short, and fear flashed across her face. "Where are we going?"

"If you recognize the route, you know the answer."

"How can you possibly know the way?"

"I don't."

"You can't do this. You'll blow us up."

"Michael?" Robert sounded concerned.

"Trust me, Robert. This isn't a suicide mission. Carolyn's waiting for me, and I intend to get to her."

Althaea laughed. "You'll fail and we'll die."

"Move it." Michael quickened the pace and pushed Althaea ahead. He pressed the gun to her back, making sure she could feel it. The closer they got to Michael's target, the greater grew his sense of urgency. They were almost running by the time they reached the door he wanted. When they stood before it, he said, "Open it" and pushed Althaea to the keypad.

"I don't have access."

"Bullshit. Quit stalling, or I'll blow your head off and get in anyway."

She punched the code into the keypad and pressed her thumb to the scanner. The door slid open.

They entered a rocky chamber, the door whisking shut behind them. Carved from the bowels of the mountain, it was a rough, cold cavern. Water sweated on the walls and glowing crystals carpeted the floor.

A low henge of stones in the shape of a Vesica Piscis—two intersecting circles, the centre of one circle hitting the perimeter of the other—lay before them. A large crystal stood within the intersection. Michael didn't recognize the composition. The crystal wasn't anything formed of this earth.

Bubbles of what looked like acrylic hung from the ceiling, suspended by thick tubes. Something floated in a clear liquid inside them. Horrified, Michael realized each bubble held a foetus in it, all at varying stages of development.

"Jesus." Had they taken babies from Carolyn and brought them here? He shivered and looked away, the whole idea unbearable.

"Mick, why are you here?" Althaea sounded terrified.

Terror surged through Michael as well, but he brushed it aside. This was Carolyn's only hope. "Cover her. If she moves, shoot her. Think you can do that?" Michael said, without looking at Robert.

"Yes," Robert replied, grief and anger in that one word.

Michael believed him. "I'm breaking the hold these bastards have on all abductees. If anyone else shows up and tries to interfere, shoot them."

He made his way to the edge of the Vesica Piscis while Robert led Althaea away from the door. Michael had a sudden urge to walk the sacred symbol before he entered it. He began at the nearest intersecting point, walked clockwise around first one circle, then counter clockwise around the other. He repeated the walk around the circles again, completing seven laps in total.

Michael stepped into the centre and placed his hands on the crystal.

CHAPTER 26

Althaea watched in horrified fascination while Michael walked the Vesica Piscis and ran his hands over the crystal. He then sat, lotus position, eyes closed. The door slid open. Three guards ran into the room, guns raised.

Robert dragged Althaea in front of him. Afraid the guards would damage the crystals and the incubators if they fired, she held up her hands, halting them. They paused, uncertain.

"Don't shoot. You're too far away."

"Come any closer and I'll kill her," Robert said.

Althaea opened her mouth to tell the guards to approach, let Holden shoot her if he wanted, when a vibration filled the room. It amplified, and humming filled her ears. She didn't recognize a specific chord—she knew nothing about music—but the sound was beautiful. Tears streamed down her face. She looked at the guards, and they were also crying.

Robert released her, but she didn't move. She sensed Robert on the ground behind her and turned to him. He'd dropped her gun and writhed, screams tearing from his throat. His eyes rolled back in his head, and his back arched. Blood gushed from his nose—more than she thought possible.

When the blood from Robert's nose slowed to a trickle, a lump crawled out of his left nostril. The blob of goo slithered down his face, leaving a gory trail of blood, snot, and bits of flesh. She looked over at the guards. One of them also ejected the thing from his nasal cavity. So even some of the Agency's own were abductees. But not her.

Althaea looked at Michael, who continued to sit, meditating. Not Michael either. The sound eased. She had to act before he snapped out of his trance. Robert lay unconscious. He wouldn't be any trouble. She shouted to the two guards, who stood dazed by the door. "Get these fucking cuffs off me."

94

***

Cornell hadn't called Carolyn to the lab in over a day. Did that mean the Agency had caught Michael? A constant knot of worry twisted her gut. She and Arnie had tried to figure a way out, but nothing came to mind. Neither Carolyn nor Arnie was a fighter, and every plan they came up with involved over-powering the guards and grabbing their guns. They'd never succeed.

Carolyn spent most of her time lying on the cot in her cell, alternating between tears and numbness. Despair blanketed her. She called on her angels and guides, but nothing happened. It was difficult to trust they were helping without evidence of it, and her faith faltered.

Part of Carolyn felt relieved when she resigned herself to captivity. If the decision to leave was out of her hands, then it wasn't her fault if the aliens took her baby. But Sam would be safe. Guilt overtook her then. She couldn't let this baby be sacrificed to the aliens to protect Sam, whose safety wasn't exactly guaranteed. Whatever Cornell told her should be considered a lie. He'd tell her whatever he needed to so she'd cooperate.

Carolyn made a move to stand and get water from the sink when she felt a dull ache in her head. The pain increased, became unbearable. She moaned, cried, and screamed. In the next cell, Arnie also screamed. The whole cellblock became a symphony of agony as the other inmates joined in.

Her head. Carolyn pressed her hands to her head. *Stop it. Stop it. I can't take it.* She screamed, screamed, screamed, but it wouldn't end. Carolyn's back arched, and she thrashed on the cot, writhing in agony. The pain burned, ripped her apart.

Red fluid spewed from her face, and her mind registered that blood flowed from her nose. Something crawled out of her nostril and slid along her face. The last thing Carolyn heard before she fainted was the wet smack the fleshy blob made when it hit the floor.

***

When Carolyn came to, she lay strapped to a bed in the infirmary. No one else was in the room. She looked for a call button, but didn't see one. "Hello?" Surely, someone was monitoring her.

The door opened and a hook-nosed man with a scar on his cheek entered the room. He wore scrubs, so Carolyn assumed he was a nurse.

"What happened?" But she already knew. She'd lost her tracking device. The aliens couldn't home in on her anymore—unless they captured her again and shoved another tracker up her nose. Carolyn blanched when she realized it'd been a living creature.

The nurse checked the monitor hooked up to her.

"Is my baby okay?"

He glanced at her. "The baby's fine."

"Why am I the only one here? Are the others okay?"

"Yes." The nurse pressed a button and two guards entered. "Doc says she can go back to her cell." He turned and left the room.

The guards—one of them was Deuce, and he walked much better—removed her restraints. "Get up," Deuce said.

Back in her cell, guards gone, she talked to Arnie, who made it clear he was more determined than ever to escape. Certain that Michael had done this, Carolyn wanted to scream the news out to the other abductees, but kept it to herself. No doubt, the others had figured out they were no longer traceable—they just wouldn't know who'd liberated them.

It occurred to Carolyn that maybe Michael would come for her now. Perhaps he'd get here before the baby's birth and help them escape. If anyone could do it, Michael could. Carolyn said nothing to Arnie—she wouldn't say anything to anyone. She didn't want to risk tipping off Cornell or anyone else in the Agency.

Where was Michael now? Had he escaped? Carolyn lay on her cot, eyes closed, trying to connect to him. She breathed deeply, trying to relax. Impressions came to her in dribbles. She saw large crystals in a cavern. Shapes. Something about a fish? Everything was too vague. Large stones. Intersecting circles.

Carolyn experienced a moment of frustration and breathed through it. In a clear flash, she saw Michael place his hands on a large crystal, and she knew the end had come.

CHAPTER 27

Althaea grabbed the gun from the ground and stepped over the still unconscious Robert. She'd almost reached the interlocking circles when Michael's eyes opened. She froze. Radiant and beautiful, he pained her eyes, and Althaea forgot what she was doing.

She forced her gaze away and searched for the guards. One lay on the floor, unconscious. Another stood staring at Michael. The last one, still holding the cuffs he'd removed from Althaea's wrists, hunched next to Robert, eyes glazed.

The gun. She looked at the gun in her hand. So archaic—a primitive weapon for a primitive people. The thought surprised her, the source unknown. Never mind. The gun would do the job.

She closed her eyes and took three deep breaths. When Althaea opened her eyes again, she looked at the floor and strode towards Michael. Slow and steady. *A sunny day's stroll in the park.*

One step at a time, she drew closer to the target, forcing her mind away from what she intended to do. Michael moved behind the stone on which the giant crystal sat. Still she kept her head tilted towards the floor.

The closer she got to the circles, the greater was the energy. It was thick, like walking through water. The energy opened for her and snapped shut behind her when she stepped into the circles.

A glance at Michael showed him glowing, filled with light. His arms embraced the crystal. Beams of light linked the crystal to the stones, to the crystals, to any living beings. A vortex of energy fed her knowledge of what he was doing.

She lunged forward—as much as she could, considering the liquid feel of the surrounding energy—and fought her way to Michael. When she reached his side, Althaea dropped her gun, and tried to push him away from the crystal.

"Stop!" Although she screamed, her voice sounded muffled.

Eyes glazed, Michael held firm, either ignoring Althaea or unable to hear her. Wind whipped around them in shrieking gusts. The cavern became translucent. Red light glowed outside their circle. One of the guards dropped to his knees and clasped his palms together. Was he *praying*?

The ground shook. Part of the ceiling caved in, burying the unconscious guard and the one who'd been praying.

Althaea put her arms around Michael's waist, hands clasped across his abdomen, feet braced. She pulled. The man was a rock. Desperate now, she squeezed herself between Michael and the stone, then pushed against him as hard as she could. She couldn't fucking do it. She screamed at him, pounded on him.

The floor rocked. Althaea watched, mouth hanging open, as her gun slid past them. The gun. She dropped to her knees and reached for it, but it slipped from her grasp. She pounced and grabbed it. Legs shaking, she stood and faced Michael. *Fuck you, Mick. I don't want to shoot you.*

Althaea raised her hand to hit Michael on the head when the floor shifted again. She lost her footing, crashing into him. A jolt went through her, and she screamed, this time in agony. The room dimmed. *No. Can't pass out.*

Michael shoved the crystal off the stone, and it crashed to the ground, shattering. Like dominoes falling, the rest of the crystals in the room split and cracked. The incubators shattered, spraying their contents everywhere. Something dripped down her face, soaking her hair. Althaea brushed it with her hand. Amniotic fluid. She gagged, trying not to think of what might be stuck in her hair.

She braced herself against Michael, pulled her arm back, and clocked him. He dropped, yanking her on top of him when he fell. She lay quiet, his warm body under hers. God how she'd missed him. She checked his pulse. It was strong.

Althaea looked around and realized she'd failed.

CHAPTER 28

Cornell hung up his phone. Something had happened at all the alien bases, but the Nahanni base was the epicentre. Near as he could tell, based on the garbled reports flooding in from around the world, the aliens and their ships were gone.

Valiant. It had to be. He called Helen and told her to have Carolyn Fairchild escorted to the lab. He had to sort this out. Without the alien technology, Earth would never be repaired. They'd be stuck underground forever, and the facilities weren't designed to last that long—two or three generations, maybe, but not indefinitely.

Next, Cornell called his wife. "Pack up, Ginny. We're heading underground."

"What happened, Jim?"

"Something no one expected. I'm mobilizing everyone. We need to evacuate before everything goes to hell."

"What about Sam?"

"Sam's coming with us. Trust me. Okay?"

"Yes." Ginny sounded reluctant. Jim couldn't waste time explaining it again. But they'd have a long talk when they were safe underground. Sam had to trust them both. If Ginny screwed this up with her petty jealousy, he'd never forgive her. "I have to go now. Tell me you'll watch over Sam. We can't lose her, or I'm screwed—we're all screwed. Understand?"

"Yes." Ginny sounded resigned.

"I'll call you later." He hung up the phone.

One last call to make. Cornell picked up the phone again. "Helen, send a memo out to the Agency heads. Tell them it's time to go underground. They must do a thorough clean up before heading out. No non-Agency personnel are to remain."

"Yes, sir."

Call ended, he rose from his desk. Time to chat with Carolyn. She'd be the exception to his non-Agency personnel rule. The Agency needed her special abilities underground, but the others would be eliminated. At least he'd spare them the coming hell.

***

"You know what happened." Cornell leaned towards Carolyn, who sat in the recliner in the lab. She'd tried to tell Cornell she didn't know, but he refused to believe her.

"What did Valiant do?" Jim asked.

Carolyn closed her eyes though she didn't bother to connect. She opened her eyes. "Michael's out of reach."

Cornell's face turned red, and he frowned. "What happened?" he asked through gritted teeth

Carolyn sighed. "I don't know. Why won't you believe me? I saw strange images—crystals, stones, fish shapes. Weird stuff. Michael was there. Then he wasn't." Carolyn refused to say Michael wasn't dead. She wouldn't give Cornell that.

An energy field surrounded Michael, but she wouldn't tell Cornell. The truth was, she couldn't connect to Michael.

The lights flickered. They'd flickered periodically for at least the last hour, Cornell growing increasingly agitated. When Carolyn had told him she wasn't getting anything, he'd left the room for a while. She'd feared at first he'd forgotten her, then she'd hoped he had. But he'd returned and now sat haranguing her.

His chair crashed to the floor when he abruptly stood. Carolyn recoiled as he rushed around the table and yanked her from the chair. "I've had enough. Let's go."

Why wasn't he calling the guards to come and get her? Cornell pulled out his gun and pointed it at her, waving the gun at the door. "Move."

Carolyn went. "You don't have to do that." It reminded her of Michael. She'd said that to Michael when he'd kidnaped her. She tried to clear her head. Best not to think about Michael now.

She stepped out into the observation area where a guard waited. He looked young—barely older than Sam. His red and freckled face looked innocent. But he was an agent, so Carolyn knew that was deceptive. The young man would be as cold and hard as the others.

"Take her to my office and keep her there until everyone else has evacuated. If anyone but me tries to get in, shoot to kill. You have your cell?"

"Yes, sir."

Carolyn's mouth went dry. *Cornell wants to take me underground with him.*

The thought sent shivers down her spine. What about Arnie? Carolyn was afraid to ask, afraid to remind Cornell of Arnie. Instinct told her to stay quiet, so she did.

Cornell didn't spare her another glance and left.

The guard grabbed Carolyn by the arm and walked her out the door.

When they entered the reception area of Cornell's office, Carolyn noted Helen wasn't there, her belongings gone. The guard released Carolyn's arm and ushered her into the office. He opened the door, scanned the room, and waved her in. Carolyn entered, the guard right behind her.

"Sit." He didn't sound mean, just brusque.

She took a seat on the couch. The guard shut the door and joined her. How long would they have to wait here? Carolyn considered asking him, but feared he'd hit her. At least he'd holstered his gun.

The silence was creepy. Beside her, the guard shifted and pulled out a cell phone. She watched while he flipped through some images. Suddenly she felt sick, and it wasn't morning sickness this time. Something was wrong. *Oh, God. They're killing everyone.* Without thinking, Carolyn jumped up.

The guard leapt to his feet and forced her back onto the couch. "What do you think you're doing?"

"They're killing the prisoners. Why?" Tears rolled down her face. *Arnie. Oh, Arnie. No.* Carolyn shook, sobs wracking her body.

He stood over her, his face impassive. "Don't move. If you get up again, I'll hit you."

Carolyn put her head in her hands and fell into grief. The lights went out.

***

When the lights flickered, Arnie had the first hint that something big was happening. Tasha and Deuce ran into the cellblock amidst shouting and clanking doors. "You do one side, I'll do the other." Tasha's voice held panic. "Don't open the doors. Just do it. We've got to go."

Arnie had never heard her sound like that, and it chilled him. Then the meaning of the words sank in, and his stomach knotted. His fears were confirmed when the begging, screaming, and shooting started.

Carolyn wasn't in her cell. What would happen to Carolyn? Did Cornell take her out to spare her this last indignity? Was he keeping her for his own uses? Arnie wished he'd had the chance to say goodbye.

Moments dwindled as Tasha and Deuce worked their way through the rows of cells, and Arnie's turn loomed. He decided not to beg. He'd done enough begging, and it hadn't helped him. These people were psychotic. At least he'd be free.

He lay on his cot, eyes closed. He'd never believed in God or the angels

Carolyn always turned to, but a little superstition couldn't hurt. Arnie asked any angels around to help him through this.

Sounds of death grew louder. He sensed Tasha's presence and waited for the bullet to hit him. A sudden urge to put the pillow over his face came over him, and he covered his head.

"Move the pillow, Arnie."

He slid the pillow off his face, but kept his head concealed from her view.

"Very funny, asshole. Remove it."

"Not if you begged me, Tasha."

"I don't have time for this shit. You'll suffer for this."

He heard her carry on the shooting rampage down the row of cells. He'd received a stay of execution, but she'd be back. Arnie closed his eyes and prayed that when she returned, he would have the nerve to fight.

Ten minutes later, he heard the rattle of keys and clink of the cell door as she entered. Everything after that became a haze of anger, instinct, and adrenaline. Tasha snatched the pillow from his face, and Arnie grabbed for the gun. She swore when he pulled her on top of him. Her knee thudded into his thigh, narrowly missing his groin.

He arched his back, trying to escape the pain from her pressing him into the cot. The gun fired, a bullet ricocheting off the wall. They both grunted and struggled. She was stronger. His hand gave, the gun pointing at his face.

Her thighs pressed into him and she loomed above him. In a burst of strength, fuelled by terror, he twisted her wrist as she squeezed the trigger, and the bullet hit the wall next to the cot. Arnie felt the ping in his side when the bullet hit him.

A scream tore from his throat. "Fuck you." He twisted the gun again. This time it pointed at her face, and his finger rested on the trigger. "Fuck you." Her face blew apart, and he thrust her away, her body slamming against the wall. "Fuck you." He bellowed it again and again, punctuating each curse with a pull of the trigger. When the anger and terror receded, he dropped the gun to the floor.

The cries of the other prisoners had dwindled into silence. Blood trickled down Arnie's side, but he remained immobile, standing and staring at Tasha's body. He shook himself and focused on taking deep breaths. The lights continued to flicker. He hoped Carolyn was still alive, but didn't expect Julie was. They'd probably killed her days ago. Was it days ago he'd last seen Julie? He didn't know. Time had no meaning here.

Silence became his world. Too tired and nauseated to walk, he sank to the cot. How long before he bled to death? The lights flickered and died. Arnie clutched the gun and closed his eyes.

***

Julie Helliwell was not dead, but she was close to it. Deuce and Tasha had tortured her, wrung what information they could from her, and thrown her into a cell. She'd spent most of her time since then surviving minute by minute, aware it'd end with her execution.

When the gunshots, screams, and pleading reached Julie's ears, she knew something had gone wrong. Instead of a formal execution, they likely planned to shoot her with the abductees. Julie smiled. Finally, she'd caught a break.

But she'd have to act fast, and with her broken ribs and toes, and her missing fingernails, "acting fast" was a relative term. She steeled herself, ignored the agony, and stood. She attempted to simulate a body on the cot using her blanket and pillow and went to the cell bars.

With luck, whomever they'd assigned to her little corner of hell wouldn't expect her to be ready and waiting. She'd be last, which was a shame. If she succeeded, she could've saved others, perhaps even Arnie.

Julie squashed herself into the wall and waited. It didn't take long before Deuce arrived. He swept to the cell door, focused on the cot where he expected her to be. In one fluid motion, Julie reached through the bars, twisted the pistol from Deuce's hands, grabbed him by the shirt, and shot him in his surprised face.

She gritted her teeth against the searing pain and yanked Deuce's body to the cell. Blood sprayed from Julie's hands when the makeshift bandages slid off her fingers, exposing raw, meaty fingertips. She kept her eyes focused on the hallway. Tasha would come soon.

Julie swiped the keys from Deuce, unlocked her door, and dragged him into the cell. Sweat poured from her body, dripping from her forehead and into her eyes. She hauled Deuce's body to her cot.

She set the guard down for a moment, dizzy. When the vertigo passed, she ripped the blanket off her bed. The pillow fell onto the floor, but she ignored it. She hauled Deuce onto the cot and draped the blanket over him. The cell looked like a Roman arena after a gladiator-lion fight, most of it her blood, but at least it looked as if Deuce had done his job.

Julie drew a raspy breath, returned to the cell door, and closed it. She listened. Where was Tasha? The silence continued for so long, Julie suspected she was alone in the cell block. She left the cell silently. Nothing moved along the corridor. Tasha was gone? Or she was hiding, ready to ambush. Only one way to find out. Julie hugged the wall and crept along, one cell at a time.

CHAPTER 29

When the lights died, and the shattering ceased, Michael came back to consciousness from a warm and cozy place. He thought it was a dream. No images, only floating in peace and darkness. He awoke, however, to Althaea slapping his face.

Michael sat and slapped her back, then instantly regretted it—not hitting her—that had been self-defence, but the sudden move. He rolled over, pressed his hot face to the cool floor, and willed the room to stop spinning.

"Why'd you hit me?" Althaea asked.

"Why were *you* hitting *me*?"

"To wake you."

"I'm awake." Michael remembered everything and jumped to his feet—another regrettable move. Bile rose in his throat and he couldn't stop it. Michael fell to his knees and vomited. "You gave me a concussion."

"Get over it. You've just killed us."

Michael ignored her. "Robert?"

"I'm here." Robert's voice seemed to come from a distance.

The room spun and Michael sat. He second-guessed the move and lay on his back, Althaea standing over him.

"This is all your fault," she said.

"Really? I had to stop you maniacs."

Robert moved into Michael's line of sight and looked at him. "What happened?"

"He phased the aliens and their ships off of Earth," Althaea said.

"I don't understand," Robert replied.

The guard joined them, looking puzzled and confused. Michael figured he was trying to decide whether to draw his gun or hang out and chat. Lying in this huddle of people turned Michael's stomach again and made him claustrophobic. "Back up or I'll puke. Althaea, explain what

104

happened."

"Mick phased the aliens and their ships back to their world, then destroyed the portal. That'll start a chain reaction of destruction here. Parts of our technology depended on the energy supplied by the alien crystals set up around the world." Althaea turned to Michael. "It'll look like Pompeii out there soon."

"How?" asked Robert.

"The main portal was here. It makes use of zero point energy, combining with the energy of the crystal in the Vesica Piscis." Althaea turned to Michael. "How did you know what to do?"

"The aliens helped me."

Althaea stood, hands fisted on hips, accusing. "That's insane. Why would they help you? Back in their world, they're as good as dead. They need to be here to survive."

"Perhaps the ones that helped me didn't like sacrificing humans to save themselves. Some of them have a conscience." Michael rubbed his head. They'd told him what to do, but not what would happen when he succeeded. Head aching, mouth dry, he turned his attention to immediate concerns. "Does anyone have water?"

"I should shoot you instead," Althaea said. But she pointed to the guard and asked him to give Michael a swig of water from the canteen on his belt. The water settled Michael's stomach, and he risked sitting, but put his head in his hands when the world threatened to spin again.

After the fog in his brain cleared, he said, "The aliens were experimenting on humans, my family included. They stole foetuses from pregnant women and ova from fertile women. It had to stop."

"They'd have reconstructed the Earth. It'll never recover now, and you've triggered the Aurora machines. That'll decimate whatever remained. Congratulations. You're the man who unleashed Armageddon, and you knew that when you did it," Althaea replied.

"You think they'd rebuild the world for us? Cornell thinks he can rule over the new world, but he's deluded. And I didn't realize sending them back to their world would trigger the Aurora machines." He'd expected the aliens to return to their world, understood their sacrifice, and expected upheaval at this end. But he hadn't realized until the moment he'd done it the extent of the damage and systems failures.

Yet this was what he'd been sent back from death to accomplish. The knowledge of it came in a burst, although he didn't remember why he'd had to do it. He turned to Althaea. "You know a lot too."

She looked puzzled. "I don't know how."

It hit him. "You're like me." He stood and approached her.

She backed away, and the guard raised his gun.

"Relax, fella." Michael waved a hand, the gesture placating. "Althaea, I won't hurt you." In fact, Michael didn't want to do what he felt compelled to do, but that wouldn't be the first time today.

She stood, rigid, and he held her face between his palms. When they drew close together, she closed her eyes, as though waiting for his kiss. His forehead touched hers, and images flowed into him.

He viewed Althaea's past. The traumas: her family's friend molesting her when she was five; her parents' denial; her angry adolescence; the drug overdose; then the self-mutilations and eating disorder at seventeen; the physical altercations—she became a violent, uncontrollable whirling dervish, in prison by the age of nineteen.

The Agency approached her during her incarceration, and she went to them gladly. Michael sensed something beneath the images pouring into his mind—a sense of corruption. But when he tried to focus on what it was, pain pierced his skull and his mind retreated.

The images continued to flow, and Michael saw Althaea's life at the Agency. Focused on work, she kept most men at arm's length, except for Michael. She let him in, and the decision ended up hurting them both. He experienced déjà vu as he relived the time they'd spent together. Her heart broke when he rejected her, and she expressed her anger inappropriately, as always. It drove him further away.

Michael pushed deeper, to her origins. He'd been right when he said she was like him. The aliens had tampered with the Althaea foetus. They spliced in alien DNA as they had with him. She hadn't fully activated yet, but her psi abilities were awakening. She knew things intuitively, especially when they pertained to the aliens and their world.

He felt her trying to pull information from his own mind and blocked her.

Althaea pulled away and slapped him across the face. "You invade my mind but won't let me see yours?" Her voice shrilled with agony.

Horrified, Michael realized he'd violated her. Without thinking, he tried to take her in his arms, but Althaea pushed him away.

"I'm sorry. I wasn't in control of it," Michael said.

Her eyes watered. "That was mind rape. Fuck you."

"I'm sorry. I didn't realize until you intruded in my head." The sense that something was wrong in Althaea's mind lingered. Unable to understand it, he let it go.

She looked as if she'd retort, but the guard who'd given Michael the water spoke. "What happens now?"

"I find Carolyn," Michael replied, his gaze meeting Althaea's.

"I can't let you do that, Mick. Cornell wants you." Althaea nodded at the guard, and he raised his gun.

"Do you plan to walk to Peterborough from Nahanni, Althaea?" Michael said.

"Were you planning to walk to Peterborough, Mick?"

"If necessary."

"There's your answer. But we won't have to walk. The choppers will work as long as the storms hold off. They'll be evacuating all the compounds now, and we need to get to the underground community." Althaea turned to Robert. "I'm sorry."

Michael moved over to Robert. "Let him go. What's he going to do? Robert will be lucky to survive out here, but he deserves the chance to try."

Althaea shook her head. "You know the drill, Mick."

"Let him go, Ally." This time, he deliberately used the nickname. "I'll allow you to take me in."

"I won't bargain. I'm taking you in."

"Have it your way." Michael lunged at her.

The guard raised his gun, but Robert jumped on him, and they grappled. Michael and Althaea wrestled, each trying to reach her gun. She grabbed it and swung around to aim it at him.

Michael forced her to the ground, and they struggled. He applied pressure to her hand, and the gun slipped to the ground. He leaped for it, but she grabbed him and dragged him back. Althaea punched Michael in the face, and he saw stars. He grabbed her in a chokehold, almost losing his grip when she slammed backwards into him. It threw him off balance, but he held on. Soon the thrashing subsided.

He checked for, and found, a pulse. Relieved, he pushed the unconscious Althaea off, rolled over, and picked up the gun. On his knees, he aimed at the guard, who straddled Robert, hands around Robert's throat.

Michael fired twice in rapid succession, rushed over, and knocked the guard's body away. Robert's eyes stared vacantly.

"No!" It was a useless gesture, but Michael checked for a pulse anyway. It wasn't there. He bowed his head. "I'm so sorry, Robert."

It was some consolation that Robert and Danny were together. How could it have ended like this? Robert had said he was supposed to come with Michael to the base. Did it mean he'd been fated to die here? Before he could think more on that, he heard Althaea stirring. He held the gun on her.

She rose on one elbow. "Are you going to kill me?"

"I'm taking you with me."

Althaea looked surprised. She stared at Robert's body. "It was nothing personal."

"Murder is always personal," Michael said. "Even when you think you're just doing a job."

"You've become quite the philosopher."

Michael didn't reply, but looked around the cavern. The door through which they'd entered lay shattered, and the ceiling had crumbled. Smoky, burnt-orange sky stretched out above, and rubble surrounded them. Michael was grateful they could breathe the air though it was thinner and blanketed with smog. They'd acclimate.

He tried to gauge the best way out. It was a miracle they'd survived. Althaea sported cuts and bruises. Michael's shoulder burned, and his head ached.

"To the right," Althaea said.

Michael turned his head in the direction she indicated. The walls had crumbled more at that end, which was adjacent to the centre stone and the greatest force of outward-directed energy. He went to the pile of debris that had been the west wall.

"I think we can climb this." He estimated the best route to take without bringing the whole thing down on them. Michael motioned for Althaea to lead. She picked her way up through the ruins, and he followed.

CHAPTER 30

When the lights went out, Carolyn raised her head. The guard remained motionless. A pale light shone in through the windows, illuminating his face. His expression told her nothing. Carolyn asked her angels and guides to help her connect to his guides, then risked speaking. "What's happening?"

The guard's eyes darkened; he frowned and made no reply.

"Please." A whisper, afraid to push, but more afraid of not knowing.

The guard shook his head.

"Why are they killing everyone in the cells? The guards are shooting the prisoners."

Startled, he turned his face away. Carolyn tried to sense anyone around him. She asked for his departed loved ones to come through and help her talk to him.

Erik. A female presence.

Carolyn cast a sideways glance at the man and said, "Your name is Erik."

Erik jumped up and yanked her off the couch. "How do you know my name? They'll think I talked to you. I didn't tell you." His voice sounded panicked, and his grip hurt.

"I'm connected to one of your loved ones in the spirit world, and she told me."

"What are you saying?"

Silently Carolyn asked the spirit's name.

Lisabet.

"Who do you know named 'Lisabet?'"

"How did you get that name?"

"I'm connected to her."

Fear crossed his face. "What are you trying to do?" He pulled out his gun, pointed it at Carolyn, his other hand still gripping her arm.

Lisabet, please help me talk to him. Who are you?

Mother.

"Lisabet's your mother. She's here. Talk to her."

"It's a trick. Stay away from me. Stop talking." Erik shook her while he spoke, and Carolyn stumbled, tripped, and would have fallen if he hadn't been supporting her. The gun in his hand oriented on her temple, and her stomach twisted.

"Please. Jim doesn't want you to shoot me, so put down the gun. I won't try anything. I want to help you connect with your mother."

"She's dead."

"Why do you think the Agency locked me up here? I have a gift that lets me communicate with spirits. The Agency wants to use it. That's why Jim doesn't want me killed." Carolyn used Cornell's first name, making it more personal, though it disgusted her to talk about him as though he were a friend.

Doubt showed on Erik's face, but he lowered the gun. Carolyn focused on Lisabet, trying to establish a stronger connection.

A young mother, fair-haired, pretty. Walks with two young kids: Erik and a little sister. Erik looks to be eight, his sister six. Mom and children walk into a convenience store.

The man behind the counter shouts at them, confusing them. They turn to see a man holding a gun. Lisabet pushes the children aside as the gun fires. The bullet strikes her, hitting her heart. She goes quickly, the children screaming and crying while she passes in front of them.

Carolyn spoke again, whispering. "I'm so sorry. She died in front of you and your sister."

Erik raised the gun. "Stop that. One more word out of you and I'll beat the shit out of you."

Lisabet, please, help him listen. Carolyn fell silent, giving it time, though she couldn't wait too long. She needed someone on her side. If Erik carried out Cornell's orders, she'd be lost forever. Her terror escalated at the thought of going underground. Fear she'd never see Sam again overwhelmed her.

Silently Carolyn thanked Lisabet for coming through and asked her to stay close. The room darkened. A storm approached. Lightning speared across the sky and seconds later, thunder rumbled. Outside the office door, everything was quiet.

In her head, Carolyn reviewed the self-defence techniques Michael had taught her when they were in Peterborough. Doubtful she could pull off an escape, but she had to try, even at the risk of a beating.

Erik checked his watch. "Let's go." He waved the gun.

Carolyn considered her options. She'd have to be quick and sure when she tried to disarm him, and Erik was a trained fighter. But Michael had shown her how to grab a gun from someone's hands even if they'd had training. *Don't over-think it*, Michael had told her. *Okay, Michael, this one's for you.*

When they approached the door, Carolyn slowed her pace, letting Erik get near her. She reached for the doorknob. Instead of opening the door, she whirled, twisted the gun out of his hands, and smashed him in the face. Erik's nose spurted blood, and his eyes watered.

Carolyn ran, slamming the door shut behind her, and sped through the office. The doorknob rattled, and the door swung open. A glance back showed Erik rushing from the office. She stumbled into the hall, straight into Jim Cornell's arms.

He grabbed the gun from her hand and punched her in the face. Blood and tears smearing her face, Carolyn dropped to the floor.

Erik caught up to them. "I'm sorry, sir."

Carolyn looked up in time to see Cornell level the gun at Erik and shoot him in the gut. He doubled over, dropping to the floor. Cornell shot him again, this time in the head, and Erik went still. Cornell snatched a pair of handcuffs from the body.

"That was your fault. I have no use for anyone who can't keep you under control." Cornell grabbed Carolyn's arm and dragged her to her feet. "Turn around, hands behind your back."

She complied, knees wobbling and hands shaking. She wanted to wipe the blood from her cut lip, but he bound her hands behind her. Carolyn watched a drop of her blood land on the carpet.

"Kneel."

"What are you going—" Carolyn choked on a sob as she had a sudden thought he wanted to execute her.

"Don't make me tell you anything twice." Cornell forced her to her knees.

Out of the corner of her eye, she watched him fish the key to the cuffs off Erik's body. When Cornell returned, he lifted her up and spun her around. "I have Sam. If you escape, she'll still be with me, and you'll never know if I killed her until you talk to her ghost. Let's go."

He led her away.

CHAPTER 31

The sound of the cell door unlocking shocked Arnie. He realized a moment of terror before he yanked the pillow off his face to confront the torn wreck that was Julie. His heart broke with grief and relief.

"Julie. Oh, God. How are you here?" Arnie tried to keep his voice low, but it still seemed loud to his ears.

Julie crouched at his side. His T-shirt lay on the floor next to the cot, and she picked it up and tore it into strips. While she talked, she bandaged his bullet wound.

"We need to hurry," she whispered. "If they find us alive, they'll finish what they started."

Arnie wrapped his arm around Julie's shoulder, and leaning on each other, they hobbled to the cell door. Shadows filled the cell, but the hallway glowed from emergency lights located every few metres along the wall near the ceiling. He listened, but heard nothing.

"Did anyone else survive?" he said.

"I haven't checked every cell yet. Help me do it, but hurry. If anyone's monitoring the cameras, we're dead."

"Wouldn't they have spotted us by now?"

"Maybe not. It's likely chaos up there. Deuce and Tasha were careless, or neither of us would've survived. But it means something terrible happened."

They slipped into the hallway. Julie closed the cell door, a slight sound of metal meeting metal. In silence, the pair limped from cell to cell, checking each one. In all cases, it was obvious the person was dead. Most of the bodies lay on the floor, or draped half on the cot. Blood spatters marked their final moments. Tears rolled down Arnie's face. What a waste.

These corpses would rot. But it told him no one planned to return to this death camp. At least Carolyn's cell had been empty. Thank God, he didn't have to see her lying discarded on her cot. He could hope she'd survived, and he'd find her though he didn't know where to look.

They reached the end of the cellblock finding no one alive. Arnie couldn't believe he'd survived. His furtive prayer to the angels came to mind. Unbelievable. But he sent a quick thank you and a request to help him find Carolyn.

Julie led him to the infirmary. "I need pills and bandages."

We both need pills and bandages, Arnie thought.

They went to the supply cabinet and grabbed whatever would be useful. Julie pulled out a bottle of painkillers, opened it, and gulped two.

She tipped two into Arnie's hand, and he swallowed them with water from the tap. He hoped they worked fast. The pain had become unbearable.

Julie found a black medical bag, and they packed it. "I need to remove that bullet from your side soon, Arnie."

He nodded, afraid to speak. He glanced at the door often, expecting it to burst open at any moment.

When they left the infirmary, Arnie carried the bag, and led the way through the corridor. Julie limped, and Arnie hoped she'd be able to run if they encountered any Agency personnel. At least she had a gun. If only he could find Carolyn.

***

Arnie and Julie hid behind a pillar near a set of stairs, the main exit to the compound up ahead. In front of the double doors and their avenue to freedom stood Carolyn Fairchild and Jim Cornell. Carolyn had blood on her cheek, chin, and shirt. Cornell gripped her arm, her hands cuffed behind her.

Outside, rain poured, and trees whipped violently in the wind. Cornell pulled out his cell phone and released Carolyn's arm. "What's your ETA? It's getting worse out there."

Carolyn stood, passive, staring at the floor. A lump grew in Arnie's throat. He'd lose her if he didn't do something fast.

Cornell hung up the phone and put his arm around Carolyn, who remained mute, immobile. He said something to her that Arnie couldn't catch. She shook her head, and Arnie saw the glint of tears on her cheeks.

"Consider it an adventure." Cornell sounded jovial, excited, his words echoing across the deserted reception area. "Wait until you see what we've done. It's a miracle. Took us thirty years to build it right." He reached out and stroked her cheek. "We'll get you a shower and clean clothes."

Carolyn wrenched her arm, but his grip on it was firm. "Behave, angel."

Arnie looked into Julie's eyes and set the medical bag at his feet. He reached out his hand and motioned for her to give him the gun. She shook her head and pointed at herself, then at Cornell. Arnie nodded. Even with her mutilated fingers, she'd be the better shot.

If they didn't stop Cornell, he'd walk out those doors with Carolyn, and Arnie would lose her forever. He couldn't let that happen. He had to at least try. *I have to try or die.* Not inspiring words, but they'd have to do.

He edged his way around the pillar. Julie touched his arm and motioned for him to stay put. She slipped closer to the side of the pillar away from Cornell and Carolyn, Arnie following close behind her. They were halfway around it when Cornell spun around and pointed his gun in their direction.

"Did you think I didn't know you were there, Griffen? Helliwell?"

They froze. Carolyn gasped and came to life then, putting her body in front of Cornell's gun, blocking him. He wrapped an arm around her and pulled her tight to his body.

A Humvee pulled up at the entrance. Cornell's ride. His head inclined towards the door, but he didn't glance at it.

"Let them go. Please," Carolyn said. "If you do, I'll leave with you. I won't fight you."

"I have Sam. You'll do what I want regardless."

"No. I won't. If you kill Arnie, you'll have to kill me, and if you kill me, I'll protect Sam from the other side."

Cornell paused, uncertain.

Carolyn pressed her point. "I won't let you kill Arnie."

"I'd be doing him a favour. He's as good as dead if I leave him here."

"Then what difference does it make?"

Two agents with assault rifles stepped from the Humvee and headed for the doors. Arnie stood frozen, watching them. The agents entered the building. Carolyn screamed, "Run!"

Cornell shoved Carolyn at the two agents. "Take her to the car."

Arnie grabbed Julie by the arm and ran. A bullet pinged off the pillar behind which they'd hid. Julie took two shots, the bullets hitting the wall. Arnie ran blindly through the doors and into the corridor, his wound burning agony.

Silence behind them told Arnie no one pursued them, but he kept moving, dragging Julie with him. A set of double doors blocked their path and Arnie pushed through them. The pair hobbled along the hallway, listening for Cornell's footsteps.

They'd made it almost to the cell block when Arnie finally stopped running and turned. No one followed. Cornell was gone, and he'd taken Carolyn away. Arnie and Julie were alone, with only the dead to keep them company.

CHAPTER 32

Michael hovered the helicopter over the Peterborough compound's deserted parking lot. Wind and rain battered them, and he struggled for control, but he landed it without killing anyone.

His heart told him Carolyn was gone even before he saw the vacant parking lot and dark building. But he needed to make sure Cornell hadn't killed her and left her body behind. He shut the engine off and turned to Althaea. "I'm going in."

"No one's left, Mick. We have to get underground."

"I'm not going anywhere until I know what happened."

Althaea scowled, but kept silent. Michael waved the gun in her face. "You first."

She rose from her seat with difficulty. "Can't you at least take the cuffs off?"

Michael ignored her, hoisted a backpack onto his shoulder, and waved the gun at the door. Together they climbed out into the wind, forced to cling together. They fought their way to the main entrance and found the place locked.

He used C4 to blow the doors, dragging Althaea around with him while he set up everything. The storm lashed at them while they huddled outside the blast radius, and Michael detonated it.

Gun held ready, he guided Althaea into the building. Shell casings littered the floor, but he saw no bodies. A trail of dried blood, maybe two days old, led away from a pillar in the lobby.

He dragged Althaea to the reception desk. The wind blew rain into the hole he'd made, and Michael had to raise his voice to shout over the noise. "I'm not carting you around this place. You're too much of a distraction."

"You can't leave me here."

Michael didn't reply, but forced her to sit, and cuffed her to the chair.

Althaea's face darkened, and she struggled against the cuffs. "You asshole. What if someone's in here?"

"Charm them with your sunny personality."

Michael jumped out of the way as Althaea's booted foot swung at him. He walked away, following the trail of blood.

The trail ended at the infirmary. Michael tried the door. Locked. He kicked it open, using the wall as cover. His heart skipped a beat when he found the room occupied. But he lowered his weapon when he realized the man and woman occupying the two beds were either asleep or dead.

He recognized Arnie, but not the woman. Both looked wounded and beaten, especially the woman. Arnie's eyes popped opened, and he groped for the gun on the nightstand, his motions groggy and feeble. Michael snatched it up.

"Arnie." Michael kept his voice low.

Arnie jerked up when recognition flashed in his eyes. He screamed in pain, and Michael grabbed his flailing fist.

"Easy. I'm not here to hurt you."

Arnie's eyes bugged out, and his lips contorted in rage. "You fucking kidnapped me. You killed John."

Michael stepped back, out of fist-flailing range, and aimed the gun at Arnie. "Calm the fuck down. I'm here to help you. Where's Carolyn? Is she okay?"

Arnie collapsed back on the bed. "Last I saw her, two of your psycho buddies were dragging her into a Humvee. Her mouth was bloody, and she was in handcuffs."

Michael winced. "Let me help you? Blood's seeping through that bandage around your abdomen."

"Help Julie. She's dying. I haven't been able to wake her for the last day." Arnie's voice broke. "Please. Do something."

Michael turned to Julie. He set Arnie's gun on her bed and shoved his into its holster. A blanket covered her to the neck, and Michael eased it down to her waist. Bandages swathed her torso, and her hands and feet were beehives of more bandages. Dark bruises decorated the skin around her eyes, a stark contrast to her pale face.

"If I check her back, will I find it covered in welts?"

Arnie nodded.

"Was she Drummond's source?"

"Yes." Arnie looked away.

"She's lucky to be alive. You must tell me one day how you two survived. I've seen the cellblock."

"Can you help her?"

"I'll try. She probably has an infection. I'll give her antibiotics and painkillers intravenously. Her breathing is regular, but her colour looks terrible. What happened to you?" Michael nodded at the bandage around Arnie's abdomen.

"A guard shot me when they executed everyone. The bullet's still in there."

"Shit. Why didn't you remove it?"

Arnie looked at Michael as if he were crazy.

"All right. I'll take it out." Michael found what he needed, talking to Arnie while he did. Arnie spoke grudgingly at first, but then told Michael everything that had happened since Carolyn arrived in the cell next to his.

"I overheard Carolyn talking to you that day," Arnie said.

Michael looked up from Julie's arm, where he was removing the needle after inserting the catheter.

"You heard everything?" Michael asked.

Arnie nodded.

He knows the baby is mine.

"Turns out we've both given her babies," Arnie said.

Michael froze, heart pounding against his chest. "What does that mean?"

Arnie smiled as though enjoying Michael's reaction. "Cornell told her the aliens had me impregnate her—in the traditional manner."

"Then I'm sorry for you both," Michael said.

Arnie's face fell.

"Don't look so disappointed. Nothing they do surprises me, and what Carolyn has done in the past isn't my business—especially when she has no memory of it. My business is leaving here and going after her before Cornell hurts her any more than he already has."

"Do you know how to find her?" Arnie's voice rose, hopeful.

"I know where they headed. I would've been going with them had I not taken a permanent detour to help Carolyn escape." He checked Julie's temperature—too high. He went to the sink, wet a washcloth, and handed it to Arnie. "Wipe her down with this, then rinse it again with cool water and apply it to her forehead. I have to get something from the lobby."

"What about my bullet?"

"I'll take care of it when I get back."

Arnie stood, taking his time, wincing with every movement.

"When did you last take a painkiller?"

"A few hours ago, I took four of whatever Julie found in the cupboard the other day. I can't handle the pain."

"No more painkillers while I'm gone," Michael said. "I'll give you more when I return and find out what you took." He handed the gun back to Arnie. "Keep this handy. Make it a habit."

Arnie nodded and turned his attention to Julie.

Michael hurried from the room and down the hall. Hopefully, Althaea was still where he'd left her. He pulled the gun from its holster though he was sure no one remained in the building. In the reception area, water pooled on the foyer floor. A fine mist covered Althaea's hair.

She looked up when she heard him and cursed when she saw him. Michael rushed to her side. She held a pin in her hand and had been trying to pick the lock on the cuffs. Michael pulled out his key, freed her hands from the chair, and then handcuffed her again, hands front. "I don't have time to screw around with you, Althaea. Get up." The gun aimed at her head reinforced the statement, and she complied.

While they walked, Michael told Althaea about the two survivors. He contemplated his next move. Until the weather cleared, he was stuck here. Althaea would try to interfere at every turn. The underground facility was locked down tight—getting in would be near impossible. But if he didn't find a way, he'd lose Carolyn and his baby daughter.

He refused to abandon them. He'd told Carolyn he'd find her no matter what it took, and he'd keep that promise. Death hadn't kept him from her, so he sure as hell wouldn't let the Agency stop him. Michael's hand strayed to Carolyn's wedding band, and it gave him hope.

CHAPTER 33

Julie slipped into the spirit world during the night. Michael dozed on a chair in front of the door, but snapped awake to the sensation that something touched his cheek. He grabbed for the gun in his holster, pulled it out. A glance around the room showed everything was normal.

Arnie slept, eyeballs rolling under the lids while he dreamed. He'd kicked off his blanket, exposing the bandages around his ribs where Michael had patched him up after removing the bullet. Althaea remained handcuffed to a bed Michael had dragged in from another room. Eyes still, she slept dreamlessly now, though she'd been restless most of the night.

Michael looked at Julie and noticed she wasn't breathing. He holstered his gun, crept to her side, and checked for a pulse. Too late, and he'd known it was even before he touched her. He wondered if Julie's spirit was still here, watching them. *I'm sorry, Julie. I wish I had Carolyn's ability.*

Arnie stirred and opened his eyes.

Michael released Julie's hand. "I'm sorry." He glanced at Althaea to make sure she still slept.

Arnie sat, grief etched on his face. He picked up Julie's other hand in both his own, gaze riveted on her face. "I dreamed I talked to her."

"What did she say?"

Tears slid down Arnie's face. "She said it wasn't my fault."

"It's not."

"It is. The Agency wouldn't have found her if I hadn't told them what I knew. It didn't take much for Tasha to make me spill my guts. I couldn't keep my mouth shut." Arnie kept his gaze on Julie's face.

"How could you have kept your mouth shut while they broke your bones and flayed your skin, then had the aliens put you back together to do it all again? It's not your fault."

"I never should have slept with Julie. If I hadn't gone along when Ralph met with her, they wouldn't have had anyone to interrogate. Ralph's dead, so they couldn't get anything from him."

Michael started. "Drummond's dead? What happened?"

"You don't know?" Arnie's head snapped up.

"No."

Arnie returned his gaze to Julie. A wisp of hair on Julie's cheek caught his attention, and he brushed it to the side and then stroked her head. He talked to Michael in a quiet voice. "Tasha told me Ralph hanged himself, and Carolyn said she'd seen Ralph in a dream." He told Michael what Carolyn had revealed.

Michael went numb. "That's why she left me in Algonquin." Michael clutched Carolyn's ring in his fist. "Why didn't she wake me and tell me?"

"She knew you'd stop her, and she wanted to keep Cornell from giving Sam to the aliens."

"I would've helped her get Sam back."

Althaea stirred. "Maybe Carolyn didn't trust you."

He turned and faced her, but couldn't bring himself to reply. She returned the stare and then looked over at Arnie. "I'm sorry about Julie. Michael's right. It's not your fault. The Agency can break anyone." She paused. "It was pointless, too, if you consider it. Whatever they wanted Julie to tell them doesn't matter anymore."

"That's not helpful, Althaea," Michael said.

"Mick—"

"Don't call me that." It came out a snarl. He grimaced.

She gave him a puzzled look, but that was all.

"What do we do now, Michael? Can we get to Carolyn?" Arnie said.

"I'm not leaving her there," Michael replied. "I'll do whatever it takes to get her back."

Althaea interrupted. "Do you feel that?"

She tried to get up, but the cuffs wouldn't let her. Michael's chair shook, the beds squeaked, and bottles rattled in the cupboards. Arnie set Julie's hand down and stood. "An earthquake?"

"Stay here." Michael pulled out his gun and rushed into the hallway. Everything was dim. Emergency lights gave off a feeble glow. He went to the lobby. The wind howled outside, the storm still raging. They'd have to patch up the hole where the doors used to be. The ground continued to tremble.

The wind roared louder and trees on the other side of the parking lot bent to the ground. One large tree snapped in half and flew onto the pavement. Michael watched, horrified, while the helicopter he and Althaea had arrived in fell on its side and slid across the cement. The ground stopped shaking, but the wind and rain continued.

Lightning speared from the sky, thunder crashing seconds later. He could forget about going after Carolyn anytime soon. Michael turned his back on the storm and walked away.

Back in the infirmary, he propped the door open and adjusted Julie's bed. Without a word, Arnie got up and helped Michael wheel it out into the hallway. From the room next door, they brought another hospital bed in for Michael.

"I hate to sound like a chicken shit, but I'm glad I don't have to sleep in a room alone," Arnie said.

"I'm sure there's no one else roaming around here, but we'll stick together for now. It'll get old fast, though," Michael replied.

Arnie shook his head. "I'm not worried about that. The Agency murdered people here. It's not the living that scare me."

They froze, staring at each other, while the building shook again.

CHAPTER 34

The next time Michael opened his eyes, it was morning. Arnie's bed was empty. Michael glanced at Althaea's bed and was relieved to see her still securely handcuffed. She was also glaring at him. "I'm sick of this, Mick. Take these fucking cuffs off me."

"I can't, even though you've asked me so nicely."

"What do you think I'll do? I can't go anywhere. Those tremors we experienced are the least of our worries. We're stuck here, and wandering around this place by myself doesn't sound enticing. Killing you wouldn't improve my situation. I can help you, but not handcuffed to the bed."

Michael shook his head. "Sorry. Can't risk it."

Arnie walked in carrying a tray of food and drinks. "I found a lot of food in the cafeteria, but if we don't find a generator, we'll lose everything in the freezers. Some of the refrigerated stuff has already gone bad."

Michael glanced at the gun tucked into Arnie's belt. "Glad to see you're carrying the gun. Scavenge a holster for it. Thanks for the food."

Arnie set the tray on the counter next to the sink and passed around Danishes, bagels, fruit, and muffins. "The stove runs on gas, so I made tea. The drinking boxes and water are room temperature, but I guess we're lucky they left it." Arnie turned to Michael. "Doesn't this place have a generator?"

"Yes. They cut the power deliberately and didn't engage the generator when they evacuated. They weren't expecting anyone to stay here."

"We have to do something about those bodies in the cellblock. Should we call someone? The cops? The fire department? I need to contact my mother, too," Arnie said.

Michael and Althaea exchanged glances.

"What?"

"You can't call anyone," Michael said.

"Why not? I have to get in touch with my mother."

"She thinks you're dead." Michael didn't want to be blunt, but he knew no other way.

"Because of you," Arnie snarled. He made a move as though to attack Michael, but pulled back when Michael stood.

"I was under orders. Besides, the phones aren't working."

"When the storm lets up, they'll fix the phones. And we've got landlines in here. They should work."

"Do you realize that storm has been raging for three days now?"

"So?"

Michael looked at Althaea again and she stared back, impassive. He'd get no help from that corner. "I don't know how long it'll last or what'll remain standing when it's over. This isn't a natural storm. It's manmade."

"Why would anyone purposely trigger something like this? How could anyone do this?"

Michael told Arnie about the Aurora machines, how they could manipulate the weather and cause large-scale destruction. "The machines triggered when I phased the aliens back to their world."

"You did this?" Arnie's hands balled into fists, and he took a step towards Michael again.

Althaea laughed out loud.

"What's so funny," Arnie snapped.

"You two. Ever since we got here, Michael's been on his guard, and Arnie's looked as if he wants to pounce. Arnie, you're just dying to find an excuse to slug Michael. Why?" She looked from one to the other.

Michael grasped Carolyn's ring, and Althaea noticed. "It's Carolyn, isn't it? Both of you want her, and this'll devolve into a pissing contest, because neither of you know who she'll pick if you ever find her."

"Enough, Althaea," Michael said and looked at Arnie. "We'll find your mother and see if she's okay."

"Mick—"

"I told you not to use that name, Althaea." Michael scowled.

"Jesus Christ, Mick—excuse me—Michael. I've called you 'Mick' for years. What's your problem?"

"Just don't use that name."

Althaea sighed. "Well, isn't this nice? What shall we do now? Shall I sit here handcuffed to the bed while you two punch each other out, or can we eat and do something productive?"

Michael stepped around Arnie, poured himself a cup of tea, grabbed a muffin, and headed to the door. "Don't leave the room. Arnie, watch Althaea. Don't go near her. If she needs to pee, throw her a cup to use."

Michael left the room, the door thudding shut behind him.

***

"What an asshole." Arnie stared at the closed door.

"He can be."

Arnie grinned. "Did you give him those black eyes he's sporting?"

Althaea grinned back. "Yes."

"Kudos." Arnie's gaze returned to the closed door. "What did Carolyn see in him?"

"I guess the same thing I saw in him."

He spun around to stare at Althaea. "You and Valiant?"

Althaea flushed, shook her head. "Almost. Mick was married at the time."

"What happened?"

"I'd rather not get into it. He has it in for me, though. That's why the cuffs. I'm not a threat, Arnie. Get these handcuffs off me. I promise, you won't be sorry." She licked her lips.

He looked her up and down. Did she mean what he thought she meant? Arnie took a step towards her before he realized what he was doing. He stopped, shook his head. "I don't think so. Michael said to stay away from you. Besides, I don't have the key."

"I'm sure we could use something here to spring the lock. Please? I have to go, and I don't want to pee in a cup."

He shook his head again, but not forcefully. She arched her back, her breasts pressing up, nipples outlined against the tight shirt she wore. He pictured himself on the bed, suckling those breasts. A drop of sweat ran down his back, and he grew hard.

Althaea's gaze locked on Arnie's. "Please. This is killing my back. I can't move."

Arnie stepped closer.

"Help me?" She beamed a smile at him.

For the first time, he noticed her deep blue, almost violet, eyes. Long blonde hair haloed her face. Arnie imagined raking his fingers through it, wrapping a fist in it to tilt her head back and ravish her throat.

He gulped and almost took another step towards her, but stopped. She continued to stare at him, lips parted. What would it be like to kiss those lips, to nibble on them?

Arnie looked away, remembering Tasha, the humiliation and pain. "I can't." *Son of a bitch, I want to, but I won't think with my dick ever again. It could be a trick.* He walked away and stepped out into the hall. When the door swung shut, Arnie leaned against the wall and covered his face with his hands.

"Well done." It was Michael.

Arnie looked up, confused.

"I heard the siren trying to lure you to your destruction. Congratulations on pushing through the pain. She was after your gun."

Arnie looked at the gun in his belt and then back at Michael. "You're an asshole." Before Michael could respond, Arnie said, "Why do you have Althaea handcuffed? What's she going to do?"

"Althaea's Agency. No matter what she says, she's programmed to follow their agenda."

"Carolyn trusted you, and you're Agency trained. Why aren't you following their agenda?"

"I decided to think for myself. Althaea has had no epiphany."

Arnie opened his mouth to speak when a crash inside the room rattled the door. Michael tried to open it, found it blocked, and forced it.

Still cuffed to the bed, Althaea had used both feet to shove Michael's bed into Arnie's, sending Arnie's bed into the door.

"You could've called us. We were right here," Michael said.

"I need to use the washroom."

Michael dug in his pocket and fished out the key, but also drew his gun. He went to Althaea and handed her the key. "Go ahead. Take off the cuffs."

She did, rubbing the liberated wrist. The other end of the bracelet dangled from the bedrail. She stood, massaging her lower back.

"Give me the cuffs and the key," Michael said.

Althaea handed both to Michael, and he waved his gun at the door. "Pull your gun, Arnie. She's getting an armed escort. If she tries anything, shoot her in the leg."

Arnie hesitated, studying Althaea's face. She stared back at him, neutral. *What the hell.* If she was anything like Tasha, Michael wasn't the asshole Arnie thought. He pulled the gun from his belt and stepped into the hallway.

"Where are we going, Mi—Michael?"

"Down to the cellblock. Arnie, do you have the keys to the cells?"

"Yeah." He located the key ring Julie had taken from Deuce and handed it to Michael.

When Althaea opened her mouth, Michael cut her off. "Let's go."

***

The smell drifted out to them as they drew near the cellblock.

"You won't lock me in here with them, will you, Michael?" Althaea spoke softly.

"No, he's not," Arnie said and turned to Michael. "I won't let you. I don't care what she's done or was thinking of doing."

Michael faced them both. "No. What do you take me for?"

Althaea exhaled loudly.

"Then what are we doing here?" Arnie asked.

"We have to remove these bodies before the stink gets any worse." Michael turned to Althaea. "You're going into one of the empty cells. Use the toilet. Arnie and I will work on getting rid of these bodies. I'll get the generator going and we'll burn them."

"I can help you," Althaea said. "It doesn't make sense to decommission me."

"Given the chance, you'd kill Arnie and try to take me in or kill me. Tell me that's not true."

"What I say doesn't matter, does it?" she replied.

"I'm afraid not." He grabbed her by the arm.

Althaea kicked out, but he was ready for it and wrenched her arm behind her back. He shoved the arm upward, making her scream. "You're so predictable." He whirled her around. She lunged forward and head-butted him, their foreheads colliding.

Michael saw stars and a flash of an image. As they grappled, the nagging feeling he'd had in Nahanni that something was wrong with Althaea's mind returned. This time, he wasn't going to overlook it. He put her in a headlock, bending her over almost double. "Stop it." He shook his head to clear it. "For fuck's sake, Althaea, did you feel that?"

"You're hurting her!" Arnie approached the struggling pair. "She's crying, Valiant."

Afraid Althaea would grab Arnie's gun if he got close, Michael shouted, "Stay back, Griffen." He heard the sobs then and almost released her. *No way. Althaea Dayton doesn't cry.*

He held her against his body, immobilizing her. Her pulse raced, and her breath came in hoarse gasps.

"Ally, listen to me."

"Okay."

He barely heard it, but she went limp against him. Michael sank to the ground with her in his arms.

She leaned into his chest, eyes closed. "What was that?" She shivered, and Michael knew it wasn't from cold.

"It's like there's something in your head, Ally."

"When we connected, it felt like my brain was shredding. I saw an animal. Am I going crazy?"

"It's not you. There's something there. I felt it in Nahanni. They did something to you. It sounds crazy, but I can feel it." Michael put a hand on her forehead.

She groaned. "That head-butt should have hurt you, not me."

"Trust me, it did. But there's something else going on. If you'll let me, I'll help you find out what."

"No. You're not doing that to me again."

126

"Do you know another way?"

"Fuck it. Lock me up."

Michael hauled her up by the arm as he stood and turned towards an empty cell. "Fine. Open the door, Arnie."

Arnie unlocked the cell, but when Michael tried to push Althaea inside, she collapsed. He lifted her in his arms, carried her to the cot, and covered her with a blanket. He left the cell and made Arnie lock the door behind them. When he glanced at her again, she was asleep.

***

Althaea awoke, alone in the cell. The racket from the corridor told her Arnie and Michael were still working. A dull throb in her skull reminded her of what had happened. She'd head-butted Michael and in that instant saw a vision of a large animal that might have been a jackal.

Michael seemed to think there was something wrong with her. Uneasiness made her stomach tighten. She had a feeling he was right. Ever since he'd connected to her in the cave, she'd felt off, like she wasn't herself. Dreams plagued her—terrifying scenes that made her wake up in a cold sweat with an unshakeable feeling of doom.

What had the Agency done to her? It had to be the Agency. She hadn't had an alien tracker in her, so that meant she wasn't an abductee. But something had been done to her. Michael had knocked it loose when he'd invaded her mind, and now she couldn't function. The son of a bitch would have to fix what he broke.

But the only way to do that would be to let him access her mind again. Did she really want to let him in? She'd have to trust him, because there was no one else who could do it. Pain swelled behind her eyes, forcing her to close them. Instantly, a parade of images scrolled through her head and nausea churned in her gut.

She used the toilet and washed her face, hoping that would help, but she continued to feel queasy. *Please, no.* Was this hideous sensation the new normal? She couldn't keep going like this. She made up her mind. "Valiant!"

He appeared at the cell door faster than she'd expected, and Arnie was right behind him.

"You okay?" Michael sounded genuinely concerned.

"I want you to do it."

He didn't seem surprised. "Okay. If you're willing, I'm willing. But I won't let you in, Ally. It'll be me probing you. If that doesn't seem fair, then I'll be back when we're done for the day."

Althaea gritted her teeth, but nodded her head. "Fine. I just want my brain to stop killing me."

Arnie watched the exchange, puzzled. "What are you talking about?" he said.

"I can probe her mind," Michael answered.

"Like some kind of Vulcan mind meld?"

"Just open the cell door and cover her while I do this."

Arnie unlocked and opened the door. Michael holstered his gun and approached Althaea, drawing in close to her. He helped her stand and steadied her when she swayed. She closed her eyes while Michael reached out his hands and drew her into the circle of his arms. He leaned forward and touched her forehead with his.

CHAPTER 35

Carolyn stopped pacing and sat at the table in the open kitchen of a small apartment where she'd spent the last two days. The apartment in the underground community was an improvement over the cell in the Peterborough compound, but she remained a prisoner. The unit had no windows, and the exit door locked from the outside.

She had new clothes; a fridge stocked with healthy food; clean, filtered water; toiletries; and actual sheets, pillows, and a comforter on her bed. But she had no books, no TV with DVDs—nothing to do but pace or eat. And no human company other than Cornell. In the cell, Carolyn could at least talk to Arnie, even if it was surreptitiously at night. Where once grasping his fingers wasn't enough physical contact, now it would be everything to her.

She didn't know where the community was located, only that it was near the city of Peterborough. They'd headed south on Highway 115 after leaving the compound, but she lost her bearings after that. They'd entered farm country, mostly fields and forests along secondary roads, and then a dirt road with forest on either side.

Above ground, the facility looked like a cement fortress with a barbwire moat. Electrified fences, security cameras, and manned guard towers ensured that no one approached undetected. She despaired that Michael could ever rescue her, and even if he managed it, they'd still need to find Sam.

Carolyn stood again and returned to pacing. Worry knotted her intestines. Her hands settled on her belly, a protective gesture she made instinctively whenever she thought about her baby.

The deadbolt in the door clicked. She stepped backwards and bumped into the table. Heart in her throat, breathing rapid and shallow, she watched the door swing open. Cornell. The devil she knew.

He frowned when he glimpsed her face. "What's wrong?"

"Are you kidding?"

"No. You look frightened. Did something happen?"

"You can't be serious."

"Carolyn, you're safe here."

"You killed everyone at the Peterborough compound. You expect me to believe you when you tell me I'm safe?"

"I didn't bring you here to kill you."

"Why am I here then? The aliens are gone. I spent all day yesterday establishing that for you." Carolyn stopped talking and tried to collect herself. Tears threatened. When she could speak without her voice breaking, she said, "Where's Sam? I want to see her."

"That's impossible. She believes you're dead. She's happy here and doing well. I don't want to do anything to traumatize her."

"You mean like tell her you're a lying psycho responsible for her father's death and her mother's disappearance?"

Straight faced, he said, "Yes."

"What do you want?" Carolyn's hands moved to her pelvis.

He set his briefcase down and walked towards her. She backed away, bumping into the table again. He smiled while he approached her—a friendly smile that made her insides churn. Hands pressed on the table, Carolyn leaned back, bracing herself. When Cornell reached her, he gripped her shoulders, steadied her, and brushed a strand of hair off her face.

Panic rose, filled her. Carolyn's mind raced. She contemplated kneeing him in the groin, but feared reprisal. Tears sprang to her eyes.

"Still so afraid," Cornell whispered. "Work with me, and we'll be able to accomplish so much. I don't want to use force on you, angel. This is a new world we're creating, and you can be a vital part of it." Cornell's breath, reeking of stale coffee, puffed in her face when he spoke.

Carolyn's stomach turned, morning sickness always close to the surface, and she averted her face. "I'll never willingly work with you. You destroyed my life, tore apart my family. How can you expect me to accept this?"

"You're smart, a survivor. On the surface, the world is in its death throes. Michael Valiant triggered that. If Sam were up there, she'd be killed along with everyone else. Do you still think Valiant's a hero?"

"Michael's doing what he has to do, and I trust nothing you tell me."

Cornell put an arm around her and drew her to him. She tried to push him away, but he held firm.

"Let me go. What are you doing?"

Cornell's other arm came up, tightening the embrace. "I'm proving a point, angel. I can do whatever I want to you or Sam, and no one will interfere." He released her and stepped back. "But I'd rather not."

"What do you want?" Carolyn's voice shook.

"A helicopter disappeared from the Nahanni base. We've located it at the Peterborough compound. I want you to remote view the place and tell me who's there."

Carolyn's heart leapt. Remote viewing wasn't necessary to know who it was. Michael. It's Michael. Michael would find Arnie, and they'd come for her. Hope swelled.

Cornell must have seen something in her expression, because he smiled, but this time, it wasn't friendly. "It's Valiant?"

Carolyn looked towards the floor, avoiding his eyes.

"Answer me."

She nodded. Cornell's finger lifted her chin so her gaze met his. "When I ask you a question, I expect you to answer me. It's Valiant, isn't it?"

"Yes." A whisper.

He took her hand in his and led her to the recliner in the living room. "Sit."

She sat, leaned back.

Cornell picked up the briefcase, set it on the coffee table in front of her, and opened it. He handed her a pad of paper and a pencil. "Go ahead. Write or draw whatever you get. Be thorough." He took a seat on the couch opposite her.

Carolyn closed her eyes and focused on the Peterborough compound. Three souls' energies touched her: Arnie; Michael; a woman she didn't know. She wrote down everything. The connection to Michael strengthened, his familiar energy easing her tension.

Something diverted his attention, and he didn't sense her. Michael focused on the woman. Images flowed past Carolyn, faster than she could see them, making her dizzy. Something snapped near her ears and she found herself in a hallway as real as the most vivid dream she'd ever had.

Carolyn barely oriented when the floor trembled, and a deep growl echoed through the corridor. Something large moved in her direction.

She turned, quickened her pace, running away from that feral sound. She sensed Michael somewhere in the vicinity. The snarling grew louder, paws padded and claws clicked on the floor behind her. Terrified, she glanced back.

A huge jackal closed the distance between them at an alarming rate. Carolyn screamed and ran. The jackal snorted, and a paw swiped at her bare ankle, a claw tearing into the skin. She screamed again and ran faster, her ankle stinging and burning.

The jackal overtook her, threw her onto the floor. She tried to roll over, but the animal pressed on her back, trapping her. Strong jaws closed on her arm and dragged her backwards. Carolyn twisted and shoved a finger in its eye.

The mouth opened just enough for her to slide her arm out. Blood streamed down the arm, but Carolyn hardly noticed. She jumped up and ran towards the sound of human voices.

Her heart skipped a beat when she recognized Michael's voice. She ran forward, rounded a corner, and there he was.

Michael looked up, eyes widening when he caught her gaze. He grinned and ran to her. "Carolyn?" His look changed to panic when he noticed the blood on her arm.

"Michael!" She collapsed into his arms. Pain lanced through her when the beast gripped her again, and she slid from Michael's arms.

She snapped back to the room with Cornell. Carolyn opened her eyes and gasped for breath, the room spinning around her. She couldn't breathe. The pencil fell to the floor, the notepad following it. Her back arched, and she bucked in the chair.

Cornell called to her, but she couldn't answer him. Blood spurted as she flailed her arms. Carolyn managed a wheezing gasp, but continued to struggle for air. His hands pressed her into the chair.

She stood next to the chair, watching, while Cornell leaned over her now limp body. Carolyn thought about Sam, tried to go to her, but she was yanked back into her body. She landed with a thud, sucking in air, grateful to breathe. Her eyes snapped open, gaze meeting Cornell's.

Carolyn said, "He's seen what you've done." She fainted.

CHAPTER 36

Althaea hears footsteps and turns to see Michael approaching. He takes her hand and leads her to a room. The door stands wide open, a mess of toys on the floor. Five-year-old Ally is there, sitting on the floor playing with toy cars. Dave, her father's friend, peeks into the room and steps inside. Uncle Dave lifts her into his arms.

When he throws her high in the air, she laughs. She's flying. The air whooshes around her, dress fluttering, legs kicking out. Uncle Dave catches her—Ally didn't doubt he would—and cradles the child in his arms. He moves over to the couch, and fear hits her.

Althaea turns to Michael and shakes her head. No, she can't watch this. She knows what happened in that room. This man molested her, one of the many times he did.

"Please, stop this," she begs and thinks, I'm always begging Michael for something. Anger bubbles up.

Michael shakes his head.

No? Can he be that cruel? Althaea looks over at the scene where the child struggles and cries, trapped, helpless in the man's arms. But the scene wavers, shatters, and reforms.

Little Ally's on the floor, playing with her cars. Uncle Dave enters the room, lifts her up, and she laughs, joyful. He sets her down and watches while she scurries over to the toys.

"Play with me?" She smiles, hopeful.

He laughs and sits in the midst of the mess, picks up a car. "I only have a moment," he says.

Her face falls. Uncle Dave is her favourite "uncle," always kind, always making time for her. He's never hurt her, will never hurt her.

Althaea looks at Michael, shocked. She can't believe it. A more authentic memory has replaced the foul one. "Did you do that?" Has Michael done something to her?

"The Agency took your memories, Ally. We're getting the real ones back." She notices Michael has used her nickname. It's reassuring.

133

He takes her hand, and they move on to the next room.

Ally is fifteen and cowering in an alley—Ally in an alley. She remembers this one too. She'd run away from home to escape her parents' denials, her schoolmates' taunts, her own self-loathing. Razor cuts cover her arms, a physical expression of her anger. She's thin, emaciated.

After she's lived on the streets for a week, a pimp finds her. He forces himself on her, but she escapes. He finds her, beats her, and drags her away. Ally's life on the streets begins in earnest.

Again the scene shatters, melts, and reforms. Ally is fifteen and playing basketball in the high school gym. She's the captain of the girls' basketball team, tall, powerful, and agile.

Althaea smiles. How she loved playing basketball. Where had that memory gone? She hadn't left home, hadn't left school, and did have friends, even a boyfriend, though not serious.

She looks at Michael. "The Agency took that too, didn't they? Everything I thought I remembered was something they wanted me to believe. None of my memories are real? Who am I?"

"Do you want to see more?" Michael's voice is gentle, soothing.

"Yes."

He leads her to another room, and she has to ask: "Whose house is this?"

Michael smiles. "Don't you know?"

Althaea shakes her head, but even while she does, she knows the answer. "My house," she says, a look of amazement crossing her face. "It's me."

Michael nods and smiles, encouraging her. "You don't need me to show you anymore. You can go through it yourself. But I need to know: what about the Agency?"

She places her hand on Michael's shoulder. "Destroy them."

Growls from somewhere down the corridor reach their ears, and the hallway trembles. Footsteps. Michael shouts, half in excitement, half in fear, and pushes past Althaea.

"Carolyn."

The woman screams in terror. "Michael."

He reaches Carolyn, embraces her. Blood drips from her arm. The thing chasing her appears. A roar, and a hairy, monstrous jackal paw reaches out and snatches her from Michael. He cries out. "Help me, Ally."

Althaea runs, the desperation in Michael's voice spurring her on.

Carolyn's screams are cut short when the beast wraps its paws around her throat, squeezing. Michael has a sword. How is that possible? *Althaea catches up to him and tries to pull Carolyn away from the jackal, but its grip on her is strong. Michael's sword whistles through the air and slices into one paw. The beast howls in agony.*

The jackal releases Carolyn, and she disappears. Michael lifts the sword and skewers the beast through the chest.

***

Michael released Althaea and stepped away from her. Hands gripped his shoulders, and he shrugged them off. He spun around to find Arnie there, concern and fear on his face. "What happened?"

Michael ignored Arnie for the moment and looked at Althaea. "You okay?"

She trembled, eyes moist, and exhaled a tattered breath. "The Agency brainwashed me to kill for them." Her pale face had a green tinge.

Michael nodded, understanding what she felt. He'd had the same revelations once. Althaea moaned. "Robert. Danny."

"I know." Michael held Althaea's face in his palms. He looked into her eyes, consoling. One repentant killer to another. "I know."

Althaea placed her hands over his. "Okay." She looked stricken, but calmer.

Michael released her.

"What was that thing?" she asked.

"I think it was a guard."

"I don't get it."

"They inserted something into your mind that would trigger if you poked around in the memories they built for you. When we dismantled their illusions, we triggered it. We wouldn't have gotten as far as we did, but Carolyn distracted it."

"How did she get there? Where did she go?" Althaea asked.

"Back to where she left her body, I assume. Maybe she tried to connect to me. When Carolyn arrived, your mind would've recognized her immediately as an intrusion."

"Was it real?"

"It was to us. I have to find her."

Arnie grabbed Michael's arm. "What about Carolyn? What happened?"

Michael recounted their experience, leaving out the details of Althaea's past, but telling Arnie everything else. Arnie's eyes bugged out. "Could it have hurt her?"

"We weren't dreaming. It was fortunate she came along, because it gave us enough time to shatter the illusions they'd planted in Ally's mind. Carolyn is strong enough to get back, but I'm worried they made her do this to track me. Arnie, you said Cornell left you here?"

"Yeah. They had to clear out before the weather trapped them. It was already storming when they left. I guess chasing Julie and me down was too much trouble."

"Now he knows I'm here too."

CHAPTER 37

Carolyn woke from a dreamless sleep to the throbbing of her arm and ankle and opened her eyes. She was in her bedroom, Cornell seated on a chair beside the bed. Her arm, swathed in bandages, lay atop the comforter. A slight brownish stain on the bandage showed where blood had seeped through and dried.

When Cornell realized she was awake, relief flashed in his eyes. He smiled, friendly again. "Glad you're okay. I feared we'd lost you."

"The baby?"

"The baby's fine. What happened?"

"I connected to Michael and a woman in a house with many rooms. A jackal attacked me." Carolyn looked at her arm. "It clawed my arm and my ankle."

"How?"

"What I experienced in my mind manifested in my body."

"Are you saying Valiant isn't in Peterborough?"

"I don't know." Carolyn lied in that, but jumped on every opportunity to fudge the truth. The longer she could keep Cornell ignorant, the more time she bought for Michael.

"Why did you say he knows what I've done?"

"What do you mean?" Carolyn didn't remember saying that.

"You said 'he knows what you've done.' Did you mean Michael? What does he know?"

"I don't know. The last thing I remember is strangling and fighting for my life, a huge jackal clawing at me. I'm unaware of anything I said."

Cornell frowned. "Can you make a guess?"

"I guess it means Michael knows what you did. I don't know everything you've done. It could be any number of awful things. Pick one."

He stood. "You're obviously feeling better. I'll bring the doctor in to talk to you, but he said it doesn't look as if there's any nerve damage. You'll have scarring, but the lacerations aren't deep."

Cornell left the room, and she heard him leave the apartment.

***

Cornell went straight to the lab. Thomas Scielo, a psychiatrist and former CIA director, and the man in charge of the research department, rose from in front of his computer. "Still intent on doing this, Jim?"

"More than ever. The aliens don't need the baby. If Carolyn loses it, we'll erase the entire pregnancy from her memory. Having said that, do everything to protect it. This child could become an asset." He went to the cooler and poured water into a disposable cup.

Scielo paused, staring at Cornell as though uncertain of what he wanted to say. "This will take a huge toll on Fairchild physically. I can't guarantee she'll retain her psychic abilities."

"What do you mean?"

"How will you prevent her from learning the truth if she can communicate with spirits? All she has to do is talk to her husband once, or Valiant's former partner or late wife, and the jig is up. If you erase Fairchild's memories and replace them with new ones, you must block her mediumship abilities."

"Can you make her believe she's hallucinating? Or schizophrenic?"

"Yes. We could give her an antipsychotic. There's a new one available that should block the mediumship, but won't interfere with her ability to remote view. That's what worries you, right?"

"Yeah. What are the side effects?"

Scielo hesitated. "Low white blood cells. The subject would need regular blood tests. This drug is only used when nothing else works. It can cause seizures, heart problems, or low blood pressure. Most of the time, it's fine, but you plan to manipulate her mind. That involves physical intervention, and I don't just mean the meds."

Uneasy at this hint of what else they'd put Carolyn through—hypnosis, verbal and sexual abuse, torture, and sensory deprivation—Cornell turned away from Scielo.

"Jim? Second thoughts?"

He shook his head and forced his mind back to the conversation. "What about one of the other antipsychotics? Something without the extreme side effects?"

"Not powerful enough. You want to stop the voices, so to speak? We need something that'll completely block her. Nothing gentle will do."

"Do what you have to do. She's wounded now. Get working on her. I want her greeting me after work with a kiss, a martini in her hand, and ready to shoot Valiant by September."

"A Stepford wife and an assassin? Really, Jim?" Scielo laughed. "That's quite the combination. What will you tell Virginia?"

"That's classified," Cornell smiled, considering it. Time with Carolyn would be like a mini-vacation, a spa visit, and not the ordeal he currently experienced.

"You look as if you're salivating, Cornell."

He grinned, showing teeth. "If this works, consider the potential. What if I wanted her to connect to a spirit? Can it be done?"

"Well, she'd have to stop the meds, which would take preparation. You can't stop it cold turkey. To control it, you'd need to put her under using hypnosis, so you could guide it. But yeah, it would be feasible. Did you have someone specific in mind?"

"No. Just trying to understand the limitations. I don't like reducing Carolyn's abilities, but it helps if we can tap into them if the need arises."

"There's one problem with the timing though."

"What's that?"

"The pregnancy. We can't give her the drugs until she has the baby. She'll lose it, or it'll be born defective. How far along is she?"

Jim frowned. "The first trimester."

"No good. But it's possible to make the subject think she doesn't believe in that stuff. We can hold her in a cell that is so strongly shielded she can't connect to anyone or anything and keep her in there until the baby is born. The mind control stuff will affect her, but not the child. When her time's up, we can induce labour and begin the drugs."

"Okay, get it implemented. I want her so far out of Valiant's reach that even if he gets her back, she'll want to kill him."

"Yes, sir. I'll have them set up her new quarters immediately, and we'll go get her. We can start this afternoon."

"I want daily updates on her progress, but I don't need the details. Your methods are disturbing, Tom. Ensure you don't kill her or the baby. Carolyn has grown on me. I don't want to lose her."

Cornell crushed the empty paper cup in his fist, dropped it into the recycling bin, and left the lab. He'd see Carolyn once more before the doctors came for her. He rather liked her the way she was. Too bad she wouldn't cooperate and they had to re-educate her. There was no telling who she'd be when they finished.

CHAPTER 38

Michael, Arnie, and Althaea stared out into the parking lot. Holed up in the Peterborough compound for three months now, the waiting became intolerable. August had come in like a *Tyrannosaurus* and had gone out the same way. Two funnel clouds passed through in that one month, along with two hurricanes, four earthquakes, and many storms with wind gusts strong enough to rip trees out of the ground.

Michael was grateful they were in a building designed to withstand almost everything. But if either of the funnel clouds had hit them, he didn't think the building would still be standing. The helicopter he'd brought from Nahanni was nothing but wreckage now.

He'd hoped August would be better, but there'd been no break in the violent weather. Now it was September, and they still hadn't been able to head out. How did others cope with the storms? The environmental upheaval would've caught most people unprepared. At least the compound contained ample stores of food, water, medical supplies, and a generator.

The group had cleaned up the bodies using an incinerator designed for such a purpose though Arnie had fallen apart when the time had come to put in Julie's body. They'd had no choice, however, and in the end, he'd let them do it.

Determined to go after Carolyn, but with the helicopter no longer an option, Michael hoped he'd find a vehicle in an outbuilding. But until the storm subsided, stepping outside would be suicide.

Arnie broke the silence. "I don't know how much longer I can stand waiting."

Michael agreed. They'd spent most of their time preparing to leave, and by now were beyond ready. Frustration permeated everyone, but at least the delays had given them time to teach Arnie how to shoot and fight. Althaea made Arnie train for hours every morning. The activity kept them fit and

139

gave them something to do.

That the two hadn't slept together yet astounded Michael, and even more astonishing, the holdout was Arnie. Althaea and Arnie had grown close, but he'd kept his hands to himself.

Though it was the middle of the day, the black clouds made everything dim and brooding, and inside, emergency lights provided the only illumination. Michael powered off the generator at regular intervals. While a substantial reserve of fuel for it existed, without knowing how long they'd be trapped here, they used the generator sparingly.

Michael turned away from the window, disgusted, and reached for the ring on the chain around his neck. He'd had no communication from Carolyn since that day they'd connected in Althaea's memories. Every moment of delay cut into his heart like a dagger. He was afraid they were already too late.

***

Michael passed the time by scouring the information on the hard drives he found rooting around in Cornell's office and in the storage room. Cornell and his people must have been in quite a hurry to have left these drives intact. The units had been erased, but not destroyed, and some weren't even reformatted. That had allowed Arnie, a former software developer and computer expert, to recover the data on them.

Cornell likely hadn't known the drives were left in storage intact. Protocol would've demanded they be destroyed, and he'd have ordered it. No doubt, the escalating storm had caused the grunt charged with securing the data to just delete and run.

One folder contained documents outlining agreements with the aliens. Michael clicked on a file in the folder. Sections of the document were redacted. He accessed another file, leaving the first one open. Perhaps if he opened all the files, he could piece together the information. He created a new file and got to work.

He was still working on it when Althaea stuck her head in to see if he wanted dinner. When he grunted at her that he wasn't hungry, she left, returning fifteen minutes later with a tray of food.

She set the tray on the desk and put a hand on Michael's shoulder. "I won't bother you, but please eat your dinner."

Michael gave her a distracted nod, and her goodbye went unacknowledged, the door closing behind her unheard. After a few minutes of staring at the screen, though, the smell of fresh bread and beef stew distracted him. He dipped a piece of bread into the hot broth of the stew and nibbled on it. Whatever else you could say about Arnie, the guy was a great cook.

The open document on the screen in front of him caught his attention again, and he leaned back in the chair. Dinner might be a good excuse to stop and pick it up again in the morning. Michael leaned forward, hand on the mouse, hovering the cursor over the close button.

It was then that all the pieces fell into place, and suddenly Michael found it hard to breathe. He was looking at a contract. Those Agency assholes had sold Earth to the fucking aliens. Michael's hands curled into fists.

The agreement stipulated that the people in the underground colonies would remain free. Any other survivors on the planet would be the property of the aliens, who could use them any way they wanted.

Michael closed the file and set password protection on it. He'd let Althaea know it was here and add it to the documentation they were creating. One day, the aliens might return, and whoever was here should prepare for that eventuality.

Desperation to retrieve Carolyn hit him, and he considered the options as he closed everything and powered down the computer. They had to go after her soon, and Sam, too, of course. *I'll have to teach Sam, and the baby when she gets older, to watch the skies.*

Michael looked over at the plate of food Althaea had left him and his stomach clenched, his appetite gone.

***

Subject's re-education complete. Please review the attached document for instructions on proceeding.

Cornell read the message from Scielo and almost cheered. He looked up, afraid Ginny might suspect something. She sat on the sofa, watching a movie, Wade seated next to her. Upstairs, Sam read George a bedtime story.

A glance at the clock showed eight o'clock. Cornell hadn't had any contact with Carolyn for three months and was eager to see her. Not wanting to witness what Scielo and his team did to her, he'd stayed away during her re-education. Now it was done, he couldn't wait until morning to visit her.

The baby had survived the ordeal, to his relief. Scielo had reprogrammed Carolyn to believe the child was Cornell's, making it easier for her to accept him as her lover.

He stood. "I have to return to work, Ginny. Tom Scielo sent me an urgent message. He's completed a complicated project I assigned him, and I need to go inspect the results."

Ginny looked at him, puzzled. He'd explained too much. He'd have to be careful not to get talkative. Typically, Cornell told Ginny he was returning to work and that was that. "I'll be late. Don't wait up."

He said good night to Sam and George, waved to Wade and Ginny on the way out, and walked to Carolyn's house. They'd set her up in a nicer, two-bedroom townhouse with all the amenities, and Scielo's team had ensured the unit was shielded.

Cornell stopped at a greenhouse and picked up a bouquet on his way. The greenhouses were spectacular accomplishments in the underground community. Constructed to simulate daylight, the vast structures grew plants sprouted from heirloom seeds collected over the last thirty years.

Birds, insects, and small animals lived in the bio dome, and if you didn't look up and see the enclosure, you'd think you were outside. Even the circulating air simulated a summer breeze.

When he reached Carolyn's door, he waited, listening. The drone of the TV filtered through the door. Cornell tapped on the door and used his key to open it.

Carolyn sat on the couch, legs tucked under her, a shawl around her shoulders. She was always chilly, even though the temperature in the house was regulated, the humidity controlled.

When the door opened, she gave him a shy smile and paused the movie she watched. His mouth went dry, and he felt a flutter in his gut. She'd never smiled at him. It made her even more beautiful and desirable.

"Hi, Jim." She sounded happy to see him. "I didn't think you'd come see me today. It's getting late, so I assumed you were working or went home."

"I couldn't stay away." He held out the flowers and caught a faint whiff of carnation.

She beamed. "Thank you. They're gorgeous." She went to him and accepted the package, taking it to the kitchen. A large vase appeared from a cupboard, and she unwrapped the paper.

Cornell watched her while she trimmed the stems and put the flowers in water. She moved fluidly, no trace of any injuries. When she set the arrangement on the table, he went to her, and gently grabbed her wrists.

He turned her hands over, examined the nails, the palms. He looked into her eyes, ran his hands through her hair, checking for lumps, checking for cuts and bruises.

Worry crossed her face. "What is it? Something wrong?"

Before he could speak, he cleared his throat. "No, nothing." He exhaled in relief. "I haven't seen you in a while, and I got worried."

"What do you mean? We saw each other yesterday at lunch. Everything was fine."

His heart thudded against his chest. Carolyn had memories of spending time together from as recently as yesterday. He'd have to read through Scielo's notes carefully, make sure he knew every lie they'd fed her.

"Yes, of course. It feels like an eternity when I don't see you." Cornell smiled.

"Why did you think something was wrong? Did something happen?" Carolyn's voice rose, and panic flashed across her face. "Is it Michael Valiant? Is he coming after me?"

He pulled her into his arms. "Shh. No, don't worry. You're safe here. It wasn't anything like that. How's the baby?"

Carolyn nuzzled her head against his neck, and then pulled back, smiling. "I think she kicked today—just a flutter—but I'm sure it was baby and not gas." Her excitement lit up her eyes.

"She? Did the doctor tell you the baby is a girl?" He felt unease though he couldn't have said what troubled him.

"Just a feeling." Carolyn leaned over and kissed his lips.

Cornell responded, desire flooding through him, but restrained himself. He wanted to take her to the bedroom, but needed to make sure she belonged to him. He couldn't afford to shatter the illusion with haste.

Carolyn broke the kiss and giggled. "Are we going to stand here all night? Let's go sit. Watch *Casablanca* with me. I love that old movie." She grabbed his hand and pulled him to the couch.

Cornell settled himself in the corner and put his arm around her shoulder. She restarted the movie, leaned into him, and curled her legs up. He ran a hand through her short hair, enjoying the softness. He'd had them cut the brown dye out of it, and it was a natural golden blonde again. Contented, he kissed the top of her head and sighed. He could get used to this.

CHAPTER 39

Sam waited until Ginny was in bed for an hour before slipping from her room and sneaking to Cornell's office. Compared to the home they'd left behind in Richmond Hill, this one was small, though still larger than the house Sam had lived in with her parents.

When the Cornells and Sam had first arrived at the underground community, everything had had a dream-like quality. She'd marvelled at the backyard, almost a replica of the Cornells' previous yard. It even had the swimming pool, though, like the house, everything in the yard was smaller. Cornell had even told Sam she must wear sunscreen if she wanted to sit "outside" for any length of time.

At first, things had seemed better here than in Richmond Hill. Virginia was nicer to her—even encouraging Sam to call her "Ginny." Cornell spent more time at home and tension between Cornell and Ginny eased.

Sam missed her friends and regretted leaving them without saying where she'd gone. But Cornell explained they'd come to the underground community because they were in danger from cult members responsible for her mother's death. He'd assured Sam that her friends were safe—she was the one in danger and why she lived with the Cornells.

The underground community, originally built for scientific research, provided a safe place for the family to hide. Sam could even continue her studies here. But then this project came up, and Cornell worked long hours, sometimes spending the entire night at the office. Ginny became moody, the boys restless, and Sam herself grew suspicious.

She guessed it was an effort for Cornell to act as if everything were normal. He seemed excited at the prospect of leaving for work in the morning. Often absent at dinner, when he did show up, he went out again after the kids went to bed. He'd lost weight, too and took extra care when he got dressed in the morning.

Yesterday, Sam had overheard Cornell arguing with Ginny, assuring her there was no one else, that he was working on an important, time-consuming project. Sam didn't believe him, agreeing with Ginny that he behaved like a man having an affair. As a favour to Ginny, Sam had decided to snoop around, though she was unsure what she'd do if she discovered Cornell was having an affair. But it angered her to think he'd do that to his family.

A nail file popped the lock on the office door, and Sam slipped inside. She didn't turn on her flashlight until she'd shut and locked the door. She went straight to Cornell's desk and sat in the chair. Without touching anything, she scanned the desk: laptop; a picture of Ginny and the boys; a stress ball; phone; pens and pencils in a stainless steel holder; and a two-tiered paper tray with papers in both tiers.

Sam shone the light on the papers, which were face down in the tray, a paperweight resting on the top stack. She tried the top stack first. Sam rifled through the pages until an email message caught her interest. It was dated two weeks ago, September 18, which was when Cornell had started acting weird.

Re: Subject 4382CF.

The body of the message was brief:

To answer your questions, 4382CF believes you rescued her from Valiant. The subject believes Valiant killed her husband and daughter and kidnapped and raped her. She does not pose a threat to you or your family. Memories can "bleed through," as you put it, but that's rare, and typically limited to minor flashes of inconsequential events.

Regarding training: start with self-defence and weapons training. It should be safe to issue the subject a firearm to keep on hand for protection. Let me know if you have any questions or comments.

Tom

Below this was Cornell's original message:

Tom, what does 4382CF believe is my connection to Michael Valiant? Is there a chance of a relapse? In other words, is it possible for old memories to bleed through and make her a threat to me or my family? Can the subject begin training, and if yes, what do you recommend? Can I issue her a Beretta to keep on hand in case Valiant makes it here when I'm not with her?

Jim

A lump grew in Sam's throat and her stomach fluttered. The new project Cornell had mentioned was a *person*. A woman. When he left here after dinner or didn't come home until early morning, he was probably with her.

Based on the messages she'd just read, the woman believed things that weren't true. But how could she believe she'd been raped if it hadn't happened? Was the purpose of the project to make her think that? Why would Cornell do that to someone?

Sam put the paper back where she'd found it and replaced the paperweight. She'd seen enough. The next time Cornell went out, she'd follow him and find out who this 4382CF person was. Then she'd figure out what to do about it.

***

Cornell awoke and checked the clock next to Carolyn's side of the bed. Just after one o'clock. A glance at Carolyn verified she was sound asleep. He slipped out of bed and reached for his pants. This routine had become tedious, but he had to go home. It was bad enough he kept falling asleep here and getting home after midnight.

After the argument he'd had with Ginny the other day, he'd sworn to go home earlier, but he'd been reluctant to tear himself away. The time spent with Carolyn was more than pleasant. She made no demands on him, had no expectations. Aware he was married, she accepted he'd never leave his family. She greeted him with enthusiasm whenever he showed up, and when he didn't, she occupied herself and didn't complain.

But he'd made sure she had plenty to occupy herself with: DVDs, including exercise videos, books, and a computer—whatever she wanted. Cornell had even gotten a few good old-fashioned games, like backgammon and chess, which they could play when he visited.

He'd set up a mini gym in the back of her bedroom, large enough to accommodate an elliptical trainer, a bench, free weights, and a rowing machine. Carolyn wasn't doing anything too hard core through her pregnancy, but she exercised each day.

She had enough freedom to leave her house, which could be unlocked from inside, though her section remained segregated from most areas. Cornell granted her access to the greenhouse, library, market, park, and cafés frequented by Agency personnel.

A patio and garden in the back of the house provided the illusion of a natural setting. The yard didn't have a pool, but it had a small pond. The gratitude Carolyn expressed for everything he'd done brought with it the occasional stab of guilt, but he told himself she was happy and shrugged it off.

Dressed, Cornell tiptoed out of the room. He disliked leaving without saying goodbye, but hated disturbing her sleep even more. She'd told him she understood. Cornell stood for a moment, listening. The fridge hummed in the background; otherwise, the house was quiet. He unlocked the front door and stepped out into the soft summery night.

When he arrived home, he silently let himself in, took off his shoes, and headed towards the kitchen. On the way past the bar, he grabbed a rocks glass and the bottle of scotch. Cornell sat at the table, using the nightlight by the stove to guide him, and poured himself three fingers. With Carolyn, he rarely drank. But when he arrived home, he'd grab one regardless of the time.

The next day's schedule scrolled through his head as he sat sipping the scotch. Carolyn had self-defence lessons in the morning, and weapons training in the afternoon. After that, he'd join her at her house and ask her to do remote viewing—the first since her re-education.

The thought of the first remote viewing made him nervous, afraid it would trigger a real memory, though Scielo had assured him that wouldn't happen. But he had to get her back into tracking Valiant. Too much time had gone by, and Valiant might be on his way, storms or not.

A sound in the hallway caught his attention, and he looked up. Sam stood staring at him. She didn't look sleepy and wore a robe over pyjamas. The bunny slippers on her feet made her look like a kid.

She is a kid. "What's up, Sam? Why aren't you in bed?"

"I couldn't sleep, and when I heard you come in, I came out to talk to you."

"Something wrong?"

"Not with me."

Cornell sipped his scotch, anticipating what she'd say next. "Then with whom?"

"You."

"Sit. Tell me."

Sam moved to the chair across from him and sat.

"Drink?" He held up the bottle of scotch.

She shook her head.

"Okay, what's so urgent that you had to confront me at this time of the ni—morning. Already." Cornell sighed. He might not get to bed after all.

"I overheard you arguing with Ginny yesterday."

"No doubt. She wasn't quiet."

"I think she has a point."

"What's her point?"

Sam stared at Cornell as if he'd said something incomprehensible. She hesitated, and when she finally spoke, she whispered. "That you're seeing someone else."

"Sam, I have many responsibilities. I don't answer to Ginny. I certainly don't answer to you." He held up his hand. "No, wait. I appreciate your concern. But you should know Ginny often accuses me of this. When you first came to live with us, she was jealous and suspicious of my relationship with you. Were you aware of that?"

Sam nodded once and sighed. "This is different. You act different than when we were back in Richmond Hill."

"I don't know what you mean, but I can tell you I'm under more stress here. I have to keep this place running smoothly." Cornell reached out and patted her hand. "Your concern is touching. I'm not seeing anyone. I'm wrapped up with my responsibilities here. Please help Ginny understand. She makes it tough for the rest of us when she has one of her jealous fits." He withdrew his hand.

Sam stared at the table. When she looked up, her eyes were guarded, but she gave him a weak smile. "Okay. I'm sorry I jumped to conclusions. You're away too much, and when you leave in the morning, you dress as if you're seeing someone special."

He smiled. "I'm not doing anything different than I've always done."

"Yes, you do. You lost weight. You dress nicer."

"That's kind of you. But I've lost weight because the diet we have here isn't as processed and unhealthy. Ginny lost weight too. You don't think she's having an affair, do you?"

Sam shook her head and smiled. "Okay." She pressed a palm to her mouth, stifling a yawn. "I'm going back to bed. The boys and I have a big day tomorrow—an outing to the library and the public pool."

"What's wrong with the pool in the backyard?"

"The public pool has activities for kids. We're meeting up with their friends, and I'll hang out with the other nannies while the boys have swimming lessons."

He nodded. "Okay. Good night."

After she left, Cornell took another swig of his scotch. He'd have to be more careful. The last thing he needed was Sam snooping into his business. He fought an urge to go back to Carolyn's and never return. If it were just Ginny, he'd do it, but he couldn't leave his boys. He chugged the rest of his scotch and went to bed.

CHAPTER 40

Carolyn slips on her long, white gown and cinches it at the waist with a gold cord. Natalia, her handmaiden, braids Carolyn's hair and wraps it around her head, then leads her by the hand into the temple where the priests wait. The high priest, whom Carolyn recognizes as Jim Cornell, takes her hand from the attendant's and guides her to a chair on the podium.

Once Carolyn is seated, Cornell stands behind her, hands gripping her shoulders. The other priests encircle her, and she closes her eyes. Motion ceases, and she hears a rustle of paper. A scribe will record everything. Carolyn clears her throat, nervous.

The incense's spicy scent fills her nose, making her nauseated. Cornell's hands stroke the back of her neck, tickling her. She shivers, and his hands slide to her bare arms. The touch repulses her, and she wants to shake him off, but forces herself to keep still. The punishment for rebelling would be brutal.

An image of the moon pops into her head, and she speaks: "I see the moon."

The scratch of a reed brush on papyrus reaches her ears as the scribe writes that down.

"A blue moon, heralding upheaval. Beware."

Screams from outside interrupt. She startles at a crash from the front of the temple. Footsteps running up the aisle close in on where she sits. Curiosity overcomes fear, and Carolyn opens her eyes to see Michael Valiant, a soldier, racing towards her. Blood seeps through the front of his uniform.

Cornell pulls her up from the chair and pushes her behind him while motioning for two priests to remove her from the room. A stream of guards run in behind Valiant, swords drawn. He makes a sound that's part growl, part wail, and runs at Cornell. Carolyn struggles against the priests who hold her.

She wants to break free, to help Michael. If she doesn't, they'll kill him. A guard reaches Valiant and runs him through with a sword. Carolyn screams in agony and despair.

Carolyn awoke, tears on her face, and touched the space next to her, looking for Cornell. Gone. She flicked on the light and pulled a notebook and pen from the night table to record the details of the dream.

The frequency of the dreams had increased, and they'd become more vivid and strange. Each one involved Michael Valiant, herself, Cornell, and a man she'd never met, who in the dreams was Valiant's partner until Valiant betrayed him.

The pattern was always the same: Michael and his partner capture her. In one series of dreams, it was during a witch hunt. In another, she was an oracle in ancient Greece. Carolyn thought she was in Atlantis in yet another.

Regardless of the dream's setting, she and Michael fell in love and one or both of them ended up dead. She'd considered telling Cornell about the dreams, but something always prevented her. Perhaps it was because in the dreams, Cornell was always the villain.

Carolyn closed the notebook and put it away. She lay back again and thought about Cornell and what he meant to her. She didn't love him. He was kind and generous to her, and she appreciated that, but she didn't love him. She missed John and Sam. The loss of her husband and daughter had been more than she could bear.

Thoughts of her family brought her around to thinking of their killer: Michael Valiant. He'd killed her husband, and before she'd even buried John, had broken into her house, kidnapped her, and killed Sam. Carolyn had lived in a constant state of terror when she was with Valiant.

First, he'd taken her to a hotel in Peterborough, where he'd raped her. Then he'd taken her to Algonquin Park, where he'd turned her over to the aliens, but not before raping her again.

Panic and fear escalated as she relived those moments. She calmed herself by remembering how Cornell had rescued her from the aliens. He'd taken her to the safety of the compound in Peterborough and gotten her the help she needed to recover. He protected her now. Yet whenever she had one of these dreams, she'd wake up longing to be reunited with Valiant, her heart breaking at the thought of losing him.

It was the residual effects of the dream, but it disoriented and confused her. This man had destroyed her, and she was having dreams of being in love with him and despising Cornell. It'd be a bad idea to tell him the dreams.

She checked the time. Almost five o'clock. She'd have to get up soon anyway. They'd begin her self-defence training today. It unnerved her to think Cornell believed it was necessary, implying the possibility Valiant could get to her here.

Carolyn climbed out of bed and headed to the washroom, a flutter of anticipation making her hurry. She'd train hard. If Michael Valiant ever found her, he'd discover she wasn't the same woman he'd abused and then handed over to the aliens. She'd make him pay for what he'd done to her.

***

Sam waited in her room while Cornell prepared to go out again. He'd come home for dinner at least, but insisted he had to return to work. She'd said good night and excused herself, claiming she had studying. Door closed, she removed her T-shirt and jeans and put on a skirt and blouse. A pair of low-heeled pumps replaced the sneakers she wore. She brushed her hair and twisted it into a bun.

When she heard the outer door close, she tucked an ID badge she'd stolen from Cornell's desk into her shoulder bag. Sam left her room and returned to the kitchen, where Marnie scraped leftover food from dinner plates into the garbage disposal. Ginny sat at the table with a cocktail and watched.

Sam told Ginny she was going to the library, and Ginny gave her a distracted nod. Getting away from Wade and George turned out to be more difficult. They begged to go along with her. She argued that she needed to study, and Ginny withdrew from her haze long enough to yell at the kids to leave Sam alone. Sam hurried outside into the tunnel, a replica of a street, and searched for Cornell.

She spotted him walking along the sidewalk, headed in the direction he took when he went to work. Sam followed him, keeping her distance. Trees lined the street, and if she didn't know they were underground, she'd never have believed the twilight sky above her was an illusion. She could see what looked like the setting sun in the distance. A slight breeze rippled her hair.

Sam pulled the ID badge from her bag and clipped it onto her blouse. Finally a practical use for the graphics degree she'd been working on for the last year. She'd doctored the ID badge to display her picture. Anyone examining it closely might spot the forgery, but she figured dropping Cornell's name would prevent most people from asking too many questions.

Earlier in the day, she'd taken a test run from the residential section where the Cornell residence was to the restricted Agency section where Cornell worked. No one had stopped her. She'd gone into their library, hung out at a café for a while, and picked up fruit at the market.

She shouldn't have any problems getting back in now. Sam kept Jim in her sights, but hung back in case he stopped and turned around. When he reached the gatepost entrance to the Agency quarter, she slowed even more. After he was through, she quickened her pace.

Sam got through security again with no issues and fell in behind Cornell through the commercial section. Residential buildings dominated the other side. Sam noted with some smugness that Cornell didn't head to his office building, but instead continued on through the core towards the residences.

She slowed her pace again, and when he turned into a walkway leading up to a townhouse complex, she crossed the street. He never looked back. She waited until he was inside, then stood across the street from the house and memorized the distinguishing features.

Roses grew on a trellis in front of the small porch. Fairy wind chimes hung from the porch roof. The wooden porch was painted a dusty blue with white accents. Lights in the living room and open curtains showed the house's interior.

A movie played on the TV. The movie paused, and Cornell moved into view. He opened his arms, and a blonde woman appeared. She went to him and they hugged. Sam's heart skipped a beat. The woman's movements were familiar.

Sam watched, entranced. The couple kissed. Ginny and Sam had been right: he was having an affair. Anger bubbled up. She had an urge to rush over and bang on the door. At that moment, the lovers parted, and Sam saw the woman's face for the first time. She staggered backwards and gave a wounded cry when she recognized her mother.

CHAPTER 41

"Why isn't Michael joining us?" Althaea called out to Arnie, who was in the kitchen cooking dinner.

"Couldn't drag him away from the windows. The wind's dying down, and he wants to get out and hunt for a vehicle. I said we'd help him after dinner, but he snarled at me, so I walked away." Arnie's voice floated out through the open kitchen doors and into the cafeteria where Althaea sat at a table.

"The wind is dying down, but he should eat something. I hope he doesn't go out alone. But he gets obsessive and needs his space. Good call."

Arnie appeared, a plate of food in each hand. He set one on the table in front of Althaea and the other across from her.

"My specialty."

"Scrambled eggs and sausages." Althaea grinned. "Breakfast for dinner. I've always enjoyed that. And not a veggie in sight."

"Now, wait. Veggies coming right up, Madame."

He returned to the kitchen and dishes clattered. A moment later, he reappeared, carrying two bowls, which he set in the middle of the table.

"Asparagus and biscuits." Hands fisted on waist, Arnie puffed out his chest, grinned, and executed a bow. "Don't forget to tip your waiter."

Althaea laughed. She laughed more often these days, and Arnie was usually the cause. "I can't deny this meal is fabulous—not when you're so proud."

The grin grew wider, and when it reached his eyes, her heart gave a thud. This time, she jumped to her feet, threw her arms around him, and kissed him forcefully on the mouth. Arnie's arms enfolded her, and his mouth opened in response before he pulled away.

"What's wrong?" Her voice sounded petulant. Hurt replaced surprise as the rejection sliced through her gut like a sickle. She'd believed the attraction was mutual, and considering Arnie's single status, she'd expected him to make a move on her sooner or later.

Michael had warned her weeks ago that Arnie was a womanizer. When the expected move hadn't come, Ally assumed he'd held back while healing from his bullet wound. But now she wondered if she was a man repellent.

When Michael had rejected her, it was bad enough, though in the end, she understood why. This was different. What about her was so repulsive that even a guy who couldn't keep it in his pants could keep it in his pants?

Arnie directed his gaze at the floor. "Ally," he said.

"Don't. Please. You have a reputation for nailing anything that moves. Yet when I'm like the last woman on Earth, on the pill, ready and willing, you don't want me." Her voice broke. *Damn it. Don't cry like a girl.* She sat and picked up her fork.

"Althaea, it's not—"

She cut him off. "Don't feed me the 'it's not you it's me' bullshit. Okay?"

Gentle, Arnie took the fork from her hand, set it on the plate, and covered her hand with his. "Listen."

The kindness in his voice made the breath catch in her throat. She looked up at Arnie, mesmerized by his eyes. With difficulty, she pulled her gaze away and stared at the uneaten eggs.

"It's not that I don't want to. You've no idea how much I want to. But I don't want to hurt you, which means taking things slow."

"That's not what I heard about you."

"You mean from Valiant?"

Althaea nodded.

"A great one to talk. He was with Carolyn for a nanosecond and slept with her. You were involved with him too, right? You told me so yourself."

She shook her head, finding it difficult to answer that question. "Sit. Eat your dinner. It looks delicious."

"You want to eat?" Disbelief and an edge of irritation were in his voice.

"I don't want to waste good food."

His shoulders dropped, and he laughed softly. "You're so practical it drives me crazy." But he sat and picked up his fork. "Shall we talk while we eat?"

Althaea speared a stalk of asparagus, shattered pride soothed while she focused on the vegetable and nibbled. "Excellent."

"Thanks. But you're not going to distract me."

"I jumped you, and you rejected me. What's to discuss? Just tell me what's wrong with me."

The fork in Arnie's hand clattered to his plate. "There's nothing wrong with you. This isn't a rejection. I want to make sure it's what you want. I've never considered the woman's perspective before, but I want to now. In this fucking hellhole, I found out what it's like to be used and abused. It made me reconsider how I treat other people, Ally, especially women."

Suddenly she felt ravenous. She shovelled eggs into her mouth, grabbed a biscuit, and wolfed it down. "I need a drink. Want one?"

Before he could reply, she stood and went to the kitchen, returning with two bottles of water. Arnie took one from her, and, still seated, pulled her to him. He hugged her tight around the thighs. She gripped his shoulders, trying not to fall on him.

"Did you love Valiant?"

After taking a deep breath to squelch her frustration, Althaea pulled away from him. "Is that why you've kept me at arm's length? I didn't sleep with him. Does it matter?"

"Were you in love him?"

"Yes." It was true. She'd been in love with Michael, or, at least, she'd loved him in the limited capacity she'd had for loving anyone back then.

Arnie's steel-blue gaze locked onto hers. "Are you still in love with him?"

"No. If I was, I wouldn't be throwing myself at you."

"I'd like to think that's true. You guys are awfully buddy-buddy."

Althaea sat in her chair again, but this time didn't pick up the fork. "I understand Michael—we're a lot alike, shared similar experiences. Yes, I was attracted to him once. He's strong, intelligent, and passionate. Qualities that appeal to me. But I'm over him. I got him out of my system, and yeah, most of that was done after we got here, but I'm over him. Why are we analyzing it?"

"I want to make sure you want me, and I'm not just a—a substitute or something." Arnie gazed at his plate of food, dejected.

Althaea sighed. "I'm attracted to you, Arnie. But I don't know if I'm looking for anything more than sex. I assumed you'd be okay with that."

"You mean because Valiant told you I'd nail anything that moved?"

"Yes."

"I'm not looking for that anymore. I'm tired of that."

"What about Carolyn?"

"What about her?"

"Are you in love with her? I see how you get when you talk about her. I can tell you hate it when Michael mentions their time together, or when he grabs for her ring, which he thinks we don't notice."

Arnie leaned forward. "I thought I was. Don't get me wrong: I still love Carolyn, but I'm not in love with her. I think I wanted Carolyn because she didn't want me. It was juvenile. But I had a lot of time to reflect since there wasn't anything else to do but navel gaze and take abuse. I want to rescue Carolyn from that asshole Cornell, but not for me. I just want her to be safe."

155

Althaea nodded. "Okay. So now what? Are we going to be okay?"

Arnie took her hand, put it to his cheek, and closed his eyes. "We'll be great."

***

Michael stared out into the storm. The wind had quieted at least enough for him to make the run to the garage. Too restless and agitated to wait for Althaea and Arnie, he'd skipped dinner and hovered at the side exit watching for a break.

Backpack loaded with C4, blasting caps, and a radio-frequency detonator, Michael planned to blow the garage bay doors open if necessary. If there were a vehicle in there, he'd get it and finally get the hell out of this place.

Rain battered the door, and Michael estimated sixty kilometres per hour winds. It would make getting to the outbuildings difficult, but not impossible. It was much better than the strong gale-force winds they had until now.

A waterproof windbreaker covered his clothes, and the backpack hung from his shoulders. The sky still showed the puke-green colour that had become the norm, but he was sure there'd be no funnel clouds.

Michael pushed his way out onto the pavement. The wind caught the door, almost wrenching it from his grasp. He wrestled nature for control and forced the door closed.

The garage, fifty metres away, loomed like a barrow mound in the murk. The hood blew off his head, and within seconds, his hair and face were drenched. He ignored the discomfort and pressed on, leaning into the wind.

Michael fought his way to the entrance and tried the insulated steel overhead door first. It refused to budge. He moved to the next door and jiggled the handle. Also locked, but he could pick that no problem—no need for C4. He set his pack down and took out a lock-picking case.

Inside, the bays before him stood empty. Worried, he jogged along the corridor. To his relief, three vehicles, two of them SUVs, sat abandoned. He reached into his pack for the car keys he'd taken from Deuce and Tasha. When he pressed the remote, the lights flashed on the vehicle in front of him.

Michael yanked open the car door and jumped into the driver's seat. The engine started, and he checked the gas gauge. Half full. He turned the vehicle off and inspected the other car, which had over a quarter tank of gas. They'd siphon the gas from this one and add it to the other SUV.

Now they had the means to leave, he was anxious to get moving. But when he returned to the exit and opened the door, his heart sank. The wind had picked up again. Michael stepped out into the storm. Lightning flashed overhead, followed seconds later by thunder. Pushed along by the wind, he ran back to the building.

As he neared the building, Althaea poked her head out the door and screamed something at him. Michael thought it involved the f-bomb. He tumbled inside, Arnie grabbing an arm to keep him from falling.

"What the fuck were you thinking? You should have let us know you were going out." Althaea's face held red fury.

"Forget it. I'm here now. Two SUVs in the garage. We can leave."

Arnie and Althaea exchanged glances.

"Don't tell me no. The wind isn't that bad."

"It's picking up again. Try the radio and find a weather report," Arnie said.

"They don't know what they're talking about. I'm not waiting. We have to get Carolyn."

From outside came a sound like an approaching freight train. Michael cursed and looked out into the storm. In the distance, a funnel cloud reached towards the earth from the roiling green ceiling headed in their direction. He froze. If the tornado hit the garage, it would turn it into rubble and destroy the cars.

Althaea touched his arm. "We'd better get to the basement."

CHAPTER 42

Sam stood rooted to the sidewalk while her mother and Cornell canoodled in the window of the townhouse across the street. Carolyn turned her back to Cornell, and he moved behind her, put his arms around her, and nuzzled her neck. Sam's legs shook and breathing became difficult.

It occurred to her to move away from the direct view of the house. She walked two metres back the way she'd come, then stopped. Should she confront them? What would Cornell do if she appeared at the door?

She recalled the message she'd seen on his desk. Her mother was the "subject" referred to in the email and thought someone named Michael Valiant had killed her family. Sam gulped at a lump in her throat. *Mom thinks I'm dead—like I thought she was dead.*

Cornell had done this.

Afraid the two would see her, Sam continued to walk back towards the gatehouse. It was best to return to the Cornells and figure out what to do next. Knees wobbling the moment she sighted the gate, Sam stopped to breathe out nervous tension.

The guards checked everyone leaving, too. If she looked too flustered, they'd stop her. She grabbed a spot at the end of the line, took a few deep gulps of air, and did another breath check. Steady, even, inhale, exhale.

People ahead passed through the gate, flashing ID badges at the guards. No one stopped or even paused. The process should be easy enough: hold up the badge, walk by the guard without hesitation, go through the gate, and head home. Sam unclipped the phony badge from her lapel and held it ready between numbed fingers.

Afraid the badge would slip through her fingers and attract attention, Sam tightened her grip. Thoughts raced, her brain trying to reconcile seeing her mother with Cornell's assertion Carolyn had died in Algonquin. *Mom is alive.*

Sam inhaled, steadied herself, and stepped up to the gate. The guard, who looked about the same age as Sam, smiled. She forced a brief return smile, flashed the badge, and continued walking, careful not to appear anxious or hurried.

"Hey, Blondie. Wait a minute."

She froze and turned to face the guard, trying to look puzzled and bored at the same time.

"Are you new here?" The guard walked over to her, peered into her face. He slipped the badge from her icy fingers and glanced at the name and photo. "Samantha Cornell. Are you related to Jim Cornell?"

Sorry now she'd used the Cornell name on the badge, Sam had assumed it would get her past checkpoints more easily. "Yes. I'm his niece. Is there a problem? I can call him." She looked into his eyes. He blushed, and her tension eased. All she had to do was bluff her way past him.

Face still tinged with red, the young man shook his head. "No problem. I wanted to meet you."

Sam flashed another smile, hoping she looked friendly and inviting. "You've met me." She glanced at his badge. "Trevor. Now we know each other."

She reached for her badge, letting her fingers brush against his hand when she retrieved it. "Is this your regular post?" Sam hoped so. If she got to know him, he'd let her come and go as she pleased. This might work to her advantage.

"Sure. Every afternoon shift for the next month, anyway. Then my shift changes back to days."

"What time does the afternoon shift start?"

"Two o'clock."

"I'm holding up the line. I'll see you again soon?"

"Can we meet for coffee before my shift?" Trevor blushed.

Sam beamed at him. "Sure. Meet me tomorrow at one o'clock at the cafe."

When he agreed, she fluttered her fingers at him and walked away. A safe distance from the gate, she exhaled loudly, relieved she'd pulled it off. The blouse she wore had soaked through under the arms though she hadn't even noticed she'd been sweating. Sam hurried home.

***

Carolyn sat on the recliner, eyes closed. The pad of paper in her lap already held sketches: a garage door, an SUV, a funnel cloud, and a mangled helicopter. Cornell was particularly interested in the SUV.

"Are they in the vehicle?" he asked for the second time.

"No. It was something Valiant saw, standing in front of it, not looking over the hood from behind the steering wheel."

She tried to sense Valiant again though the thought of connecting to the man who'd murdered her family repulsed her. "Jim, it's too difficult. They went to the basement, which blocked me. That's all I can get."

Carolyn opened her eyes, and Cornell took the paper and pencil from her. A smile played across his lips, and he grasped her hands and pulled her from the chair. He held her, kissing her lips and her neck. When he spoke, his lips moved against her skin. "You don't have to worry about Valiant anymore today, okay?"

She sighed, relieved. "Okay. Thank you. I hate thinking about him. It brings it all back as though it happened yesterday."

Cornell slid his hand up her shirt, under her bra. "Then forget him for now." His voice was thick with desire. He pressed against her, and she let him. Having Cornell with her felt comforting though not exciting. When he wasn't with her, emptiness and longing closed in, and his presence eased her loneliness.

He took Carolyn by the hand and led her into the bedroom. They stayed there the rest of the evening.

***

He's cute.

Sam accepted the coffee Trevor handed her, and he sat opposite her at the table. She'd chosen a booth at the back of the café with a direct view of the door. Even though she was positive Cornell was at the office, she had to be careful.

No longer terrified of Trevor, Sam studied him and decided she liked what she saw. His dark hair was too army cut, but that wasn't his choice. He had a nice face and kind eyes that reminded her of a puppy her friend Vanna had.

"Are you here visiting your uncle?" he asked.

For an awful moment, Sam didn't understand. Then she remembered she'd told Trevor the day before that Cornell was her uncle. "No. I came here to visit you. Uncle Jim would be mad if he knew I was here. He doesn't want me coming here unless it's to see him, and he doesn't want me to date. Don't mention you saw me if you talk to him. Okay?" Trevor might run into Cornell and mention seeing his "niece." She'd better plaster over that hole right now.

"Why does he have a say in who you date?"

"The Cornells are my guardians. I live with them, and I play nanny to their kids. The boys have school now, though, so I slipped away."

"I won't say anything."

"Thanks." Sam fell silent and sipped her coffee. She'd been without a friend for a long time, and she'd better be careful. Trevor could never be a confidant. *God, I miss Jack and Vanna.*

"Why are you living with your uncle? Where are your parents?"

Sam stared at her coffee. *Half full.* She glanced at Trevor.

He waited, patient.

"They're dead. Dad died of a heart attack. Mom killed herself when she got involved with a UFO cult." Safest to perpetuate the lie, she decided.

"I'm sorry." He sounded sincere.

She wondered if he knew what was happening. Perhaps she could get information from Trevor. That would mean less snooping in Cornell's office. "How did you get hired?"

"Recruited out of university." Trevor sat straighter, puffed out his chest.

Wide-eyed, Sam said, "Wow. They noticed you? What were you studying?"

"I majored in math at the University of Waterloo, but had more than a minor in astronomy. They also liked that I'm a black belt in Judo."

"That's impressive. Are your parents here?"

"No. They died in a car accident when I was in my second year at university."

"I'm sorry. So you understand what it's like for me. How old are you?"

"Twenty-four. You?"

Sam smiled. "Twenty."

Trevor checked his watch. "I have to go. Can we meet again?"

"I'd like that. What time do you finish work?"

Trevor raised his brows. "Ten-thirty. Would the Cornells have a fit if I called on you then?"

"Yes, that's too late." Sam let him hear her disappointment. "Let's meet tomorrow before you start work?"

"Sure. Same time?"

Sam nodded and beamed a smile at him. Trevor grinned back, and Sam thought she could happily spend the rest of the day sitting here watching him smile. She tossed back the rest of her coffee and stood when he did.

Butterflies fluttered in Sam's stomach when he touched her hand as they said their goodbyes. A woman in army fatigues bumped into Trevor as he headed towards the door. Jealousy pinched Sam for a second when he held the woman to steady her.

She shook it off. He was nice, but she couldn't trust him, and a crush on him might make her careless. But it would be nice to have someone.

Sam left the booth and stood inside the café entrance, which was open to the sidewalk. Before stepping out, she searched for any sign of Trevor or Cornell. She caught sight of Trevor's back as he headed towards the gate.

Only a handful of people wandered about, and no sign of Cornell. Sam left the café and walked to her mother's house.

CHAPTER 43

Michael stood at the exit and tried to determine how severe the damage was to the outbuildings. The tornado had munched the right side of the garage, but the left side containing the SUVs remained intact. When the funnel cloud had passed, it took the gale-force winds with it, and the rain fell in a straight sheet. If the SUVs survived the damage, they could leave today.

"Grab the bags we packed while I get the vehicle," Michael said.

Arnie and Althaea headed down the hall, and Michael pushed the door open and stepped into the rain. Hair and clothes already soaked, the downpour wouldn't add much to his discomfort. He didn't bother to put his hood back up.

The building groaned as if on the verge of collapse. Michael ignored the ominous sounds and heaved open the bay door. He jumped into the SUV and started it. At the sound of the engine turning over, his heart soared.

Michael estimated an hour drive to the underground community. He'd outlined a plan with Althaea for getting them in. If all went as planned, they'd have Carolyn before day's end. He drove up to the main building, pulled over, and jumped out to help the others load the bags into the car.

Everything stowed, they hopped into the vehicle, Michael driving, Althaea, wearing Agency-issue military-style gear, riding shotgun, and Arnie in the back. Michael grasped Carolyn's ring for a moment before putting the car into drive. He manoeuvred around the damaged helicopter and the downed trees.

The road was an obstacle course, and they frequently stopped to move trees and other debris out of the way. He tried the radio. Most of it was static, but a military station broadcast on one of the AM channels. A recorded message played:

"Stay in your homes until further notice. The storm is expected to end soon. Power will be restored in your area in order of priority. A state of emergency has been declared. Those requiring evacuation will relocate to government-run shelters. Stay in your homes until further notice ... "

Michael turned off the radio. So they'd declared a state of emergency. The Agency had abandoned the Aurora Project equipment. Considering the ferocity of the storms since they'd gone underground, Michael guessed it'd taken this long for the military to discover what triggered the cataclysms and deactivate the machines. The drop in wind force told him they'd finally managed it.

"We taking back roads?" Althaea said.

"Yes. It'll double the time we take to get there, but if they stop us, they'll never let us go."

Arnie leaned forward between the two front seats. "Why would anyone stop us?"

Michael remained silent. After a moment, Althaea responded. "Both cops and military will stop anyone on the roads. Once they identify Michael and me as agents, they'll ask questions we won't want to answer. You're supposed to be dead. When they figure out who you are, they'll lock us up."

Arnie slid back in his seat. "How long until we get to where we're going?"

"About two hours. I want to arrive by dusk," Michael said.

"Will you tell me what you plan to do once we get there?"

"No."

"Did you tell Althaea?" Arnie sounded annoyed.

"It's 'need-to-know,' Arnie."

"Who do you think you are? James Bond?"

"If I don't tell you, you can't blab if you're interrogated. I won't risk Carolyn's life just to let you feel included. You know your part. Leave the rest to Ally and me."

Arnie fell silent. Althaea turned and faced the back. "Don't worry. It'll be fine."

Michael stopped the car. Another tree blocked their path. "I'll get this one." He jumped from the vehicle.

A birch tree lay strewn across the road, and Michael dragged it to the ditch. His feet slid through the mud at the side of the road, and he almost fell. The air smelled of dirt, swamp, and cedars. Rain hitting the roof of the car, a constant rat-a-tat that was louder inside the vehicle, drowned out any other sounds.

Arnie stared out the side window. Guilt bolted through Michael. Maybe he should tell Arnie the truth about what they'd planned. But that would be like telling the dog you were taking him to the vet for neutering—it'd freak him out and not change the outcome. Michael shook his head, wiped his hands on his jeans, and returned to the car.

***

Carolyn poured tea from an insulated, stainless steel pot. The aroma of chai and vanilla wafted up from her mug. It was late afternoon, and Cornell wouldn't be coming over until after dinner. He'd been spending more time at home since the argument with Ginny. He'd told Carolyn about the fight, confiding much of his personal life to her, but little of his work life.

She didn't mind the former, but sometimes resented the latter, especially since she contributed to that work with her remote viewing. Perhaps that's why she still refused to tell him about her dreams.

She'd had another one last night—the witch dream again. She'd stood on a scaffold, about to be hanged. Cornell had whispered in her ear that if she gave herself to him, he could save her. She'd spit in his face, and he'd dragged her to the noose. Michael Valiant had pushed his way towards the scaffold.

The sight of him had raised both hope and fear in her. The hope had been that he'd reach her in time, and the fear had been that he'd be captured and they'd both die. In her dream, she'd wanted to die rather than have harm come to him. She always woke from these dreams confused, missing Michael's touch, and loathing Jim Cornell.

She pushed the confusing thoughts and feelings aside and reminded herself Cornell was taking care of her. Without his help, the aliens would've held her captive for the rest of her life. He'd rescued her.

As always when she got reflective, the images bubbled to the surface. Carolyn tried to push them away and failed. John dead in the hospital. Michael shooting Sam. Michael raping Carolyn in a hotel in Peterborough. She'd fought him, but he'd beaten and raped her. The terror escalated and tears welled up. Would she ever rid herself of these cursed memories?

Carolyn jumped when she heard a knock at the door. She grabbed a tissue and dabbed at her eyes while she walked to the door. Hand out to open the door, she stopped, fear making her cautious. Cornell wasn't due yet. Her martial arts trainer came over in the mornings.

Her stomach fluttered. She rushed to the bedroom and got the gun Jim had given her. Another knock, louder this time. She ran to the door and stuck her eye to the peephole. A young woman stood on the other side of the door, and Carolyn's heart skipped a beat. The young woman looked like Sam. Impossible, but what if? Cornell's cautions forgotten, she threw open the door.

"Mom." Sam's voice broke, and she rushed inside, throwing herself into Carolyn's arms.

It was Sam. How could it be? The gun slipped from Carolyn's grasp and landed on the foyer floor. She hugged her daughter, sobbing, hands sifting through the golden-blonde curls, verifying they were real and solid and not part of a glorious dream. Carolyn inhaled, caught the scent of lavender and roses. Sam was real.

Carolyn pulled herself away. "I thought you were dead. How are you here?"

"I thought *you* were dead, Mom. I *buried* you."

"Michael Valiant shot you. I saw it. Your heart wasn't beating. I tried to give you mouth-to-mouth but Valiant dragged me away."

Sam turned her head and looked behind her at the open door. "Wait," she said and closed the door. "I don't want anyone to see me here. Jim Cornell can't know about this."

"How do you know Jim Cornell?" Carolyn asked. Something fluttered in the back of her mind, like a moth against a window screen.

"I'm living at his house."

Carolyn stumbled backwards, bumping into the back of the loveseat at the edge of the foyer. "Sam, how did you get here? How did you survive?"

"Sit, Mom. There are things you should know about Jim Cornell."

CHAPTER 44

They were close. Michael saw a tall, grey structure sticking out above the trees ahead. *Wouldn't they have wanted to hide it?* But no, in their arrogance, the Agency didn't care who saw it. What would people do, anyway? They'd assume it was a government building, and they'd be partly right. But if they tried to gain access, they'd be shot.

Michael had already ignored the "Danger," "No Trespassing," and "Keep out" signs and driven around sawhorse barricades. Those were the weakest deterrents. The warnings and threats might keep out Mr. John Q. Public, but not Michael Valiant.

He dropped a hand to his holster and then touched the ring lying against his chest. *Bring it.*

A "Trespassers will be shot" sign loomed up, and Michael drove past it without slowing. When he saw the fence in the distance, he turned off the dirt road into the trees. The SUV wove around elms, maples, beeches, and varieties of evergreens, some lying on the ground, others standing only because they'd snagged on another tree when they toppled. When the trees became too dense, he backed up, turned the SUV around to face the road, and cut the engine.

"End of the road." He glanced at Althaea, whose face was stone. She relaxed when her gaze met his. Michael turned to Arnie, whose face was less grim than Althaea's, but white with fear. His eyes had glazed over, and he looked as if he wandered somewhere in the nine circles of hell.

"Arnie," Michael said. "Come back."

Arnie blinked, focused his eyes, and gaped at Michael, jaw slack. Althaea shifted in her seat and reached a hand out to stroke Arnie's cheek. "Don't worry. We'll get through this."

She turned back to Michael. "Better to blow it when we have Carolyn, Michael."

Michael frowned, irritated that Althaea was reviving an argument they'd had earlier. "It makes little sense to destroy the one place where there's hope of survival. I want payback too. But we can't kill innocent people, and we don't want to destroy the only place that offers a chance to rebuild."

She shook her head, mouth curling up in a sneer, disgusted. "You should've thought of that when you destroyed the crystals."

"The crystals were Trojan horses with aliens, and you know it. Enough. We can't keep debating this." Michael looked at Arnie. "We're far enough off the road you shouldn't be noticed. This rain will give good cover. Stay alert. Keep your gun handy, and remember the fence is electric."

Arnie nodded.

"Don't nod. I need to hear you're with me."

"Yeah. I'm fine," Arnie said.

"Understand what you're supposed to do, how to time it?"

"Yeah. I said I'm fine."

"Great. Get out of the car. Give us at least two hours. Got the night-vision goggles?"

Arnie held up the pair he'd kept next to him on the seat, and Michael gave a thumbs up. Arnie grabbed his backpack and stepped out of the vehicle.

Althaea lowered her window. "Arnie."

He went to her.

"Good luck."

"You too," he said and turned away, but stopped as though reconsidering. He leaned through Ally's window, pulled her towards him, and kissed her on the lips.

Michael stared into the forest, allowing them their moment. Arnie muttered something to Althaea, and she leaned out and kissed him again. When she pulled away, her eyes were moist. Head bowed, she raised her window.

Michael threw the vehicle into drive and left Arnie behind.

***

Carolyn sat on the couch next to Sam, holding her hand, and still not daring to believe her girl was here. Eyes wide, Carolyn listened while Sam told her everything that had happened since the last time they saw each other. When Sam finished speaking, a haze enveloped Carolyn, numbness spreading up from her solar plexus. *Sam lives at Jim's house, and he told me she was dead. Oh, God, why would he do that?*

"I have your engagement ring, Mom. They said it was on your body, but they didn't find the wedding band."

Carolyn stared at her bare fingers. "I thought I'd lost them in

Algonquin. I fell into a ravine and later noticed they'd disappeared. Valiant wouldn't let me go back to find them." She stopped, frowned. "Why am I remembering things that contradict everything you're telling me?"

Hope sprang into her eyes. "Sam, maybe your dad is still alive. I remember going to the hospital and seeing him there, dead, but perhaps that's a lie too." What if John were alive? *Oh, please let John be alive.*

But Sam shook her head, sadness and grief etched on her face. "No, Mom. The funeral was open casket. No mistake. You told me after Dad died that you'd seen his spirit. Dad's dead." Sam put a hand to her mouth as if to hold in the heartache.

Something fluttered again in Carolyn's mind.

"Seen his spirit." Carolyn tested the words, repeating them slowly. The concept seemed at once strange and familiar.

Sam reached into her purse and removed a piece of paper. "This might help. I found it on Jim's desk and stole it before I came here so you'd have evidence."

Horror rose as Carolyn read the email communications between Cornell and someone named Tom Scielo. She stared at Sam, a lump in her throat. "Brainwashing?" Disbelief oozed from the word.

Her pulse thudded in her ears, and she felt numb. Everything was a lie, every memory untrustworthy. Disoriented, she took a deep breath and attempted to focus. Carolyn squeezed Sam's hand, and it helped ground her.

"What about Michael Valiant? Have I even met the man? Sam, they've been training me to kill Valiant if he shows up here. I remember him as—" Carolyn's dreams popped into her head and she felt sick. Perhaps her unconscious held the truth.

"As what, Mom?"

"Your killer. Your father's killer. My kidnapper. He gave me to the aliens." It was a litany repeated often while she prepared to face him someday.

"I know nothing about Michael Valiant."

Carolyn jumped off the couch. "Jim will come back."

"When?" Sam's voice held panic, and she too leapt to her feet.

"Not for another two hours, but we should leave now. How long before the Cornells notice you're gone?"

"I have time. I told Ginny I was going to the library to study. The kids are at school."

Carolyn considered their options. "I can't leave this area. My ID badge only allows me access to a few places in this section and nothing else. For my own protection." She spat it out, tasting the lie. *I'm a prisoner here.*

The loathing she'd felt for Cornell in her dream surged through her. She'd let him touch her, make love to her. *Not make love. He fucked you. He used you.* Grief competed with pain, and she put her hands over her belly, cradling it.

"I can't pretend everything's normal when he comes back." The panic she'd heard in Sam's voice now reflected in her own. Cornell would know. He'd walk in, look at her face, and know. Her gaze darted to Sam, then landed on the gun lying on the floor. She looked again at Sam. "I know what we can do about Jim Cornell."

CHAPTER 45

Althaea pulled up near the gate and stepped from the SUV. Through the open window, she glanced into the back seat where Michael slumped as though unconscious. He leaned against the door, hands cuffed in front.

Infrared cameras had picked up their approach. A guard tower thrust out of the front of the building, and she saw movement. They waited. It didn't take long. A vehicle approached—she didn't see from where it came.

"Humvee." Althaea muttered. "Two occupants."

The Hummer pulled up to the gate, and the agents stepped out. Both wore military gear and carried automatic rifles. Althaea turned off the engine and took the keys from the ignition. She stuffed them in her pocket when she approached the gate.

The two agents levelled guns at her.

"Althaea Dayton, fellas. I'm bringing in a prisoner."

The guards kept the guns raised and waited.

"Radio it in to Jim Cornell. I've got Michael Valiant here, drugged and unconscious."

The guard on the right, who appeared older than his partner, inclined his head towards the SUV. The partner lowered his rifle and went back to the Humvee. Althaea couldn't see what he did, but assumed he used the radio.

The guard stepped from the Humvee and waved the older man over. After a moment spent conferring in hushed tones, the older guy returned to Althaea. "Cornell says to let you through to the east entrance. I'll ride with you."

The partner climbed into the driver's seat of the Humvee while Althaea returned to her vehicle. The older guard signaled to the tower, and the gate slid open. Althea drove through the entrance, and the gate closed.

The older guard jumped into the SUV next to Althaea. He was tall, but not as tall as Michael, and fit and muscular, though he looked at least ten years older than her. A faded scar ran along the left side of his face and hooked under his chin.

He nodded his head in Michael's direction and said, "I heard he'd escaped. How'd you find him?"

"He took me hostage. I turned the tables. It wasn't easy. You don't know what I've been through these past few months."

The guard looked her up and down. "Impressive. You don't look as though you could take him."

"Maybe I'll show you my moves sometime." Ally licked her lips. The guard flashed a shark-like grin. In her imagination, she slammed her gun butt into his face. Instead, she steeled herself and leered back.

Typical fucking man. If she kept acting as if he were God's gift, she could keep the blood concentrated away from his brain. Then it'd be easy to take him out. "What's your name, soldier?" she said.

"Call me Pistol. I'll show you why later." Wink.

"Pistol. Okay." She ignored the wink. *If he makes a crack about me getting pistol whipped, I'm knocking out those goddamn teeth.*

Althaea glanced at Michael using the rear view mirror. To his credit, he continued to appear unconscious and kept a straight face. They were around the building's east side now. The vehicle ahead pulled up by a steel door. Althaea parked the SUV behind the Humvee and looked over at Pistol. *Fuck, what a stupid nickname.*

"What's your buddy's name?" Althaea asked.

"We call him Shift, 'cause the guy loves the overtime." Pistol jumped from the car and motioned for Althaea to do the same.

She stepped out into the rain and mud, leaving the keys in the ignition, and moved to the passenger side. She stood next to Michael's door. Something felt off, and she tensed, loosened the gun in her holster. "Cornell coming out here?"

Pistol smiled. "Later." He raised his gun and swung it at her face.

She ducked under it and hurled herself at his chest. The SUV's passenger door opened, and she felt, rather than saw, Michael hit the dirt. The handcuffs rattled when they dropped to the ground.

A pistol fired—the weapon, not the guy—and Michael had fired it. Beneath Althaea, Pistol pushed his fingers into her face, trying to stick them in her eyes. She hauled off and punched him in the head. When the fingers slipped from her face, she kneed him in the groin.

He howled. Althaea slugged him with her gun and pulled back for another blow. Michael leaned over and waved his hand in her face. "He's down, Dayton."

She looked. Pistol's nose and mouth gushed blood. He was still conscious though he'd stopped fighting. She dragged him to his feet. He spat and a tooth went flying.

Shift lay on the ground, holding his gut, which oozed blood. Michael moved to stand over him and raised his gun.

"Don't move, Valiant. We've got you both covered."

Althaea recognized Cornell's voice coming over a loudspeaker and looked around. "The towers, Michael. Sharpshooters."

The steel door opened and six agents trotted out. Two went to Althaea, each grabbing an arm, and another two went to Michael and did the same. Pistol staggered to his feet, went to Althaea, and punched her in the face. "Cornell said not to trust you."

She rubbed a hand across her mouth. "I told you I'd show you my moves."

"And I told you I'd show you why I'm called Pistol. We've got a date later, bitch." Pistol punched her in the stomach.

He turned to Michael, who struggled to shake the two guards holding him back. "Perhaps I'll let you watch."

Michael kicked out, but Pistol had turned and walked to the door. "Take these traitors to interrogation."

***

Carolyn retrieved the gun from the floor and set it on the coffee table. Sam's gaze met Carolyn's. "No, Mom," she said. "You can't shoot him."

"No, Sam. But I can make him help us escape."

"That's not a good idea. We can't even let him know I found you. Let's just leave. We're on the right side of the gate."

"What do you mean?"

Sam sighed and took Carolyn's hand. "Did you see the gate separating the family housing from the Agency sector?"

"Yes. I can't go through. Jim told me it was to protect me. I know now it was to keep me contained." She hugged Sam, relieved at having her close.

"The exit to the surface lies on this side of the gate."

"Okay. Good. I have to tell you something else."

Sam pulled away, concern on her face. "What?"

"I'm pregnant."

Eyes wide, Sam looked at the slight roundness under the baggy T-shirt.

Carolyn took Sam's hand and pressed it to her pelvic area. "I know it doesn't look like much, but soon it will."

"Mom. Who?"

Carolyn went into the living room and sank to the couch, tears falling. "I think it's Jim Cornell's. At least, that's what I remember. I hope it's not true, but what if it is?"

"We'll live with it. I thought Jim was nice, too, and I trusted him. He pretended to help me."

"I don't know who I am. I'm missing pieces of myself." Carolyn put her head in her hands. She wiped away the tears as Sam put an arm around her, but jumped at the loud tap on the door. "Get in my bedroom. Hide."

Sam ran for the bedroom.

"On the left."

Sam disappeared into the bedroom as the front door swung open. Heart thudding, Carolyn turned and faced Cornell.

CHAPTER 46

When Cornell's gaze landed on the gun, Carolyn froze.

"Why do you have the gun out? Did something happen?"

She licked her lips. "No. I set it there when I returned from target practice earlier. What are you doing here? I didn't expect you until after dinner." She kept the tremor from her voice and the guilt from her eyes.

"I have something to tell you." He strode to her side, breathless, eyes shining.

Carolyn strove not to flinch when he put his arms around her. Reluctantly, she returned the embrace, struggling to suppress the fear that she broadcasted her distrust, and focused on acting normal. "What is it?"

"Good news, darling." Cornell pulled back and studied her face. "Michael Valiant is in custody. I want you to confront him in the interrogation room. It's good you've got the gun here. Valiant will be executed. Maybe you'd do the honours? Payback, for what he did to you."

The blood drained from her face. At first, she experienced a surge of excitement and anticipation at the thought of confronting, and even killing, Valiant. It's what she'd trained for. But the realization they'd manipulated her followed, and she tried to squelch her hatred. She was certain of one thing: Michael Valiant hadn't killed Sam, regardless of what Carolyn remembered.

"You can do this, honey. I'll help you."

She tried not to recoil from the endearments. "I can't kill anyone."

Cornell went rigid. "What do you mean? We've discussed this, prepared for this. You've been looking forward to it. Valiant is a menace. He shot your daughter in cold blood. Valiant killed your husband, raped you. He turned you over to the aliens."

As he reviewed the list, Carolyn shuddered, and her hatred swelled. Without conscious thought, she reached for the gun, picked it up. Blackness filled her, and she wanted to smash something.

Cornell put an arm around her. "Come on. I'm here for you. We'll face him together."

Carolyn tucked the gun into her belt and allowed him to lead her from the house. It wasn't until they were almost to the sidewalk she remembered Sam was still in her bedroom.

***

When Sam heard her mother and Jim Cornell leave, she stepped into the living room. She didn't know what to do. What if he returned to the house with her mom? She couldn't stay here. Sam found a pen and paper and wrote a note to her mother: *Be back tomorrow, same time. S.*

Afraid to write more, she glanced around the room, searching for somewhere only her mother would find it. Sam went into the bathroom and opened the medicine cabinet. She closed it again when she saw the men's razor and toiletries, confirming the intimacy between her mother and Cornell.

She returned to the bedroom and opened drawers in the dresser until she found where Carolyn kept her underwear. Relieved to find no boxers or men's briefs in there, she set the note on top of the panties and slammed the drawer closed. Sam hurried to the front door and peeked out. Coast clear, she stepped outside and headed for the gate.

***

Carolyn followed Cornell past the guard and into the interrogation room. Her heart skipped a beat when she saw the man and woman tied to chairs, gagged, faces swollen, eyes bruised. She waited for a surge of hate at the sight of Michael Valiant. It trickled up while she stared at him.

Images of their past flowed into her mind and passed in a flash: Valiant shooting Sam and dragging Carolyn away while Sam bled out on the carpet; Valiant pinning Carolyn to the bed in the hotel room, punching her, ripping her clothes off, ramming painfully into her; and doing it again in Algonquin; Valiant dragging her, broken and bleeding, to the clearing in the forest, to hand her over to the aliens.

Carolyn's pulse quickened and tears sprang to her eyes. She cried out in pain when he looked up and locked his gaze on hers. Hand trembling, she raised the gun and would've shot him, but in the moment's hesitation, Carolyn saw her pain mirrored in Michael's eyes, and she remembered her daughter lived.

Cornell placed a hand on her shoulder. "Do it. No one would blame you."

Jim Cornell, her lover, moved behind her, embraced her. His hands slid around to her belly and stroked it. Warm breath whispered in her ear and soft lips kissed her cheek. "Do it for us, darling. Do it for the baby."

Michael growled through the gag, his palpable rage flowing over and past her, its target Cornell. The agony in Michael's eyes found Carolyn and stabbed at her. She shuddered and choked on a sob.

Valiant strained to speak, groans of despair leaking through the gag. Tears flowed down his face.

Other images flashed into Carolyn's mind: standing on a scaffold, wanting to die rather than allow harm to come to Michael; lying naked, stretched out on a rack, Cornell molesting her, forcing his fingers into her, until Michael burst into the room and interrupted; Michael dying in her arms in a temple, an attempt to rescue her failing. These were her dreams, but they felt closer to the truth than her memories.

Cornell raised his voice now, telling not only Carolyn, but also Michael. "Michael Valiant killed John. Valiant killed Sam. He raped you and gave you to the aliens."

Valiant killed Sam. It echoed in her skull. Carolyn had a flash memory of a man standing over her, repeating this to her.

Valiant killed Sam.

Rage at Cornell's lie overpowered the rage programmed into the lie. She raised the gun, stepped towards Michael. Turned. Faced Cornell. "Sam is alive, you bastard." Carolyn pulled the trigger.

CHAPTER 47

Cornell's face contorted in horror, and he fell to the floor, shouting for the guard. Carolyn fired again and silenced him forever. The door swung open, and the guard entered the room.

He had enough time to glance at the two prisoners, still restrained in the chairs, before she shot him as well. He staggered back, pushing the door shut, and she shot him again. The guard dropped, leaving a smear of blood on the door when he fell.

Carolyn shoved the gun into her belt and crouched next to Michael. Fingers shaking, she pulled the gag from his mouth. The gag fell loose around his neck.

"Oh, God, Carolyn. What have they done to you? Please, untie me."

Brown eyes. A funny thing on which to focus, under the circumstances. Carolyn didn't move, but simply stared into those brown eyes and waited for something, a feeling, to tell her what to do.

The woman next to Valiant struggled and made angry noises. Carolyn ignored her. She turned her head, and her gaze landed on the bodies. "I killed Jim." Her voice sounded like a little girl's.

"Please, untie me."

Carolyn faced Michael again. Maybe she should leave. She'd run back home and get Sam, and they'd leave as planned. But he knew what she'd done. Should she kill him, too, before he hurt her again? What about the woman? She gripped the back of Michael's chair and searched his eyes.

"Carolyn, please. Hurry. There's no time."

The bruised face brought to mind another dream, and an echo of love for him pressed on her. "I don't know what's real," she said. What if this was a dream? The woman's frustrated grunts and struggles intruded, but Carolyn kept her gaze on Michael.

"Carolyn, listen. I can help you. We were together. Don't you remember that? Cornell lied when he said I killed your husband. I didn't kill anyone you love. I didn't rape you. Remember, please. When I died, I came to you, and you saw me. Cornell had you in a prison cell."

Michael's eyes lit up then, and his voice rose with excitement. "Reach into my shirt and get the chain around my neck. Your wedding band is on it. You gave it to me, because you wanted me to find Sam and give it to her."

"My ring?" It came out thick, slow. She shook her head, trying to clear the fog and confusion, but couldn't think. Nothing he said made sense.

"You put your wedding ring in my backpack when you left me in Algonquin Park. Sam's still alive. I'll help you find her, and then you can give it to her yourself. Please. We have to hurry before someone finds us here. Get the ring."

Carolyn touched the collar of his shirt and gently felt for the chain. Michael closed his eyes, as if savouring her touch, though she tried not to and recoiled whenever a finger brushed against him. She lifted the chain over his shirt, and the ring appeared.

Her wedding band. She recognized it: a plain gold band, not too thick, with a single, tiny diamond in the centre. She looked at Michael. "Can I take it?"

He smiled. "Of course. I've been waiting so long to get it back to you. But Carr, we have to go."

The use of her nickname jarred something loose in her memories. Carolyn started untying Michael, and when his hands were free, he nudged her away and finished the job. The last bit of rope fell to the ground.

Michael moved towards Carolyn, and she scurried backwards.

He winced. "I'd never hurt you. Please believe me. I didn't do what that bastard said." His voice broke.

"Sam showed up at my house. They did something to make me believe you ... " She trailed off, unable to say the horrible accusations aloud. "But now you're a stranger. Cornell said you came here to kill me. Why did you come here?"

"To get you away from Cornell and the Agency. Now we're together, we can get out of here."

"Sam. I left her at my home. Oh, God, I hope she's still there."

"We'll get her. Don't worry." Michael turned to the woman next to him and slid the gag from her mouth.

"About fucking time. Get these ropes off me. Hurry."

Michael shook his head, flashed a half-smile. "I shouldn't have started with the gag. Carolyn, meet Althaea."

Carolyn recognized the woman she'd seen with Michael when she'd done remote viewing. Freed, Althaea jumped up and went to Cornell's body. She grabbed his gun and tucked it into her waistband.

Michael took a pistol from the guard and turned back to Carolyn. "I know the layout of this place. Arnie's outside waiting, and we have to get back."

"Arnie." Carolyn hadn't thought about Arnie for ages. Confusion made her frown. Arnie was alive, too, but she didn't know how that was possible. He should've been dead. She'd thought he was dead. Carolyn glanced at the guard's body, nauseated she'd been the one to kill him. "How will we get away?"

"Leave that to us," Althaea replied. "Ready?"

Michael shoved the guard's body to the side and peeked into the hallway. Carolyn looked over his shoulder into the empty corridor. They headed out, guns raised, Michael leading, Carolyn second, and Althaea bringing up the rear.

Carolyn's heart raced. If Sam wasn't at the house, Carolyn didn't know what they'd do. When she found Sam, she'd never let her out of her sight again.

***

Wrapped in a thermal blanket, Arnie huddled under the trees. He put the night-vision goggles on when the sun set and checked his watch. More than ninety minutes since the others had left. Arnie put away the blanket, shouldered his pack and assault rifle, and headed towards the road.

When he sighted the road, he veered to the left, keeping to the shelter of the trees. Michael had coached him on how to spot booby traps, and Arnie maintained a slow pace. The thought of the traps Michael described sent chills up Arnie's spine.

The sick fucks running this place didn't mess around. Risks included pits full of spikes, land mines, and beer cans resting on grenades that would explode if kicked. He gulped, fear escalating. Sweat melded with the rain running down his face.

He stopped walking twenty metres from the gate and hunkered down in the brush to watch the road and the gate. Nothing moved. So far, no alarm had triggered. Arnie settled down to wait.

***

Sam reached the Cornell house, ran inside, and threw herself on the bed in her room. George stuck his head in through her doorway, and she smiled. "Hi, George. What are you doing?" She'd miss George, though she wouldn't miss Wade so much.

"Nothing. I'm bored. Play a game with me?"

"Where's Wade?"

"He's at Joey's. They didn't let me go." George's face fell.

"It's okay, Georgie. I'll play." It would be a good distraction.

He perked up and ran to the living room. She followed at a more leisurely pace. By the time she reached the couch in front of the TV, he'd already set up the game. Sam picked up a paddle and let George take the lead. She glanced at him out of the corner of her eye. "Where's your mom?"

"In her room."

Ginny spent a lot of time in her room these days. Sam was sure Ginny had started cocktail hour early. That was good news, as far as Sam was concerned. It meant Ginny would stay out of sight, and Sam wouldn't have to act as though everything were okay.

She repeatedly checked the time, worrying about her mother. What if her mother was in danger? What if Mom came back to the house to find Sam gone?

George laughed, a loud, raucous bleat, and Sam jumped.

"Ha, I'm winning," George squealed. "I'm beating you, Sam. I never beat you."

She smiled at him. "I guess you're getting better. Soon you'll be beating Wade, too." Part of her wished she could stick around and see that happen.

The two played for twenty minutes. Sam was about to suggest they take a break and get a snack, when the doorbell rang. She looked at the clock. Just after seven. Sam waited, anticipating Ginny to come rushing from the bedroom.

When she didn't appear, and the doorbell chimed again, Sam dropped her paddle and went to the door. Two men stood outside, both wearing short-sleeved, white T-shirts, khaki caps, and military pants, rifles slung over their shoulders. The shorter one sported a tattoo of a bulldog on his upper arm. The taller one suffered from a raging case of acne and was skinnier than bulldog guy.

Sam paled, took a step backwards, and gulped air. Her thoughts flew to her mother, and she shivered.

"Is Mrs. Cornell here, ma'am?" Bulldog asked, and the two men stepped into the house.

Sam gaped at them in wide-eyed silence, not daring to breathe.

"Ma'am?" He frowned. "Can you get Mrs. Cornell, please?"

Sam nodded. Someone approached behind her, and she turned to face George. She gripped him by the shoulders and bent her face to his. "George, get your mom. Quick." She gave him a small shove towards the stairs. He ran.

She faced the two men. "Is something wrong?"

"We're here to speak with Mrs. Cornell."

They waited. Sweat trickled down Sam's back, and her underarms dampened. She lowered her head and stared at the floor. A strand of hair slipped over her right eye, and she raised a shaking hand to tuck it behind her ear.

At last, she heard footsteps and turned to see Ginny walk towards them. She stumbled a little, confirming Sam's suspicion Ginny had been in her room drinking. George loped along behind her. When Ginny reached the little group at the door, Sam caught a whiff of alcohol.

The older woman's expression tightened. An attempt at a smile failed, and her mouth formed a combination sneer and grimace. "Gentlemen," she said, a slight slur in her voice. "What can I do for you? If you're looking for my husband, he's not here."

"Mrs. Cornell?" Bulldog asked.

"Yes. What is it?" Fear crept into her eyes.

"I'm sorry. There's been an accident. Your husband is dead."

Ginny gasped. "What happened? Are you sure?"

"Mr. Cornell was shot trying to prevent an escape."

"No. Jim's supposed to come home for dinner," Ginny said. She raised fisted hands to her mouth and shook her head. "He has to come home for dinner."

The two men stared at Ginny, uncomfortable. Bulldog spoke. "I'm sorry, Mrs. Cornell."

Sam's heart almost stopped beating. "Was anyone else hurt?" *Mom. Oh, God, please. I can't lose Mom again.*

The agent glanced at Sam and shook his head. "I'm not at liberty to say."

"Does that mean someone else was hurt?" Sam's voice rose to a near shriek.

"Mama?" George went to Ginny, wrapped his arms around her legs, and burst into tears.

Ginny looked at her son as if she didn't recognize him. "Sam, take George to his room and stay with him."

"Okay." Sam led the boy towards the bedrooms, but slowly, trying to hear what the man had to say.

"I want to see Jim," Ginny said.

"Yes, ma'am." Bulldog sounded detached, and Sam hated him for being so cold.

"Sam," Ginny called out.

Sam stopped and turned.

"Stay with George while I go?"

Sam heard the pleading behind the words and hesitated. She couldn't stay here when she didn't know what had happened to her mother. "Please, can we come?"

"No. I need you here with George. He can't come and I have to hurry." Ginny's voice broke. Sam forced herself to hold back her own tears and nodded.

Ginny didn't waste another moment. She rushed outside, the two agents following her, leaving Sam staring at the closed door.

CHAPTER 48

Sam hurried to George's room. He lay on his bed, staring at the ceiling, and didn't look up when she entered.

"My daddy isn't coming home anymore." His voice was steady. "Wade will like that."

"Of course, he won't."

"Yes, he will. Wade said if Daddy wasn't around, he'd be the man of the house." George's hands lay clasped on his chest.

She sat on the bed beside him. "Wade was teasing, bragging about being the oldest. He loves your daddy." Sam didn't believe everything she told George—Wade could be a dick, sometimes even making her wonder if he was a budding sociopath.

"Sorry about your daddy, George. I know what it's like. My daddy died, too."

George's face contorted, and he bawled. "I want Daddy. I want him now."

Way to comfort the kid. What could she say? *It's okay, George. Your dad was just as big a dick as Wade?* Sam reached out and stroked his arm. George's crying intensified.

"It's okay to cry," Sam said. *Useless. What do you say to a six-year-old kid whose dad just died?* "Can I get you something? Maybe a chocolate milk?" *Sure. A sugary drink should fix him right up.* She winced. "Or water."

Who could she call? Sam had to get back to her mother's. Carolyn would go home eventually—unless something had happened to her, too. Sam stood. "I'll be right back."

Without waiting for George to reply, Sam left the room. It was Marnie's afternoon off, but Sam thought the housekeeper was in her rooms. Sam pounded on Marnie's door. Nothing.

As she raised her fist to knock again, the door swung open. Marnie stood there, cream coating her face. Sam arched her brows, and Marnie, through clenched teeth and tight lips said, "Facial. Can't talk." She waved her arm, inviting Sam inside.

"I can't. Marnie, I need a favour."

"Afternoon off."

"It's an emergency. Something terrible happened." She told Marnie about Cornell's death and asked her to stay with George.

"Wade's not home and I have to find him." She forced herself to look Marnie in the eye while she told the lie. "He's at the market with friends. Ginny went with the soldiers, so she told me to find Wade. George is too upset to go."

Marnie agreed to watch George and told Sam to bring him to her rooms. Sam bolted back to get George and tried to be patient while she coaxed him off his bed and over to Marnie's.

George safely ensconced in the housekeeper's quarters, Sam rushed outside and ran all the way to the gate. A longer line than usual greeted her. She pushed her way through the crowd, ignoring the glares of those she jostled in her haste. At the front, she saw the line wasn't moving.

Sam turned to a woman standing near her. "What's going on?"

"The guards aren't letting anyone through who doesn't have high-level clearance. Someone said two prisoners escaped, so we're stuck here. Some of us have to get to work." The woman raised her voice while she said the last piece, and a guard glanced in their direction.

Sam's hopes rose when she recognized the guard, and she rushed to him. "Trevor."

He gave a distracted smile. But when he recognized Sam, he stepped away from the man whose badge he inspected and waved her over. "What are you doing here? I heard about your uncle. So sorry for your loss. Are you okay?"

"No, I'm not okay. The boys are devastated. I left them home with the housekeeper to find Mrs. Cornell. They brought her here, and I have to go to her. Please, Trevor. Let me go through." Sam worked to inject grief into her voice, but had no trouble getting her panic across. Terrified they wouldn't let her through, it took an effort of will not to sound hysterical.

"I'm not supposed to let anyone through, but you're a logical exception. Come into the guardhouse. Keep walking and act as though you belong here." Trevor took her arm and guided her through the gate. "You're lucky I'm still here. Most of the guards will join the search, so a few more minutes, and I wouldn't have been here to help you."

"Thank you." The flutters in her stomach calmed as he led her into the guardhouse.

Once inside, Sam glanced around. They were alone. She threw her arms around Trevor and hugged him tight, fighting a sudden fear she might never see him again.

"Okay. Okay." He stammered it. His arms went around her, and he pressed his lips to the top of her head. After a moment, he released her. "You have to go. If the supervisor walks in here, he'll send you home. Just go. When this mess clears, we'll talk."

He opened the door to the Agency sector, and Sam hurried through it. Without looking back, she ran towards her mother's house.

***

Carolyn knew the second she stepped into the house that Sam was gone, but she shouted Sam's name anyway. Michael and Althaea appeared at the patio door, making Carolyn jump, even though she'd expected them. She let them inside.

"Sam's not here," Carolyn said, an edge to her voice.

"They'll search for us here, and they've probably found the bodies," Althaea said.

Michael went to Carolyn and looked at her belly. "Is everything okay with the baby?"

Fear prickled through Carolyn. "Why do you care about my baby?"

He stepped closer to her.

She stepped back.

"Our baby," Michael whispered, his face pale.

Carolyn took another step back. She tried to speak, but only managed a strangled cry. *The baby is Michael's?*

"Carolyn." Michael made as if to step towards her again, but stopped mid stride, face contorted into a mask of agony. "Whose baby do you think it is?"

"Jim Cornell's."

Michael's hands tightened into fists, and he gritted his teeth. "No, Carolyn. The baby is ours. Try to remember our time together. That memory has kept me going—helped me survive."

"I remember you raped me." Carolyn's voice was low, challenging.

"My God! I didn't rape you. Don't you remember how amazing it was?"

Althaea touched Michael's arm. "Not now. There's no time for this."

Michael rounded on her. "I have to. She has to remember. It's killing me, Ally."

Vertigo made the room spin, and Carolyn thought she might faint. She stumbled to the couch. Her head fell into her hands, and she sobbed. The memories Michael insisted were there wouldn't come. When she thought of Michael, only images of pain and brutality came to mind.

"Michael." Althaea's voice held a warning.

Carolyn raised her head. Michael stood before her. "Althaea's right,

Carr. We have to go. Regardless of who you believe is the father, please tell me the baby's okay."

"The baby's fine."

Michael held out a hand to her.

Carolyn stared at it. Reluctantly, she put her hand in his. A vision of Michael punching her in the face popped into her head, and Carolyn wrenched back as if his touch burned.

"I regret that that son of a bitch had but one life to give for the Agency." Michael grimaced.

Carolyn stood. "I can't leave without Sam. She's staying at the Cornell house, but that's not in this sector. I assume that when I left with Jim, she went there."

Michael looked to Althaea. "Any thoughts on how to get across to the residential sector without walking through the gate?"

"Let me think on it." Althaea went to the patio door and stared outside. "The main walls have—"

A knock on the door stopped her.

"Into the bedroom, quick." Carolyn waited until the two were hidden, then rushed to the door and peered out the peephole. Sam! Carolyn threw open the door and yanked the girl inside. "Oh my God, I'm so happy to see you." She hugged Sam tight, flooded her face with kisses.

Sam gave a return squeeze, then extricated herself. "Two men came to the Cornells' and told Ginny Jim was dead. What happened?"

"No time to explain now. We have to go."

The bedroom door opened, and Michael and Althaea stepped out.

"Sam, Michael and Althaea will help us."

Sam gaped. "Michael Valiant?"

A flush crept up his face, and he nodded.

Sam put a protective arm around Carolyn, pulling her close. "You okay, Mom?"

Carolyn kissed Sam's cheek. "Yes."

"Through the back." Michael opened the patio doors and waved to them to follow.

When they were all outside, he slid the door closed and joined them. "We'll go through the backyards. That whole back part is foliage, no fence. Althaea, you lead." He turned to Carolyn. "Keep your gun ready. I'm happy you know how to use it now. When we were together, I could barely convince you to pick one up."

She nodded, just to agree with him. Her memories didn't include Michael offering to give her a gun to use. She also didn't want to tell him Cornell had trained her specifically to use it to kill Michael. Carolyn touched the wedding band now back on her finger. She looked up and caught Michael watching her.

He smiled. "Shall we ask the angels and guides to help us find our way out?"

Carolyn frowned, confused. "I don't understand."

Michael frowned and his hand rose as if to touch her cheek, but he stopped himself. "It's okay. I'll explain later." He closed his eyes for a moment. When he opened them again, he glanced around and nodded his head at Althaea.

The group headed to the back of the yard, where a row of bushes camouflaged the wall of stucco that rose and disappeared into the fake sky above. Althaea pushed between the leaves and branches and held the opening for them. Carolyn gripped Sam's hand, and they stepped into the breach.

CHAPTER 49

The group reached the elevators that would take them to the upper world and crouched behind bushes fronting the Agency offices. Two guards blocked the doors. A siren wailed, shrieking like a deranged harpy.

Michael motioned for Althaea to take the guard on the left. She nodded. He raised his hand and counted down on his fingers. They fired on one and both guards dropped. Sam and Carolyn remained hidden while Michael and Althaea raced to the elevator.

He pressed the button to summon the lift, and when the doors slid open, they fired, killing two soldiers inside. Althaea held the doors open while Michael dragged the bodies out.

A wave from Althaea brought Carolyn and Sam running. Michael pushed Carolyn to one side, Sam to the other, and then motioned for them to lie on the floor. As the doors closed, Michael and Althaea raised their weapons.

The moment the doors opened, they fired, knocking down two guards, while two more shot at the group from the hallway. Michael aimed and picked one off, but the other continued to shoot. "Cover me, Ally. Let the doors close, but hold the elevator. Give me thirty seconds and open the doors again." Michael's voice was almost inaudible over the gunshots, but Althaea nodded.

She rapid-fired her gun while Michael ducked under her arm and launched himself into the hallway, rolling behind a wall. The elevator doors whisked shut. The guard who'd been firing at them peeked around the corner.

Michael fired and winged her when the bullet ricocheted. She ducked back behind the wall. He peered into the hallway. If they didn't get her soon, more soldiers would arrive. He gauged where to strike.

When the thirty seconds were almost up, he fired. A pain-filled cry told him he'd made a hit, but the guard held her ground. The elevator doors slid open. The guard leaned out to shoot, and Michael fired again, multiple times. Chips flew off the wall, but when the dust settled, she lay on the floor, arm stuck out into the hallway. A gun lay on the floor next to her hand.

Althaea jumped into the corridor and relieved the guard of an automatic rifle, scanned the hallway, and waved Carolyn and Sam out. Michael ran to them. "This way," he said, urging them to take the corridor leading right.

He led the group to the exit, Althaea bringing up the rear, and again guards confronted them. Michael hung back with Sam and Carolyn, letting Althaea lead the attack with her rifle. She reduced the number of guards from six to three, and Michael joined her, using the more accurate pistol to target each guard. Two guards remained.

Sam shrieked. "Trevor!"

"No, Sam!" Carolyn screamed in response.

From his periphery, Michael saw Carolyn throw restraining arms around Sam as she tried to break cover.

"No, Michael. Don't shoot. Trevor. Stop." Sam struggled against Carolyn.

Althaea and Michael pulled back. He didn't take his eyes off the corner where the guards hid though they'd ceased firing.

"Sam, explain," Michael said.

"One of the guards is my friend. Please, don't kill him."

A male voice called out. "Sam? Are you okay?"

"Answer him," Michael said. "Tell him you're okay and we only want to leave."

"Trevor, I'm okay. We just want to leave. Please, let us go."

"I'm sorry, but I can't do that. I know you're being held against your will. We'll get the prisoners back, dead or alive."

"You don't understand. Jim Cornell was holding me, and he had my mother. Mom wasn't dead. I found her. She's with me. Please. Let us go."

Trevor paused, spoke again. "Drop your weapons, and we'll take you in. Sam, these people killed Jim Cornell. They'll answer for it. We won't negotiate. Drop your weapons."

"You drop 'em. We're leaving. If you don't stand down, we'll fire." Michael shouted back. He lowered his voice, and, keeping his eyes on the targets, said, "I'm sorry, Sam. If it comes to a choice between us or them, I choose us."

Sam sobbed and made another effort to break Carolyn's hold.

"Hold her," Michael said.

Carolyn shifted behind him, likely trying to comfort Sam. He heard heated whispers, Sam's protests.

"We've been standing here too long," Michael said. "Watch the rear,

Carolyn. We might have company soon. If you hear or see anything, alert Althaea. Have your gun ready. We might need your help."

Michael had deduced which guard was Sam's friend when Trevor had spoken. He'd take out Trevor's partner. Maybe then, Trevor would step aside though Michael doubted it. He assumed this wouldn't end well. "Drop your weapons. You have ten seconds," Michael said.

"No!" Sam cried.

Michael ignored her and fired, ricocheting the bullet off the wall and into the back of Trevor's partner's arm. When the man cried out and lurched forward, Michael fired again, shooting the man in the head.

Sam screamed, "Trevor!"

"He's still standing, Sam," Michael answered, voice calm. He felt the struggle behind him.

"No, Sam! Michael, I can't hold her."

"Althaea, cover him," Michael yelled. He turned and grabbed at Sam, who'd slipped from Carolyn's arms and ran at Trevor. Michael caught her arm and yanked her back. "Do you want to get us killed? Your boyfriend will do his job. He's programmed to." The words came out gruffer and colder than he'd intended, but he was getting sick of this standoff. He pulled Sam into his arms and held her while she sobbed.

Carolyn wrapped her arms around Michael's, burying her face in Sam's back. "Please, Sam," she said. "We have to get moving."

Sam lifted her head. "Just let me talk to Trevor."

"I'm not letting you go near him," Michael said. "He'd use you as a hostage."

"No, he cares about me."

Michael looked over Sam's head at Carolyn. She met his eyes and shook her head. *No.* At least Carolyn understood.

"Drop your weapon, Trevor." One more chance. "You're out numbered and we've got more experience. I don't want to shoot you, but I will if I have to."

"Trevor, please. Don't let him kill you."

Michael hoped Sam's interjection would help, but thought it could go either way. Trevor might take what she'd said as a challenge.

"Let Sam come over here."

"I'm not that stupid, son," Michael replied. How long had they lingered here? He'd have to go at Trevor. Michael raised his gun.

Sam screamed.

Trevor fired at them, and Althaea and Michael fired back. Trevor went down in their hail of bullets. Sam broke away from them and threw herself at Trevor's body.

"No, Sam. He might not be dead," Michael shouted. He lunged after her, but was a few seconds too late. Trevor lurched to a sitting position, wrapped his arms around Sam, and stuck a pistol to her head.

Tears streamed down Sam's face. She tried to pull away, but Trevor tightened his grip. "You're not going anywhere. One move and I'll shoot her." Trevor's voice was hoarse, his breathing laboured.

"Then what, Trevor? You'll only get one shot."

"That's all I need."

Sam leaned her head against Trevor and sobbed. "What are you doing? Let me go. I cared about you. How can you do this?"

"Sorry, I can't. Not if it means letting prisoners escape."

In a flash, Michael raised his gun and shot Trevor in the head. Blood splattered onto Sam, and she screamed. She pushed the body away from her, fell forward on her knees, and threw up.

Michael grabbed her by the arm and hauled her to her feet. "No time for that. Move." He dragged her, ignoring her choked sobs.

Carolyn caught up to them. "Michael, let me."

He handed Sam off to Carolyn, who put an arm around her daughter, and guided her forward.

"I thought he liked me," Sam said, sobbing.

"Forget him, Sam," Michael replied. "The job comes first for these guys. I know. I was one of them."

The group stopped in front of the exit doors. Michael peered through the window and saw more men and women with automatic rifles. The SUV still sat along the side of the building. He hoped the keys were still in it.

CHAPTER 50

Arnie heard the commotion, saw the armed agents running to the east side of the building, and understood Michael and Althaea were on their way back. He snatched up his pack, tucked the gun into his belt, and grabbed the rifle. He'd have seconds to blow the gate when they were out and in the vehicles. But if he acted too soon, he'd be spotted, and then he'd never be able to help his friends.

Shots fired without pause and guards fell. Other guards returned fire. Arnie could only watch and hope the Agency bullets didn't hit their mark. More shots. The group at the east door thinned, Michael and Ally picking them off. Arnie held his breath. Maybe soon he'd see Carolyn again.

The frenzy at the door continued unabated, and Arnie wished he had a grenade. Michael hadn't trusted Arnie with one, though—had been reluctant to leave Arnie with the C4 and the blasting caps, but there was no one else. Althaea had to go in with Michael.

Arnie would've felt offended, except that deep down, he knew Michael was right: Arnie didn't have enough training to be left with grenades. They'd practiced the hell out of using the C4 though. Arnie no longer feared handling it, even with the unwieldy rubberized gloves he'd have to wear to protect him from the electric fence. While he wasn't the commando Michael was, he'd come a long way.

A whirring sound reached his ears. Helicopters. *The Agency's choppering in more guys? From where?*

Arnie removed the C4 from his pack and stuck the blasting caps inside each wrapped piece. Should he blow the gate now and join the fray? He thought better of it when an explosion rattled the copter and half the guards flew into the air in little pieces. Michael, apparently, had a grenade.

There they were. He'd recognize Althaea's style anywhere. That woman even made kicking ass look beautiful. Arnie rose into a standing crouch, ready to run to the fence. He cried out in horror when more men rounded the opposite corner of the building.

One newcomer fired off a quick round. Althaea cried out, dropped her gun, and then fell on it. Terrified they'd killed her, Arnie broke cover and raced to the gate. He focused on planting C4 on the hinges and handle of the gate, except for one quick glance in Althaea's direction when it was all in place.

To his relief, she was on her feet again, though one hand dripped blood. She used her left hand now, but still picked agents off with deadly accuracy. Two blonde heads appeared. Carolyn and Sam. His heart leapt.

He backed away, giving himself the distance Michael told him he'd need. *Ready or not, guys, here we go.*

A hit to the detonator emitted a radio signal, triggering the blasting caps. The blast put Arnie on his ass and made his ears ring though he wasn't hurt. The gate ripped open. Shrapnel and debris flew everywhere, but he was far enough away.

Arnie jumped into a crouch and tried to get his bearings. The Agency goons would come for him now they were alerted to his presence. Arnie hoped to Christ Michael and the others were on their way.

***

Michael heard the blast. They'd better get to Arnie before the Agency soldiers found him. The helicopter veered close again, teetering in the air, the pilot struggling to keep it steady. Michael raised the rifle he'd swiped from a guard and fired at it.

Something pinged, the helicopter plummeted, and then veered in their direction. Michael screamed "Duck!" at Althaea and pulled Carolyn and Sam down with him. The helicopter landed in a fireball, killing the agents who were attacking them. Heat washed over Michael, and he covered Carolyn and Sam with his body.

Debris rained down around them, a piece of flaming metal landing close enough to feel its heat. He jumped up and yanked Carolyn and Sam with him, dragging them to the SUV. He yanked on the door, and to his relief it opened, and the keys were still in the ignition. "Get in!" he screamed over the noise.

Althaea grabbed the passenger door and jumped in. Carolyn opened the back, shoved Sam in, and then climbed in after her. Michael threw it into drive while the women slammed closed the doors. "When we reach Arnie, get him into the back," Michael yelled.

They neared the open gate. Arnie crouched, rifle raised. Michael glanced in the rear-view mirror.

A Humvee closed in.

Michael braked when he pulled up next to Arnie. Sam threw open the door, and Arnie scrambled in as the vehicle rolled forward. Althaea lowered her window, turned around in her seat, and leaned out. She fired at the Humvee. Michael wove along the road, flooring it, determined to outmanoeuvre them.

"Keep your heads down," Althaea yelled.

Michael glanced into the rear-view mirror, and fear raced through his gut when he saw Carolyn, Sam, and Arnie all sitting.

"Get the fuck down," he shouted. The heads in the mirror disappeared, and Michael breathed again. He glanced at Althaea. *Fuck*. She was bleeding. "Ally, get in here. You're bleeding."

She ignored him and kept firing. "It's nothing."

"It's not nothing. You're leaking blood from your arm."

"A bullet grazed me. I'm fine. I can't stop now. They'll close the gap."

"I'll fire at them." Arnie popped up in the rear-view mirror again, worry etched on his face. He leaned forward and touched Althaea's hand. "Get in, Ally. I'll do this. Please, God, just don't—" He stopped talking when she slid back into her seat.

"Okay," she said, "but if you get shot, I'll kill you."

While Althaea took off her shirt, tore it into strips, and stanched her wound, Arnie lowered his window and leaned out, firing at the vehicles behind them.

They reached the end of the road, and Michael barrelled onto the highway without slowing. "Get in," he yelled at Arnie. "Hold on tight. The roads are slick."

Back in his seat, Arnie closed the window.

Michael pressed on the gas pedal, and they sped along the road at a hundred and twenty clicks. He headed west, taking the road towards Toronto. Downed trees blocked the road, and Michael swerved around them without slowing. No oncoming cars to worry about.

Night fell. What streetlights there were along town roads they crossed didn't come on.

Michael checked the rear-view mirror: only darkness behind them. They were okay. No one would risk driving without headlights with all those trees down. But he wouldn't feel safe until they'd put a great deal of distance between themselves and the underground community.

"Arnie, thank God, you're okay." Carolyn.

"Yeah, Cornell never came after us when he dragged you away from the compound."

"What do you mean? I thought they found your body in your car. They said you committed suicide."

"What the fuck? I'm sorry, but the Agency locked us up together for weeks at the compound. Last time we saw each other, Cornell was dragging you away and shooting at me and Julie. What happened to her, Michael?" Arnie asked.

"They took her memory." Michael's heart ached to say it.

Carolyn burst into tears, and Arnie hugged her. His gaze met Michael's in the rear-view mirror. "Can we help her get it back?"

Michael opened his mouth to reply when Althaea spoke. "Yes," she said, "we can."

CHAPTER 51

Carolyn awoke from a fitful doze, an arm around a peacefully sleeping Sam's shoulders. Arnie held Carolyn's other hand. She'd clutched Arnie's hand while Althaea had outlined the idea for triggering Carolyn's memories and hadn't let go after Althaea stopped talking.

Arnie's warm, comforting grip helped Carolyn stay anchored. Terrified to think she couldn't trust anything she remembered from before Sam showed up at her door, Carolyn's mind raced. How could the Agency have not only erased memories, but also have substituted them with false ones?

Both the engagement ring and the wedding band were back where they belonged. Michael hadn't forced her to abandon them in a ravine in Algonquin Park. With the pad of her thumb, Carolyn rubbed the rings on her left hand, and tension eased at their familiar feel.

But the disturbing thoughts continued. Sam had gone through a funeral for first her father and then her mother, which sickened Carolyn. What nauseated her most was that one of those deaths had been faked so Cornell could keep the two of them for his own uses. It brought her close to breaking.

She opened her eyes and studied the back of Michael's head. They'd been driving for over an hour now, heading to the homes they'd left behind. Michael had remained neutral from the moment they'd lost the Agency vehicles. He hadn't tried to talk to Carolyn, or convince her of anything, and she appreciated he'd let her be.

Carolyn had tried to dredge up recollections of her time with Michael that didn't involve beatings, rapes, or betrayal. At least now when she thought of him, she found favourable memories. During the escape from the underground community, he'd risked his life for her and Sam. No trace existed of the sadistic psycho she remembered from the trip to, and through, Algonquin.

An urge to hear his voice, to talk to him, made her break the silence that'd hung over the group since they'd left the Agency behind. "Michael?"

His gaze met hers in the rear-view mirror, and he smiled. "Yes?"

The warmth he exuded brought a surge of affection Carolyn found encouraging. "Back there, you said something about angels and told me you'd explain later. Will you tell me now?"

So he did. She listened, rapt, while Michael told her who she used to be, what she used to do. How she'd talk with people's departed loved ones, their spirit guides, their guardian angels. How she'd always called on her own angels and guides to help and protect her and connected to her own departed loved ones. And how the Agency had blocked it to manipulate and control her.

Story told, Michael fell silent. A squeeze on her right hand made Carolyn glance at Arnie. She squeezed back and listened to the drone of the engine, the swipe of the wiper blades, and the patter of rain on the roof. The shock at hearing of Arnie's death came back to her then. But she couldn't remember any of the details, like what she'd done or how she'd reacted.

She took a deep breath and calmed. She had to stop dwelling on this. But no sooner did Carolyn tell herself that than the image of her shooting Cornell popped into her head. That bullet had been meant for Michael. What if Cornell's plan had worked? What if Sam wouldn't have found Carolyn and put doubts in her mind? Michael would be dead, and Carolyn back at the Agency, sleeping with the real enemy.

Breath shallow again, stomach tense and knotted, Carolyn went rigid, her arm sliding from Sam's shoulders, her hand releasing its hold on Arnie's. This had to stop. Frantic, she could almost feel Cornell's hands on her body. "Michael, when can we fix this? Please. I need to get my real memories back—get myself back. I don't know who I am anymore, and I think I'd like who I was better than I like who I am now."

Michael cleared his throat, then spoke. "We can pull over in Port Perry." His eyes fluttered to the mirror and met hers again. "We're almost there."

She settled down to wait.

***

Port Perry nestled at the bottom of the hill through which 7A led. The highway sliced through Lake Scugog, a manmade lake that had barely recovered from massive fish deaths in 2007 when the Aurora machines triggered. Michael had already been doing less than the eighty-kilometre speed limit, but when they approached town and the speed limit dropped to fifty, he slowed to forty.

No cars approached. No cars followed.

Michael slowed again and then stopped when he saw water flowing up from the swampy lake across the highway. The streetlights were dead. The darkness and teeming rain made it impossible for Michael to determine how deep the water on the road was. He pulled over and unhooked his seatbelt. "I'll check it out."

"Want me to go with you?" Althaea reached for her gun.

"No. Stay with them."

Michael checked his gun. Cocked and ready. He stepped from the car and walked the few metres to the water's edge, then placed a foot into the water and found it didn't cover his shoes. Michael went to the guard rail to look into the lake.

Bulrushes and grasses rose from the depths. Nothing moved. It smelled like raw sewage, the surface dotted with dead fish. Michael wrinkled his nose in distaste and looked across the strip of roadway into the town. Everything was still. What cars he saw were empty. The stores and restaurants before him were dark. Somewhere across the lake, he saw a soft glow of light, perhaps from a flashlight, lantern, or candles.

The place looked deserted. Until they'd hit Port Perry, they hadn't gone through any large towns. They'd stayed on dirt roads or secondary highways surrounded by farmers' fields, forests, and blink-and-you-miss-'em towns, where it wasn't unusual for everything to be dark and quiet even in the early evening. But the ambience here gave him the willies. For a moment, he was glad Carolyn had lost her ability to talk to the dead.

Michael returned to the car. "We're going in. There's a restaurant on Queen Street where Torque and I used to go sometimes. I know the owner. We can stop there."

***

Carolyn stood, arms crossed over her chest, facing Althaea in the banquet room upstairs at the King's Castle Restaurant. Arnie and Sam sat at a nearby table. The establishment's owner absent, Michael had jimmied the lock, and they'd entered to find the place deserted, but unmolested.

Warmth wafted from the gas fireplace, but Michael had just lit it, and the air in the room was still icy. Carolyn shivered and rubbed her hands up and down her arms, trying to warm herself. Goose bumps prickled her arms and legs, and she wished she had warmer clothes, but she'd run away wearing only shorts and a T-shirt.

Michael stepped close to her and put his jacket around her shoulders. She smiled her thanks.

Arms now bare, Michael wore a khaki-green T-shirt tucked into military pants. He'd found another shoulder holster in the SUV and wore that and a gun. When he smiled at her, warmth and kindness replaced the air of tough-guy seriousness under which he usually operated

Carolyn suppressed an urge to fold herself into his embrace.

"Ally and I will both do this with you, Carr," Michael said. "I guess you don't remember what happened when I helped Ally, but you were there."

Carolyn shook her head, and Michael told her about the creature set to guard Althaea's memories, a trap that triggered when they accessed Althaea's mind.

"We might face something similar when recovering your memories. Ally's coming along to help hold off anything planted in there. That should give us enough time to retrieve some of what's buried, and then you can recover the rest on your own."

Carolyn clutched the jacket tight around her and trembled, feeling exposed. She watched his mouth move while he spoke, appreciating the shape of his lips. She shook her head. Being this near him awakened something in her.

His voice faltered, and he stopped talking.

"Carr." He tried to speak again, but his voice cracked. His eyes grew bright in the dim glow of the candles scattered around the room. He stepped closer to her, their bodies almost touching. Michael raised a hand and touched her cheek, stroking it with the outer edge of his fingers.

The touch brought with it that moth-wing flutter in the back of her mind as though of something familiar. She closed her eyes and inhaled the scent of melting wax from the candles, of Michael, of oiled wood from the dark beams of the rafters above. Gentle fingers brushed her lips and without thinking, she kissed them.

Carolyn opened her eyes, now damp with tears.

"Ready?" Michael's voice was husky.

"Yes," she said, her own voice thick. The others forgotten, she was alone with him.

Michael explained what he'd have to do, and Carolyn agreed. She removed his jacket and set it aside. He placed his hands on either side of her head, leaned his forehead in to touch hers, and called out to Althaea.

Carolyn sensed Althaea step up and join their connection. Althaea placed one arm around Carolyn, and the other, Carolyn knew, was around Michael. The triangle completed when Althaea leaned in.

Pulses fired into Carolyn's forehead, into the space between her brows. *The Ajna centre.* That thought popped into her head, but she didn't know what it meant or from where it came.

Carolyn stands in a hallway. Michael takes her hand and leads her to a large, wooden door. It opens, and she recognizes the room she and Michael had rented in Peterborough when Michael had kidnapped her—the room in which he'd raped her.

She glances at the bed and sees herself there, handcuffed. Michael stands next to the bed, removing his clothes while Carolyn sobs, pleads. He's ignoring her, a fierce, predatory light in his eyes. When he's naked, he climbs into the bed and rips at her clothes, one hand stifling her screams.

Her anger and hate well up, and she turns away from the scene. When Michael puts his arms around her, she struggles, fights him. "Shh. It's okay. Look."

She doesn't want to, but something in his voice makes her lift her head. The scene shatters. Melts away. Changes. Another forms.

Carolyn sees herself in the room, in the bed again, but she's sleeping, undisturbed. No cuffs restrain her. Michael sleeps on the couch in the living area. Light snoring reaches her ears, and she feels a surge of affection.

The Carolyn in the bed stirs, cries out, eyes darting frantically under their closed lids. She moans and cries out. Michael leaps from the couch, naked except for a pair of briefs. He runs to the bed and cradles her in his arms, reassuring, telling her it's just a dream.

Her eyes open, and she melts into his embrace. The words tumble out, and she tells him how afraid and alone she felt in her dream. Michael soothes and comforts her. She raises her face from his chest, hugs him, and her lips seek his. He hesitates, but only for a moment, and then returns her kiss.

Carolyn watches the couple on the bed for a moment longer, knowing everything about to happen, drawing it from her memory. "I remember. Oh, God. I remember. You. Us." She looks at Michael, her smile radiant, Michael's smile reflecting hers.

He tries to speak, chokes, and takes her in his arms. "Oh, thank God." He hugs her tight, and his lips brush hers. "I was so afraid I'd lost what we had together."

She kisses him, and her hands stray to his hair. She wants to touch him, wants him to touch her.

Althaea's harsh cries break through their joy. "A hydra, Michael. Get out here."

He releases Carolyn and runs towards Althaea's voice. Carolyn follows him out of the room and into the hallway. Althaea holds a sword and slashes at a three-headed beast in front of her. "When you pull out your gun, it turns into a fucking sword. What the hell, Valiant?"

Frozen in horror, Carolyn stares while Althaea hacks at the beast.

Michael catches up to his former partner as one of the hydra's heads tumbles to the ground. When two heads pop out of the stump of neck, Michael steps back. "No good," he says. "We can't kill it by cutting off the heads."

Something about that sounds familiar to Carolyn. It's a story or a myth. "You have to stab it in the heart," she shouts. Carolyn pulls out her gun and finds a sword in her hand.

A scream from Althaea jolts Carolyn and she runs to the other woman, whose shoulder and arm ooze blood and ragged flesh. She pulls Althaea away from the creature and steps forward.

"Carolyn, no." Michael, afraid for her.

Eyes fixed on the monster, she stands her ground. "It's mine, Michael. Back off." She knows she can do it. Carolyn raises the heavy sword with ease and swipes the air with it.

The monster's heads orient on her.

She pulls herself up to her full height, standing tall. The beast seems to diminish before her strength and power. Is that a glimmer of fear in its eyes? The hydra bares four sets of teeth, four throats growl, four mouths slaver, and flecks of spittle hit her exposed arms.

Carolyn chokes down the rising bile and scans the hydra's chest. Where's its heart? She'll take a stab at it. Carolyn smiles a little at the joke, but it's grim. She hopes she'll get the chance. In her periphery, she sees a blur, Michael's arms, waving, distracting the monster for her.

The tactic succeeds, and now she's afraid for Michael as all the heads turn to face him. A lunge forward, and Carolyn's sword drives into the tender flesh where all the necks converge at the top of the body. A roar bursts from the heads.

She draws the sword back out of the monster. It takes more effort to remove the sword than it did to shove it in. When the last of the blade clears the body, she hears a sucking sound and blood spurts from the wound, splattering both her and Michael. Instead of rolling clear of the monster, Michael draws closer to it and stabs the sword upward into its belly.

The heads howl and thrash, the clawed feet stomping around Michael. One foot makes contact, tearing at Michael's stomach. Carolyn screams when blood flows from Michael's abdomen. She lunges forward again and shoves her blade back into the monster, lower down the body this time.

Its thrashes weaken, and it staggers.

Terrified the beast will collapse on Michael, Carolyn drops the sword and grabs Michael under the arms. She hauls him away, and the monster falls, missing Michael by a hair's breadth.

Althaea crawls to Michael and presses both hands onto his wound, attempting to stop the blood. "Finish the fucker and let's go."

Carolyn picks up her sword again. The monster lies dying before her. She raises her sword and plunges it into its body up to the hilt.

Carolyn opened her eyes. She lay on the floor, head cradled in Sam's arms.

CHAPTER 52

Carolyn shook off vertigo as she jumped up and ran to Michael, who lay on the floor as if unconscious. Arnie had his balled-up shirt stuffed against the wound in Michael's abdomen. Althaea rummaged in the packs, pulling out gauze and first aid supplies. Blood trickled down her arm, seeping through the towel she'd wrapped around her own injured shoulder.

"No. Oh, God, please, no." Carolyn knelt by Michael's side.

Michael's eyes opened, and he flashed a weak smile. "Hi. Good to have you back." He winced and closed his eyes again.

Carolyn clutched his hand and put it to her cheek. "Don't you dare leave me."

Althaea leaned over him. "He'll be okay. The wound is not as bad as it looks. It's not deep, just long, and hit no internal organs. It was close though. Arnie, I'll need your help. You two," she said, indicating Sam and Carolyn, "step away."

Carolyn hesitated. Althaea stared at her, refusing to budge. Reluctantly, Carolyn stood and went to Sam, hugged her.

"Almost everything came back to me," Carolyn said. "I remember Michael breaking into the house to kidnap me, and you came home and left that note for me. Michael helped me escape, and we grew close during our time together."

She studied Sam's face, trying to gauge her reaction. Sam's eyes were wet, but the tears had already stopped flowing.

"You know now the baby you're carrying is Michael's, don't you?"

Carolyn nodded. "It doesn't mean I forgot about your father. I love your dad, and I always will. Michael and I have a connection that goes deeper than anything I've experienced. It was as if we'd picked up the thread of something started a long time ago. We both thought I couldn't get pregnant."

"I guess it was meant to be, then, right? Isn't that what you used to say?"

Carolyn smiled. "It's what I still say."

***

Carolyn sat next to Michael, who'd stretched out on the bench seats along the back wall of the banquet room. A blanket covered his torso. Althaea rested on another makeshift bed across the room. Sam and Arnie sat at a table, heads together, absorbed in low conversation.

The night deepened, but Carolyn couldn't sleep now that Michael was awake. He'd slept for four hours while she'd dozed in the chair at his side, holding his hand, longing to talk to him. Every once-in-a-while, Carolyn raised Michael's hand to her lips and kissed it. The last time she'd done that, he'd opened his eyes and smiled at her. Carolyn's heart almost burst at the sight.

"I can't believe we're together," he said. "Do you have any idea what you've put me through?"

He teased, but she frowned. "Althaea told me most of it. Arnie told me more. I remember seeing you in my cell. Michael, you'd died. What if you hadn't come back?"

"But I did. Don't think about the 'what ifs.' That's pointless."

"Yes. But the thought of losing you—"

Michael cut her off. "Stop. We won't do this."

The front door creaked and Carolyn tensed. "Didn't we lock the door?"

He sat up, wincing when he moved, and grabbed his gun from the nearby table. Arnie and Ally both stood, guns ready.

They walked towards the stairs, Michael taking the lead. The floor creaked when they hit the landing.

Carolyn held her breath.

From below, a man's voice called. "Someone up there?"

"Dylan?" Michael lowered his gun. "It's okay. It's the owner." He moved down the stairs and called out again. "It's Mick Valiant."

"Valiant, you old fuck. What are you doing trespassing on my property?" Dylan appeared in the mirror above the landing where the staircase curved up to the second floor. A flashlight reflected off the mirror and shone onto the suit of armour that stood in the corner. His rubber boots squished and squeaked on the polished wood stairs.

It surprised Carolyn to see how young he looked—thirty, maybe. The gravelly voice had made her expect someone older. Dylan wore his long hair tied back in a ponytail, but it was sleek and black, with no touch of grey.

He removed his raincoat while he walked, revealing a red flannel shirt and jeans. Carolyn couldn't decide whether he looked more like a hippy or a farmer. She settled on hippy farmer. The closer he got to them, the more energized she felt. Carolyn decided she liked him.

"What happened here, Dylan?" Michael jumped to the heart of it as soon as Dylan reached them.

A red satin cloth appeared from the pocket of Dylan's jeans. He removed his glasses and wiped the rain off the lenses. "It started a few months ago. Storms. Earthquakes. The power's been out for months. At first, people holed up in their houses. The news reports told us to stay inside, so we did. But then the lake flooded. Scugog just rose up and swallowed most of the beach, blocked the 7A."

"We came in from the east, over Lake Scugog. There's about a centimetre of water covering the highway," Michael said.

Dylan nodded. "Yeah. Now. If you'd been a week earlier we wouldn't be standin' here talkin'. After the rains started, the fish died, floatin' so thick you couldn't see the water. Looked like 2007 all over again. 'Course, when the rain was heavier, you couldn't see nothin'. Then the waves got big and tossed stuff around."

He went to a table and sat. They grabbed chairs and grouped around him.

"The people started dyin' after that. Somethin' in the water, might be?" He studied them, frowning. "Haven't been drinkin' the tap water, have you?"

"No," Michael said. "We have bottled water."

Dylan looked around for the first time. "So who's 'we?'"

Michael made the introductions. Dylan stood and went to the back room, returning with a bottle of bourbon and glasses on a tray. "Speakin' of drinks: late night drink? Might help."

Arnie and Althaea exchanged glances. The two sat next to each other, Arnie's arm encircling Althaea's waist. Odd seeing Arnie show affection to a woman other than herself or his mother, Carolyn thought, and smiled at the sight. She pointed to her belly, shook her head, and held up a water bottle when Dylan offered her bourbon.

Drinks distributed, he raised his glass. "Cheers, friends."

The little group clinked glasses, but it wasn't celebratory.

Dylan continued the story. "When folks first got sick, they went to the hospital. Docs couldn't figure out what was wrong with 'em though. A flu-like thing. Fever. Stomach cramps. The squirts. Pukin'."

He paused, looked around. "Ella, my wife, caught it. She still feels tired all the time and has bad moments—sometimes so bad I'm afraid I'll be on my own. We've prepared for the worst, but she's hangin' in."

Dylan took a long draw on his drink, draining it. He set the empty glass on the wood table, the sound echoing through the room. Another couple of fingers of bourbon splashed into his glass.

Carolyn peeked at Sam and noted Sam's glass was almost empty. The urge to tell her to slow down hit Carolyn, but she decided it didn't matter. They were lucky to still be alive and together.

Dylan's eyes met Carolyn's, and he nodded as though reading her mind. "Most people who had somewhere else to go left town. We weren't hearin' about shit like this anywhere else—not at first, anyway. Might be we're ground zero for this thing. I have the restaurant here. A house. I drop by and check this place every day, make sure no one's broke in. Don't matter much, I guess. What can they do here? You can walk into the liquor store and help yourself to booze if that's what you want. Food's spoiled. I salvaged what I could and figured I'd get a rebate or something on the rest. But there's no one left to get the rebate from, see? They're all gone."

Dylan stopped talking. Michael egged him on. "Who's all gone? What do you mean?"

"Everyone. You go through town, no one's left. Many died, sure, others fled, but they would've had to have flown somewhere, yes? I drove to Newmarket one day. Went through Uxbridge. Know what I found?" He looked at each of them. They gaped back.

"Nothin' and no one. It's as if they dropped off the earth. Sure, there's the odd person. It's not deserted. But close to it. And lots of bodies. It'll be a hell of a cleanup one day. But they're not all dead. I didn't even get sick. It's weird, Mick. Some of us are fine, never got sick. Others are just gone. That's all I know." Dylan took another gulp of bourbon.

After a pause, he looked at Michael. "So what do *you* know? That's what I'm wonderin'. 'Cause you ain't told me everythin'. Give." Dylan leaned forward and glared at Michael. "What the fuck happened to our lives, Mick?"

CHAPTER 53

Michael met Dylan's gaze without flinching. "We came from the northeast. I sheltered in a military compound during the storms. We're heading home."

Dylan ignored that. "What do you know, Mick? I know it's more than you're sayin'." He pointed at Althaea. "You and your gal pal here have nasty wounds. You didn't get those drivin' from the northeast." Dylan's eyes glinted black, shiny from bourbon and candlelight. "Where's your buddy? Torque? That motherfucker was up to no good. I don't care how polite he was or how much money he spent at my restaurant. Butter wouldn't melt in his mouth, and he was a dangerous S-O-B. I always liked you, Mick. But that buddy of yours? Wouldn't turn my back on him."

Michael sighed. "Torque's dead. What do I know? I doubt you'd believe me if I told you. It's safest just to say we're on our own. The government can't help anyone anymore. We should consider banding together, because if we don't, we might not make it."

"That sounds mighty ominous, dude."

"It's the truth. We're heading to Aurora in the morning. But we need to find a central place to hole up and organize ourselves. The compound from which we came is the best prospect for shelter through the winter. We'll be returning in a day or two. I'll catch up to you and Ella then, and we'll talk. Fair?"

"Yeah, man. I'll head home now. Ella hates bein' left alone, and I don't blame her. By now, she'll be worried, I expect. Can't call the house and tell her I'm okay, so I have to git. Lock the door when you leave. You know where I live. If you don't find me here when you return, you'll find me there. Help yourself to whatever you need."

After Dylan left, the group settled down to sleep. Arnie and Althaea pushed two benches together and were asleep within minutes. Carolyn told

Sam to do the same and then went to Michael, who was back on the bench on which he'd slept.

"Does the wound hurt much?" Carolyn sat on the chair next to him, cupped his face with her palm, and sent him a Reiki boost.

Michael nuzzled into her hand, eyes closed for a moment. The bristles on his unshaven face tickled her.

"I'll be fine, Carr. Go sleep. Stay close though. Don't go anywhere without telling me. Sam too."

Carolyn lowered her voice. "What do you think made people sick?"

"Not sure, but I'd bet money Dylan is an abductee."

"What about his wife?"

"Good question. Maybe Ella's lucky she survived. Just promise you'll stay inside the restaurant. No telling who's out there. At the least, there might be scared people with itchy trigger fingers."

"Are you afraid the Agency will find us?"

"I don't assume they've let us go. Promise me you won't even go downstairs without telling me."

"I promise." Carolyn stood and went to where Sam had pushed two benches together. She'd already snuggled under a blanket and yawned when Carolyn climbed in beside her.

"Thanks, Mom."

"For what?"

"Staying with me even though you want to be with Michael. I'm twenty, but I don't want to be alone. This place is creepy."

Carolyn looked around as if for the first time. A dark-haired woman in a long, blue dress stood near the women's restroom. Carolyn could vaguely see the restroom door through the woman's body.

Eyes closed, Carolyn connected to the woman. *Do you mind our presence? We don't want to impose, just sleep.* When she opened her eyes, the woman had disappeared, but her voice echoed: *sleep well.*

The return of Carolyn's memories had unblocked her mediumship abilities, and she found it reassuring. She asked the spirits in the restaurant to alert her if anyone tried to enter the building.

Light flashed at the corner of Carolyn's eye, and when she looked, a young girl appeared at the top of the stairs. The girl held up a hand, placing her index finger to her thumb, forming a circle. *Okay.*

A man on the main floor positioned an ethereal chair by the door and sat. Carolyn sent thanks to him, but told the man she didn't want to put him to any trouble. His wheezy laugh reached Carolyn's psychic hearing, and she caught a whiff of pipe smoke as he settled in for the night's vigil. *My pleasure, ma'am. No trouble.*

Carolyn lay her head on a rolled up jacket she used as a pillow, sent her thanks out to the spirits around them one more time, and closed her eyes. A few minutes later, she slept.

***

Carolyn's eyes open to find Jim Cornell lying next to her in bed. Cornell's mouth forms a toothy grin when he notices she's awake. She struggles to stand, wanting to get away from him, but can't move.

Head whipping from side to side, she tries to find the others. Cornell snickers. The sound reminds Carolyn of a wheezing dog in a cartoon she can't quite remember. He puts a hand over her mouth, stifling a shout. "Think I'd let you call Valiant?" Cornell leans in to her ear. "Keep your mouth shut. One word, and I'll butcher Sam like a hog. Understand?"

Carolyn whimpers, nods her head. The hand retreats from her mouth, and she stares at him. He's dead. What's he doing here if he's dead?

Cornell smiles again and gags her mouth. "I need you quiet, still." A hand slides up under her clothes, touches her breasts. Carolyn wants to struggle, but she's locked in place.

"You used to like this. Remember?" Cornell waits for a response.

A tear slides from Carolyn's eye, and the hand travels to her belly, stroking, caressing. "I would've cared for the child as if she were mine. Now I'll make it difficult for you. She's trying to come through, and I can keep her from getting to you. Perhaps she'll be stillborn."

Carolyn tries to scream, but the gag stifles it.

"Did you forget Sam? I told you to be quiet." Fingers pinch her nipples.

She tries to pull away. Can't.

He makes a sudden move, sliding a hand inside her pants, between her legs.

Carolyn attempts to pull her thighs together, fighting the paralysis, but fails.

He plays, touches, probes. "I've missed this. Can't let that fucker have all the fun."

She tries to clear her head, to think. Carolyn hears the sound of a zipper and Cornell shifts and fidgets next to her. The gag drenches with saliva and stifled screams, and she shakes her head, the only movement she can make.

At last she remembers and says silently, "Archangel Michael, I call upon you now. Please come and remove any entity attachments from me, any lower vibrating energies, any toxic energies." In a vision, light fills the room, and she senses the angelic presence.

Cornell rages. "You bitch. You can't win. I'm not done with you."

She screams against the gag, tries to claw with her still paralyzed hands, tears streaming down her face. The bright light behind Cornell silhouettes his body. When he disappears, Carolyn finds her voice and screams.

"You're okay, Carr. You're dreaming." Michael.

Thank God. Carolyn opened her eyes, clutched at him. "Sam. Where's Sam?" She sat. Sam's bench was empty, and Carolyn leapt up. "Where's Sam?" She said it louder, ran towards the women's washroom.

"What's wrong?" Michael asked. "Sam went to look around downstairs. I made her promise not to venture outside. She's fine."

Carolyn calmed when he said that, but wanted to verify. Though her bladder felt ready to burst, she hurried past the women's washroom and rushed down the stairs. "Sam? Where are you?"

"Here, Mom. What's wrong?"

Carolyn landed at the bottom of the stairs and raced into the dining area, almost knocking over Sam, who gripped Carolyn's shoulders and peered into her eyes. "Why are you freaking out, Mom? I'm only checking the place out. I was bored and didn't want to wake you."

Carolyn sighed. "Nothing. A bad dream."

Footsteps on the stairs made her look up. Michael hurried towards them, face troubled. "What happened, Carolyn? What did you dream?"

"Later. I have to hit the washroom." She turned to Sam. "Stay inside. Promise?"

"Yes. I already promised Michael. I'm not going anywhere." Sam clenched her jaw and put her hands on her hips.

Carolyn hurried to the washroom on the main floor, the mundane motions of using the toilet and washing up helping to calm her. Refreshed, she went upstairs with Michael and told him about her dream.

"Was it Cornell or a nightmare from your unconscious?" Michael asked. The two sat at a table and picked at the food Arnie and Althaea had scrounged from the packs they'd brought and the stores Dylan had on hand.

"It was Cornell," Carolyn said. "He's angry and vengeful."

"I don't get it," Michael said. "Torque wasn't like that. He wanted to help us. Why doesn't Cornell? When I had my near death experience, I regretted everything I'd done that hurt anyone, no matter how small my mistake, and I wanted to atone for it. Why wouldn't Cornell want to do the same?"

"He hasn't gone into the light. He's earthbound, full of resentment and hate, and he wants to hurt us, so he refuses to cross."

Michael chewed a handful of trail mix and considered what she'd said. "What about when you called on Archangel Michael? Did that force Cornell into the light?"

"There's a chance. I got him away from me for now, but the angels can't go against free will. If someone refuses to go into the light, that person may stay earthbound."

Michael moved his chair closer to Carolyn's, put an arm around her, and kissed her cheek.

"May I touch the baby?" Michael hovered his free hand above her belly and waited. When she nodded consent, he put his hand on the bulge below the waistband of Carolyn's track pants.

"Can you feel the baby move?" Michael asked.

"Sometimes—more often in the last week. At first it felt like little flutters. Now it's a definite kick."

"Can Cornell hurt the baby?"

"I won't let him."

"But can he prevent her from coming through? Will she be all right?"

"I've got protection around her. I'll always protect her, Michael. Cornell can threaten all he wants, but I'm not helpless." She thought about how he'd bound her in the dream. She'd never drop her guard like that again. Carolyn turned to Michael and pressed a hand over his, kissed his mouth, gently parting his lips, pouring her love into him.

After a moment, she released him, and he kissed her forehead. The arm around Carolyn's shoulders drew her into a tight hug. "The thought of that bastard harming you or our baby terrifies me. How do I fight a ghost?"

She pulled back, met his gaze. "Ghosts can't hurt us. They're not in the physical. Play on our fears, give us nightmares, annoy us, yes—but they can't hurt us unless we let them. I won't allow Cornell access to our baby, and now I'm aware he's around, I'll always have protection around us."

Something occurred to her. "Don't let Cornell suck you into anything on his turf. If you have a dream with him in it, ignore him and call in Archangel Michael. Cornell can harm you in your dreams. But we don't have to play his game."

When Michael promised, Carolyn taught him the words to call in Archangel Michael for help, and the steps to put up energetic protection. He smiled while repeating the words and gestures she taught. "I feel silly," he admitted.

She returned the smile. "I understand. But you'll want to have this protective energy around you. An entity can harm you by clinging to you and muddling your thinking. Cornell's anger can infect you and make you angry. Keep him away."

Michael nodded. Both looked up when Sam appeared at the top of the stairs. "The car's packed. No one wanted to interrupt you, but Arnie's eager to find his mom."

"We'll be right down," Michael said.

Sam turned and left.

Carolyn looked around. She stuffed the few belongings still lying around into a bag. Packed up and ready to go, Michael helped Carolyn put her backpack on her shoulders. Once again, she wore another woman's clothes. Althaea had lent her a pair of camouflage pants and a black tank top. It reminded her of the days they'd spent running from the Agency. Then she remembered Arnie's mom and shuddered. "It won't be good, Michael."

"Is that your intuition talking?"

Carolyn nodded. "I don't want to tell Arnie because I can't say what's wrong. When I try to sense her in spirit, I'm not positive she's there. But I doubt we'll be happy with what we find."

"All we can do is be there for him. Let's go. It'll take us less than an hour to get to the condo." Michael took Carolyn's hand, and they walked down the stairs.

CHAPTER 54

They arrived at the southeast section of Aurora, where Arnie's condo was located in a complex built less than five years before. It was a mix of apartments, offices, and retail spaces. Locals opposed to having the zoning bylaws changed to allow high-rise buildings in what until that point had been single-family dwellings had almost blocked the new development. But when the permits had gone through and units went up for sale, Arnie had lined up to purchase.

The developers had promised a design that would blend buildings into the landscape, and Michael thought they'd succeeded. All the structures sported rooftop gardens, and they'd generously dotted the surroundings with green space. Michael remembered the protests, but hadn't been a part of them. He hadn't cared what they did, knowing it would all end anyway.

When he recalled his former attitude, he felt ashamed. Standing in the drizzle in front of the demolished building and seeing the stricken look on Arnie's face increased the shame tenfold and added guilt.

"Are you getting anything, Carolyn?" Arnie asked for the third time.

Carolyn leaned on a cement block, eyes closed. She took a deep breath and winced. Michael wanted to touch her but feared distracting her. When Arnie reached a hand towards her, Michael intercepted and shook his head.

"She was inside, with her nurse. I can feel them both in spirit, Arnie. I'm so sorry." Tears spilled down Carolyn's face, and she opened her eyes.

Arnie fell to the ground. Michael waved Althaea over and indicated he'd take over for her as lookout. He moved away from the rubble and took up a position near the road.

Althaea dropped next to Arnie and hugged him. He wrapped his arms around his knees and buried his head. His muffled voice drifted up to them. "My home is her tomb. We can't even retrieve her body for burial." Arnie looked up at Carolyn, his face a mask of fear. "Is she earthbound?"

Carolyn shook her head. "She crossed. So did her nurse. Your mom visited you, Arnie, and she's here now. She says you've seen her in your dreams."

"Yes. She looked young. I thought it was just a dream."

Carolyn sat on the ground next to Arnie. "No, that was your mom. She wants you to know she's with your dad, and she's never been happier. Both watch over you."

They sat there a while and let Arnie come to terms with his loss. The earthquakes had been strong in Toronto, the aftershocks so great that buildings as far north as Bradford were destroyed. Millions of people in Toronto and the GTA had died.

Carolyn went to Michael and put her arms around him. She looked up at him, so full of sorrow his heart lurched at the sight. "I feel Steve in spirit, Michael." She whispered it, so the others wouldn't overhear.

When Carolyn's husband had died, Carolyn's friend, Steve, lost his wife, Shelly. Losing Shelly had scared Steve into terminating his friendship with Arnie and Carolyn.

Michael put a hand on Carolyn's head and pressed her face into his chest. "I'm so sorry."

"I don't want to check on anyone else right now. What if Sam's friends are dead too? She won't be able to cope with that."

"They might have survived, if they were in houses and not apartments."

"I hope they're okay. She'll ask me sooner or later."

Michael looked up to see Sam walk away from the demolished building and climb into the car. Perhaps she was thinking about it and was as afraid as Carolyn of knowing what happened. He thought about his own house and decided he didn't need anything there. All he needed was Carolyn, the baby, and Sam.

He called over to Althaea. "We have to get moving."

She looked up and nodded. One of Althaea's hands stroked Arnie's hair, and she leaned forward and whispered something to him. He kept his head lowered. Althaea talked to him some more, and Arnie allowed her to lead him towards the SUV.

Michael stopped him. "I'm sorry. For whatever part I played in this."

"You shouldn't have let them take me away."

A vision of being Arnie, forced into the trunk of Torque's car, fearing for his life, Carolyn's life, and his mother's life flashed into Michael's head. He swallowed, tried to control the sense of being two people at once, a remnant of his near death experience.

Not knowing what would come out, Michael started to speak. Arnie turned away and left Michael standing there, mouth hanging open.

"Give him time. I'll talk to him later."

Michael jumped. He'd forgotten Carolyn was there though her hand still held his. "He's right, Carr. There's a lot on my conscience."

"Forgive yourself, then, before you expect Arnie to." She tugged on his hand, and he followed her to the car.

***

This time, Arnie stayed in the car while Michael, Sam, and Carolyn went up to the wreckage left of Carolyn's house. Most of the charming century home had burned to the ground. Althaea stood next to the car, rifle slung across a shoulder, on lookout once more.

Michael kept an arm around Carolyn while she made her way to the front steps. He remembered forcing her down those stairs, rejecting her attempts to convince him Jessica, his dead wife, was with them. A glance at Carolyn told him she relived it too. Sam went to the bottom of the stairs, looked up towards the front porch, and turned away.

"Mom, where's Vanna? And Jack? Are they okay?"

Carolyn's body went rigid against Michael's side.

"Do you know?" he asked.

She nodded. "They're alive, Sam."

"Is that true, Mom?"

"I can't sense them in spirit. That doesn't mean everything's fine. It means they haven't passed. I can't tell you where they are without focused remote viewing, and I can't do that here."

"That's all I need to know," Sam said. "Let's go. I hope the people renting this place got away." She turned and headed back down the driveway.

Carolyn and Michael watched her until she climbed into the car. Michael looked up at the sky. The drizzle had stopped. Fat, grey clouds threatened more rain, but for now, it had stopped. "We'll stop in Port Perry—let Dylan know where we're heading."

"I'm glad we came here. I had to see. Maybe we can come back someday and rebuild."

Michael didn't answer her, just kissed her on the forehead.

"You don't think that'll be possible."

Damn her abilities. Sometimes it made life with her difficult. "Not for a long time. Things will get worse as people discover the infrastructure they took for granted is gone." He sighed. Some things she couldn't see, and it was just as well. They returned to the car holding hands. Michael wondered if there would ever come a time when he wouldn't need her touch reassuring him she was still there.

***

214

Michael didn't need psychic abilities to tell him something was wrong when they pulled up in front of the King's Castle Restaurant in Port Perry. The door leaned open and two of the windows on the main floor were smashed. He grabbed his gun from its holster. "Ally, with me. The rest of you stay here."

"Michael, no." Carolyn's voice registered fear.

"I have to check it out, Carr. Wait here. Have your gun ready. You too, Arnie. Lock the doors when I get out and don't leave the car for any reason."

Sam whimpered, but Michael ignored it. Carolyn would have to deal with it. He hoped Dylan was okay. Althaea stepped out of the car, gun ready, and they made their way to the patio together. Michael motioned for Althaea to stand to the left of the front door. He pushed the door open wider. It made a slight creaking sound, but everything else was still and quiet. He waited. Nothing.

Inside the restaurant, shards of reflective glass stuck to the wall behind the bar, remnants of a mirror. The rest of the mirror lay strewn on the floor and the counter in crunchy, glittering fragments. Barstools marinated in a pool of what smelled like beer and wine.

Althaea indicated she'd take the main floor. Michael nodded and moved up the stairs, pausing on the landing. The suit of armour lay in pieces on the stairs, the shield and sword missing. The floor creaked when he took another step. He froze. Still nothing.

He continued the journey up the stairs. When he reached the top, he scanned the banquet room. Michael's group had cleaned everything up when they'd left, but now food wrappers and broken glass littered everything, the floor sticky with more booze.

A sound behind Michael made him spin around, gun ready.

"Don't shoot." Althaea gazed up at him from the landing. "Main floor's secure, and I peeked into the cellar. It's creepy down there—locked from this side, but I went down anyway. No one's here."

Michael suggested they move on to Dylan's house and the two returned to the car. Relief showed in Carolyn's eyes when they appeared.

Dylan lived nearby. The businesses and homes along the way appeared deserted, the streets empty. Michael thought he caught a glimpse of movement in the window of one house, but couldn't be sure. The SUV pulled up in front of a two-story century home, one of a dozen on the short crescent. Michael jumped out of the car, and the others followed.

The house looked vacant, curtains closed over the windows. Michael climbed the steps to the wrap-around porch and knocked on the wooden screen door. It opened as the others joined him on the porch.

"Dylan, what happened?" Michael recoiled at his friend's appearance.

Dylan's hair, usually tied back in a neat ponytail, hung loose and greasy.

Sweat beaded along his hairline. He wore the same clothes he'd had on when they last saw him. He pointed a shotgun at them, but lowered it when he recognized Michael. Eyes dark rimmed and hollow, Dylan waved them in.

The odour hit Michael as soon as he stepped inside. Somewhere in the house lay a dead body. He stopped the others and asked everyone except Carolyn to wait on the porch. She gave Michael a puzzled look and entered.

Sorrow replaced puzzlement as soon as she was through the door. They followed Dylan into the living room. The heavy curtains in the picture window gave the room a stifling, stagnant aura. The cloth-covered couch held a blanket and pillow. Dylan had been sleeping here.

"When did Ella die, Dylan?" Carolyn said, voice cracking.

Dylan dropped his rifle and sank to the couch. Michael and Carolyn sat on the matching loveseat.

Head bowed, Dylan said, "Ella was dead when I got home from the restaurant. I shouldn't have dawdled." He looked up. "It was good to see you, Mick. I enjoyed our visit. But while I was away, Ella took a turn. That disease got her. I know no one who survived it once they got it. I shouldn't have left her alone. My Ella died alone." Dylan broke into wracking sobs.

Carolyn went to him, put an arm around him. She glanced at Michael and he nodded. "Dylan," she said, "Ella's here. She wants to tell you she's okay."

"What are you talkin' 'bout?"

"Carolyn can communicate with spirits," Michael said. "She helped me connect with Jessie. I didn't believe it at first, but it was Jess all right. Carolyn can help you get closure."

"Ella came to you after she passed. She wanted to see you before she went into the light. She crossed just fine. Her parents were both there to meet her. There was also a dog—a black lab." Carolyn tilted her head, listening. "Spike? Was that your dog?"

Dylan gaped at her and nodded. "Spike died a few years ago. It crushed Ella. She loved that dog." He paused a moment, said, "Tell her I'm sorry I wasn't here. Tell her I love her."

"Ella knows. She can hear you," Carolyn said. "Have you found pennies around the house in weird places?"

"Yeah. I thought I was going crazy. After the government stopped makin' pennies, we got rid of the ones we'd had, or so I'd thought. I'd rolled 'em up and took 'em to the bank. But I must've found ten in the last two days in crazy places."

"That's Ella, letting you know she's around." Carolyn smiled, and Dylan beamed back.

"Will Ella always be near me?"

"Not always. But she'll pop in and visit sometimes."

Michael hated like hell to break this up, but they needed to get moving. "Dylan, come with us. We're returning to the Peterborough compound. It's a safe place to hole up and winter's coming."

"You're askin' me to walk away from my home? The restaurant?"

"For now that would be best. The place was prepared for a shutdown of the grid. We can survive the winter there. If we have numbers, we'll be safer, too. After a while we'll return and rebuild. But you need to be somewhere safe where there's clean water and food."

"What about Ella's body?"

"We'll help you bury her. Then we'll go. You can join us or not."

Dylan remained silent for a moment and then gave Michael a single nod. "Okay," he said. "I'll come with you."

CHAPTER 55

They buried Ella in the garden behind Dylan's house and returned to the Peterborough compound the next day. The moment Carolyn saw the vast structure looming ahead in the grey light of afternoon, her breathing shallowed and sweat bloomed on her palms. Lips pressed together, she tried not to let the fear show.

When Michael pulled up in front of the garage, Sam jumped out, but Carolyn remained sitting in the SUV. Eyes wide, Sam stood transfixed by the wreckage of the helicopter. Dylan pulled up behind Michael in a Matrix, and Althaea and Arnie climbed out. The others unloaded bags, while Carolyn watched, fighting to quell her anxiety.

"You okay?" Michael touched her arm, gave it a rub.

She nodded, but he wasn't buying it. "Don't worry, Carr. We secured the place, but we'll go through and verify no one's waiting to surprise us. I see no vehicles around, so I'm sure we're alone. Everything looks the way it did the day we left."

Carolyn looked at her knees. "Michael, it's not that. Memories are flooding back, and it's difficult to enter that prison."

Concern flashed across his face. "I'm sorry. Arnie lived here for months after everyone else evacuated. I didn't consider how returning here might affect you." Michael took Carolyn's hand. "We have to make sure you'll be able to give birth safely when the time comes. Ally and I can help deliver the baby in the infirmary. It's well stocked, and you'll have a better chance here than at a hospital."

The group had visited the Aurora hospital after leaving Arnie's condo. It was standing, but had been vandalized, the only people in evidence squatters, the staff dead or gone.

"I'll be fine." Carolyn got out of the car, giving Michael a half-smile before slamming the door closed.

Arnie and Althaea opened the garage-bay doors, and Michael and Dylan parked the vehicles. The front entrance was boarded up, so they'd go inside through the side doors. Carolyn was glad the main entrance was unrecognizable. It helped push from her head the vision of Cornell dragging her away while Arnie and the woman with him ran for their lives.

The padlock and chain Michael had left on the side entrance door were still intact. He removed them and held the door open to let everyone file into the building. Michael and Althaea had weapons drawn, but neither one seemed concerned.

The moment Carolyn stepped inside, the heaviness pressed in. Not all the souls who'd died here had departed. The farther the group went into the building, the closer they got to the cellblocks, the thicker became the air. Feet dragging, energy draining, and head pounding, Carolyn halted, stumbled, and sank to the floor.

"Mom," Sam cried out and crouched next to her mother.

"Carr?" Michael said.

She pressed hands to her forehead, pain stabbing through her eyes. "Too much spirit activity in here. Headache."

"Sam, sit with her while Ally and I scope the place out. Arnie, draw your weapon. Dylan, keep that rifle handy. It'll take us a while to check the place out," Michael said.

Carolyn relaxed and leaned back against Sam. "Need to clear myself and put up protection. There are so many." Her breath hitched. "I'll cleanse the whole place when I'm feeling better."

She followed the steps to rid her body of entity attachments and put protection around herself and the others though none of the others were affected. Slowly the pressure eased and her energy returned. Carolyn took deep breaths, and though the air she sucked into her lungs was stale, her head unclogged.

Sam helped Carolyn stand, and they waited for Michael and Althaea to return. When almost an hour had passed, Carolyn became worried. They'd heard no shots, which was reassuring, but the two should have returned by now. She opened her mouth to suggest searching for them when Althaea burst through the doors. Carolyn's heart skipped a beat, but she realized Althaea didn't appear worried. In fact, she smiled. "Everything's great. Michael's getting the generator up and running. We'll have light and we can cook something."

"I thought this place had solar power?" Dylan said.

"Enough to keep the freezers and a few other things operating. We still need the generator for lights and heat. But we'll have a home-cooked meal tonight." Althaea took a bag from Arnie and led the way back to where they'd set up the sleeping quarters. Carolyn sent a silent message ahead to the spirits waiting in the cellblocks. *I'll visit you as soon as I settle in. You're not alone. I'm here to help.*

***

The compound contained a dormitory. The four sections, each with five bedrooms and a shared bathroom and shower, would be their sleeping quarters for the foreseeable future. Michael had claimed one section for himself, Carolyn, and Sam.

Dylan settled into another section alone, in a room farthest from the others. "Nothin' personal," he explained. "Want my space while I can get it."

Althaea threw her bags into a bedroom in a third section and removed her weapons, dropping them on a desk next to the door. Her movements were stiff, her shoulders sore, the wound throbbing.

The door slamming shut behind her didn't get her attention, but the lock sliding into place did. She turned and stared at Arnie without speaking. He got the point. "I want to share your room, Ally."

Althaea sucked in her breath. "Arnie—"

He didn't let her finish. "When you drove away with Valiant and left me in the forest at the underground community, I was afraid I'd never see you again. That was bad enough. But when I did see you, I didn't know if you'd get through that battle alive. I watched you get shot and fall, and the time it took for you to get up was the longest moment of my life. It's as though we've been given another chance, and I want to grab it."

He licked his lips and continued. "I hope you want me, too. Valiant warned you about me, but if it takes the rest of my life, I want to show you I'm not that person anymore. Move in with me, Ally. I want to go to bed with you every night and wake up with you every morning for as long as we live. If we had a priest here, I'd want to get married."

Althaea sank to her bed, not sure how to respond. They hadn't even slept together yet, but that could be rectified right now. Arnie waited. Butterflies flitted in Althaea's stomach. "Remember I told you I wasn't interested in a relationship? That I was okay with just sex?"

Arnie nodded.

"Before Michael and I left you behind, you said 'come back to me. I love you.' Those words, for all I knew, were the last words I'd ever hear you say." Ally's voice broke, but she continued. "Then the whole time we were on the road, we took care of one another. I've never experienced that kind of caring and affection—neither giving it nor receiving it. When you're not with me, I miss you. No. I ache for you. Being without you hurts and being with you makes me happy. Yes, I'd like it if we could live together, and someday, if we can find a way, we'll talk about marriage." Now it was out, Althaea relaxed and gave him a smile.

Arnie exhaled loudly. "Christ, Ally, you scared me. You do over-think things." He sat next to her. "But don't ever change." Arnie smiled, put an arm around her, and when Althaea lifted her face to him, he kissed her.

She parted her lips, and he thrust his tongue between them, exploring. Nervous, she pulled back. "Are we going to sleep together now?"

Arnie smiled. "No sleep involved in what we're about to do, Ally."

She laughed, a full, throaty laugh and joy spilled from her.

The smile on Arnie's lips grew wider, and without a word, he helped her out of her tank top. She noticed how careful and protective he was of her injured shoulder. Next, Arnie helped remove her bra and, her torso bared, he kissed first one breast then the other. When Althaea reached out to embrace him, Arnie stopped her with a whisper. "Not yet."

Self-conscious, Althaea fidgeted. "I'll turn off the light."

"No. Please? I want to look at you."

She hesitated, not wanting Arnie to see the ugly scars on her body, though she told herself he wouldn't care. A wisp of hair fell into her face, and Arnie brushed it aside with fingers soft and gentle. "You're so gorgeous. I want to see all of you. Let me, Ally?"

When Althaea gave an uncertain nod, he smiled, reassuring. "You're the most beautiful woman in the world, Ally."

Althaea parted her lips, but didn't speak. Arnie took Althaea's face between his palms and kissed her again, then broke the kiss, and removed his shirt. He closed his eyes while her hands stroked his soft skin. He undid her cargo pants and shoved them to the floor.

Naked, except for a thong, Althaea shivered. Arnie slid the thong down in a swift motion and it joined the pants on the floor. Her arms wanted to cover her nakedness, and when Arnie saw them rising, he reached out and captured them in his.

His gaze roamed over her body, taking in the muscles, the curves, the long, lean look of her. Goose bumps prickled her skin though more from nerves than from chills. "It's okay," Arnie said. "Relax. I'll warm you up."

What was wrong with her? She wasn't usually this nervous. Then again, usually it was just sex. She tilted her face forward to look into Arnie's eyes, those blue eyes she could get lost in.

He removed his clothes, revealing a strong, muscular body. Althaea reached out and touched his bullet wound, now healed, and then kissed it. Warm hands stroked her skin, travelled down her back to cup her ass.

Arnie parted her legs so he could kiss her thighs, and she dropped her head back and moaned. Her whole body ached for him. She craved his touch and whimpered, the sound thick with lust. Her hands grasped his shoulders, massaged them, and then sifted through his hair.

Arnie lay next to her, and she turned on her side and faced him. Her hands wandered over his body. When she stroked the rough terrain of his back, the spell broke for a moment, and sadness overwhelmed her at the reminder of what he'd suffered in this place.

But then she looked into his eyes, and the love and desire in them brought her back to the moment. Her fingers continued to explore, and he lay back and let her touch him. She watched his face, delighting in his changes in expression, which flitted through varying degrees of ecstasy.

Arnie groaned, pulled her into his arms, and rolled on top of her, gentle, watching out for her shoulder. She opened her legs to him, and when she felt him nudging at her entrance, she thrust her pelvis forward to help him.

His eyes mesmerized her as he guided himself inside, watching her face intently while he did. Althaea tried to keep her gaze locked on his eyes, but when he thrust into her, she closed her eyes and cried out. He leaned forward and kissed her, greedy, demanding. He pumped into her faster, harder, as if he owned her.

She cried out, and he paused, lips releasing her mouth, expression a question. She cried out again, in protest. "Don't stop. Please."

Mouth pressed to Althaea's once more, Arnie thrust into her again, his rhythm quick and full of need. Her legs wrapped around his hips. Whimpers escaped her and spilled into his mouth, and she gasped and thrashed under him. "Oh, God, Arnie."

Her muscles contracted around him, taking her over the edge, and she felt his release within her. When the tsunami receded, Arnie collapsed on her. After a moment, he rolled off, but pulled Althaea to him and held her tight.

Heart pounding in his chest so hard she could feel it, he panted, catching his breath.

"Arnie?"

A squeeze. "Yes?"

"We'll need a bigger bed."

CHAPTER 56

They made the place home. Carolyn cleared out the trapped spirits, and Michael set up the infirmary to be ready for the coming birth. The baby's estimated due date was mid-February.

Each member of the group took a turn monitoring the radio, which played nothing more than static as time went on—even the pre-recorded messages disappeared into limbo. Once a week, Michael and Althaea went out to find people who were good candidates for joining the group. Already, four men, three women, and one child had joined them.

When Carolyn asked Michael why he wanted to bring strangers here, he told her they'd need the safety of numbers while things continued to deteriorate. The new people brought with them a variety of skills and knowledge.

Karen was an expert in edible wild foods, with knowledge that went deeper than even Michael's. John, his wife Mary, and their young son Alexander were farmers. Troy was a mechanic.

"But how will we feed them?" Carolyn said. The greenhouses grew fresh herbs and vegetables, but they'd need to find a source of fresh meat and fruit when frozen stores ran out.

"There are enough supplies to get through this winter, and we pick up more non-perishables on every run to a town. In the spring, we'll farm. The sun will return by then. Have you noticed? We're getting fewer days of darkness, fewer wild storms and earthquakes."

She hadn't noticed. But she'd noticed a lightening of everyone's mood. Carolyn was well into the second trimester of her pregnancy and was as comfortable as she'd ever be while pregnant. She'd passed the morning sickness and weakness of the first trimester, and had the heavy, unwieldy final trimester yet to come.

Most of her days she spent snooping around in the offices, wanting to learn as much as possible about the underground community. One day, she worried, the Agency might come after them, or things would get so bad on the surface they'd need to find shelter underground themselves. When she mentioned this to Michael, he shrugged off her concerns, though he first asked her if she acted from a premonition or from anxiety.

She admitted she'd had no premonitions, but simply worried. She also told Michael about Torque's warning, months ago, that the ionosphere was heating. Michael seemed more interested in that information than anything she'd found in Cornell's files, but he didn't explain what it meant. He was in the midst of preparing for another outing with Althaea.

"I'm glad you're digging around in the offices. If you find hard drives or memory sticks, get Arnie to help you hack into them. If you see anything that mentions the ionosphere or the aliens, give it to me immediately. But I don't want you stressing yourself about stuff that probably won't happen. Are we clear?" Michael leaned over and kissed her forehead.

She pushed the rifle he'd slung over his shoulder out of the way so she could kiss him back without the thing bumping her. She wasn't afraid of guns anymore, but she still didn't like them. Everyone in the group spent part of their days doing target practice, and even Sam was learning martial arts.

Carolyn sat at a table in the cafeteria leafing through the latest pile of file folders she'd brought from Cornell's office. "What if the Agency finds us here? Don't you think that's a possibility?"

Michael shook his head. "If they venture out, we'll be ready."

"Please be careful." Carolyn said this to him every day, at least once.

Michael cupped her face in his hands. "I will. I love you, Carr." He kissed her, making her heart flutter.

The fear rose again, and she asked the angels to protect him and Althaea. She removed her wedding band, and Michael held out his palm. The ring dropped into his hand, and he pulled the chain from his pocket.

She insisted that anytime they were apart, he take the ring with him, and give it back to her when he returned. He pretended to indulge her superstition, but Carolyn knew he liked carrying it with him. The gesture made them both feel better.

"Ready?" Althaea appeared in the doorway.

Michael gave Carolyn's cheek one last stroke before he turned and walked away. Her heart went with him as it always did. She lowered her head, opened a folder, and busied herself.

***

Michael hopped into the SUV's passenger side. Althaea waited for him to shut the door and buckle up before she pulled out.

"The ionosphere's heating." Michael said as Althaea drove out of the parking lot.

The rain pelted down, but the wind had stopped blowing. She flicked on the wiper blades and their rhythmic clicking made the only sound. He waited, let her process the information.

"How?"

Michael shrugged. "Nothing related to what I did in Nahanni. Carolyn said Torque told her about the ionosphere before I destroyed the crystal. Cornell understood what it meant, and she said it panicked him, but he never told her why."

"Of course, he didn't." Althaea frowned. "If that's true, we'll need to go underground. No one could survive that without help from the aliens."

Michael flinched. Was she accusing him of killing everyone above ground by sending the aliens away?

Without looking at him, she said, "I'm not blaming you for anything. It is what it is."

Michael smiled. She always seemed to know what he was thinking. It'd made them a lethal combination when they'd worked together at the Agency. He was glad to have her by his side again.

"I've asked Arnie to see if he can get satellite hookup. I can monitor the ionosphere myself if I can access the correct satellite. When we figure out what's going on, we can decide what to do."

"Okay. What'll we do if the aliens return? Have you considered that possibility?"

Michael waited while Althaea manoeuvred the SUV around a downed tree. "I try not to, but yes, I've considered it. The threat will always exist. The aliens wanted Earth for themselves. They're not likely to give it up that easily."

Althaea nodded. "I agree. We should tell the others."

"No. Don't even tell Arnie."

"They deserve to be informed. We need to warn them the danger exists. What if something happens to us? Besides, they can help us figure out a contingency plan."

"I don't want them worrying over nothing."

Althaea thumped a hand against the steering wheel. "You're assuming the aliens won't be able to recreate the technology to phase back, but you don't know. They've done it once, they can do it again."

Michael tried to catch her eye, but she didn't glance at him. He sighed. "They took years to figure it out the first time. It won't be easy to rebuild."

"Stop making assumptions. I get you don't want to deal with this, especially with Carolyn's pregnancy distracting you, but you'd better face reality, Michael. The others think they're safe and free, but that could change."

"What do you expect they'll do if we tell them about this?" He didn't let her reply. "They'll worry and they'll panic. But if we keep this to ourselves, we can figure out a way to handle it. We'll document everything we do. If anything happens to us, they'll have the information."

Althaea slammed on the brakes. Inertia threw him forward, and the seatbelt pulled tight against Michael's chest. "Jesus Christ, Ally. What the fuck?"

"Why are we going to Port Hope?"

Michael didn't reply.

"It's the CFS, isn't it?"

"Yes." Michael had wanted to check out the Canadian Forces Station in Port Hope for months now, but this was the first opportunity to do so. He hoped they could use the Signals Intelligence, or SIGNIT, capabilities there to set up a way to detect changes in existing electromagnetic or light signals. They'd use it as an early warning system to alert them to alien presence on Earth.

"Drive, Ally. We need to do this."

She put her foot back on the gas and continued heading towards the highway. "Okay. I'll keep it to myself for now. But if we ever find evidence they've returned, we tell the others immediately."

"Deal," Michael relaxed into his seat, confident it would never happen.

***

Arnie sat in the cafeteria and watched Carolyn and Sam chatting while they munched on cookies and drank hot chocolate. An empty mug sat in front of him, but his cookie lay untouched on the plate.

"Arnie, they're okay," Carolyn said for the third time.

Distracted, Arnie nodded. "I know." But he didn't. He wished he had Carolyn's confidence in his intuition. All he felt was unease. Arnie had allowed Carolyn to help him practice using his intuitive abilities—he refused to call them psychic abilities—but he still couldn't distinguish between a premonition and needless worry.

Restless, he had to do something and decided to go tinker with the satellite feed. It hadn't taken him long to get the satellite hookup Michael had asked him to do three days ago—three days. That's what bugged him. Valiant and Ally had been gone for three solid days. Arnie's chair screeched across the floor as he pushed it back and stood.

"Arnie." Carolyn's voice was firm.

"I said 'I know.' I'll check the satellite."

"Don't worry."

"I know!" He hadn't meant to snap at her. "I'm sorry. I wish they'd return."

"They're on their way. I checked in with them again."

Arnie's jaw dropped. "While you were talking to Sam?"

Carolyn nodded.

"Teach me how to do that?"

She smiled. "Baby steps, Arnie. But yes, I'll teach you."

Arnie relaxed. Hearing her say Michael and Althaea were on their way eased the worry. He sat again and scarfed the cookie.

Two hours later, Ally was back in his arms where she belonged. They lay in bed, Arnie dragging her there as soon as she'd stepped out of the shower. Her head rested on his chest, and the scent of fruit wafted up from her hair. How long before he could get it up again and go for round two? He couldn't get enough of her.

When he thought about the last three days, he frowned. "What took you so long? I went crazy with worry." He'd sat on the question for as long as he could. "Port Hope's not even an hour away." He hoped he didn't sound angry or accusing.

She nuzzled his neck, kissed his cheek. "I hate we can't keep in touch when we're on the road. We had to set up surveillance at a military station."

"Surveillance of what?"

Ally didn't reply for a moment. "Nothing specific. Just monitoring the airwaves. We'll have to go back to check up on it. Eventually, we'll settle people there to monitor full time."

Tension eased from him. Tech stuff. Arnie could understand that. "I recovered data from the drives Carolyn found in storage. I also got data flowing from the satellites while you were gone. Valiant can get whatever info he wants now."

Ally's hand went to Arnie's chest and stroked his skin, sending shivers down his body. "Michael will be happy to hear it. Did you collect data on the ionosphere?"

"Yeah. The numbers were a little higher than Valiant said they should be."

Ally exhaled loudly and her hand froze on Arnie's chest. A prickle of fear traced its way up Arnie's spine. "Is that bad?"

She didn't reply, but sat and grabbed her clothes.

"Ally?"

"I don't know. We'd better go talk to Michael."

Arnie got out of bed and reached for his clothes.

CHAPTER 57

Michael reviewed the printout for the second time. Arnie and Althaea perched on the edge of Cornell's desk and waited.

"How bad is it?" Althaea asked.

"Not as bad as you first thought," Michael replied. "It's not great, but it's not lethal. We have to monitor it. As long as the numbers don't trend up, we'll be okay."

Althaea and Arnie both looked relieved.

"So we don't need to worry?" Arnie asked.

"Worry wouldn't help," Michael said.

"Now you sound like Carolyn." Arnie smiled.

"We need to keep an eye on it, not freak out about it. The industries causing this to happen have shut down. We're no longer contributing to environmental destruction, though there are still risks. But it'll take time to reverse what we've done. If you're in a car doing 120 kilometres per hour and you slam on the brakes, you'll still get forward momentum before you stop." Michael plugged another hard drive into a port and waited for the computer to recognize it.

Arnie nodded. "Okay. I'll make sure the data continues to download." He took Althaea's hand. "I've missed my training while you were away. Shall we go to the gym?"

Michael caught Althaea's glance and waved her away.

"You sure?" she said.

"Yeah. I want to review these drives. We'll talk later." Michael stuck his face back to the monitor and clicked through the folders displayed on the screen.

Althaea smiled and slid off the desk. "Okay, Arnie. I'll enjoy kicking your butt again."

Michael's gaze followed them out the door, enjoying their camaraderie.

Althaea had never been so happy before, amazing, considering the circumstances. She'd become a brand new person the day they'd recovered her true memories. Michael even approved of this relationship she had with Arnie.

Folder structure open in front of him, Michael navigated to where he'd left off the day before. So far, he hadn't found anything as staggering as the contract with the aliens, but he continued to troll. No telling what secrets Cornell had tried to obliterate here.

***

Carolyn opens her eyes when she realizes her tormentors are no longer in the room. She's naked, lying on the cold, stone floor in the foetal position. They'd raped her again and had left her broken and humiliated on the floor. After the rapes, and before they'd left her, they'd asked her who'd raped her. As always, if she were to say anything other than "Michael Valiant," they'd beat her. This time they hadn't had to beat her. She'd answered correctly and without hesitation.

Carolyn rolled over and sat up, sweat drenching her naked body, memories of the brainwashing keeping her up again. She'd been getting clusters of memories returning ever since Michael and Althaea had helped her recover what the Agency had stolen. But along with the beautiful memories, the ones of making love with Michael, were the foul ones of the brutal treatment at the Agency.

Michael slept peacefully next to her. She reached out and touched his hair, still marvelling they were together after so much.

The group had been living at the compound now for two months. So far, no Agency personnel had shown up to reclaim Carolyn, no aliens had tried to abduct her, and she'd gotten comfortable. She worried less that someone would snatch her away again. There were more nights where she didn't wake up screaming than nights where she did. She was grateful.

The little group had grown to twenty. Michael and Ally no longer went on their forays, Michael saying they had enough people to look after for the winter. Carolyn noticed he'd stopped the scavenging trips as soon as he'd found a doctor to join their group.

She was in the third trimester of her pregnancy. The baby kicked wildly, especially at night, making sleep even more difficult. Sometimes Tina came to Carolyn in dreams though most of the time, she couldn't remember what they'd discussed.

Jim Cornell's spirit no longer intruded on her dreams, and Carolyn made sure she cleared and protected herself every day. She drew her legs up and rested her chin on her knees. Perhaps she should get up so she wouldn't disturb Michael.

"Carr?"

Too late. She was sorry she'd woken him, but not sorry he was awake. The sound of his soft voice brought a tingle to her core. She let her hand stray to his shoulder.

"You okay?" Michael whispered.

Michael and Carolyn had a room to themselves, but Sam's room was right next door. It was both a curse and a blessing that the walls were thin. If something happened in the night, a shout would bring everyone running. But it made lovemaking and late night conversations a challenge.

"I can't sleep. It's nothing." The memories still threatened, but she could push them away more easily when he was talking to her.

"Come here." Michael pulled her into his arms, and she rested her head on his chest.

Carolyn raised a hand to his face and stroked it, fingers sliding over the smooth, soft skin. She kissed his cheek. "I can't stop touching you."

"Fine by me."

Carolyn smiled and pinched his arm.

"Ouch. What was that for?"

Carolyn giggled quietly. "I wanted to make sure this wasn't a dream."

"I think the protocol for that is pinching yourself." A wry smile appeared, making him look young in the moody dimness.

She touched his lips with a finger, returned the smile, but then grew serious. "When I was locked in my cell here, I'd sometimes dream about you. Then I'd wake up and you weren't there after all. Do you think we did it this time? Will we be able to stay together?"

Carolyn raised herself on one arm and watched his eyes. A faint glow came from a clock radio on the bedside table. It was enough to see shadows and outlines and the dark pools of his eyes.

Michael took her hand and kissed it. "I think we did. No more Torque. No more Cornell. They were always the ones who kept us apart—at least they were in the dreams I had. When you killed Cornell instead of me, you broke the pattern."

The thought that she'd come close to killing Michael brought anxiety shooting up and she frowned. Another memory she had to keep at bay, though it was the memory of only what might have been, so she felt relief in it.

Carolyn leaned down and kissed the softness of his lips. "I think so too," she mumbled into his mouth.

Against her lips, Michael's curled back in a smile. "No talking." He kissed her back, gently at first, then more insistent. Aroused, she ran her hand down his naked body.

When they'd first arrived at the compound, their lovemaking had been fast, frantic, with an aura of desperation and fear, as if bracing themselves against losing it all again. Now it was different, more slow and languid, the undercurrent of fear gone.

Carolyn felt now as though they had all the time in the world and their only concern was pleasuring each other. A nip at his bottom lip, and then she turned her attention to his ear lobe. She nuzzled his neck, and a hiss of air escaped his lips.

All she wanted was to please Michael, make him happy. She peeked at him. Michael had relaxed into the pillows, eyes closed. They clasped hands, and Carolyn continued her journey down his body. She liberated her hands from his, and used her mouth. Michael groaned, and she giggled again, self-conscious of the thin walls.

When he was close to release, Carolyn straddled him, wanting to see Michael's face, to look in his eyes. They clasped hands again while she moved on him, her rhythm picking up speed. She squeezed him with her thighs, mindful of the depth of his penetration. They gazed into each other's eyes while first she climaxed, then he followed suit. She dropped onto his chest, not letting him withdraw from her.

It didn't last long. Her unwieldy belly quickly became uncomfortable. "I have to move," she said.

Michael helped her shift onto her back, and she looked up at him, his face hovering over hers. He opened his mouth to speak, but she beat him to it. "You're beautiful."

He smiled. "Hey, that's what I wanted to say about you."

"Well, you are. You're so beautiful." Carolyn didn't know how else to say it. She stiffened when the baby kicked and grabbed Michael's hand, placing it on her belly. "Feel that?" she asked.

Her belly jumped again when the baby punted it. Michael started, but his hand stayed pressed to her abdomen.

"Oh my God. So strong." Michael kept his voice to a whisper, but Carolyn heard the excitement in it. When they finally fell asleep again, their hands rested, fingers entwined, on her rounded belly.

CHAPTER 58

Ready, Mother? It's time.

Carolyn opened her eyes. The voice, Tina's, echoed in her head. Ripe with baby and more than ready to deliver, she hoped it wasn't a dream and today was the day. Movements slow and awkward, she eased into a sitting position and swung her legs over the side of the bed. Carolyn shoved her feet into a pair of slippers and glanced at Michael. His soft snoring continued uninterrupted. She smiled, though some nights he'd get an elbow in the ribs for doing just that.

The building was difficult to heat, and Carolyn shivered in the chill air. To conserve energy, they lowered the thermostats at night, so she'd worn a nightgown to bed, much to Michael's dismay. The pressure in Carolyn's lower back motivated her to get moving and grab her robe. She'd walk to the washroom first, then the cafeteria. No more sleep for her now.

She took three steps and then her abdomen clenched. A contraction. Carolyn slipped out the door into the hall. Let Michael sleep for a while longer—labour could take all day.

The realization that things were moving faster than expected hit her when she used the toilet and lost her mucous plug. *Still not an emergency. That can happen days before the birth.* But her stomach felt queasy, and she considered waking the doc.

Carolyn checked the time: just after four in the morning. Too early. Nerves and excitement made her jumpy, and she wished she could talk to someone. The thought she'd be holding her baby soon filled her with anticipation, and she longed to share the news. Michael could have another hour, and then they'd wake the doc together.

Dr. Randy Waters was military, and at first, that had made Carolyn suspicious. But when she'd accepted that he wasn't a spy for the Agency, she'd found she enjoyed his company and trusted him with the welfare of her unborn baby. The last checkup with him had gone well. Three days ago, he'd told her the baby was in position, and she could go into labour any time.

In the cafeteria, she got a drink of water from the cooler. Though her stomach growled for food, she figured she shouldn't eat. Her belly tightened again, a long, forceful spasm. Carolyn gasped and doubled over. She should get Michael.

She turned to leave, but froze when liquid trickled down her legs. Between her feet, a puddle grew. Her water had broken. Definitely time to get the doc. She'd have to ask Sam to come and clean up the water.

Carolyn groaned when the next contraction hit and gripped a nearby table until it passed. The door seemed farther away than she remembered. She took two steps in its direction and stopped when another contraction hit. The pains were coming faster than she remembered it with Sam. *Every baby is different.*

Yes, but she'd been in labour with Sam for *two days*. This was happening too fast. She shouldn't have walked to the cafeteria by herself. Carolyn cursed herself for not waking Michael. But she'd assumed there'd be more time and had wanted to let him sleep before the coming ordeal.

The room spun, and she pulled out a chair to sit for a moment. She lowered her head onto her arms and closed her eyes, but speared up again when the next contraction hit. The pain wrenched a whimper from her. Michael. She needed to get to Michael.

Carolyn stood, and something warm trickled down her legs again. Expecting more water, she looked and was shocked to see red. Blood. She cried out, staggered to the door, and braced herself on it. She'd have to use the wall to support herself while she walked through the hall. She lurched away from the door into the hallway, colliding with the wall, leaning on it, the exertion forcing grunts from her.

The double doors leading to the dormitory seemed far away. A glance behind showed a trail of blood following her. *No.*

Carolyn took a deep breath and called on Archangel Raphael, the healing angel, to help her and to keep the baby safe and healthy. *A few more steps. Stop.*

Why had she come here? If she could do it again, she'd wake up Michael and tell him it was time. Carolyn tried to focus on getting back to their room. Michael would help her. He'd get Dr. Randy, and together they'd deliver the baby, and everything would be fine.

Another contraction made her take three hurried steps. Teeth gritted against the pain, she took four more steps. Carolyn looked towards the doors. Still so far away.

***

Michael awoke and his hand drifted to Carolyn's side of the bed. When he didn't feel her there, his eyes popped open. "Carr?" He sat.

Carolyn wasn't in the room. He checked the clock—not even five yet. Maybe she was in the washroom. Michael turned over to go back to sleep, but couldn't do it without her in the bed. It was silly, but she was so pregnant, the thought of her wandering the halls alone bothered him. When ten minutes passed, and she still wasn't back, he got out of bed and went to find her.

Not in the bathroom. He'd check the caff. Surely she wasn't wandering around the building. A glow of lights came from the hallway leading to the cafeteria, and he rushed to the double doors. Relief washed over him when he spotted the lights and realized she was there, but it was short lived. When he pushed open the doors, he found her lying on the floor.

He cried out and ran to her, his pulse thudding in his ears. A trail of blood led up to her and pooled under her. He scooped her up in his arms and ran for the infirmary.

"Michael?"

Her voice startled him. He hugged her tighter to his body. "You'll be fine, honey. I won't let anything happen. We'll get you to bed."

"The baby's coming."

"Okay. It'll be fine." Michael looked at her white face. His throat constricted and worry knotted his stomach.

They reached the infirmary where Dr. Randy had set up everything they'd need for the delivery. Michael laid her gently on the bed. "I'll go get Randy now. Please hang on. I'll be right back."

Carolyn nodded her head, eyes closed. Michael banged through the doors and burst into Randy's room without knocking. Randy took one groggy look at Michael's face and was up and following without question.

When they reached the infirmary, Michael ran to the opposite side of Carolyn's bed and took her hand. "Carr." He kept to a whisper, afraid to disturb her. But when she didn't answer, he called out loudly, fear amplifying his words. "Carolyn, baby, please. Wake up."

Randy shook his head. "She's unconscious, Michael. You can hold her hand while I examine her. Relax. She'll be fine." But Randy's brows furrowed when he opened Carolyn's robe and lifted her nightgown.

"Mamma."

Michael gazed towards Sam, who stood in the doorway, Arnie behind her, hugging her. He glimpsed Althaea in the background.

"Michael?" Arnie asked everything with that one word.

Randy didn't look at them, but when he spoke, the doctor's voice was kind. "Take Sam to the cafeteria, Arnie. Wait there while I examine Carolyn. Ally, come in here and scrub up." He turned to the sink behind him, scrubbed his hands, and slipped on a pair of latex gloves.

Althaea rushed into the room, pushing past Sam and Arnie, who hadn't moved.

"Arnie." Randy's voice was sharper. "Close the door. We need privacy."

Arnie led Sam away, the door slamming shut behind them.

Michael's eyes grew moist. He closed his eyes and suppressed his emotions. He'd make sure she was all right. She had to be. They'd come through so much. He couldn't lose her now.

***

"Placenta abruption," Randy said. "The placenta detached when she went into labour. She should be okay. The baby is full term, growing on schedule, and Carolyn's healthy, though she tells me she's been through abuse. But she insists any checkups she's had during her pregnancy showed everything was fine."

Her eyes were open, but drowsy. Michael held a cool, wet cloth to her forehead.

Randy continued. "You'll be able to deliver vaginally, Carolyn. You lost blood, but the abruption seems minimal."

Michael frowned. "The baby?"

"Is fine. If the baby's in any distress, the monitor will show us. So far, everything looks all right." Randy looked at Althaea. "Take a break. Carolyn is only five centimetres dilated. Tell Sam and Arnie to stop worrying."

Althaea nodded. "Call me if you need me. Otherwise, I'll be back in half an hour to check in. Can I bring Sam and Arnie back with me? They wouldn't want to miss the birth."

"If Carolyn and Michael are okay with that, sure," Randy replied.

Carolyn looked up at Michael, and he smiled at her.

"Whatever Mom here says is okay with me."

"Please, Ally, bring them back with you, if they want to come." Carolyn clutched Michael's hand, and he leaned to kiss her.

***

Carolyn looked at the baby in her arms, suckling at her breast, and then at the baby's father snuggled up next to them on the bed. Michael's eyes were closed, and he breathed deep and slow. One arm curled around Carolyn, protecting her and the baby, even as he dozed.

The baby gripped Michael's index finger in her little hand. Sam beamed at them from her perch on the end of the bed. Althaea and Arnie stood beside the bed, their arms around each other. It was good to see Arnie in a monogamous relationship.

Carolyn smiled at them. "You guys were great. Thank you."

"We're happy for you," Arnie said.

Althaea nodded, glanced at Arnie. "We should go. Give them time." She yawned. "I could sleep for a week now. I'll eat something and go back to bed."

Arnie and Althaea said their goodbyes and left.

Sam reached out and stroked the baby's cheek. "I can't believe I watched a baby being born, and I didn't faint," she said.

"Same here," Michael said, grinning, though his eyes remained closed.

Carolyn glanced from one to the other, happier than she could remember being for a long time.

Sam stood. "If you don't mind, I'll grab something to eat. When I return, I'll bring you breakfast."

"Okay, sweetie,"

Sam left and Carolyn turned her attention back to the miracle in her arms.

Michael sighed and pressed his lips to the top of Carolyn's head. Melancholy swept over Carolyn then, followed by fear. She hitched a sob from her throat. "Michael, into what kind of world did we bring this baby?"

"I don't know, Carr. But during my near death experience, I saw her. Tina was a young woman, beautiful. We were with you in that cell. Do you remember?"

"Yes," she whispered. "She was beautiful, wasn't she?"

"Do you remember I told you Jess appeared in a dream after she died? I saw the baby, too. Jess told me to name her 'Christina' when she was born. Jess said the baby wanted to be called 'Tina' and she'd see me soon. I didn't know what that meant—just thought it was part of a crazy dream."

Carolyn suspected she knew where he was going with this.

"When she appeared in your cell, I knew we were bringing back my baby with Jessica. Tina belongs to the three of us, Carr. Do you think that's possible?"

She leaned into him, relishing the warmth from his body, and drew in a deep breath, catching his scent mingled with the baby's. "I know it is. She worked so hard to get here. She's supposed to be here now. We have to trust things will improve and she's got a role in that." Something else came to mind. "We survived it all and we're together. We broke the pattern."

Michael studied her for a moment and gave her a slight nod. "I think we did. But what about Tina? What pattern does she have to break?"

Carolyn gazed at baby Tina, who'd fallen asleep on her nipple, Michael's finger still hostage to her tiny fist. "That's her journey. We can't walk it for her."

Michael used his free hand to tilt up Carolyn's chin. He kissed her lips, and she let his warmth and love flow into her. After a moment, he released her, eyes shining. "I love you, Carolyn."

She rested her head on his shoulder, tired, but happy. "I love you, too, Michael."

Carolyn closed her eyes, unafraid of going to sleep. There'd be no more dreams to disturb her peace. It'd be tough, but she thought they could carve out a life for themselves, despite the threats continuing to hover over them. Whatever confronted them, they'd handle, she was sure of it. Sam and Tina had hope for a future, and it would be in a world of their making. It felt right.

Exhausted, she dozed off, but as she tumbled into dreams, she muttered a word she didn't know and would forget by morning: SIGNIT.

The End

SAMPLE CHAPTER
INJURY

Eyes closed, sheet covering her face, Daniella Grayson groped for the phone and dragged the receiver to her ear. "Hello?"

"This is Tobey Ames from TNN, Miss Grayson. Do you have any comment on last night's arrest of your mother?"

Were she not so hung over, Dani would've bolted up. Instead, she drew her legs to her chest, assuming the fetal position. "No comment." The hand that held the phone dropped to the bed. Thumb probing for the "End" button, she found it and disconnected the call.

The phone rang again as she contemplated whom to call first. This time, she let it go to voice-mail. The machine in the living room clicked on after the third ring. The message and beep played, and John Madden, her manager, came on, sounding intense. "Dani. Are you screening? Pick up. I've been getting calls about your mother ... "

Dani sat this time, resting her aching head on bent knees, and answered. "What's going on, John? Tobey Ames just called, asking about my mother's arrest."

"I don't know the details yet. They're accusing your mother of killing your father twenty years ago. You would have been what, then? Five?"

Silence. Dani tried to understand what John was telling her. "My father left us when I was five." Dani's mouth went dry, and her hands and feet grew cold. "Lilli was a bitch from hell." Nausea threatened and her spine prickled as she processed the awful news. *Could it be possible? Oh, God.* "She's capable of it. If they've arrested her for killing Daddy, she probably did it." An edge of hysteria had crept into her voice.

"Listen," John said. "Don't answer the phone or open the door until I get there. I'll call the lawyer on my way over, and we'll figure this thing out. There must be a mistake."

Dani said goodbye to John and hung up the phone. She shivered as she slipped out from under the covers and got out of bed. A glance at the clock on her nightstand showed seven-twenty in the morning. No wonder she felt like shit—she'd just gotten *into* bed at four-thirty, helped up to her apartment once again by her trusty chauffeur, what's his name? She always had trouble remembering. Oh, yeah, Cope.

Good looking as hell, but too young for Dani's tastes, and her employee, so she barely gave him a second glance. But he was kind and helpful and made sure she got home safely no matter how drunk she was.

Dani grabbed her bathrobe and snuggled her naked body into the warm terry cloth. As she slid her feet into a pair of slippers, the phone rang again. She returned to her nightstand and disconnected the phone. It continued to ring in the living room until the machine kicked in.

She listened for the caller's voice.

"Hello, Miss Grayson. It's Mark Rutherford of ASN. John Madden suggested you give me an exclusive interview. I'd love to hear your side of the story. Please call me back at ... "

Dani shook her head in disgust while Rutherford recited his phone number. She pulled the plug on the living room phone as well. Anyone she'd want to talk to could call her cell.

She sank onto the couch, switched on the TV, and clicked over to the news channel. An eternity seemed to pass before the stories cycled to the one about her mother. Finally, the newscaster returned to the headline news.

A somber Toby Ames faced the camera, eyes filled with compassion. "Ms. Lillian Capshaw, mother of Oscar-nominated actress Daniella Grayson, was arrested last night in her apartment in Toronto on charges of first degree murder in the death of her husband Paul Grayson. Grayson's skeletal remains were discovered yesterday morning in a capped well at a Sharon, Ontario residence once rented by the family. Ms. Capshaw was taken into custody late last night."

Dani's childhood home flashed on the screen behind the reporter. Plywood covered the windows, and two police cars sat in the driveway. Video footage of Dani appeared on the screen next, showing her exiting a limousine.

The newscaster continued in voiceover. "Miss Grayson, seen here arriving at the premiere of her movie, the Academy Award-winning best picture *Injury*, lives in Los Angeles and has not commented on last night's events. We will update you as the story progresses."

Dani flicked to a channel that focused more on entertainment news. After a few minutes, her photo appeared behind the news anchor, and he gave the same spiel as Ames had though without the premiere clip.

The footage then switched to a taped interview with Gregory

Henderson, caught leaving a restaurant with a date. Dani swallowed past a lump in her throat and hugged herself, terrified of what Henderson might say.

Always an attention hog, Henderson leaned toward the female reporter and into the microphone. "No, I haven't talked to Dani. She's not speaking to me these days."

Dani noted the slight slur in his speech. Henderson's arm rested around the shoulders of a gorgeous blonde, who looked delighted to be with him, getting her fifteen minutes of fame.

"Did you meet Lilli Capshaw when you were dating Miss Grayson?"

"No ma'am." Henderson swayed and steadied himself by leaning on his date. "Dani kept me all to herself." He looked into the camera. "Call me, sweetheart. I'm here for you, baby."

The date lost her look of delight.

After a few more inane questions from the reporter and more slurred responses from Henderson, the interview wrapped up.

What an ass. Dani switched off the television, recalling the premiere. She'd stepped out of the limousine and had smiled for the cameras while voices of people she didn't know had cried out for her to look their way.

She hooked her arm through Greg Henderson's and hoped her four-inch heels wouldn't catch on the red carpet. "Greg," she whispered, "don't let go of my arm."

He smiled at her. "Relax, baby. I've got you covered."

Dani loved tall men. At five-foot-ten, she usually looked most men in the eyes—looked down on them, let's be honest—especially in four-inch heels. Henderson was the perfect height for her, and their chemistry on screen and high-profile romance off screen had helped make *Injury* the hit of the season.

She tried to get in front of the cameras as much as possible and had worked hard at looking particularly stunning for that premiere. Her body-hugging gown had shown off her slender figure. She'd let her long, dark hair hang loose in a wild and carefree way that took hours with a curling iron to achieve.

Maybe my father is watching this, she'd thought, as she always did when she put herself on display in public. It's *why* she put herself on display in public.

Daddy's never seen me. All those times, I thought he'd see me and feel sorry he left us, and he wasn't even alive.

The doorbell rang. *John.*

She unfurled from the couch and waited for him to enter. When the door didn't open, she walked over, reached for the deadbolt, and then remembered John's warning to not open the door. She checked the peephole. Nothing there. If that was John, he wouldn't be hiding. She waited. The doorbell rang again, but whoever was there took pains not to be seen.

Dani left the door, went to her room, and opened her closet. *There'll be a media feeding frenzy. What am I going to wear?*

Did it matter? Yes, she supposed it did, but it felt strange to know that her father wasn't out there somewhere perhaps noticing her and thinking about contacting her.

At eighteen, she'd tried to find him, to ask him why he'd turned his back on her. She could understand that he'd want to escape controlling, abusive, obsessive Lilli. Dani herself had moved out of her mother's home at sixteen. But Dani was a child when her dad had disappeared, and she'd taken the rejection and ensuing lack of contact personally.

The knocking on the door penetrated her thoughts. *How'd that asshole get into the building?* Multiple fists pounded the door, she realized. More than one asshole was out there in the hall stalking her. Then she heard voices arguing, demanding. She hopped back into bed, pulled the covers under her chin, and waited.

A key rattling in the door told her John had arrived. Dani sighed and slid out of bed. Peering out of her bedroom, she waited for him to step inside. John, handsome, rugged, older. But assertive, protective, kind. She itched to touch him.

Would he sleep with her now she was over twenty-one? It'd been five years since she'd tested those waters. When she'd first hired him to be her manager, she'd thrown herself at him.

She'd almost fired him when he'd rejected her, then had decided she didn't give a shit after all. One by one, she'd seduced his associates, until she'd gotten it out of her system. The older men had been eager to accept the offer of her young body.

When John had complained, like he had any right to say anything about whom she fucked, she'd told him to butt out. He'd almost quit on her then, and she'd had to beg and plead and promise the moon to keep him as her manager. Fear of him abandoning her reined in her reckless, wanton behavior, and she'd battled to keep him in her life.

They'd had a holy alliance since then, focusing on her career, which shot through the stratosphere. She'd kept her attraction to him locked away, taking it out only in the darkest of nights when she took comfort from and pleasured herself on thoughts of him.

But now that ache for him was back, fierce, hot. Dani slid a hand down her robe and loosened the knot on the belt at her waist. The robe parted slightly, exposing her body in a thin, vertical line of curves and shadows. Her nipples hardened, and she parted her lips.

She tilted her head to the side and watched John struggle to shut the door as hands holding microphones jammed themselves into the opening, and voices shouted her name. John pushed against the door, and a man cried out in pain. The arms disappeared, and the door slammed shut.

"Don't worry, Dani. I've alerted security. They'll be gone soon," John said, his back to her.

The normality of seeing him there shook her back to reality, and she closed the robe. When he turned to her, she faced him head on. "John." Her voice caught in her throat, and his name came out low and throaty, but it was grief, not lust that did it. "What happened to my father?"

ABOUT THE AUTHOR

Writer Val Tobin also owns and operates Serenity Now Gifts and Services, an in-home business providing Reiki and other holistic services, in Newmarket, Ontario. She lives with her husband, Bob, and Scully, their cat.

Other books by Val Tobin:

Angel Words by Doreen Virtue and Grant Virtue
Val contributed a story to Doreen and Grant Virtue's *Angel Words: Visual Evidence of How Words Can Be Angels in Your Life*

The Valiant Chronicles Series
Book One: *The Experiencers*
A black-ops assassin atones for his brutal past by trying to help an alien abductee escape her fate.

Book Two: *A Ring of Truth*
A rogue assassin returns from the dead to rescue alien abductees and triggers Armageddon.

Injury
A young actress at the height of her career has her personal life turned upside down when a horrifying family secret makes front-page news.

Short Stories by Val Tobin

Storm Lake
A girl and her little brother struggle to save themselves when trapped in an isolated marina by flesh-eating creatures.